Limelight

A HOLLYWOOD STARDUST NOVEL

by

Kim Carmichael

Published by Rebel Romance,
An imprint of Irksome Rebel Press
Los Angeles, California

KIM CARMICHAEL

Limelight

A NOVEL

Published by Rebel Romance, an imprint of Irksome Rebel Press

Cover Design by JWORX Designs

Book Design by Tamara Eaton

Dedication

To all those who had to wait for something,
not knowing if they would ever get it.

Acknowledgements

My Husband – You were worth waiting for.

The Sons – Thank you for letting my characters share me.

The Fur Balls – Everyday you make me smile.

Tamara Eaton – My sister-editor, you make me better, what else can I say?

Emily Smith-Kidman – You always have my back and you always make me look great.

Teresa Neeley-Martin – My proofreader you are the person who gives my stuff its starburst!

Vicki Rose – Love how you think outside the box.

Traci Hyland – You are incredible, and I thank you for everything.

Julia Clare – When someone loves your work and then jumps in, the results are amazing!

Marissa & Laurie – Looking forward to seeing what you can do with this!

Short Glossary of Film Terms

Cut
A change in either camera angle or placement, location, or time.

Director
The principal creative artist on a movie set. A director is usually (but not always) the driving artistic source behind the filming process, and communicates to actors the way that he/she would like a particular scene played. A director's duties might also include casting, script editing, shot selection, shot composition, and editing. Typically, a director has complete artistic control over all aspects of the movie, but it is not uncommon for the director to be bound by agreements with either a producer or a studio.

Dissolve
An editing technique whereby the images of one shot is gradually replaced by the images of another.

Exterior
AKA: EXT
Used in a slug line, indicates that the scene occurs outdoors.

Fade
AKA: Fade To Black, Fade In, Fade Out
A smooth, gradual transition from a normal image to complete blackness (fade out), or vice versa (fade in)

Filtered
Post production term to add a filtered sound effect as over the phone.

Idolized
To regard with blind adoration or devotion. To worship as a god.

Interior
AKA: INT
Used in a slug line, indicates that the scene occurs indoors.

Limelight
The center of public attention, interest, observation, or notoriety.

Off Screen
AKA: O.S. Dialogue spoken off screen and is heard by the character.

Producer
The chief of staff of a movie production in all matters save the creative efforts of the director, who is head of the line. A producer is responsible for raising funding, hiring key personnel, and arranging for distributors.

Slug Line
A header appearing in a script before each scene or shot detailing the location, date, and time that the following action is intended to occur in.

Stardust
A naively romantic quality

Typecast
1. to cast (a performer) in a role that requires characteristics of physique, manner, personality, etc., similar to those possessed by the performer.
2. to cast (a performer) repeatedly in a kind of role closely patterned after that of the actor's previous successes.

HOLLYWOOD STARBURST

FADE IN:

INT. LOS ANGELES, CA – STUDIO STAGE - DAY

ROXY – eighteen years old. Beautiful, but not a standout among the other beautiful girls auditioning for movie or television roles in California. ROXY opens her eyes and looks out at the director and producer and holds her breath.

DIRECTOR – typical Hollywood type doesn't even look up from the table.

                    DIRECTOR
               (voice flat unemotional)
               Thank you Ms...

DIRECTOR lifts a piece of paper and squints.

                    DIRECTOR (CON'T)
               Ms..?

ROXY licks her lips.

                    ROXY
               Shore

                    DIRECTOR
               Yes, Ms. Shore.
               (Tosses paper aside.)
               We will be in touch.

ROXY shifts weight from one foot to the other.

                    DIRECTOR
               Thank you Ms. Shore.

ROXY pauses and finally exits into:

INT. STUDIO HALL – DAY

ROXY passes all the other people up for the part. She makes her way to

INT. STUDIO LOBBY - DAY

ROXY goes up to

WILLIAM - typical eighteen-year-old caught between being a man and being an adolescent. Clean-cut and good looking, the type of man parents want their daughter to be with.

WILLIAM waits by a window.

>   ROXY
>   Let's go.

WILLIAM continues to stare out the window and wipes his hand over his face.

>   WILLIAM
>   I agree it's time to go.

ROXY steps back.

>   ROXY
>   What do you mean?

WILLIAM lifts a backpack and slings it over his shoulder.

>   WILLIAM
>   Exactly what I
>   said. It's time to go.

WILLIAM pauses, looks down at the ground and kicks his foot.

>   WILLIAM
>   I'm getting out of
>   here. I'm going home.

                    ROXY
               (whispers)
          You're leaving me?

               WILLIAM
     You can't leave what you never had.

ROXY looks up. She and WILLIAM stare at each
other.

                    ROXY
          I don't know what to
          do. I want to be
          together.

                    WILLIAM
          If that was what you
          wanted then we would
          be. I can't compete
          with your thoughts of
          Steven, I can't compete
          with this.

WILLIAM swipes his hand around the room.

                    ROXY
          This is my dream. I'm
          not going with you.

                    WILLIAM
          I didn't ask you to.

WILLIAM reaches in his pocket and hands her
some cash. When ROXY puts her hand in his, he
holds on, pulls her in and kisses her cheek.

                    WILLIAM
          I'll always love you
          Rox. I think you need
          to figure out what your
          dream really is.

WILLIAM lets go of her, hoists his backpack
higher and walks away.

ROXY watches WILLIAM leave.

                    ROXY
              You left.

Chapter One

FLASHES FROM THE CAMERAS created lingering silver, glowing starbursts in Drew Fulton's eyes. The media frenzy started almost instantly, derailing the 20th anniversary screening of the one and only movie he filmed, *Hollywood Stardust*. For someone who successfully remained hidden for two decades, he chose the ideal subtle moment to come out of his self-imposed exile, or maybe not.

"Drew, where have you been all these years?" called out one of the reporters gathered for the gala.

Once the studio executives realized what happened, they stopped the festivities and with a bit of movie magic, made the stage into a spot fit for a press conference in record time.

Before showing up at the shindig, Drew promised himself to go for it. Now was the time for full disclosure, and he leaned down to the microphone. "To encapsulate two decades into one sentence—I changed my name, went to school, earned my doctorate, and opened up a small nutraceutical laboratory." All right, it wasn't the world's best sentence, but it would suffice. In the next two days he would have to show up at his business and do a lot of explaining, something he sort of pushed aside when he made his snap decision to come here to find her.

A woman waved her hand. "Why did you feel the need to change your name and disappear?"

Drew wasn't sure if she was part of the media or not, but if he didn't answer her, someone else would force the issue.

He searched for the only woman he wanted to see in the studio set converted to look like the inside of the Hollywood Stardust Theatre, the destination for the four characters in the movie. In the film, their quest took them across country. The road was a metaphor for the trip one takes to transition between adolescence and adulthood.

In real life he, and the other actors, faced the same challenges.

Once more, he looked for the reason he came tonight. With her knowledge of all things smoke and mirrors, no doubt she managed to squirrel away where she could watch everything, yet not be seen. For the first time since he met her, she shied away from the limelight.

Drew swallowed and took hold of the microphone stand. While he wanted to offer the fans of the movie the truth they sought all these years, the answer as to why he disappeared was better left unspoken, at least in public.

"Sometimes you need to just get away from everything and everyone and start over." More lights flashed, leaving him blinking to see.

"But how did you hide your identity?" The question came from a male in the crowd.

An easy one. "During the movie I wore prosthetics to appear more like the producers wanted the character and they asked me to stay in costume for public appearances. It was very easy to fade away once the costume came off...and the weight came off."

Some chuckles went through the audience.

Yes, he was the chubby kid. During filming he lost weight, causing a whole host of issues for the movie. They had to keep adding padding to his costume to retain continuity. He hid for a while, let the fanfare of the movie die down and then went abroad for college. By the time he returned with a different name, no one ever put it together. He still found it incredible that he pulled it off. Maybe he was a real actor after all.

"Have you kept in touch with your cast mates?" Another question barreled toward him.

Drew glanced off to the side of the stage. While he might not be able to find her, his best friend, Logan Alexander, was always there for him. Logan nodded, giving him the okay to answer. "Only Logan Alexander." The quote unquote villain of both the movie and of real life was one of the best people he knew. One might even say a hero.

Some mumbles went through the crowd.

"Drew, why did you decide to come back now?"

Again, he looked for her. Where did she hide herself? On the other side of the stage he located Ryder Scott, their leading man. The poster boy for a movie star, he always had everything. After the film, Ryder went on to a successful career and now also dabbled in directing and producing. Additionally, he was a complete and total ass. However, Drew couldn't locate the last of their four. The reason he came out of hiding.

"I have some unfinished business." He needed to go find her. "I can take one more question before we should probably let you all get back to the movie."

"Can we get a picture of the four of you together?"

Well, the promise of a picture that would be all over the world should bring her out. He turned left and right. Ryder joined him first, shaking his hand and taking center stage to thunderous applause. Logan, who only moments before proposed to his fiancée on this exact stage, came out next and the clapping grew to the point where it vibrated the building.

Logan shook his hand and raised his eyebrows.

"Where is she?" Drew attempted to ask the question without moving his lips.

"She'll be here." Logan patted his back and took his place.

The crowd stilled as if holding its collective breath, waiting for the one female of the group.

Drew ground his teeth together. After everything he just did, would she not reveal herself?

And then she appeared.

Damn him to hell for his breath catching at the sight of her. Though he followed her career, watched her in her movies, her television appearances, and even clips of her in a stage play, nothing compared to her in person.

She stepped to the edge of the stage and the applause began once more. Yes, even with his news of showing up after twenty years, Erin Holland would always steal the spotlight.

The color that overtook her cheeks would be gorgeous in the pictures, but he knew better. He knew the blush came from her being flustered, unsure and taken off guard. If they were alone, away from the scrutiny of the public, she would be crying. Not that it mattered. Crying, flush, with or without makeup, and even with twenty years behind them, he had never seen a more beautiful woman.

Instead of tears, she nodded toward the audience and made her way to her once co-stars. Her silver form-fitting dress moved like liquid metal, fluid and flowing. She wore her blonde hair down, smooth and cascading over one shoulder, but pulled back from her picture-perfect face. Her doe-like blue eyes and heart shaped lips were all natural and the envy of many a teenage girl way back when.

She stared into his eyes, asking questions, shooting accusations. In short, being Erin through and through. The one woman he couldn't stand, but couldn't get out of his mind. He could never move forward if he only looked back, and the second she came within reach, he held his hand out to her.

"Drew." She licked her lips, put her hand in his and gave him a hug. Her trembling betrayed her cool outward demeanor.

"I came here for you." He inhaled. Her perfume might have changed, but the aroma enveloping him was the same. It was just Erin. "We need to talk."

Without a word, she pulled back and took her position between Logan and Ryder. The three made up the love triangle of *Hollywood Stardust* while Drew's character, Charles, was always left standing on the edge, just like him.

Again, the lights flashed and he found himself posing with the rest of them. Old habits returned, subtle changes in his position to catch the light, show off a better angle, allow the photographers to get the ever-important shot.

He needed to get to the person he came here for and raised his hand, the universal signal for stopping the show.

"Drew, one more question before you leave," a woman called over the mumbles, the claps and the oohs and ahhs.

He waited.

"What unfinished business brought you back? Is this a publicity stunt for the movie or was it something, or someone, else?"

"It wasn't a stunt. In fact, I didn't even know I was going to do this until about an hour before I arrived." He turned, wanting to catch Erin before she ran away licking her self-perceived wounds.

As usual, he was too late. Erin had already vanished and he almost fought a laugh. Once more, he changed his life for her, and again she wasn't around. "As for the rest, stay tuned."

HOLLYWOOD STARBURST

FADE IN:

INT. LOS ANGELES, CA — STUDIO SET - EVENING

ROXY holds up a can of cat food.

> ROXY
> And that is why if I
> want a pretty kitty I
> only give my baby the
> best with Purrrrfect
> Blend Kitty Food.

ROXY leans over and spoons cat food into a
crystal goblet and three different cats
congregate and begin eating the food.

DIRECTOR — a middle-aged woman with a hat and
glasses stands up.

> DIRECTOR
> Cut!

ROXY sneezes and sniffs.

> DIRECTOR
> I'm not sure you're
> believable as a cat
> owner. Have you ever
> owned a cat?

> ROXY
> Back home we have a dog.

ROXY looks down.

                    DIRECTOR
               Where is back
               home? Kansas?

                    ROXY
               It was California, then
               it was Indiana, now...

ROXY shrugs and sneezes.

                    DIRECTOR
               I think they may be
               casting an antihistamine
               commercial in the next
               building. I'm looking
               for someone whose cat
               ownership bubbles out
               through their pores.

                    ROXY
               Thank you for not
               leaving me hanging.

ROXY walks across the set and picks up her
purse.

                    DIRECTOR
               Ms. Shore.

ROXY turns

                    DIRECTOR
               Maybe you need to find a
               home before you play
               act.

                    ROXY
               I need to go searching.

Chapter Two

"DRIVER, CAN YOU HURRY?" Erin turned on the light in the back of the limo and held up her mirror. She seemed paler than normal and why shouldn't she? A ghost she chased for twenty years finally decided to appear with no warning, no sign, not even a note on a Ouija board.

Why tonight? Why now?

Though he told her differently, deep down she knew Logan was in constant contact with her love. For twenty years she begged him to reveal Drew's whereabouts, but the man proved to be unbreakable, even after she tried just about everything. She gave her reflection one last glance and tossed the mirror in her evening bag.

After all this time she refused to allow Drew to call the shots, show up when he was damn good and ready, and blurt out he needed to speak to her. When they connected it would be under her terms.

No, she wouldn't make him wait years or days. She wouldn't torture Drew as he had her, though the thought was appealing. At the end of the day, she wouldn't put herself through any more pain. The last hour provided a long enough wait, and she still had more obstacles in front of her before she reached her goal.

The traffic from the studio to her home crawled. Heated energy surged through her, and she breathed in to get a good yell out at the driver.

Wait.

She stopped her outburst and inhaled deeply as if she were getting into character. Many, many times in life required stomping and screaming, but there were still some moments that necessitated the wide-eyed sweetheart. Whatever the role required.

"Sir?" She called out to the driver.

"Yes, ma'am?"

She shuddered at the old lady term, but continued using her best innocent, helpless high-pitched voice. "Do you know if there's a shortcut or anything that we can take? I really need to get home, um, it's sort of an emergency."

"I'm doing my best, ma'am."

"Oh, I know you are." She pressed her hand to her chest and licked her lips to make sure they maintained a shine even if matte lipstick was in style. "But something tells me that you excel at everything you do."

The chauffeur straightened up. "I will get you home, ma'am."

"Erin. Darling, please call me Erin." Once more she reached into her bag to retrieve her phone.

Her breath caught. For the first time in twenty years, potentially the one person she wanted to hear from would contact her. At least this time she could turn on the device and have the information she quite literally crawled on her hands and knees for.

When she first got in the vehicle, she'd texted Logan for Drew's phone and address. Still waiting for a response from her co-star, she closed her eyes and tapped the button. It seemed all she did was seek out information about one Drew Fulton, down to the first time she laid eyes on him at his screen test.

She and Logan had arrived early and peeked into the studio housing their rumored newest cast member. "Is that him?"

"Who else could it be?" Logan had rubbed his hands together. "He'll make a perfect minion."

"He looks like he's nice. Don't be a jerk." She stared at the guy who the studio hired just for her. Sweet face, nice smile, a little chubby and he carried himself with a humble demeanor, especially with the way he stood by the person she assumed to be his mother with his hands in his pockets. In a world where everyone was taught to be outgoing and stand out, he was refreshing.

"I'm only stating the obvious. If anyone should be worried about being a jerk, or may I use the proper term for a girl, a bitch, it should be you, since you got that Stacy fired."

No sooner had Logan let out a low chuckle than the director motioned for them. "Erin, Logan, come on in. You're right on time."

Once the director turned his back, she elbowed Logan. "I'm not a bitch." She held her head up high and gracefully walked into the studio.

"Keep believing that, princess. Someone has to," Logan snarled under his breath and passed her, making his way to the newcomer first and held out his hand. "Logan Alexander, your new best friend and leader."

Unable to hide her emotion, she rolled her eyes and waited. Though she wanted to be the first person to meet the potential fourth, now she thought it might be better if she stood back and waited to take center stage.

"Drew Fulton." The newbie shook Logan's hand, but his focus was most definitely on her. "I don't think it's you anyone will be following."

Again, Logan let out a laugh and though Drew wasn't her type, her cheeks heated.

After allowing the moment to stretch a little more, she stepped forward, joining the boys.

"Erin Holland, no doubt." Drew offered his hand for a shake.

"Our resident bitch." Logan elbowed her.

Jutting her jaw out at Logan, she put her hand in Drew's. Warm, soft skin encompassed her hand it almost felt like safety.

"I am a fan of your work." He let go of her and pushed his glasses up on his nose.

"Well then, you have excellent taste." With a bit of attitude, she pursed her lips and glanced at Logan. Except for Ryder, she had more experience than anyone.

"I think I also have great instinct, and mine tells me you're not a bitch." Drew tilted his head, but was one of the few people who didn't seem timid to look her in the eye.

She smiled, a genuine one, not one forced or rehearsed, and they studied each other. Besides the calming deep brown color of his eyes, she glimpsed something else there.

"Should we get on with the screen test?" The director interrupted them.

Though she never really had a friend before, she wondered if she found one in Drew Fulton, and she held her hand up. "We need to give the part to Drew."

Everyone in the room focused on her and this is where she shined.

The director narrowed his eyes. "We haven't seen you act together."

"He's perfect, you'll see." Before turning to the director, she licked her lips to give them a shine, widened her eyes, and hooked her arm in Drew's. "Please, you said that Roxy and this character had to have an underlying trust and friendship, and I think I can have that with Drew. He belongs to me. You said that about this character just the other day."

The director crossed his arms and tapped his foot. "Hold on." He went to a phone across the room and spoke in muffled tones.

Without letting go of what she rightfully claimed, she winked at Drew.

The director returned. "Well, we have heard Drew read for the part of Charles. Sometimes chemistry is inherent among cast mates, and we feel that is the case here. Drew, we'll draw up your contract."

Yeah, right. Erin just kept up the good girl act, her favorite role. The director, the producer, and everyone else knew there would be hell to pay if they didn't give her the actor she chose. She had leaned over to her new partner in crime, the one who would protect her, even if he didn't know it yet. "I need to talk to you."

With a start, she opened her eyes. Now, Drew needed to talk to her. The word talk reverberated in her mind over and over as if someone hit the repeat button in her brain. Until this precise moment, she didn't consider the possibility he wanted anything except to talk about them, but what if it were something different? Her stomach twisted, but before she let her mind race off, she glanced down at the screen.

Nothing. No Logan. No Drew. No Brian.

Brian?

She straightened up. Her agent, also known as her significant other, who wasn't so significant, didn't attend the anniversary party for *Hollywood Stardust*. Where was he anyway? Anytime she needed him, he seemed to go missing. If he had the information she wanted all these years, she swore the man would live to regret it.

At long last the limo pulled up in front of Brian's home south of Sunset Boulevard, the house that *Hollywood Stardust* built. Funny, how he ended up with the seven-figure home, while she did all the work. All agents were the same.

The car stopped and the chauffeur got out and opened the door.

"And here we are, Erin." The man gave her a huge grin. "How did I do?"

Reaching in her bag again, she bypassed a hundred dollar bill and grabbed two twenties. She got out of the car and shoved the bills in the man's hand. "You should have taken the proper way to begin with."

Without looking back, she headed straight to the front.

Before she ever put her key in the lock, the door opened.

Apparently, tonight was the night her life changed. She always figured the second she and Drew were reunited would be earth shattering.

If the suitcases didn't tell her what she needed to know, the fact Brian stood with his arms crossed blocking her way filled in any gaps. The strange thing about it all was that the first thought to go through her head was this little disturbance would delay her in getting to Drew.

"You weren't there tonight." She stated the obvious.

"When exactly did you notice?" He tilted his head.

Throughout her entire career they attended functions separate yet together, mostly arriving in different vehicles in order for her to attend to business. Even the most social events were work events. She didn't dare tell him the truth and admit she didn't notice his absence until she practically pulled up to the house. "It was a big event."

"It's always a big event. It's never *not* a big event."

She smiled. "You used to love that about me."

"You used to search me out no matter where you were." His tone lowered, he never could act.

"Do we have to do this tonight?"

"It's never a good time." He sighed.

"Then I'll pencil you in for the morning. I'm going to head up to bed. It's been quite a night." Her ploy usually worked or delayed the inevitable. She simply needed some time with Drew before pulling up roots.

"Not in my bed, not in my house, not on my property." He continued to block her way.

"You sound like a nursery rhyme." She stepped forward.

"I need to speak in a language you will understand." He held up his hand.

Stupid. She stopped and put her hands on her hips. Everyone always thought she was stupid. "Have you been online? Drew showed up at the gala."

"I'm actually surprised you bothered showing up here this early. This is what you waited for and wanted for two decades. I've always been a placeholder, like those people that fill the seats at the Oscars so the audience looks full."

Again, she withheld some truth. If she had Drew's information she might not have come home at all. "I didn't talk to him yet."

"I'm sure he's waiting for you, and you'll have plenty of time." He rubbed his neck. "You didn't get the Cushing part."

His words dropped on her with a sad thud. For the millionth time tonight tears heated the back of her eyes, and she swallowed to stop any from falling. "I've had a bit of a dry spell."

"You're quickly becoming a has-been." He picked up the suitcases and brought them to her. "You're letting yourself go, you spend money like you're an A-lister, and you lay around here like you're retired."

"I've worked for over thirty years." The statement caused bile to sting the back of her throat. Two seconds ago she was under thirty and never had to audition for roles. In a heartbeat, she was nearing forty and living with a man over twenty years her senior because she had nowhere else to go.

"You better keep working because that's all you're good at. You don't love me, and I can't help you anymore. We need to separate our lives, starting now."

"That's not what you said when you slept with someone underage."

"I'm not saying I'm perfect." He inched closer. "I'm only saying I'm done."

"So, without any warning you're kicking me out and dropping my contract?" Jutting her jaw out, she lifted her face to him.

"You never heed any warnings unless you want to." As if deflating, he exhaled. "If I don't do it this way, we'll only end up back in the same cycle."

Her phone vibrated and ignoring the fact Brian stood in front of her, she took her time opening her handbag and reading the message on the screen. Finally, Logan came through with the information she wanted most in the last two decades.

"Erin," Brian barked.

Without moving her head, she looked up at him through her eyelashes. "I think you're right, we're done." If he wanted to see a has-been he should look in the mirror. The man held her back, her past held her back. Well, now with Brian wanting her gone and Drew wanting to talk, all barriers vanished. Since her driver for the evening already left, she found her keys, spun on her heel toward the open door, and threw her hair over her shoulder. "Load up my bags, will you?"

They didn't speak as he put her suitcases in the trunk of her luxury sedan. She slipped into the leather seat and strummed her fingers on the steering wheel while he finished.

Brian slammed the trunk lid closed and came to the side of the car.

Right on cue she locked the doors, cranked up the music, and sped out of the driveway. The man wasn't even worth her time to glance back at in her rearview mirror.

Once around the corner, she stopped, plugged the address into her navigation system and lowered her head.

The consequences of her actions always hit her a few minutes too late.

She left without knowing how much, if any, money she had and without a place in the world to stay. All Drew said was he needed to talk to her.

HOLLYWOOD STARBURST

FADE IN:

INT. HOLLYWOOD, CA - AGENT'S OFFICE - EARLY
MORNING.

ROXY sits in a dingy waiting room wringing her
hands.

SECRETARY points to the agent's door.

>   SECRETARY
>   You can go on in
>   now. Hand Mr. Snyder
>   two copies of your
>   resume and headshot and
>   wait for him to address
>   you.

ROXY stands and pulls her papers and pictures
out of her bag. She goes to the door, opens it
and tiptoes inside.

AGENT sits behind desk reading a magazine and
holds his hand out.

ROXY shoves the documents into the agent's
hands and sits down in the chair across from
the desk.

>   AGENT
>   I'm sure my secretary
>   didn't tell you to sit.

ROXY presses her lips together and stands.

AGENT glances at papers and pictures and tosses
them on a pile.

>   AGENT
>   Well, you sort of take
>   direction well,
>   minus one for sitting.

ROXY opens her mouth.

AGENT looks up and raises his eyebrows.

ROXY Shuts her mouth and wraps arms around her
shoulders.

>   AGENT
>   You're learning. You
>   also don't stand up for
>   yourself.

>   ROXY
>   What does that mean?

>   AGENT
>   (raises voice, agitated tone.)
>   That means that you will
>   get trampled on. That
>   means you're just
>   another pretty
>   face. That means you
>   are only good for porn
>   if you want to get paid,
>   an extra if you want to
>   think you're legit.

ROXY puts hand to chest. Her lower lip
quivers, and she shakes her head.

AGENT stands and leans over the desk.

>   AGENT
>   Look at you, even now I
>   just used your dreams to
>   wipe my ass and all you
>   can do is look at me
>   with your tear filled
>   eyes.

>   ROXY
>   What do you want me to
>   do?

                    AGENT
          Learn to be an
          actress. Learn to
          fight. Learn to
          lie. Learn to get what
          you want.

                    ROXY
          I need to learn what I
          want.

Chapter Three

DREW'S HOME IN PASADENA looked exactly like what she pictured when she used to dream about their life together. Erin gazed up at the perfectly manicured Craftsman style home, complete with a yard, an SUV in the curved driveway and probably an obedient dog sitting by a fireplace. At least there was only one car. Of course, a second one could easily be in the two-car garage.

At last, she allowed the thoughts she brushed aside earlier to come to the forefront. Here she stood in front of Drew's home. Along with the dog by the fireplace could be a wife and maybe children. Heat flashed over her and she froze. Coming here was stupid, insane. She was one step away from stalking the man. Logan also gave her Drew's phone number, she could have texted or called.

For the second time in one night, a door opened before she had the chance to even get to the threshold.

As she predicted, a beautiful black dog ran outside.

She put her hand over her mouth. If some woman joined the animal, she would definitely pass out.

The dog barked and ran up to her.

"Don't bite me." Her voice came out muffled by her hand, and she stepped back. Though she worked with countless animals on set, for some reason she only co-starred with one dog, a little Yorkie who didn't do much and reminded her of a muff she once had to wear for a winter scene. "Please don't bite me."

A whistle rang out and suddenly the dog turned and trotted back inside.

She tightened her hold on her purse.

Drew appeared at the door.

Back at the party she barely saw him because she was too focused on making it through the motions. Before she found out why he had to speak to her she took her chance to simply look at him

Most people who didn't see each other for long spans of time always commented on how they looked the same, didn't change one bit. However, Drew had changed. Gone was the boy with the beautiful brown eyes and shy smile. In his place was a man with sultry dark eyes and matching hair simply combed back as if he didn't have a care in the world. His smile possessed a little more knowledge behind it.

Time had transformed him, gave him some edge, allowed him to come into himself. Tall and slender, he stood there leaning against the doorjamb as casual as ever in a pair of jeans and a blue t-shirt. Of all the cast, he was always the one to stop and take everything in, something she never learned to do.

"You said you needed to speak to me?" Though she trembled, she forced her voice to come out even.

He nodded.

Again, she glanced around his front yard. There was even a hummingbird feeder hanging by one of the windows. "Did you hang that?" Maybe her question would give her a clue to what she walked in on.

"It came with the house, but I refill it when it runs out." He continued to stand by the door.

Well, his answer didn't offer her much. "What do you want to talk to me about?"

"Not hummingbird feeders." He let out a laugh.

She couldn't do this. Everyone always accused her of living her life like a movie. Somewhere in her head she assumed she would show up, he would run out and lean her back in a kiss fit for a final scene of an epic romance, pick her up and they would figure out their happily ever after. "I should have called. When I got your address, I just had to come see you."

"I knew you would come here."

As always, his voice caressed her, calmed her. Yes, it was deeper now, but she still wished she could wrap herself up in his voice and go to sleep. "Tell me what to do."

"No one tells you what to do." Again, he laughed.

She waited.

"We can start with you coming inside."

With a nod she walked forward, stopping after two steps. "Will the dog bite me?"

He shook his head.

She took another step. "Are you sick?"

"No." As if trying to guide her, he opened the door a little wider. "I also don't need money. Keep going."

While she wanted to know where he got a copy of her script, she continued to forge ahead. "Drew."

"Yes?"

She stared into the face she missed. The scent of his soap wafted around her and she longed to touch him, but she needed to know something first. "Are you married?"

His eyes seemed to dart to different parts of her, as if he needed some time to absorb her or didn't want to tell her.

Her heart seized. "Drew."

"I'm not married, divorced, engaged, in a relationship or even dating someone." He leaned forward. "I thought I needed to talk to you."

She took her first full breath. "May I come in?"

"All you have to do is step over the threshold."

She glanced down and stepped inside.

After twenty years, they were finally in the same spot.

The inside of his place was as pristine as the outside. The period pieces matched the house's architecture coupled with some antiques.

The dog approached her again, sniffing and assessing her. "You always wanted a pet." She tensed at the dog's analysis.

"I got Beaker once I opened my business." Again, Drew whistled, but added snapping his fingers. "Go lay down."

In less than an instant, the dog ran over to a cushion. She sort of wished Drew commanded her like that. There would be no better way to get to know each other again.

"Would you like a drink?" Drew motioned toward a couch.

"Sure." The whole place was almost too homey. Still in her cocktail dress from the gala, she took a seat on the comfy sofa. She prayed he produced a bottle of vodka or something.

Rather than sitting next to her, he took a chair across from her and poured them each a glass of sherry from a decanter on the coffee table.

She lifted her glass and stared at the dark liquid. Once upon a time they never had awkward silences. What did he want? Why was she here? This reunion was nothing like she planned and she spent twenty years going through every scenario.

"I suppose I should propose a toast." He picked up his glass and tapped it against hers. "To old friends."

Without taking a sip, she put the glass down.

"You don't like the drink?" Drew sampled some of the alcohol.

"After twenty years, I would have thought you had something more to toast to than old friends." She sat back and crossed her legs making sure her skirt rode up her thigh.

He gave her leg a glance and took another drink. "What would you like?"

"I would have thought you would have found a better place to sit than the furthest position from me."

"All right." He walked around the table and sat down on the couch. "Better?"

The man was set on making her suffer. She turned to him. "Why don't you tell me why I'm here? Tell me what you need to talk to me so badly about you show up after two decades in the middle of an event."

"You're here because you couldn't stay away." He narrowed his eyes. "I asked to talk to you because I wanted to take advantage of an opportunity while I had it."

Somewhere the words she wanted to hear didn't happen. She didn't respond.

"I think you heard I run a laboratory. I make nutraceuticals." He continued. "Like vitamins and drinks and other nutritional supplements."

"I understand what they are." She waited, wondering how she ended up here for what was appearing to be a work related conversation.

"I am coming out with a line of products called Hollywood Glow. I want you to be the face of the line."

In movie magic, right about now would be the moment where a boulder fell on her and did her the favor of killing her or at least ending this scene. While that might not happen, her background in storytelling gave her a little insider information. His motivation made no sense. "You came out of hiding and showed up at a public venue where you made quite a scene all so you could ask me to be the spokesperson for a vitamin?"

"Well, it's a supplement, but yes." He reclined back on the couch. "Were you expecting something else?"

He knew damn well she expected something else. He knew it twenty years ago, the night she told him she wanted something else. He knew it right before he vanished. When she chased after his car, she wanted something else, and he knew it right now.

Fine, this would be how he played the game. He wanted two things, to make her suffer and to make love to her, but needed to make her suffer first. They said payback was a bitch, and she was a bitch. She decided to call his bluff. "I don't know. I have to think about it. You know I can't just go endorsing any product."

"Of course, of course." He retrieved his glass and downed the rest. "Strange thing with expectations, it's like hope wrapped in a fancier word."

Nothing ever went as she hoped. At what point in her life would she understand? Thus far, in the same time it took to see a double feature, she'd gotten thrown out of her home and thrown for a loop with Drew only asking her to hock a product for him.

She stood. "Well, I must get going." She went toward the door, counting down her options of where to go tonight, tomorrow night, and the next.

"You're going to leave so soon? We haven't even had the chance to catch up." He came up behind her.

"I think our business is concluded. I'll have my people contact your people." Only thing, she didn't have any people anymore. She put her hand on the doorknob.

"You know I could have called your people myself, but I wanted to deal with you personally." He put his hand over hers.

Maybe it was only because she craved it, but his touch sizzled through her body. "What did you expect to happen?" He moved in closer. "I don't know. I try not to have expectations."

Shivers consumed her and she glanced at him out of the corner of her eye.

"So, what do you say? Will you be my...spokesperson?" He

raised his eyebrows. "No agents, no people, just you and me?"

Now she would make him beg as she did too many times to count. "What if I say I'll think about it, and I'll give you an answer in the morning? In fact, if you let me stay the night, I'll give you my answer in person."

"What expectations do you have for that?" He stood close enough for her to feel his breath on her neck.

"Nothing, except a bed. I'm going through some renovations." She didn't exactly lie. "Since you found me, I sort of don't want to let you out of my sight. Maybe we can talk about something other than work."

"I take it you have a bag in your car?" He opened the door. "It'll be like old times."

"I'm not expecting a thing." Yes, she lied.

HOLLYWOOD STARBURST

FADE IN:

INT. INDIANAPOLIS, IN - HIGH SCHOOL HALLWAY
OUTSIDE PRINCIPAL'S OFFICE - MORNING BEFORE
SCHOOL STARTS. DAY.

STEVEN - Eighteen-year-old going on
thirty. Bad boy with an edge, the type that
girls think they can change because their love
will make a difference. He leans up against
the wall by the office door twirling a pen
between his fingers.

CHARLES - The scholar of the bunch, he's
overweight, awkward, only interested in
graduating. He plays the role of Steven's
minion. He paces up and down the hallway,
reading a textbook barely missing bumping into
other students. Every once in a while, Steven
reaches out and redirects him from disaster.

WILLIAM exits office and stops the moment he
spots Steven and Charles.

                    STEVEN
          So what's the verdict?

CHARLES stops pacing and lowers his book.

WILLIAM lifts his chin towards Charles.

                    WILLIAM
          Academic probation. If
          I do everything right, I
          can make up my lost
          credits at summer
          school. I won't be able
          to walk in the
          graduation ceremonies,
          but I'll get my diploma
          and still make it to
          college in the fall.

CHARLES shakes his head.

STEVEN pushes Charles' book back toward him.

>   STEVEN
>   It will be okay Chuck,
>   it's not you.

WILLIAM starts walking away.

STEVEN grabs Charles' sleeve and follows,
catching up to William and elbowing him.

>   STEVEN
>   Why did you leave?

WILLIAM stops, but doesn't answer.

The first bell rings and the students around
them start rushing to class.

>   STEVEN
>   Well?

>   WILLIAM
>   I couldn't stay.

STEVEN glances at CHARLES who shrugs.

>   STEVEN
>   Was it worth it?

WILLIAM pauses, looks around then up at the
ceiling.

>   WILLIAM
>   I don't know.

WILLIAM goes to leave, but STEVEN snatches him
by the collar and pulls him back.

                    STEVEN
              Where's Roxy?

WILLIAM shrugs.

STEVEN yanks William and slams him up against a
row of lockers.

                    STEVEN
              (Angry low tone)
              You left her there in
              Hollywood by herself?

                    WILLIAM
              You left her first.

STEVEN puts his face right in William's.

                    STEVEN
              What are you saying?

WILLIAM stares into Steven's face.

                    WILLIAM
              You drove away and never
              looked back.

Chapter Four

HOLLYWOOD GLOW?

When the words Hollywood Glow fell out of his mouth, Drew had no choice but to continue the farce.

Wasn't it every day that someone came out of their self-imposed witness protection program to ask a star to endorse their product?

No, he didn't want to create a line with her as the spokesperson, but the minute she entered his home and they were reunited, he felt himself being sucked into the black hole that was Erin Holland.

For once, they were in the same place at the same time, both physically and mentally. She didn't hold back in basically saying she wanted him and the fact of the matter was he had always wanted her.

Of course, last time he thought they were here, they missed the mark, resulting in him changing his name, his life and recreating himself.

Something about seeing Logan and his now fiancée, Ivy, overcome every obstacle in their quest to be together coupled with knowing Erin begged to see him for years made Drew make the snap decision to come out of hiding.

Then suddenly she was here, in his home and he froze. History could simply repeat itself, and to make matters worse he couldn't vanish a second time.

He needed to get to know her, needed to see if she'd changed. Maybe he even needed a little payback. Most of all, he had to figure out a way to keep her close, but leave some breathing room just in case.

In that instant of uncertainty, Hollywood Glow was born.

No doubt the renovations she spoke of weren't on a property, but like his fib, he went along with hers. It seemed like the right thing to do.

Like a little duckling, she followed him around as he moved her car into the garage and carried her numerous bags up the stairs, nearly bumping into him when he hesitated on bringing her either to the master bedroom or the guest room. While they both seemed desperate to keep the other in their line of sight, he had to remember to maintain some distance and forced himself toward the guest room.

"Here we go." He flipped on the light and glanced around the room that only the night before housed Logan until his best friend realized his place was with his own love.

"Thank you." She took one of the bags, put it on the floor and kneeled down opening it.

From the neat stacks in the suitcase, he knew instantly Erin did not pack her own bags. Interesting.

Also interesting was the contents, including her bras, underwear and lingerie.

His focus alternated between Erin and her bag of tricks.

"I think I'll get out of this dress." She lifted a couple of pieces.

The entire contents of the case included satin, ribbons and lace, and he ran his hand through his hair. Was he insane? Here she was basically planning on wearing strings for clothing, and he brought her into the guest room rather than his room.

With her selections in hand, she stood, slid her hair over her shoulder and backed up to him. "Would you mind?"

Every fantasy he had about Erin over twenty years began with this precise moment. How many times had he been in this exact position? She always asked the same way, as if anyone would mind undressing her. The first time she asked, maybe he should have taken action.

It was on their first location shoot about a month after they started filming. The first night the studio had booked them rooms at the only motel in a small town in Colorado. At the end of the day, he had finally finished scrubbing his face of the makeup and put on a pair of pajamas when a soft knock came at his door.

Figuring it was either one of the crewmembers needing to give him something for the next day or Logan wanting a partner in crime, he didn't even ask who it was before opening the door.

He sucked in his breath at the sight of Erin.

"May I come in?" Still in her outfit from the set and holding a pillow and various other things, she gazed up at him.

"Of course?" A jolt shot through him at his visitor. As he backed up, he clutched the edge of the door and watched her dart inside. After pausing to collect himself, he turned to her. "Everything good?" Somehow along with the role of Charles, he also had a secondary part as Erin's confidante and friend, a position he coveted and hated, but couldn't quit.

She shook her head and sat down at the edge of the bed, hugging her pillow to her chest. "I like your pajamas."

If he knew it was her on the other side of the door, he would have tried to wear something less, less... he glanced down at his pjs, less plaid. "Thanks." He stumbled, but covered it up by plopping down on the bed next to her. "Tell me."

"What do you think of the movie so far?" She ran her fingernail along the edge of her pillowcase.

"I don't have anything to compare it to, so you would know better than me." Trying to be casual, he leaned back on his elbows. Though he knew she was covering up for something else she wanted to ask, he went along with her. Eventually, she would tell him.

"I think it's good. It would have been better if the story was based off a book or something then it would already have a following." She shrugged.

He never thought of the movie that way, actually he only did this film to appease his parents. "You really know a lot about the industry."

"Most people think I'm stupid." Her voice lowered.

"Then most people are stupid themselves." A cramp taking over his side, he sat up and stared straight ahead.

Out of the corner of his eye, he saw her turn to him.

Strange, he could have a camera pointed at him all day, but the minute one particular set of eyes was on him, he froze.

"You're different than everyone else." She moved his hair away from the side of his face.

Though he willed himself to have no reaction, it was nearly

impossible and he strummed his fingers on the bed, tapped his foot. All he did was think about her. "Yeah, Logan and Ryder I'm not." He wasn't stupid either. They looked like stars, while he wanted to be sucked into a black hole.

"Stop worrying about them." She slid over and leaned her chin on his shoulder.

Easy for her to say, she had all three of them panting after her like a pack of wolves, but he swore he was the only one who really knew her.

"I don't feel safe with them. I only feel safe with you."

While these were words all guys wanted to hear from the girl they crushed on, he already knew his sentiments wouldn't be returned the way he wanted. His only choice was to remain staring at the dark wood dresser in front of him, fidgeting at her mere presence.

"Drew?" Her voice caressed his ear and her tone told him that at last she would reveal what she wanted.

He nodded.

"May I stay here with you tonight, please?"

"Y-y-you want to stay here?" He needed to repeat the words to make sure he heard her right.

"I'll never sleep all alone, I only feel safe when I know where you are."

He gazed into those huge blue eyes. Many, many people would kill to have his dilemma. How could he tell her no? He had sighed. "All right." With the sudden urge to run out of the room, he had stood and rather than running, tried to make a plan for a single queen bed.

"Thank you." Along with her pillow, she had put her bright red nightgown on the edge of the bed. "Do you mind?"

He turned to find her back to him and her hair pulled up. "Mind what?" Right now he would mind if she saw the erection he would be nursing the entire night and wished he had thicker pajamas.

"Unzipping me so I can change." Her giggle made the world sparkle.

He'd never undressed a girl before, or had a girl in his bed. There wouldn't be any sleeping on his part. Most likely he would end up passing out.

At least he had a little piece of Erin, even if it wasn't the part he wanted.

"Drew."

At the sound of his name, Drew blinked and was jolted into the here and now. "Mind what?" He spit out the first thing that sprang to mind.

"Unzip me, you're an expert." A low laugh escaped her throat.

With a bit more knowledge of the female body than the first time he performed this action, he swallowed and lifted his hand to the tab of the zipper. Slowly, tooth by tooth, he slid the zipper down.

Apparently, this particular dress didn't require a bra even though Erin had always been well endowed. Instead, she presented him with a stripe of perfectly smooth skin with no interruption.

Unfortunately, the zipper ended right at the small of her back, but damn, he wanted to know if she wore underwear, and if so, what color.

He cleared his throat. While he may have pulled a couple of zippers down in his lifetime, nothing compared to those belonging to Erin Holland. "All right, why don't you get comfortable and I'm going to go get you some sheets. There are clean towels in the cabinet."

"Thank you, Mr. Fulton. When you return, will you tuck me in?" She turned back to him, a one-sided smile gracing her face and one arm across her breasts holding the dress up. "Maybe you can tell me a bedtime story?"

Before he thrust her arm away and let her dress fall so he could see what had always been denied him, he nodded. "I'll be right back."

She wiggled her fingers at him, collected her pajamas and a toiletry bag and disappeared into the bathroom.

Once the door closed, he dashed into the hallway and found one of his better sets of sheets. Beaker trotted up the stairs and the two of them exchanged knowing looks before he rushed back into the guest room.

He tore the old sheets off the bed, tossed them into the hallway, gave Beaker a thumbs-up and then redressed the bed. By the time he finished his last hospital corner and folded the comforter down, she reappeared.

Like every time he saw her, he found himself momentarily speechless, one of his downfalls. She slithered out in a green, spaghetti strapped clinging nightgown, her hair pulled back, her face scrubbed clean and glowing, and her nipples showing right through the flimsy fabric.

"Multiple sheet sets, towels in the cabinet, you're all grown up." She put her dress over one of the chairs and made her way to the far side of the bed.

"I think that title goes to Isaac Abrams, not Drew Fulton." He couldn't take his eyes off her.

"Is that the name you went by?" She slid in between the sheets and her hair fanned out on the pillow.

"I go by and yes." He sat on the edge of the bed.

"I should have guessed the Isaac part." She bit her lip.

"Why's that?"

"You taught me all about Isaac Newton. What goes up must come down." She pulled back the sheets on the other side of the bed and patted the mattress. "Your favorite scientist."

He glanced at the space reserved for him. Did she think about it as often as he did?

"You know, every night no matter where I was or who I was with, the bed always felt empty," her voice was barely above a whisper.

They looked into each other's eyes.

"I have no expectations, I just want you to be next to me for a few minutes," she whispered. "I finally feel a little safe."

He swore her eyes glazed over. With her, he could never tell if the tears were real or not, another one of his downfalls. Still, he couldn't stop himself from kicking off his shoes, turning down the lights and joining her.

"Where did the Abrams come from?" She kept up the conversation.

"First last name I saw in the phone book when I was choosing a name that seemed to fit me." He laughed and she let out a giggle as well.

"Tell me about Isaac Abrams." She turned on her side. "I want to know him."

"He got his degrees and opened up his business and then one day he decided to crash a party from his old life."

"All so you could get the perfect spokesperson for your

products?" She ran a nail over the stitching on his sleeve.

"Exactly. You know how it is when something has to be just right and you can't wait," he said.

"Oh, I know that feeling all too well. I haven't felt like anything has been right in a really long time." She moved her nail up to his shoulder. "Tell me about the nutraceuticals."

"I was always interested in nutrition, especially with..." He really didn't want to talk about his past weight issues at the moment.

"I know, keep going." Her fingers traveled up to his neck.

Of course she knew, one of their bonds of their fledgling friendship all those years back was that they dieted together.

"I studied chemistry, studied how the right mix of things could truly make a difference in someone's life. We haven't yet begun to explore non-prescription solutions, and you know how I feel about drugs." To no avail, he tried to stop the words from exiting his mouth.

"I am well aware." Her voice softened and she continued with her caresses.

"Anyway, one of my professors was also into manufacturing, and I interned with him at his plant. I decided I wanted to try to make some truly therapeutic supplements and the rest is history." To abate the sensations coursing through him at her touch, he closed his eyes. Yes, he could have simply told her to stop, but he couldn't.

"Do you make everything yourself?" Now her fingers grazed his jaw line.

"I come up with the initial ideas and do the research. I have a couple of formulators and chemists who work with me." He attempted to keep his breathing even and ignore his body's natural reaction to her.

"Well, by the looks of things, your products work." Her finger outlined his ear as she moved closer to him. "I need to try them out. "I was told recently I was letting myself go."

He faced her. Whoever said that was either blind or wanting to hurt her. "Don't listen to them."

"I haven't had anyone else to listen to, everyone leaves me." She slid her hand over to his chin.

"Well, I'm here now and trust me, you look gorgeous."

"Drew. I missed you so much." She pressed her palm to the side of his face. "I thought about you every day."

The small amount of light coming into the room twinkled off the tear running down her face.

He rested his hand on her waist. Twenty years ago his entire life was centered on kissing her.

He never reached his goal.

At long last, he finally had her here and wanting him.

This time he would do the denying.

"It's really late." He kissed her forehead and used every last bit of his will to get out of the bed.

"Drew?" Her voice broke.

"I want you to know you can stay as long as you need." He backed up toward the door. "Good night, Erin."

He shut the door behind him and exhaled.

Promises were broken. Trust breached. He was a coward in too many ways.

Through the years he asked himself over and over again why he wanted her, why it was always her and even now he couldn't define it. Maybe it was what some called chemistry, and maybe that's why he studied that particular science.

If he allowed it, they could kiss. No doubt it would set off a reaction of epic proportions.

On the other hand, there was always the possibility it could always fizzle out.

He didn't need another downfall.

A KNOCK AT THE DOOR at nine o'clock on the Sunday morning after he revealed his true identity to the world and the woman he wanted since he was eighteen moved in with him, meant only one of three things. One, he had the tabloids knocking his door down, two, he had his employees knocking his door down, or three, he had the one last member of the *Hollywood Stardust* cast coming to check on the situation.

Since the paper and the Internet were already stuffed full of his story and he was quite sure his employees were going to give him hell tomorrow, he decided to let the third option wait for an extra moment while he popped a couple of his custom supplements into his mouth and downed them with some coffee.

After glancing toward the stairs for his houseguest, he stretched and took slow steps to the door.

A quick peep in the hole designed for exactly that purpose revealed he was right about his hypothesis.

While he almost wanted to tell Beaker to go ahead and attack, he didn't need a lawsuit and instead opted to open the door. The sight before him would probably have every woman between the ages of 16 to 50 squealing with delight. He stood back and let Ryder Scott into his home, or he would definitely have the paparazzi stalking him.

The leading man personified, Ryder flipped his overpriced sunglasses up on top of his coiffed shock of black hair and gave Drew a slight nod as he walked inside. Actually, it was more of a strut.

Beaker ran over, but ever the faithful pet, the dog gave a glance to Ryder and then ran over to his master with his toy.

"Cool dog." Ryder stopped and looked around, taking his time and making sure to build the suspense.

Drew picked up Beaker's toy and tossed the knotted rope. "I suppose I should ask you to have a seat."

"Then I suppose I should accept." Ryder made his way into the living room, nodding as he took in this or that and finally sat on the couch, arms stretched out, legs spread out, taking up as much surface area as possible.

Not sure if he wanted his houseguest down here or not, Drew joined the superstar and took the chair across from him. In a strange twist of fate, he could lay claim to the fact that each one of the *Hollywood Stardust* stars sat on his couch in less than forty-eight hours. He wondered if the piece of furniture was worth more now. "Coffee?"

"You're an excellent host, but I never touch the stuff. I drank some alkaline water before I drove over." Ryder finished his assessment of the room and turned to him. "I can bring you a case if you want. It's much better for you than regular water. It'll change your life."

"I'm familiar with the concept, and I'm good, thank you." He sat back. "Did you come here to meet my dog and offer me beverages?"

"It's been a while. You missed a lot."

"Maybe you missed a lot." In truth, Logan kept him updated.

As far as Ryder went, he didn't miss too much.

"Logan owns the sequel." Ryder squared his jaw.

"When did you find out this little tidbit?"

"Same as everyone else. Yesterday at the gala."

"You know when I found out?"

Ryder raised his eyebrows.

For the first time in his life he was going to best the man and he smiled. "About seventeen years ago when he called me after he bought it."

The star let out a grunt. "So, let's get down to business. I want to know if Erin is here."

Heat overtook him. It was always Ryder who threw his relationship with Erin at him. Though Logan played the third point in a love triangle Drew had no part of, somehow his best friend managed not to rub the situation in his face. "That's none of your business."

"Listen." The calm façade melted right off the man and he leaned forward. "For twenty years I had to hear about you and where were you, and what happened to you. Then, out of nowhere you appear and suddenly she doesn't answer texts or phone calls. Since I'm the one who cleaned up your mess for the last two decades, I just want to make sure she's okay before I officially transfer the pink slip."

No doubt Ryder rehearsed that entire little diatribe before he sped into his driveway in an Italian masterpiece, but Drew wasn't eighteen anymore and he knew Ryder was only using Erin as an excuse to get here for some reason.

"So what made you reappear after all these years anyway?" Ryder narrowed his eyes.

As if someone cued Erin, she came down the stairs. "Drew?" She made it to the bottom and stopped, grabbing on to the railing. "Rye, what are you doing here?"

Both he and Ryder stood and Beaker trotted over to her.

She appeared like a slice of morning sun in the room, a beam of light, all done up in skin-tight black pants and a white shirt, her hair cascading over her shoulder, her make- up light and casual.

"I came to check on you. I tried calling and texting." Ryder went toward her. "Are you all right?"

"I don't think it was a secret where I was headed." She patted

Ryder on the shoulder, gave the same attention to Beaker, and with her hand held out went right to Drew. "It feels so weird to see you. I woke up at five like I always do, and I didn't want to wake you up, then I was so tired I fell back asleep."

Did she really give his dog and Ryder the same attention in front of him? Drew took her hand. "Then you slept well?"

She moved up against him and put her lips by his ear. "As good as could be expected without you there, but we were under the same roof. I may have finally learned to sleep in my own room, but that was before you returned to me."

He glanced down at her, his body taking on a life of its own.

"I also came to discuss a few things with both of you." Ryder raised his voice and returned to the couch. "Everyone, sit."

Without thinking of logistics, Drew resumed his seat on the chair, leaving Erin either in a chair across the room or on the couch with Ryder. He would never learn.

"What's wrong?" Erin scanned the room.

Ryder moved over and patted the cushion next to him. "Did you see Logan's message to us?"

"I never even saw your text, what would make you think I saw his?" Without skipping a beat, she grabbed the ottoman from the other chair dragged it over by him and sat down, putting her hand on his knee.

Like an obedient pet, Beaker went to Erin and sat down at her feet, a picture perfect moment. Drew only wished he had a camera to capture it.

"It was to the three of us. He invited us to the bar later to discuss the sequel for Hollywood Stardust." Ryder lifted his phone.

"Well, he has a built in cast." The energy around Erin changed, sizzled with excitement.

Drew tensed. He sort of forgot about the movie.

"Erin, he also wants to discuss the dissolution of our contract with him. Should we go in the other room or something?" Ryder tilted his head back as if directing her away.

Drew ground his teeth together. If Erin agreed to a secret conversation, he might as well tell her to go pack her bags.

The damn contract had ruled Logan's life for too long. A moment of desperation among the three of them caused the under aged Logan to take the rap for Ryder and Erin's typical

Hollywood indiscretions. His best friend was arrested for a crime he didn't commit and, upon Ryder and Erin's prodding, managed to get the sequel cancelled when it was originally meant to start shooting right after the first movie's success.

With Logan's career effectively ruined, since then Ryder and Erin paid him a percentage of their earnings, as long as he handled all *Hollywood Stardust* dealings so no mistakes were ever made, no slips of the tongue. However, now in love, engaged, and with a movie to make, Logan wanted a fresh start and the contract over.

The contract was also the last straw before Drew's back broke. Before the ink dried he decided to get out there and Isaac Abrams was born. Once Logan was released from the rehabilitation center when he didn't need any rehabilitating, Drew disappeared and Isaac left for college.

"Aren't you glad to finally have it over?" Drew shook his head.

"I am and I don't need to go into the other room to discuss it." Erin blurted out the words and her hand trembled, vibrating on his leg.

Drew exhaled, hoping her words weren't an act, actually hoping this whole thing wasn't an act. Still, he couldn't stop from rubbing his hand across her back.

"I suppose Logan has no reason to cross us. I'm sure confidentiality will be in the dissolution agreement." Ryder turned away.

"Why would he say anything?" Erin dug her nails into his pants. "He has a movie he wants to make and a new life. He would look just as ridiculous as us and even more so. He took the money. In all truth, we are the victims and he should be terrified we don't talk."

And there was the bare truth in its most raw and simple form. She had everything, men literally falling at her feet, fame, beauty, and she considered herself the victim. Though she was the instrumental person behind the entire contract, she was the one doing the drugs, she was the one who wanted out of the sequel. But having to pay the piper was the toughest on her, and she suffered no matter what.

"Yes, this is the way things should be. We celebrated a major milestone, so the timing is right to end something such as the contract, and have a renewal with the sequel. Hopefully this will all bode well for my own movie." Ryder almost seemed to take a cleansing breath. "This is right."

Not the actor the other two were, Drew had to make a huge effort not to wrinkle his nose as Ryder spewed his rhetoric. Some things never changed.

"I agree. Now that we have Drew back, I think we need to start over with everything." She took his hand. "I still can't believe you're here, or I'm here. I carried around this hole in my chest everyday and for the first time in twenty years I woke up and it wasn't there."

Like all things with Erin, there was always the other side. The way she gazed at him with glossed over eyes and the smile she only reserved for real life, not the camera, shining across her face.

True to his nature, he couldn't stop himself from squeezing her hand, though he knew deep down even though she eviscerated him twenty years ago, she considered herself the victim there too.

"Just don't disappear again." She intertwined their fingers.

Then again, maybe he gave her all the right reasons. Somehow he ended up right back where he started, only two decades older.

HOLLYWOOD STARBURST

FADE IN:

EXT. HOLLYWOOD, CA - OUTSIDE HOLLYWOOD STARDUST
THEATRE - LATE NIGHT.

The place is now a construction site, with
warning signs and a chicken wire fence around
the theatre. The ruckus of Hollywood surrounds
the area.

ROXY stares out at the theatre, her fingers
interlaced in the chicken wire.

A gang of women and men dressed in leather and
rough attire come up to her.

>   GIRL IN GANG
>   Oh, look what we have
>   here, another little
>   starlet looking at a
>   dream. She's going to
>   end up just like that
>   building getting ready
>   to be torn apart.

ROXY tightens her grip on the fence and presses
her lips together.

GIRL IN GANG gets right up in ROXY'S face.

>   GIRL IN GANG
>   Do you think I'm going
>   to hurt you?

ROXY swallows and shakes her head.

The others in the gang surround Roxy.

>   GIRL IN GANG
>   Then why don't you
>   talk? Say something
>   princess. What are you,

                         too good to talk to
                         us? What are you doing?

ROXY faces the girl in a sudden move.

                              ROXY
                         I'm playing a role.

GIRL IN GANG leans back.

                              GIRL IN GANG
                         What kind of role?

                              ROXY
                         The girl who wants to be
                         an actress. You know,
                         the one who drove across
                         the country with three
                         boys just to see a
                         theatre and then thought
                         I could stay. You know,
                         the one who abandoned
                         her friends and family
                         and now her parents
                         won't talk to her cause
                         she ruined her life.

ROXY steps closer to the girl and then takes
her time to look around all the other gang
members.

The men in the gang smile and come closer, the
other girls frown, one puts her hand on a
knife.

                    ROXY
          Yes, I am playing a
          role. Everything is an
          act. The truth is no one
          really knows anyone,
          right?

The girl lifts the knife.

                    ROXY
          You may see a princess
          staring at a theatre not
          sure what to do with her
          life, but maybe in
          reality I have nothing
          more to lose and I don't
          care.

Roxy swipes her own knife out of her pocket and
flips up the blade.

The group stands around, no one speaks.

                    ROXY
          What? Are you scared of
          me? Think I'm going to
          hurt you? Am I too good
          for you?

Behind Roxy, a cop car slowly rolls down the
street.

GIRL IN THE GANG backs up, elbowing a couple of
the other gang members.

                    GIRL IN THE GANG
          (Laughs)
          You need to go take more
          acting lessons,
          princess. Come on, let's
          go.

ROXY stands straight up and watches the gang
leave. Once alone, she turns to the Hollywood
Stardust theatre.

                ROXY
          (Whispers)
           I'm the girl who tried
           to play a role. It just
           didn't work.

Chapter Five

DRIPPING IN EVERY DESIGNER LABEL she could put on her person, Erin felt her heartbeat increase the moment she and Drew got within a mile of Logan's brother's bar. She pulled the visor down and glanced in the mirror. No matter how many times she looked, it didn't get any better.

"The last time I was here was for the opening party, and I could have sworn I felt you there." She wrung her hands together.

"I heard the ruckus when they announced you and Ryder had arrived, and I snuck out the back door." Drew turned down a side street.

"Well, I always thought we were connected, I felt your energy." It wasn't the best night in the world. Paparazzi had followed her and Ryder, she and Brian were fighting, and when the photographers asked her and Logan to recreate the dance from the movie, he insisted on performing it with his now fiancée.

"It's possible."

She chewed the inside of her mouth. Of all of them, she had to be doing the worst. How did that happen? For the last two decades it was her and Ryder on the race to the top, with Logan coming up behind them keeping things tidy. Drew was gone. Now she was truly alone with no agent, no significant other or even an other who wasn't significant, and no jobs. Wait, one of those items she could fix before they ever walked inside. "Drew, we have something to discuss before we go inside."

He entered the small parking lot behind the bar and stopped the car. "All right."

"I told you I would give you an answer about your project this morning, and I wanted to let you know that I've decided to be the spokesperson for your Hollywood Glow line." She nodded. Even with the sequel, she needed to have something in the works.

"Don't you have to talk to Brian before you decide that?"

Yes, Brian. He finally directly mentioned her agent or whatever title he once held. One more time she pulled down the visor and caught a glimpse of her reflection in the mirror.

She opened her mouth, about to lie, telling him she spoke to Brian already, but stopped and shut her eyes. Drew gave her a second chance, and he knew she used to be with Brian. Maybe that's why he wouldn't make any move forward. Plus, Ryder and Logan would find out, if they didn't know already. "I can make my own decisions. I'm not with Brian anymore on any level. I had to make some changes about a lot of things. Maybe Ryder was right about timing and such. I didn't say anything last night because it seemed like a lot to drop on you, since I already dropped myself on you."

"So, at last you're an independent woman, completely free." He chuckled.

She faced him. "Not entirely, I heard I'm associated with the number one nutraceutical laboratory in the United States. They want to put out an amazing line and use me as the spokesperson. That's a big responsibility." As an added bonus, it would tie her to Drew and his life.

"Well, then I guess you're taken." With the words out, he exited the car.

Her stomach twisted, but in a good way, and she no sooner put her hand on the door handle than Drew darted around the car and opened the door. "Oh, I'm not used to a gentleman."

"Then you've been with the wrong people." He stood back to let her out.

She supposed she deserved his teasing and flirting, and truthfully she was enjoying it, she only prayed it paid off. "Well, I guess we're going in."

"I'm here. You'll be fine." He closed the door and put his hand on the small of her back, guiding her to the rear entrance. She sort of wished it was the other way around and he put his hand on her rear. At her own joke she managed to at least crack a smile by the time they entered through the kitchen and were slapped right in the face with the soon to be bride and groom.

"It's a miraculous day." Logan lifted his chin in Erin's direction and held out a glass of champagne. "I'm engaged, I get to call my best friend by his name, Ryder is already here and Erin is early. Seriously, I am blessed."

"Thank you for everything." Logan's fiancée, Ivy, went right to Drew and gave him a hug.

"All in a day's work." Drew gave her a kiss on the cheek and then grabbed her hand. "Now, that looks even better on you than it did in the box."

Ivy's brand new diamond ring sparkled, practically blinded Erin, but she couldn't stop studying the pear shaped diamond surrounded by a multitude of smaller diamonds. The stone itself was large enough one could take a bite out of it and she bet it tasted much better than the fruit.

Every time she witnessed someone she knew get engaged or married, a strange emptiness overtook her. It was hard to celebrate when her personal life was never up to par. She knew she better say something and forced herself over to Ivy. "The ring is magnificent, congratulations." With the champagne glass held out of the way, she gave Logan's fiancée a light embrace.

"Thank you." Ivy returned the gesture. "We didn't mean to take over yesterday's event, it sort of just happened."

Erin pulled back and assessed the woman in front of her in a stunning blue 1950s form fitting designer dress. Ivy was an interesting choice for Logan, a bit quirky with her vintage clothing, extremely smart with her degrees, and beautiful in a good girl way. Then again, maybe she was the perfect choice for the presumed bad boy of their bunch. "Well, between you and Logan and then Drew, we certainly got the media coverage."

Wanting to finish her rounds as fast as possible, she side-stepped over to Logan. She leaned in and hugged him as well. There was no woman alive who wouldn't envy the position Ivy now possessed. Gorgeous in a naughty way with his dark blond hair pulled back in a ponytail and a bit of scruff, he always seemed as if he were ready to get into trouble.

Between his appearances on Ivy's webcasts, his engagement and the movie, he would now be redeemed from the past she and Ryder had created for him. "I really am happy for you."

"Looks like we both won last night." He gave her a wink.

"It's getting there." She kept her smile, turned to Ryder and paused. Oh, Ryder Scott, the unattainable man. Stock photo leading man, he was charming on the outside, jerk and manipulator on the inside. The public loved him, but then again they didn't know him. Most women were terrified of him, and they had every reason. With his black hair that covered up a mind that absorbed everything and never forgot, clear blue eyes that observed the world and looks that didn't even seem real, women flocked to him like a drug until they realized they couldn't handle him.

More than Logan, at one point she thought Ryder was the one. Though younger than her by six months, Logan was always the big brother, but Ryder was the catch.

"Long time no see," she said.

He leaned down to her ear. "We are going to come out of this on top."

If that's what Ryder deemed, then it would be so. She patted him.

"Everyone grab your glass and let's go into the main room. We have a lot of business to take care of." Logan made his announcement, took his queen by the hand and left the kitchen.

With a shake of his head, Ryder followed.

She turned back to Drew.

Drew.

Maybe she didn't have enough time to reflect on him. Everything happened so fast. Unlike the bad boy and the leading man, in the movie that played out in her mind, Drew was the superhero. The best friend by day who would change his identity to turn into anything he wanted and no one would ever be the wiser, and she supposed that's exactly what he accomplished.

Drew was the man who silently took over. The actor who played the sidekick, but was the one who would ultimately save the day and in his own way would take over the movie.

"Shall we?" He motioned forward.

"I suppose." She went through the door, but looked behind her to make sure Drew stayed with her, something she should have done long ago.

They entered the bar done up like a classy 1920s speakeasy. The place might belong to his brother, but the vibe had Logan written all over it.

"Before we get down to business, I propose a toast." Logan stood in the middle of the room and held up his glass.

They all gathered around in a circle.

"To thrilling beginnings, breathless endings, and stories that need to be continued." He kissed Ivy first, tapped his glass to hers, and then they all proceeded to complete the ritual, clinking their glasses, saying cheers and sipping their drinks.

"We've already covered the thrilling beginnings." Logan motioned toward a table already set up with platters of food, note pads and pens.

The five of them took their seats. For the first time since she could remember, she had Drew next to her.

"Let's get on to endings. I think we'll all agree this one is ready to go away." Logan passed her and Ryder documents. "This will effectively dissolve our arrangement, but keep intact all the confidentiality agreements we have. That's our story and it's over and unlike other things it doesn't need a sequel. Take some time and read it over."

Through all the years and in all the contracts she signed, she always had someone by her side to read them. Her mouth went dry. This paper ended a huge part of her life. No longer would she have Logan to lean on. She and Ryder would no longer have that bond no one else understood from their past, what they went through together or their reasoning. The words on the paper blurred together, and she put her hand to her forehead. "Drew."

"Are you all right?" Drew whispered in her ear.

"Will you read this for me?" She pushed the document toward him.

"Of course." He took the pages.

"I don't know why we're bothering with confidentiality." Ryder flipped through the papers. "Who cares if the three of us don't say anything? Why would we?"

"Are you implying something?" Logan stared Ryder down.

She clenched her fist. How easily they all fell back into their old habits.

"Yeah, I am. We need to cover our backs." Ryder leaned forward.

"Good, for once you are thinking." Logan smiled and tossed Drew a paper. "My love already signed her confidentiality agreement this morning, and I even made Brian sign one."

Ryder broke out into laughter, and the men shook hands.

She shuddered at her ex-agent's, ex-significant other's, ex-everything's name.

Drew scanned the confidentiality agreement, signed it and slid it over to Logan. Then he resumed reading her contract.

After several minutes and flipping back and forth through the pages a couple of times, he leaned over to her. "Everything here is standard. It just states that any debt is paid in full, and of course, the confidentiality clause." He pointed to the different sections. "Basically you are all three free entities."

"Somehow this feels like a divorce." With mixed emotions, she swiped the pen out of Drew's hand and signed her name.

Ryder did the same, and they all signed each other's copies.

For all the times she cursed the contract, having to pay Logan and everything to do with the situation, a strange emptiness consumed her at the ending. At least Logan and Ryder had the class to not begin cheering or high-fiving. In fact, they all remained rather silent for a moment as if each caught in their own reflections.

Of course, the contract was the final act that drove Drew away, and it seemed fitting that the end coincided with his return. She turned to him. "Thank you."

He nodded and put his hand around the back of her chair, leaving it there.

"Well, on to better things." Logan handed his papers to his soon to be wife, leaned over and lifted what was clearly a script onto the table. "Such as stories that still need to be told."

She slid her chair closer to Drew's and held her breath. At least in the land of *Hollywood Stardust*, she was a shoo-in for the role. Not only did she want to reprise her famous character, she needed to as well.

"*Hollywood Starburst*." Logan held up the typewritten pages. "In less than twenty-four hours after the future Mrs. Alexander and I announced the sequel will be made, we already have heard from our original studio wanting to back it."

With a studio would come the money. "Well, I for one am ready to reprise my role as Roxy." Having never seen the script, she itched for the chance to put her hands on it. Like other fans of the movie, she had to know who Roxy ended up with.

"What is the scheduling?" Ever the poker face, Ryder sat back. "I'm in the middle of directing my movie and I have another film coming up."

"I have commitments as well." Not to be outdone, she sat up. "On top of it, I'm going to be the spokesperson for one of Drew's product lines, and I am determined it will be a success, however I believe this project is important and much anticipated."

"Well, I am glad to hear that." Logan put the script down on the table, placed his hand on top of the pages, and turned to Ivy. "We have a bit of a situation."

Erin's whole body tensed. If he gave her role to his stage frightened fiancée, she didn't know what she would do.

Once more Logan faced them. "The sequel picks up from where Hollywood Stardust ends."

Neither she nor Ryder said a word. Of course the movie started there.

Again, Logan reached under the table, this time holding up a blown up picture of the four of them on the set of the original movie. She smiled at the famous image of them standing in front of Logan's BMW.

He then retrieved one more oversized print from under the table, revealing a picture of them from the night before and held them side by side.

"Boy, do we look better with age." Ryder sat back. "Especially me."

"While I agree we all aged exceedingly well, especially me, I think we would all be in agreement that we can't pass for these people any longer." Logan lifted the first picture. "I believe it would make the film into a mockery. The movie starts where Roxy opens her eyes to watch Steven drive away."

She glanced between the two photos. Unless Roxy completely changed in the blink of an eye, she couldn't pass for that girl, but she and Roxy were one. "You own the script and the rights. Have her open her eyes twenty years later."

"Actually, that was a thought, but the story needs to be told the way it needs to be told." Logan put the pictures down. "We're going to cast younger actors in the lead roles."

A strange heat invaded her body, and all she knew was it better not be any sort of hot flash. She shot up out of the chair and crossed her arms. "Logan, with the right makeup we can play the characters synonymous with us."

"Erin." Logan shook his head. "Do you really want to be known as the actress who tried to play her twenty-year younger self? It would be ridiculous."

"Roxy is my role." She crossed her arms.

"You will always be the original Roxy, but if we want to see the sequel come to life, we have to do it right." Logan countered. "We had our chance, but it passed us."

Her eyes filled up. After she played Roxy, she wanted to anything she could to distance herself from the role for fear she would be typecast. Now, she would give everything to play her again. "Don't you think the fans of the movie will protest to having our roles hacked by others?" She glanced at Ivy, the woman who studied the movie would understand.

Ivy looked down at the table.

Erin ground her teeth together and stood her ground. She needed the role, and she needed Roxy. No one could take her away.

"Wren." Ryder piped up. "Logan's right."

"Then why did he call this meeting?" She put her hands on her hips and faced down the man who held her role in his hands.

"We want you in the movie. You just can't be Roxy." Logan stood. "We want you all in the movie, because we think it will more than add to its appeal to have all of us in the movie in cameo appearances. People will come just to see us."

"That is the perfect solution." Ryder got up as well. "That's how things should be. We're all busy. This way we can come and do our scenes, be involved in the movie and yet pass the torch. I give it the green light."

Now Logan and Ryder both stared at her.

"I don't think you understand." She didn't know how else to plead her case.

"We're not teenagers. We're not even in our early twenties where we could pull it off." Logan always tried to be the voice of reason, make sure everyone was taken care of, but with no contract to bind them anymore, he just wanted to toss her away.

"It's going to be all right, Erin." Ryder came in right on cue to be the hero.

Unsure of what to do and with no other offers besides Drew's endorsing job, she shrugged. "If I decide to do this, I'm not auditioning." She returned to her seat. Drew put his hand on her shoulder and gave her a squeeze. At least she had Drew. Maybe she could convince Logan to put them in the same scene. She put her hand over his.

Ryder and Logan laughed and returned to their chairs.

Logan pointed at Drew.

"Not only am I not going to audition, I think I'll have to take a pass on this one. I have a business to run." Drew's words possessed the finality of a clapperboard on the final scene.

She spun toward him. "No, you have to be in it. We'll be together." This would be the perfect opportunity for them to reconnect.

"No, I called cut on my acting career twenty years ago. I don't need a retake on that part of my life." He didn't look her in the eye, only continued to face forward.

The time of his life he didn't want to relive was the time he spent with her. "I'm not doing this." She shot up out of her chair and walked away. With each step she took, she counted off all she lost, her agent, her home, her contract, her role, her place.

HOLLYWOOD STARBURST

FADE IN:

EXT. HOLLYWOOD, CA — PAY PHONE ON HOLLYWOOD
BLVD — SUNSET

ROXY shoves coins into the payphone slot. She
dials the phone and waits while it rings.

PHONE RINGS.

>   CHARLES (O.S.)
>   (Filtered)
>   Hello?

>   ROXY
>   It's Roxy.

>   CHARLES (O.S.)
>   (Filtered. Panicked tone)
>   Are you all right? Where
>   are you?

ROXY grips phone tighter.

>   ROXY
>   I'm fine I think. I'm
>   still in Hollywood.

>   CHARLES (O.S.)
>   (Filtered)
>   Are you going to come
>   home?

ROXY shuts her eyes.

                    ROXY
          I...Did William get
          home?

           CHARLES (O.S.)
          (Filtered)
          You're not calling about
          William.

ROXY shakes her head.

                    ROXY
          I just asked about him.

           CHARLES (O.S.)
          (Filtered)
          If you wanted to know
          about him, you would
          have asked about him
          first.

Silence.

                    ROXY
          Charles?

           CHARLES (O.S.)
          (Filtered)
          If you come home soon
          you can make up the time
          you lost in summer
          school. You won't be
          able to be in the
          graduation ceremonies,
          but you won't be behind.

                    ROXY
          I'm always behind.

                    CHARLES (O.S.)
                    (Filtered)
                    Come home and we'll get
                    you ahead. Do you want
                    me to talk to your
                    parents?

ROXY stands up straight.

                         ROXY
                    No. I have to prove to
                    them I can make it on my
                    own. If I come back
                    they'll know I failed.

                    CHARLES (O.S.)
                    (Filtered)
                    It's only failure if
                    that's not what you
                    want.

                         ROXY
                    I want to find my place.

                    CHARLES (O.S.)
                    (Filtered)
                    You called me. Doesn't
                    that tell you you're
                    place is back here?

                         ROXY
                    I don't know what to do.

                    CHARLES (O.S.)
                    (Filtered)
                    What about Steven?

                         ROXY
                    Steven has nothing to do
                    with this.

                    CHARLES (O.S.)
                    (Filtered)
                    He's why you really called.

ROXY presses the phone to her chest and stares off into nothing.

Chapter Six

WITHOUT TRAFFIC, THE DRIVE from Hollywood to Pasadena took about twenty-five minutes, maybe thirty if they were unlucky with stoplights. During traffic, the same ride could take anywhere between an hour to ninety minutes.

No matter the traffic conditions, the drive from Hollywood to Pasadena took several thousand years with Erin not speaking to him, and Drew was not exaggerating in the slightest.

However, he could have a conversation with her silence. If he addressed the quiet, he would say that he couldn't commit to a movie after only being reunited with her less than twenty-four hours ago. He didn't know where they stood and didn't know if he wanted to be stuck with months and months of having to see her if things didn't work out. Maybe he wanted to know if she could accept him without acting binding them together.

It wasn't that he didn't want her, he was afraid of how much he wanted her.

At long last he pulled up into his driveway. After she walked away from the table and announced she wouldn't be in the movie either, he braced himself for her to tell him she needed to leave.

Damn. He couldn't give in and he couldn't let go. No wonder she wasn't speaking.

He shut off the car. "Erin."

"Would it be all right if I took Beaker for a walk?"

Though he heard her, he had to make sure he didn't make up her question in his head. "What?"

"Does Beaker like to go for walks? I just wanted to take him out and get some air."

She wanted to take the dog for a walk, not leave. It took him a moment to process the information.

"Never mind." She opened the car door, got out and stomped to the front of the house.

He followed her. "I am quite certain Beaker would love for you to take him for a walk. I just didn't think that was something you would want to do."

"What you don't know, Andrew Jordan Fulton, is a lot. You need to read your cues better." She tapped her foot and pointed at the front door. "May I go inside, please?"

"Since you're going to be staying, would you like me to get you a key?" He unlocked the door.

"Absolutely not. That's all I need. If you don't want to do a movie with me, and you can't trust me with your dog, how could you trust me with a key to your home?" She pushed her way inside, stopping the moment Beaker greeted her.

Drew almost tripped over them.

She kneeled down, gave the dog a kiss on his nose and entered. "I was going to offer to make you a sandwich or something since we didn't eat, but we don't have an official food taster here, so if you don't mind I think I'll just go upstairs and figure out what to do with my career now that I gave up a role for you."

He had been meaning to ask her about this exact subject. "You gave up a role for me?"

She straightened and spun toward him. "Why did you come back?"

"What?" He told her last night. Well, actually he lied, but still.

"Why the sudden reappearance? Were you that desperate for a spokesperson and Logan didn't know anyone else?" She put her hands on her hips. "When you came back and sought me out last night didn't you think the acting may be part of it? You had to know about the sequel before any of us."

"Erin." Though he said her name, he had nothing to say after it. When he made the decision to go to her, he knew what it would entail, wanted what it would entail. Erin was a lot, all emotion and passion, and he needed it all.

"Wait." She held up her hand and let out a chuckle, one that said nothing was funny. "Here I thought I was the actress."

"What?" The muscles in his neck tightened.

"This is part of my punishment. A little payback though you can truly never make it equal, so anything you do to me will always be justified." She shook her head. "It worked and now you can put another notch in your belt, let me know if we will ever even out."

Her words washed over him and he took a second to absorb them. At the gala, he could have snuck out. He didn't need to go on stage, he knew what would happen when he walked into work tomorrow and yet he still moved forward. His decision wasn't a snap decision.

Before he had the chance to retort, the grind of tires on asphalt echoed in his driveway as Logan's computer on wheels pulled up. With only what Drew would call Hollywood flair, his best friend got out of the car, adjusted his sunglasses, checked his signature ponytail, and sauntered around the car to open the door for his fiancée.

Like in a movie, first a pair of smooth legs exited the car followed by the rest of the glamorous girl. Though only engaged about twenty-four hours, Ivy seemed different, not only in the light radiating from her, but a bit of the magic touched her, the glitz, the shine.

Logan, Ryder, Erin, they always possessed that one quality, the one that made them larger than life. On screen or off, it didn't change. Damn, he missed what he never had and deep down that was one of the reasons he came back.

As he approached, Logan lifted his chin.

"I need to talk to you." Drew motioned for them to hurry up.

"I would also like to talk to you." Erin huffed behind him.

"Well, then it's a good thing we're here." Logan guided Ivy up the porch and they all went inside.

Ivy waved to him and Erin and gave Beaker a pat.

"All right, there is only so much of me to go around. So, I will buck tradition and go with men first." Logan tilted his head.

Drew turned back to Erin, resisted the need to tell her to play nice and followed Logan into the laundry room.

Before saying a word, Logan slid the door closed, encapsulating them in the tiny space, made even more miniscule by Drew's twenty-first century washer and dryer in a 1918 designed room. He backed up against the wall.

Logan held up his finger and looked in the laundry basket,

opened the lid to the washer and then the door to the dryer.

"What are you doing?" He kicked the door to his dryer closed.

Logan straightened up and crossed his arms. "Seriously."

"Do you want to talk about the movie or not?" Drew narrowed his eyes.

"First, I want to know if you slept with her, but I guess I got my answer by the lack of any dirty sheets." Logan huffed. "You waited twenty years for this and you didn't do the deed?"

He ground his teeth together. "I want to be in the movie."

"People want a lot of things, but I want to know why you didn't sleep with her."

"We have a complicated past."

Logan nodded. "More than wanting to know if you slept with her, I wanted to make sure everything was copacetic here."

"As copacetic as getting your fiancée back for you and outing myself to Erin and the world can be." Waiting for an answer about the movie, he tapped his foot.

"I did mean to thank you for that." His best friend bowed in his direction.

"Logan." He held his hands out, telling his friend to get on with it.

"I came here to basically beg you to be in my movie. I don't beg for anything, so now at least let me have the fun of making Erin wait an unusually long time before I tell her she can be in the movie as well." Though Logan didn't smile, his eyes sparkled with mayhem. "I thought once you showed up last night at the gala and then arrived today with Erin, the movie was a no brainer. I was shocked when you declined. What made you change your mind?"

Drew looked out the window into his yard at his lemon tree. He remembered thinking on the day he saw the house for the first time that Erin would love that tree. While they filmed the movie, she always sought out the shade of a tree on breaks, and the first time she saw fruit hanging from a branch, she seemed mesmerized. Sometimes he would sneak over with her, wishing their few stolen moments would make it into the movie, but it wasn't his role, his path.

"It's time," he said.

"Then this time, make some dirty laundry." Logan strummed his fingers on the washing machine, the metallic tapping ringing through the room. "Don't disappear."

No, this time he couldn't vanish.

THE DOOR TO THE LAUNDRY room slid open and one half of their famous quartet exited. All smiles, Logan elbowed Drew. "After much convincing, I have managed to convince Mr. Fulton to take his place amongst the stars."

Erin focused on Drew and her cheeks heated. What he wouldn't do for her, he would do for Logan. Why even bother with her at all?

"Yay!" As Ivy clapped, the reflection of the light off her diamond sparkled over the room. She ran over to Drew and hugged him.

Erin fought the need to walk away. No one begged for her, sought her out, made sure she was all right. Somehow, she ended up D-listed in her own group. In a need to reclaim her spotlight, she stomped into the middle of the lovefest, put her hands on her hips and faced Logan.

"Are you ready for our one on one, Miss Holland?" Logan's tone took on authority laced with sarcasm for good measure.

"I don't need my private time, Mr. Alexander." She channeled a heroine she once played, a small town waitress who finally learned to take control of her life. To this day she could still balance a tray of water glasses in one hand and wipe down a table with the other. "We all know people would talk if I didn't make my appearance, so I'll be in your little film."

"Thank you." Logan bowed to her. "I promised my future wife she would have all four of us as a wedding present."

"Well, just remember I can't be returned, and I won't be put on any registry." She held her head high.

"Thank you. It wouldn't have been the same without you." Ivy leaned in and hugged her. "You know, in my thesis I wrote why Roxy is such an important female character and how you personified the role. No one will ever be you, but I think having your energy in the movie will make all the difference."

Erin pulled back and took a moment to assess the other female. With this one, she couldn't throw a temper tantrum and get the role switched to a guy. Ivy would be here to stay and she wondered if maybe the woman's understanding of the movie could make her valuable in the end.

Erin could have a girlfriend, she just never found the right match. "I'd like to read your thesis."

"You would?" Ivy's face glowed brighter than her diamond with a smile.

"Yes, I would and I think we should go to lunch." Women lunched. It was a verb and a completely appropriate activity for two females.

"Lunch?" Ivy let out a giddy laugh and turned to Logan.

Logan tilted his head. "Well, considering that would probably make for some sort of media frenzy, why don't I make you two ladies a gourmet lunch at the bar and it will give Drew and I a chance to catch up on manly things."

Well, it was more than obvious Logan needed to brush up on his acting skills. Like Drew with the dog, apparently she wasn't fit to take Logan's fiancée out for a salad. She also refused to be the odd couple with Drew who wouldn't so much as kiss her.

"We'll have to set up a time. Excuse me, but I'm going to go change." She spun on her heel and headed toward the stairs, making the exact exit she wanted.

Alone in Drew's guest room she shimmied out of her dress and heels, found a pair of yoga pants and a shirt and waited until she heard some doors close, hopefully indicating Logan's departure.

Ready to take her walk alone, she bolted down the stairs only to find Beaker sitting at the front door with his leash in his mouth. Wagging his tail, he trotted over to her.

With Drew nowhere to be found, and not caring anymore, she took Beaker's offering, fastened the leash to the dog's collar, adjusted her sunglasses, and left the house.

She allowed Beaker to lead her down the street and took in her surroundings. Pasadena was a beautiful city, part vintage and part modern. Drew's home was nestled in one of the nicer residential areas with larger lots and kept up to perfection. Majestic trees lined the streets, creating peaceful, cool shade, ideal for a walk in the late afternoon.

Lately her life had been a swirl of activity. Not only had she finished a couple of projects and been trying to book new work, but the festivities leading up to the *Hollywood Stardust* anniversary filled her time.

If anyone would have told her last week at this time she would have walked away from her agent and her relationship without even glancing back and she would be staying at Drew's place, she would have called that person a bold-faced liar.

She always knew eventually she and Drew would be reunited. In fact, she might even say she waited for it. She'd put so many things on hold in hopes he would return to her.

The moment had come and gone without the fanfare and explosion she thought would come of their reunion.

She looked up to the rays of sunlight sneaking in through the tree branches. How come nothing in life ever lived up to the dream?

Drew's appearance was straight out of any romance story. They should have spent the night in each other's arms, kissing and exploring each other until the world faded to black, the perfect Hollywood ending.

Instead of coming in at the happily ever after, she found herself right in the middle of the movie and she wasn't sure what genre they were in anymore.

Beaker turned yet another corner, and she stopped. Caught up in thoughts of Drew, her job situation, or lack thereof, her non-existent housing situation, she sort of lost track of their location. She turned, glancing up at the signs. They weren't on Drew's street anymore and she'd walked out of the house without as much as a cell phone or a homing pigeon.

The dog gave the leash a tug.

"You know how to get home, right?" Though Beaker might not know it, he was part of Hollywood history and therefore should respond to questions like any other well-trained working animal.

Beaker continued forward and with no choice, she followed. They made their way up and down a few more residential streets. The homes became more spread out, the sun lowered in the sky and her legs started protesting. Her canine companion made one more turn and suddenly they were facing a vacant land full of bushes and trees and dark tunnel with some graffiti.

"Whoa." Again they stopped. With the leash coiled in her hand, she glanced around. She knew this place. In every horror movie, this was where the heroine was grabbed from behind and her throat slashed with a knife. At least she knew what genre she'd gotten herself into.

"Erin!"

On automatic, she spun in the direction where Drew's voice broke through the silence. "Over here!" she called.

As if also answering, Beaker barked. He had pretty good timing.

From around a bend, Drew appeared and jogged toward them. "I was starting to get worried." He bent down and gave Beaker a scratch behind his ear. "You got an extra walk didn't you?"

"I didn't lose him or hurt him." She unfurled Beaker's leash from her arm and handed the dog over to his rightful owner. "I never would."

"I know you wouldn't." Rather than taking the leash, he motioned forward.

"Well, since you felt the need to check up on us, I beg to differ." Not wanting to admit she had no idea where she was, she let Drew guide her away.

"I actually wanted to join you." He put his hands in his pockets and slowed his steps. "I thought I would answer your question."

"Which one?" She kept her focus on the dog.

"About my sudden reappearance."

She stopped and waited.

"I want my life back." He stood in front of her and stared into her face. "I want it back. I don't want to hide anymore. I want what I missed."

"What does all that involve?" She pulled the dog closer to her.

"That's the problem." Drew inched closer.

"What's the problem?" Her breath quickened.

He put one hand on her waist. "I don't know what it all entails."

She wouldn't be kept at bay while he figured out what he wanted to do. She also had her own set of timelines and troubles. "Well, when you figure it all out, you know where to find me." A glance up at the street sign let her know she found the right road. With a smile, she walked forward exactly like the heroine in that one movie who left her love before the film faded to black.

<u>HOLLYWOOD STARBURST</u>

FADE IN:

INT. INDIANAPOLIS, IN - STEVEN'S HOUSE GARAGE
LATE AFTERNOON

STEVEN hunches over the hood of his BMW,
working on the engine. He holds his hand out.

CHARLES absentmindedly hands Steven a wrench,
but continues to read.

OLDER model non-descript car drives up and
stops in front of Steven's house. WILLIAM gets
out of the car.

CHARLES puts his book down.

                    CHARLES
          Hey, look who's here.

STEVEN glances over his shoulder and returns to
his car.

WILLIAM approaches, lifts his chin to Charles.

CHARLES returns the gesture.

WILLIAM shoves his hands in his pockets and
waits while shifting weight from one foot to
the other.

STEVEN holds his hand out again.

CHARLES lifts a socket wrench.

WILLIAM grabs tool away from Charles and slaps
it in Steven's hand.

                    STEVEN
          You're wrong.

CHARLES shakes head

>   WILLIAM
>   It's right.

>   STEVEN
>   The tool is right, it's
>   you who is wrong.

>   WILLIAM
>   What am I wrong about?

STEVEN pushes away from the car, throws tool
off to one side and spins toward William.

>   STEVEN
>   When I drove away, I
>   left her with you. She
>   belongs with you and you
>   ditched her.

>   WILLIAM
>   Why does she belong with
>   me?

>   STEVEN
>   You're the right
>   choice. I'm just going
>   to sleep with her and
>   drive away. Oh, yeah I
>   did already.

STEVEN bends down, picks up his tool and
returns to the car.

               WILLIAM
          (Lowers voice.)
           I didn't sleep with her.

STEVEN doesn't turn around, but he stops what
he's doing.

               WILLIAM
           Not that I didn't
           try. She said she
           wanted to, but couldn't.

               STEVEN
           Well, I thank you for
           this moment of true
           confessions, but why
           don't you tell me why
           you're here?

               WILLIAM
           Cause you're the only
           one who gets it.

STEVEN turns back around.

               STEVEN
          (Sarcastic)
           If you were so in love
           with her, why don't you
           know where she is?

               WILLIAM
           Because I am so in love
           with her.

               STEVEN
           I'm the wrong person to
           be talking to.

               WILLIAM
           I don't agree.

               STEVEN
           You need to find her.

                    WILLIAM
              We need to find her.

CHARLES steps forward.

                    CHARLES
              I've already found her.

WILLIAM and STEVEN both spin around to face
Charles and lean in as if to attack.

CHARLES holds up his hand.

                    CHARLES
              Think before you act,
              you only get one more
              shot at this.

WILLIAM and STEVEN look at each other. WILLIAM
holds his hand out for a shake, STEVEN pauses
and puts his hand in William's.

Chapter Seven

DREW PARKED IN HIS SPOT at Fluent Word Nutraceuticals and looked in his rear view mirror. Under Logan's guidance, he had purchased the building and it proved to be a wise investment. In fact, he owned everything from the property to each piece of equipment, giving him the opportunity to be an extremely nimble company. They were able to compete with larger labs because of his lack of overhead.

He exhaled and got out of his SUV. Two days ago he left work as Isaac Abrams, Ph.D., today he would enter as Drew Fulton, ex-star of *Hollywood Stardust*. There was no telling how his handpicked crew would take his deception.

Once he opened the door to the building, he got his answer.

The soundtrack to *Hollywood Stardust* blared through the space and oversized prints from the movie, including close-ups of him in character, hung on almost every available space.

Everyone from the front office staff to the production crew gathered around and applauded.

"And the award for the best hide your identity goes to none other than our very own lord and master, Isaac Abrams." James, his operations manager, stepped forward with makeshift trophy made from a 20th anniversary DVD case, a beaker, and some containers of vitamins they taped together.

"Now is the time that we would like you to make a speech." His lead chemist, Bambi, approached, handed him a bouquet of flowers and put a toy crown on top of his head.

All the employees started chanting "speech."

He held up his hand, nodded and waited for the fanfare to die down. "All right, all right. As you have heard, in a former life I was Drew Fulton, star of the silver screen."

They clapped again.

"Aren't you still Drew Fulton?" James called out.

"In this building I am still Isaac Abrams, understood?" He glanced around.

His employees nodded.

"What about the sequel?" someone asked.

"Well, in a small bit of luck, I am much too old to play Charles in the sequel." He paused before letting out the next part. Once the words left his mouth, it would be real. "However Drew Fulton will be making a cameo appearance in the film."

His statement was met with laughter, cheers and more clapping, but now he needed to let the rest of his news out. "In a couple of hours, Erin Holland will be coming here." It felt strange to leave her in his home by herself, but he did manage to give her a key. Actually, he put it on her key ring for her. Nothing like giving her mixed messages.

The crew let out a series of gasps and mumbles. After their walk, Erin decided that she needed to see the lab since she would be working with him.

"She's going to be endorsing a new line of products I have been working on called Hollywood Glow, so I just wanted to let you know." More like give them a warning. He glanced over at Bambi, the poor woman had her brow furrowed and was staring off into space. No doubt she was wondering where her project notes were, and he would have to lie yet again and tell her he had them. Once one lie started, they piled up.

"I don't have that on the schedule." James shook his head. "We never even had a production meeting on it. What products are you looking to do? What package? What's the lead time? Do you want this to come out with the sequel? What are you talking about?"

Damn qualified staff. He used one of the oldest tricks in the book and decided not to answer the question. "While I would like to stand here all day and talk about my sordid movie star past, I have some work to get done. Please send Erin straight back to my office when she arrives." He waved to them and rushed to his office to create the notes for an entire product line.

Once inside his inner sanctum, he rushed to his desk, turned on his computer. He barely got a chance to sit down and pop a few vitamins in his mouth before someone knocked on his door. "If you're Bambi come in."

The door opened and in came his chemist. Tall, blonde and willowy, the woman should have been in movies herself. Too bad for him he liked them short, built and bitchy.

He motioned for her to come over. "I need help." Good thing for him, she was one of the smartest people in the business. He knew this for a fact, he trained her himself.

"Isaac." She put her hand over her mouth and shook her head.

"I'm still Isaac." After working with her for five years, he could read her mind. Unfortunately, for her and her shy sensibilities, he didn't have time to waste. "Just let it out, I can feel the questions."

As if she were terrified anyone would hear her, she took her seat next to his desk and leaned over. "I have seen that movie more than once, and I would have never guessed."

"I wanted it that way." With an idea forming in his mind, he typed a few key words into the computer.

"I don't have any notes for a Hollywood Glow project."

"It's a project I've been working on privately." He stared at the computer screen. "I'm thinking of ampoules. Erin would like ampoules, maybe gold ones. Maybe a dropper bottle? Maybe she wants to choose." When Bambi didn't respond, he faced her.

"Well, now I'm here. Let me get a few details down so I can help." With a pen at the ready, she opened her notebook. "How long have you been working on this?"

The answer varied depending on how he looked at it. If he took into consideration the time he'd been working on Erin, the answer would be going on over twenty years. If he only counted the time since his mind lit up with the actual Hollywood Glow concept, then the answer would be less than 72 hours. So, the answer was somewhere between twenty years and less than three days. More than once he tried to take his business relationship with Bambi to the next level, but it never worked, and he was the reason. Or maybe the woman he was trying to create an entire line for was the reason. "It's been gelling for a while."

"Is this contract manufacturing or is this a line we're going to sell?"

At last a question he could answer. "This will be part of our line." Contract manufacturing was when an account had a custom formulation run for them. The investment on the account's part was large and the price high. Those deals were few and far between.

"We're adding this line to our physician offering, spa line, or what?" She tapped her pen on the paper.

Erin would want the products to go retail, something he hadn't cracked yet. He took another vitamin, a new chewable he had been working on. The acid tang of citrus took over his mouth and he nodded. Now in order to keep Erin around him he would be investing in an entire line and marketing with a celebrity spokesperson. "I'm still exploring that."

"A celebrity would denote retail, right?" Bambi fired another question at him. "Isn't it customary that when we hire anyone to endorse the products that we show them the finished products since she's not contracting us to make them?"

If he didn't personally train her to ask such questions, he would have been furious. He wanted to tell his protégé to mind her own business. If he wanted to sink money into a line so Erin could play spokesperson, it was his name on the door. Instead, he inhaled and smiled. "You can consider it more of a collaborative effort between Ms. Holland and myself."

"Why don't I collect some packaging samples, and you can pick a few ingredients for her?" She stood.

"That sounds good." He continued to grin at her. "I appreciate that."

"Do you want me to grab some of our stock samples for her to try?" She hugged her notebook to her chest.

"No, I'll pick some things for her." Somehow he couldn't meet Bambi's eyes. Eventually, he wanted to take Erin back to the lab and show her how it was done. Wait. He corrected his own thought. What he wanted was to show her the process of creating a nutraceutical. He didn't even believe his own thought.

Right as Bambi made her way to the exit, there was a knock and the door opened.

His receptionist, Jennifer, peeked her head in, a huge smile and blush across her face. "Isaac, Drew, whatever, Erin Holland is here for you and she gave me an autograph!" The woman held up a yellow pad with Erin's dramatic signature scrawled across it in her signature metallic ink. He remembered sitting with her while she practiced to perfect her E, she explained how the letter H was already sexy, but E needed some help.

"Well, send her in." In a last ditch effort to save his behind on this product line, he quickly grabbed an ingredient catalog and flipped it open.

The Holland whirlwind entered his office. In sleek black leggings and a form-fitting shirt, she swooped inside and the energy in the room electrified.

If having her in his home was strange, her appearance at his workplace was beyond over the top.

"Drew." She held her hand out.

Instinct, need, or training, on automatic he stood and practically tripped over his own feet trying to get to her to take the token. Somehow he made it across the room and grabbed her hand. He wanted to tell her she was early, but a quick glance at the clock told him she was actually right on time. "Welcome to Fluent Word Nutraceuticals."

"It really is a big huge business, like something you would see in a movie." She let go of his hand and curled her arm around his.

In Erin Holland land that was her topmost compliment. "Thank you."

"Do I get a grand tour? Will I see the products..." She gazed up at him and snapped her fingers, an old habit from when she tried to remember one of her lines. "Will I see the products on the line?"

Out of the corner of his eye, he watched Bambi shake her head.

Trapped from leaving his office by him and Erin, Bambi finally approached. "Isaac, I'm going to go gather those items you wanted."

Being used to always being in the limelight, Erin rarely introduced herself to anyone not in the industry, but the way she didn't even glance in Bambi's direction told him two critical things. One, Erin didn't like her, and two, she was threatened by his chemist who didn't fall all over herself trying to get the star's attention. Erin never got along well with other females.

In order to set Bambi free before Erin shot her, he motioned toward the woman. "Erin, I would like to introduce you to Bambi Larue, one of my chemists."

Without a word, Erin waited.

He tried to silently will Bambi to say anything smacking of a fan. Even a mention she liked the movie, anything.

Anything.

"It's a pleasure to meet you." Bambi put a weak smile on her face.

"Because you've heard so much about me?" Erin giggled and squeezed his arm tighter.

"Actually, until today, no." Bambi's facial expression did not change one iota.

He winced and made his way toward the door, bracing himself to get ready for the whirlwind soon to become a hurricane. "How about we take that tour?"

Erin let go of him and turned toward Bambi. "Well, you will now, since I'm one of your spokespeople." She spun back and tangled her arm in his again. "I'm ready for my tour now, Mr. Fulton."

"It was nice meeting you." At last Bambi left the office.

Erin chose not to respond.

"Ready?" Now that she was here, he really didn't know what to do with her.

"For you, always." She continued to gaze up at him.

"Let's go." He guided Erin through the building. Fine, he puffed up his chest a bit at showing her what he'd built.

She smiled and nodded at everyone, signed a few autographs, and laughed at the few remaining pictures his workers kept up of him from *Hollywood Stardust*.

To her, everything was a wonder. She oohhed and ahhed at the office area, she seemed fascinated by their shipping manager's oversized tape dispenser commenting on how she rarely taped anything, but if she needed to this would be the tape she wanted. She even posed for a few pictures.

In the packaging area, she handed one of his workers her phone. "Would you mind taking a picture of Drew and me? Always hold the camera so you are looking down at us."

Everyone in the department gathered around as she positioned the two of them next to a stack of boxes and product.

"Take at least five shots, and wait until I tell you we're ready." She directed. "The rest of you get your phones up, this one's for free."

The crowd laughed, but damn if not all of his people lifted their phones to capture the image.

Never being the one next to Erin in a photo shoot, he froze trying to remember how Ryder or Logan stood.

One thing Erin possessed was a sixth sense with photography and filming. She twisted her body so she was up against him, took one of his hands and put it around her, grabbed the other and positioned it on her waist, turning him in the process. "It's about time this spot belonged to you." She titled her head for the camera. "Now."

At her words, he could only keep his focus on her. Through her lashes, she peeked up at him, micro adjusting the two of them for several shots. Then she held up her hand and bowed. "Thank you."

His worker returned her phone, and she scrolled through the shots. "This is the one." She turned the device to him.

He stared down at the captured moment in time. Any image of just the two of them together happened over twenty years ago. While she was always gorgeous, no doubt he'd changed and for the first time he looked like he could almost belong with her. "Will you email that to me?" If nothing else, he wanted a record.

"You never gave me your email and no one else would either." She laughed, but then shrugged and handed him her phone. "If you want to put in your address, I'll send it now."

For too long everything he did was to keep her away. He paused before typing his email and returned her phone.

She sent the picture and, with a little less playfulness and joy, took his arm again. "Should we continue?"

"Yes, I want to show you the actual manufacturing facility." He guided her to the back.

"That sounds exciting." He led her to the back to a giant viewing window that looked out over all the different machines.

She went to the window and pressed her palms against the glass. For several minutes she simply stood there gazing out at the machines doing their job.

"If you want to go inside we will have to put on jumpsuits and hair nets." He didn't know if she would want to do that or not.

"Is anything happening with Hollywood Glow today?" She touched the top of her hair.

"Well, it's not really near production yet." Though he was pretty sure Erin didn't come equipped with her own personal spotlight, one felt as though it were shining down on him now.

"Oh." She looked between the viewing window and him. "How about when it runs we can go back? I'm not really prepared, plus maybe then we can film it for publicity."

"That's a good idea." At least they had plenty of connections, but he had to remember they weren't a *they*.

"May I see the products?"

Her question was innocent enough. Like Bambi said, if a spokesperson was used in marketing, the products were usually finished. "I wanted to talk to you about that."

"All right." A faint hint of a smile lit up her face.

"Regarding the products, I really wanted your input. I believe if you are going to put your face and your name to the line, you should be intrinsic in the creation of the products." He tried to match her smile with one of his own, but his acting skills were sorely out of practice.

Her smile broadened. "I would love to do that with you." Once more, she turned toward the machines.

"Excellent." He had to say he enjoyed the way she watched the machines and stood next to her.

"Drew." She took his arm. "If I ask you a question, will you be honest?"

"Yes." He wondered what horror show question her mind might conjure.

"Did you only create Hollywood Glow so we could have something to do together?"

Well, her question cinched it, he was never meant to act and he couldn't live the lie. "Yes, but I do want to do the project."

"I'm so glad, now I'll be able to learn everything about you and your work." She turned, and moved his bangs off his forehead. "If I ask you another question will you still be honest?"

He was done for when she did that bang swiping thing and nodded.

"Since we know you didn't come find me to be a spokesperson, why did you show up that night and say you wanted to talk to me?"

Although he promised he'd be honest, he couldn't quite yet say the words. Instead, he tilted his head and grabbed her hand.

"Drew." Closing the distance between them, she wrapped her arms around his neck. "That's what I wanted, what I dreamed about, why did you make this all up?"

Unable to look at her, he diverted his attention to the ceiling. "Because once you arrived at my home, you were there and I wanted you and all I could think of was..." His muscles tightened, and he tried to figure out how to word what he wanted to say.

Her arms fell to her side and she backed up. "It was twenty years ago, can't you forgive me? Haven't I proved how sorry and wrong I was?"

While his mouth opened to speak, he had no answer.

"Why did you show up the other night?" She put her hands on her hips.

"I just told you."

"You disappeared on me." Shaking her head, she continued to move away. "If I was so repulsive that you felt the need to change your identity to stay away from me and you still can't move on from what happened twenty years ago, I want to know why you came for me the other night."

How did he tell her he didn't know, but he had to? "Obviously, you can't get over the fact I left for twenty years because what you did nearly killed me."

"Screw you." In a show of pride, she lifted her head high. "I don't need this. I was just fine without you."

Without allowing him to retort, she walked away.

He shut his eyes, wondering if he would come home to find she'd vanished this time.

HOLLYWOOD STARBURST

FADE IN:

INT. FLAGSTAFF, AZ - INSIDE A BUS - DAY.

Every available seat is filled. A baby is
crying, people are fanning papers and the sweat
on their brows is visible. An old lady throws
up in a brown paper bag in the seat right in
front of ROXY.

ROXY

Sits in her window seat next to an old man
staring at her. The child behind her won't stop
kicking the back of Roxy's seat. She shudders
and looks out the window, pressing her palm to
the glass.

THE WOMAN IN FRONT OF HER vomits into the bag
once more.

GUY ON BUS dressed in all leather with makeup
and a passed out girl slung over him waves
hand.

                    GUY ON BUS
               Stop the bus! It reeks
               in here, have some
               mercy!

The passengers on the bus grumble. The woman
throws up once more and at last the bus driver
pulls into a gas station. All the patrons on
the bus clap. The door opens and people begin
filing off the bus.

ROXY wipes her brow and turns, shuddering at
the way the old man continues to stare at her.

                    ROXY
               Excuse me.

                    OLD MAN
          You don't want to leave
          me, do you?

                    ROXY
          I need some air.

                    OLD MAN
          It's hard for me to get
          up. Well, not some of
          me.

OLD MAN looks down at his lap.

ROXY Her jaw drops open and she stands, getting
up on her seat and climbing over to the row in
front of her, stepping right into the bag of
vomit.

                    ROXY
               Oh God!

ROXY grabs her backpack from the overhead bin
and darts out of the bus. Once outside, she
kicks off her shoe, hobbles into the
convenience store and goes right to the
refrigerated section, pressing her face against
the cool glass.

                    ROXY
               (Whispers)
          I'm more lost than ever.

GAS STATION WORKER Older female in uniform
comes up to her.

               GAS STATION WORKER
            Miss, can I help you?

                    ROXY
          Can you tell me where
          I'm going?

                    GAS STATION WORKER
                     Well, if you're with
                     that bus, you're going
                     wherever that bus is
                     taking you.

                         ROXY
                     I just got on the first
                     bus out of Hollywood. I
                     have no plan. I want
                     someone to rescue me.

                    GAS STATION WORKER
                     Yeah, I know that
                     feeling. Been waiting
                     for that same thing
                     since the bus dropped me
                     off here twenty years
                     ago.

ROXY glances at the woman.

                         ROXY
                     I can't get back on that
                     bus. The wheels just
                     keep spinning and I'm
                     going nowhere. I need
                     to go home, but I'm down
                     to my last twenty
                     dollars.

                    GAS STATION WORKER
                      Well, sounds like you
                      need a fairy
                      godmother. I'm not sure
                      if we have that in out
                      here.

ROXY scans area, her eyes stopping on a picture
of meatloaf and mashed potatoes.

                         ROXY
                      Mashed potatoes.

                    GAS STATION WORKER
                        I don't think
                        mashed potatoes are
                        going to help you.

ROXY stands up straight.

                         ROXY
                      These type will. They're
                      not made by a fairy
                      godmother but a
                      grandmother and they're
                      more than mashed
                      potatoes. One day she
                      told me I would want a
                      second helping, and I
                      think she's right.

                    GAS STATION WORKER
                      You have a fairy
                      grandmother?

                         ROXY
                      No, but Steven does, and
                      I need some help.

ROXY limps toward the payphone.

Chapter Eight

NO MATTER HOW HARD she tried, Erin rarely slept passed 5:00 am. Over thirty years of having to be on set in the wee hours of the morning had trained her to the point where at 5:00 almost on the dot her eyes would pop open. Sometimes if she were exhausted she could drift back to slumber land. Of course, if she were in the warm embrace of someone she cared about, she could definitely sleep. If nothing else, she simply enjoyed lying there.

Unfortunately, that had not happened for many, many years and looking back, the times she thought she cared for someone, she knew whoever she was with was only filler material for the man in the next room.

Not wanting to wake Drew, she took her time in the bath and applying her makeup then cuddled up with her computer on the bed. The next thing she knew it was after nine o'clock. Anxiety and feeling like she had no place in the world exhausted her.

She hadn't seen Drew since she left his laboratory. Terrified he would ask her to leave, she rushed back here and holed herself up in his guest room with a diet soda, a bag of popcorn and an orange. Part of her expected him to come and talk to her, but she must have fallen asleep. By the time she woke up, the house was dark and his bedroom door closed.

After checking, she appeared presentable and with a plan on how to at least fix part of her life, she tiptoed out of the room.

Beaker stood up from his position on the stair landing and barked at her.

"Good morning." She smiled at her new favorite person. Yes, she decided Beaker was definitely more a person than some people she knew.

He wagged his tail, picked up a knotted piece of rope he used for a toy and dropped it on her shoe.

She moved her foot back and inspected her footwear for any scratches or slobber. "These are very expensive shoes. Show a little respect for the designer."

Beaker used his nose to push the toy closer.

She shrugged, since she met the designer once and the man wasn't all that. In fact, Beaker seemed much more intelligent. With two fingers she picked up the toy and tossed it.

The dog leaped into the air and caught it.

"Impressive." She clapped. "Mr. Beaker, you passed your audition, we will be booking you right away." Her stomach twisted. She hoped she would be as lucky with what she had to do today.

Beaker stayed by her side as she made her way down the hallway. Drew's door was partially open and she gave a quick peek inside. The room was completely empty.

Though the urge to snoop overwhelmed her, she didn't need any more strikes against her and went down stairs.

Strange being in someone's home without them. Even with her canine companion, the whole place seemed eerily quiet, as if the energy of the rightful owner left with his absence.

All in all, Drew's house oozed with hominess, a place where one could curl up on a couch or in a bed and be safe. This was the kind of home one had a family in with ideal spots to mark the children's heights as they grew, a gleaming kitchen to make soups and stews that would warm one's heart, and a yard aching for a swing set. Brian's home, though grand, never had this feeling. No place she'd ever been did except those perfect couples in the movies or on TV.

Evidence of Drew's morning lay around in various places. Some mail tossed on the table, a bowl in the sink, coffee still warm in the pot and a little note by the mugs with her name on it.

She glanced back at her star canine and with her chest tightening approached what had to be her eviction papers. Her hand trembled as she picked up the paper.

Erin –
Long time since I wrote you a note. The coffee is
hot, help yourself. Also left you a vitamin if you
want one. Please make sure you lock the door
when you leave.
~~Isaac~~ (Oops)
Drew

She ran her fingertips across his name and almost laughed at his mistake. However, the note didn't indicate if she were to lock the door on her way out or lock the door and never return. The only thing in her favor was he didn't ask for his key back.

Part of her wanted to stay here all day, change into casual clothes and play house. Maybe cook Drew dinner and open a bottle of wine while she waited for him to come home. Then, when he returned, they would eat, maybe watch a movie and go upstairs together.

Tears clouded her vision. Yesterday he made it clear he could never trust her. He even paused before giving her his email. She knew he wanted her, but he was smart enough to keep his distance. Last time she got close she destroyed him and it served her right.

Once helping herself to a cup of coffee and taking her vitamin, she sat down at the breakfast bar and prepared for her day. The last few days with Drew served as a sort of blinder to her life, but alone and most likely in need of finding a place to live right away, she had to face the rest of her life.

She set her bag down and pulled out her laptop, her list, the envelope of paperwork Brian kindly packed for her, and her phone.

Only two things graced her to-do list. Neither one she wanted to deal with, but she had no choice.

First, she needed to figure out how much money she had.

Second, she needed to work, a real job, not one endorsing a product line that didn't exist and not an extra in a movie.

She opened the envelope with the paperwork.

Apparently today was a day for notes. The neat stack came topped with a letter from Brian.

Erin,
I hope you didn't wait for weeks before opening
this.

She stuck her tongue out at the sentence.

Enclosed you will find a spreadsheet of your bills, due dates and balances. For the most part everything has been set up on auto pay so you only have to keep track of your personal spending. To the best of my knowledge, I have balanced your checkbook. All your residual payments will go directly into your account as I will no longer be taking my percentage. A copy of all the necessary dissolution papers is included. You have made me a lot of money through the years, so I think it is best we separate completely.

She shrugged and glanced over at the spreadsheet and formal paperwork before continuing.

On a personal note, I know you may hate me now, but in time I think you will find it's best we both moved on with our lives. Since we met, we have been in two different places in our lives, and we are out of intersections.
Brian

She pursed her lips and reread the last paragraph. They never loved each other, they were just there when she needed someone and he needed to feel young. The last few years they were more like roommates than anything else and even if she ended up in a hotel tonight, or sleeping in a booth at Wilson's Bar, after being here, she could never go back to Brian's. She didn't even miss him, which told her everything.

Well, at least things were organized and automated. She simply needed to take a quick peek at her balance, though she never really had to do that before, and she found the check register, opening it up to the last entry.

Before deciding on an appropriate reaction to the number, she blinked, glanced over at Beaker and took a sip of her coffee.

Inhaling, she read the number again, praying somehow she didn't understand the data.

Unfortunately, many, many moons ago when she and her mother lived in a dank Hollywood apartment, she was tasked with the job of making sure the rent was paid on their roach infested stink hole, especially during the times her mother went "out." An old lady across the way took kindly to her and gave her a lesson on balancing a checkbook.

Once old enough to manage her own affairs, she vowed never to worry about money again. Brian and accountants and teams of people took care of these things and through the years she became slack and comfortable.

However, at the moment the shoes on her feet were worth more than the balance in her account.

They weren't the most expensive shoes either.

Brian complained over and over again about the money she spent, told her to stop, but she knew the next role would take care of any debts she had and she would be back to normal.

She just didn't realize things were this tight.

Sweat broke out over her body and she closed her eyes and the checkbook. With Brian and Logan both out of her finances, she would have much more coming in and thankfully, a couple of her television series were going strong in syndication.

Refusing to panic, she gulped the coffee down and decided to move on to the second item on her list...work.

She picked up her phone and found the casting director to the role she lost. Brian had fixed these little inconveniences before and the man had cast her numerous times. They were friends, as much as anyone was friends in this industry. Her plea would be even better coming from her personally, and she pressed the button to call him.

"Well, well, well if it isn't Ms. Holland. Baby, I'm sorry I couldn't cast you, you weren't a good fit." Carl Kline's voice boomed through the phone.

In order to save her eardrum she put him on speaker. "Maybe you need to try me on again."

He chuckled. "My closet is full."

"I'm sure most of your items are out of season." She shook her head at the stupid metaphors. "At least tell me why."

"Baby, on this one, you were out of season. The producer decided he wanted the part to go to a lead who could look like she was attending college."

A shudder ran through her. Brian usually found out the reasons for any rejections and managed to either not tell her or say it in such a way where it didn't feel like acid was being poured on her body. Twice in the last few days her age had been mentioned. She wasn't forty yet!

Again, she looked over at Beaker. Maybe she needed to learn how to catch in mid-air. "Do you have anything else?"

"Sweetie, is everything okay? These aren't the kind of calls you make."

"I've decided to go independent." The back of her throat stung at the word.

"It's been a while since you had a role." His tone lowered, lost the Hollywood good ole boy swagger.

"I have some things coming up, a cameo in the *Hollywood Stardust* sequel and an endorsement deal." Her forehead began to pound.

"Can I give you some advice?"

She stayed quiet, no doubt she would get the advice no matter if she wanted it or not.

"Reinvent yourself. You have been playing the same role for the last ten years. Not that you're not good at it, but you have no breadth."

His words fell on her like a boulder, flattening her to nothing.

"Also, you can't be independent. You may as well go get a job as a waitress then."

"Thanks for the tips." She tried to sound upbeat, but her acting wasn't good enough to fake it. Maybe she needed to consult one of the roles she played during the last ten years and figure out her stock reaction.

"I'll call you if I have something. In the meantime, why don't you call Rick Southern or Shelly Terry and get yourself represented."

"Thanks." The agents he suggested were for actors on their way out. She hung up.

Without even thinking, she got up and went to the refrigerator, opened it and spied a bar of chocolate. Drew's favorite. Her favorite.

True tears heating her eyes, she kneeled down, allowing the cool radiating from the appliance to wash over her.

Last week she celebrated the 20th anniversary of one of the most beloved films of all time. She was the star. This week, she was a broke, worn out actress. Drew didn't trust her, and he had every reason to doubt her. Look at the mess she made. No matter what, she couldn't tell him what happened with her finances or her acting, or anything.

Everyone thought she wanted him because she couldn't have him. He had to think the same and worse.

If anyone ever bothered asking her, she would tell them she wanted him because he was the first to ever love her, the first to listen to her, the first man to be her friend.

Her friend.

She shook her head. Maybe that's where all the trouble started. They became friends. What she needed was a friend and he didn't want that, and she knew it from the get go.

Hollywood Stardust filming had ended for the day and she was stuck. Both Ryder and Logan continued to flirt with her off set and both had asked her to meet them later. She really didn't know what to do, because how could one choose between them?

In a small stroke of luck, or perfect timing, the leading men got detained and she bolted to a place where they would never find her, the shade of the trees that lined the mall they were using for a set.

She hid behind one and sat down with her knees pulled up to her chest, peeking over her shoulder.

Then she saw him and smiled.

Maybe Logan and Ryder didn't possess the connection to find her, but Drew Fulton seemed to always know her whereabouts.

Still in the prosthetics they forced him to wear, he took the long way around the trees.

Right when she thought he was going to pass her, he spun on his heel and faced her. "Hiding out?"

Since he knew the answer, she held up her hand instead.

He took her offering, sat next to her and held up a finger telling her to wait.

The anxiety of Logan and Ryder disappeared as Drew pulled a dollar out of his pocket and proceeded to continue a series of intricate folds.

His hands worked with precision and every once in a while, he would lift his little craft, assess it and continue.

Enthralled with his work, she leaned up against him and hooked her arm in his.

At last, he finished and held his palm out, presenting her with a perfect little dollar daisy. "For you."

"You're magic." She smiled her first unforced smile of the day, clapped and plucked the gift out of his hand.

"How do you figure?" He leaned back and scratched at the artificial nose they put on him.

"Well, only you can transform a dollar bill into a flower. Only you can bring Ryder to his knees using nothing but the power of your brain, and actually silence Logan." Technically, he was supposed to wait for the makeup crew to come and properly pull those things off, but she knew he was horribly uncomfortable and couldn't stand seeing him that way. She leaned up on her knees and carefully pried off the fake thing. "Also, only you can become unrecognizable with a few little pieces of rubber."

He took off the glasses and rubbed his hand over his face. "I think making you smile is pretty magical."

Her heart swelled. Dare she say only he said things like this to her and meant it? "I think that's cause only you can stand me and want to know more about me than what color bra I'm wearing."

His cheeks changed color, and he shrugged. "I just want you to be happy."

Once more, she cuddled up to his side. "Well, right now I am happy. When I'm with you I can relax and I can tell you anything. See? You are magic."

"I want those two to stop pressuring you already." He groaned.

How did she tell him that part of her welcomed the pressure? The rest of her simply wanted to stay here and enjoy the comfort and safety that surrounded all things Drew. "Don't worry about them." Why did she feel as if she were cheating on him every time the other two were mentioned?

"That's easy for you to say." With a shake of his head, he looked up into the trees.

She had laid her head on his shoulder and he had patted the top of her head. Fine, maybe there were some things she didn't tell him, but she couldn't lose her friend. They had stayed silent together under the tree as the cool breeze of the evening had washed over them.

A cold nose nudged her hand and she looked into Beaker's face. "He was my best friend." She closed the refrigerator door and returned to the kitchen island and opened her wallet. Back then, she refused to admit she wanted him as more than a best friend.

She rooted around in her wallet until she found the little flower he made all those years ago and pressed the little piece of art to her chest.

Even after all she put him through, he still took her in the first night they were reunited. Wasn't that the kind of man someone wanted to be with? Too bad she didn't see that before.

No, he couldn't know anything, and he couldn't kick her out before they had their chance.

He couldn't know, but she had to go to him anyway.

HOLLYWOOD STARBURST

FADE IN:

INT. INDIANAPOLIS- STEVEN'S PARENTS' HOUSE,
LIVING ROOM. DONE UP WITH ALL MODERN
FURNISHING AND VERY HIGH END.

STEVEN, WILLIAM and CHARLES sit around the
room. STEVEN and WILLIAM play a video game,
CHARLES has several books sprawled out on the
coffee table.

THE PHONE RINGS.

STEVEN tosses his controller aside, reaches
behind him and grabs the phone.

                STEVEN
           What?

        STEVEN'S GRANDMOTHER (O.S.)
           (Filtered)
           Don't talk to me that
           way, use some manners.

STEVEN rolls his eyes, but he still smiles.

                STEVEN
           (sarcastic tone)
           Hello, Granny.

CHARLES waves.

WILLIAM gives thumbs-up.

                STEVEN
           The guys say hi.

        STEVEN'S GRANDMOTHER (O.S.)
           (Filtered)
           What about Roxy?

STEVEN forces himself off the floor and stands.

>   STEVEN
>   What about her? I told
>   you, she stayed in
>   California.

Both CHARLES and WILLIAM turn to
STEVEN. STEVEN takes the phone and walks
across the room.

>   STEVEN'S GRANDMOTHER (O.S.)
>   (Filtered)
>   Why is it that everyone
>   thinks they know
>   everything when clearly
>   they know nothing?

>   STEVEN
>   (groans)
>   Okay, I'll bite. What's
>   the riddle? Do you
>   somehow know where Roxy
>   is?

WILLIAM stands and goes to Steven's side.

STEVEN shoos him away and turns his back to
everyone.

>   STEVEN
>   Grandma.

                    STEVEN'S GRANDMOTHER (O.S.)
                         (Filtered)
                    She called us yesterday,
                    took a bus out
                    here. She's been
                    through it.

                         STEVEN
                    Is she all right?

WILLIAM stomps over.

                         WILLIAM
                    Is she all right?
                    What's going on?

                         STEVEN
                    Let me hear.

STEVEN elbows William away.

                    STEVEN'S GRANDMOTHER (O.S.)
                         (Filtered)
                    Well, by the tone in
                    your voice, and in
                    William's, you both
                    care, so I'll tell
                    you. She's okay,
                    exhausted and starving.
                    She needs to feel as if
                    she has a place.

                         STEVEN
                    Her place is back here
                    with...with us.

                    STEVEN'S GRANDMOTHER (O.S.)
                         (Filtered)
                    Do you mean with you?

                    STEVEN
              Is she with you?

          STEVEN'S GRANDMOTHER (O.S.)
                 (Filtered-huffs)
              You are so like your
              father. Yes, of
              course. She stayed the
              night. She's going to
              stay with us for a bit
              because right now that
              is her place.

                    STEVEN
              Does she have money?
              I'll come and get her.

WILLIAM Grabs Steven's shoulder.

                    WILLIAM
              If anyone is going to
              get her I am.

                    STEVEN
              She went to my
              family. I think that
              says it all.

                    WILLIAM
              If she would have been
              in Maryland she would
              have been with my
              grandparents. Any port
              in a storm. I'm going
              to get her. We were
              together and I screwed
              up.

STEVEN holds phone away from his ear.

                    STEVEN
              I need to fix your
              screw ups and
              therefore I'll get
              her.

                    WILLIAM
               All you'll do is
               screw her.

                    STEVEN
               Screw you.

WILLIAM and STEVEN stare each other down.

               STEVEN'S GRANDMOTHER (O.S.)
                    (Filtered)
                    Stop!

WILLIAM and STEVEN stop and stare at the phone.

STEVEN lifts the phone and holds it so both he
and William can hear.

                    STEVEN
               Yes, Grandma.

               STEVEN'S GRANDMOTHER (O.S.)
                    (Filtered)
                    Listen here. She
                    is staying here,
                    neither of you is
                    coming here. She
                    is going to learn
                    her place and her
                    worth and she will
                    make it back to
                    where she
                    belongs. Do you
                    understand me?

STEVEN and WILLIAM nod.

                    WILLIAM
               What are we
               supposed to do?

               STEVEN'S GRANDMOTHER (O.S.)
                    (Filtered)

                    The two of you are
                    going to learn
                    patience and what
                    you want. Only
                    when you act like
                    men can a woman be
                    a woman.

                         STEVEN
                    We agreed to find her
                    together.

               STEVEN'S GRANDMOTHER (O.S.)
                         (Filtered)
                    If you were ready to
                    confront her, you would
                    have known where she
                    was. Now tell me you
                    love me.

                         WILLIAM
                    I love you.

STEVEN wrinkles his nose and shakes his head.

                         STEVEN
                    I love you.

               STEVEN'S GRANDMOTHER (O.S.)
                         (Filtered)
                    Go figure it out.

A dial tone echoes through the room and William
and Steven stare at each other.

Chapter Nine

ERIN DIDN'T DISAPPEAR.

Drew hovered his fingers over his keyboard. Work eluded him, concentration left him, and focus didn't exist.

No, Erin didn't disappear. Instead, she stayed.

Not wanting to face if she had left, he arrived home late. When he spotted her car in the driveway, he braced himself for the conversation they needed to have, but while she didn't disappear, she ended up being a no-show. She remained in his guest room completely and utterly silent.

In the morning, he snuck out of his house, leaving her nothing but coffee and a note and ran for the office under the guise he had a ton of work.

Actually, he did have an enormous amount of work, but none that would get completed while he sat at his desk contemplating if she would be there when he arrived home today.

Since she showed up on his doorstep, they tiptoed around the other as if they were terrified to break any sort of bond they managed to forge together. In all truth, except for her running off at the *Hollywood Stardust* gala, she'd faced him and his reappearance head-on, being completely genuine about what she wanted.

On the other hand, he had morphed into the game player. If he didn't want to explore anything with her, he shouldn't have appeared in the first place. Did he want to be with her or did he want to prove a point?

With a glance at his blank screen, he finally admitted work defeated him, lifted his phone right as someone knocked on the door. It wouldn't be out of character for Erin to simply show up once she rehearsed her lines. "Come in."

Bambi peeked inside. "Do you have some time?"

He slumped back in his chair. "Sure." While he may have been defeated by work, work wanted to make sure it knocked him out.

"I just wanted to go over some projects with you." She sat in the chair across from his desk. "I'm working on all the things for the road trip next week. Am I still going with you?"

"The road trip?" The road trip. His mind cleared enough for him to remember his job, the one where he owned a laboratory and had clients, clients he needed to visit, hence the road trip. Bambi had taken to coming with him. The last trip they'd tried to resume their relationship. The whole road trip and the fact he invited Bambi sort of slipped his mind, and he pulled at his lower lip. "If that's what we planned." He didn't know what to answer.

Bambi nodded. "What do you need done with Hollywood Glow? I collected some containers, but without knowing the ingredients or formulas it's a little difficult."

He stared off at his far wall filled with pictures of construction of the lab and Beaker as a puppy. With his secret out, he could add his pictures of him and Logan, and even the one with him and Erin. Maybe he would keep that one on his desk. "I'll be working on that with Erin."

"Oh, I see." She turned her face down to the composition notebook she always carried with her.

"Bambi?" He had only seen her like this twice before. Once when she messed up an order for a customer, and the other time when she came to his office the day after they decided they weren't going to be anything other than coworkers.

"She's the one, right?" Her voice came out barely above a whisper.

"What?" he asked, even though he heard her. Maybe he needed some time to stall.

"She's the one, right?" Bambi raised her head. "The reason you changed your name?"

"Partially." He grabbed the arms of his chair. "Mostly."

"Also the reason you revealed your true identity?"

Somehow, she made him sound like a superhero, but he was far from that. "Yes."

"She's also the reason we..." Once more she lowered her head.

"I haven't seen her in twenty years."

"But she was still there." She spoke to the notebook.

"I'm sorry." He couldn't even deny her statement. At the time he wanted them to work, he tried, but as she said Erin was there. Bambi knew it even if she couldn't name the person.

"Will you do me one favor?"

"Anything." Life would have been easy with Bambi. Their work, their lifestyles, their interests were all compatible. They meshed everywhere but where it mattered. If he could figure out how to put that intangible in a capsule he would be a billionaire many times over.

"Whatever she did to cause you to change your name and hide, don't let her do it again." She stared into his face. "I, for one, would really miss Isaac Abrams."

The only response he could muster was a nod, and thankfully the buzz on the intercom of his office phone interrupted them.

"Isaac," Jennifer chimed in through the speaker.

"Yes?"

Bambi went to the small conference table in his office and began setting up the container samples.

"Erin Holland is here for her meeting with you."

He narrowed his eyes. If they didn't speak, how did they make a time for a meeting? "All right. Send her in."

"I'm going to go check some things with QA." Bambi gathered up her notes and scurried to the door.

"Thank you." Unsure if he should remain sitting or stand, he decided to stay in his chair and appear nonchalant. Then he wondered when he entered adolescence again for having these thoughts. Not only did he stay seated, he turned to the computer, but kept one eye on the door.

At last, it opened and Bambi stopped dead in her tracks. His chemist held her notebook up as a shield and stepped back.

"I have a meeting with Mr. Fulton." Erin's voice rang through from the other side, in her perfect imitation of an executive. "Are you part of the product development team, Barbie?"

"Bambi." She turned back to him.

Without waiting for Bambi's answer, Erin entered. Though short in stature, she filled up the room. Always a lover of all things fashion, today she played the role of sun kissed starlet and swooped inside in a short, but flowing lace dress, sunglasses and a canvas tote bag.

"Erin, what are you doing here?" At last he stood.

"We need to talk about Hollywood Glow and get this moving." She marched straight for the table and put her tote on one of the chairs.

Curiosity alone made him join her at the table. "You want to work on Hollywood Glow right now?"

"Drew." She faced him. "I cancelled other things so I can devote my attention to this critical project. I spent a good part of the morning researching your laboratory, your brands and the competition, and I think it is imperative that we have a meeting post haste."

Unsure which script she read from, he called her bluff. "What makes it so imperative?"

"While I have absolutely no doubt your formulations are perfection, that is merely one small piece of the marketing pie. I browsed some of your other lines and may I say the packaging and the marketing copy are a little to be desired." She lifted her chin.

"The packaging is fine and chosen for that product. The copy has to be approved through our compliance department." Bambi backed up.

"Every one of your competitors is in the exact same situation, so don't feed me some line." Erin continued to look at him. "If you want Hollywood Glow to shine, we need to have a meeting, and we need to get it out on the market while the sequel is hot. Right now talk of *Hollywood Stardust* is abuzz with the anniversary, Logan's engagement and your coming out, so to speak. We need to fast track this."

Damn if the woman didn't have a point. At least if they worked on Hollywood Glow he would not only be privy to her whereabouts, but he would also be getting some work done. "All right, let's have a meeting."

"Excellent, can your assistant take notes? Your writing looks more like a squiggle, and I can never read my own writing."

He glanced between her and Bambi. "Well, she isn't my assistant, but perhaps she should stay."

Bambi returned to the table and took the seat furthest from where Erin stood. "I have not been kept abreast of this project."

"Good, then we can start all fresh." Erin glanced down at the chair in front of her and then over at him.

Without a thought, he pulled out Erin's chair for her.

She touched his cheek and sat. "Drew has always been such a gentleman."

"So has Isaac." Bambi opened her notebook.

"Drew has the name." Erin sat back and crossed her legs.

"Again, so does Isaac." Bambi took a pen out of her lab coat pocket.

He couldn't allow this to turn into a sparring match, or more of a sparring match, not that part of him didn't enjoy it a miniscule amount. "Why don't we talk about what we envision for the product line?"

"Maybe one simple supplement. We could get that out quickly." Bambi clicked her pen.

"That is simply boring and not at all anything like Hollywood." Erin turned her chair to face only him. "It needs to be a system, a complete regimen so that we can sell multiple steps. That will enable the customer to customize the products for their particular issue. The customer can decide how basic or complex they want to make it."

Erin held up a finger and reached into her tote bag, pulling out some skin care and makeup. "Let's take the Fluency line that you currently sell to physicians. That is your most extensive product with supplements treating a whole host of other medical issues."

"We don't treat, we support." Bambi held her hand up. "Treatment infers we offer a cure."

Erin blinked and continued. "Anyways, your Fluency line offers one, possibly two, support systems for each ailment when there could be so much more."

"What do you mean?" Without taking his eyes off her, he got up and grabbed a yellow pad and paper off his desk. Out of the corner of his eye, he noticed Bambi scribbling notes.

"Here's my current skin care regimen." She lifted a box housing about seven different items. "There is the cleanser, the exfoliant, the treatment products, sunscreen, eye cream, night cream and extra special boosters should the need arise."

"So what are you saying?" He almost didn't want to speak for fear she would stop.

"We need several steps of all different mediums and then we will have a well-rounded line. Everything you offer for Fluency is in capsule form, but clearly you have other ways to deliver the ingredients including drinks and powders."

"Customize your glow." He studied the products she brought with her and his mind went off in a million different directions.

"What if we named the different conditions after film genres?" She leaned in and put her hand on his shoulder.

They stared at each other. There it was, the spark, the chemistry, the intangible something. No wonder no one could ever compare to her, the woman was strong and smart, and once she harnessed her energy she could light a city.

"No one is going to do all that." Bambi shook her head. "Maybe for the spa lines, but even then, we are built on simplicity."

"I can assure you that the type of woman who would purchase Hollywood Glow would most definitely do anything if it offered results." She didn't bother glancing Bambi's way. "Why don't we get the marketing department in here and we can discuss it?"

The room went silent.

"Drew. Where is the marketing department?" Erin asked.

He stared at her.

"Marketing person?" She prodded.

"We focus on the formulas here," Bambi interjected.

"This is why none of your lines have gone retail." Erin smoothed down her hair. "I can see this situation is much more desperate than I thought."

"Erin?" He needed to grab a hook and reel her in. "We are a small specialty boutique formulator."

She stood and paced the room. "This is all right, completely fixable. Many luxury brands are boutiques, but they are still retail. We will run it like any other high end fashion item."

He swore she could be on a sound stage.

She slinked around the back of his chair. "I am so glad you told me the other day how you thought this product line was important and you wanted my input. In fact, I think the word you used would be that I was intrinsic to the process."

Bambi pressed her lips together.

He never wanted to make this worse for his chemist. Somehow, he needed to stop Erin before she went further.

"I'll take over the job of all aspects of marketing for the line. I can work right here." She returned to the table. "Of course, it's a good thing I'm staying at your place so we can really make this happen quickly."

"You're now going to be a marketing department?" Bambi asked what he wanted to know as well.

Finally, Erin bothered looking at her. "My dear, I have been working since I was a child. An actress is nothing if not a sales and marketing expert and I have been a spokesperson for lines that thrive today. At the end of it all, everyone and everything narrows down to sales. Since *Hollywood Stardust* hit the screens, I have been a trendsetter."

"Isaac, I need to go do some planning for the road trip." Bambi stood.

He stiffened, not wanting to explain trips.

"Good, that will give Drew and me a chance to discuss the terms of my contract." Essentially dismissing her, Erin smiled and waved her away.

Contract? Of course she wanted to get paid, and of course he planned on taking care of her as she said in her own words. Everything came down to sales, which meant money. He was surprised she didn't bring an agent along to negotiate a better deal.

He went to her because he wanted her, he dangled carrots in front of her to prove a point, and at the end of the day he got beaten at his own game. Maybe she didn't disappear, but nothing really changed.

FADE IN:

EXT. STEVEN'S GRANDPARENT'S HOME OUT IN THE
ROCK GARDEN - DAY

ROXY wipes sweat off her brow and smooths out
some pebbles.

>   ROXY
>   Why do they call it a
>   rock garden? I mean
>   it's not a garden.

STEVEN'S GRANDMOTHER comes over with a
wheelbarrow, drops more rocks near Roxy and
sits down next to her.

>   STEVEN'S GRANDMOTHER
>   Why is it not a garden?

ROXY shrugs

>   ROXY
>   Well, there's nothing
>   growing. No trees or
>   plants or flowers. Not
>   even grass.

>   STEVEN'S GRANDMOTHER
>   How can you be so sure?

ROXY picks up a rock and a lizard darts out
from underneath the stone.

>   ROXY
>   (Screams)
>   Help!

STEVEN'S GRANDMOTHER bursts into laughter and
pats Roxy.

>   STEVEN'S GRANDMOTHER

                    And you said nothing was
                    living in the rocks.
                    It's okay. This is
                    their land.

ROXY waits for the lizard to scurry away,
returns the rock to its place and presses her
hand to her chest.

                         ROXY
                    I guess what I meant is,
                    it's not a traditional
                    garden.

                    STEVEN'S GRANDMOTHER
                    Nothing is
                    traditional. At one
                    point even the
                    traditions weren't
                    traditional. I tried
                    growing something here
                    so many times, and
                    nothing would take root.
                    You have to make do with
                    what you have.

ROXY faces Steven's Grandmother.

                         ROXY
                    Does that mean it's okay
                    to give up?

STEVEN'S GRANDMOTHER brushes Roxy's bangs out
of her face.

                    STEVEN'S GRANDMOTHER
                       It is never okay to give
                       up. It is okay to
                       redefine your goals. I
                       may want a garden with
                       lush fragile plants and
                       flowers, but a rock
                       garden can be just as
                       beautiful and much more
                       fitting.

ROXY looks down and runs her fingers across a
few of the jagged edges of the rocks.

                         ROXY
                       I gave up.

                    STEVEN'S GRANDMOTHER
                       Did you? Or did you
                       just decide to
                       redefine yourself.

                         ROXY
                       My parents won't
                       speak to me. William
                       left. Steven...
                     (shakes her head)
                       Everyone gives up, I
                       guess.

                    STEVEN'S GRANDMOTHER
                       Steven drove away.
                     (Takes Roxy's hand.)
                       Let me tell you
                       something. No one gave
                       up. When I spoke to
                       your parents I could
                       tell they are hurt.
                       There is nothing like
                       being hurt by your own
                       child.

ROXY stares into Steven's Grandmother's face,
her eyes well up with tears.

STEVEN'S GRANDMOTHER
    Both Steven and William
    are concerned. They
    don't know what to do.
    Both wanted to come here
    to get you, but I
    stopped them.

            ROXY
    I don't know what to do.

STEVEN'S GRANDMOTHER
  (chuckles)
      Of course you don't.

            ROXY
  (silently crying)
  What do I do?

STEVEN'S GRANDMOTHER
    You don't give up, you
    work hard and you make
    it on your own, then
    when you are ready you
    decide if you want to be
    a flowerbed or a rock
    garden. Both are
    beautiful.

Chapter Ten

IN A CARBON COPY of the night before, Erin hid out in her room until Drew arrived home.

She heard him playing with Beaker and moving around downstairs. When his footsteps on the stairs echoed through the house, she froze, refusing to move a muscle.

Maybe she came off a little strong at his office, but she just didn't know what else to do. One moment she had a career and Drew seemed ready to kiss her, the next he pulled away, and she was being told to go to some two-bit loser agent for the has-been actors of the world.

After her money fiasco, she panicked and went to her one safe place. What would she have done if Drew hadn't returned to her life? She didn't know the answer and didn't want to know. All she wanted was to feel secure and have Drew. Neither was happening for her. Once Barbie or Bambo or Bimbo left the office, he simply told her he would have an agreement drawn up, practically threw some bottles of capsules at her to try, and then went to go fix a machine. She had yet to find out about some road trip.

He must have forgotten that she knew him, even if it was the him of twenty years ago, and she knew when he didn't return to his office that he was furious.

All those years ago, their downfall started with furious. She could deal with furious, she thought or hoped. Furious held emotion and potential. Ambivalence and silence held nothing. Before this went further, she needed to fix the furious.

She pressed her ear to the door and willed Drew to come to her. When she heard him speak to the dog then go into his bedroom, she sunk to her knees, closed her eyes and made a plan.

With only the past on her side, she checked her face in the mirror, collected the few things she purchased on her way home in case of an emergency, and left her room.

Like a girl sneaking to see her boyfriend, she tiptoed down the hall. With her treats in hand, she stopped just short of knocking on the door, watching her hand tremble.

Along the way, he filtered out every good memory and only recalled the worst. She chose to remember the first time he made her shiver instead.

Days on the set of *Hollywood Stardust* could be long, boring and tiring. As the veterans of the group, she and Ryder were more accustomed to drudgery of movie making, but Logan and Drew were not. Where Logan seemed to automatically fit in with the cast and crew, making his experience that much easier, Drew, like his character, had a tougher time.

The day had been grueling all around, punctuated by take after take of her and Ryder kissing. In fact, the only one who had seemed to be enjoying it was Ryder. Logan went into mega jerk mode and Drew wouldn't say a word unless it was a scripted line, and he had continued to flub those the minute he looked at her.

"Let's try it one more time!" the director yelled out.

Ryder pointed at Drew. "You're the only one who doesn't have to do any heavy scenes. Let's just get this one."

Erin bit the side of her mouth. Last time she defended Drew in front of the other two they didn't stop making fun of him for having a girl come to his defense.

Drew jutted his jaw out.

"Everyone back at their marks." The director raised his voice even more. "Come on."

"Let's do it, poor Erin has the hardest job, hopefully this will be the last one," Logan said, then elbowed Drew and they took their positions around the corner.

"Erin is just fine." Ryder flipped them the finger.

"Come on." She tugged Ryder's sleeve and they went over by a huge brick wall. The makeup lady ran up and fixed her lipstick once more, and gave Ryder a glare.

"What?" Ryder stretched and leaned back on the brick.

"Are you having lipstick for dinner?" With a shake of her head, the woman walked away.

"I would rather have you for dinner." Ryder raised his eyebrows. "After this, let's go back to the hotel and order room service."

She pressed her lips together. No doubt he was horny after all the kissing. The only problem was she didn't feel the same.

"All right, let's get this one." The director yelled.

From behind her, one of the assistants yelled the scene and the take and like a trained dog, the moment the clapperboard snapped, she turned into Roxy.

"Come on, give me something to go on." Ryder instantly transformed into William and held his arms out to her. "We are supposed to be together."

Her character, Roxy, walked the tightrope between both male leads. This movie sometimes seemed like documentary of her real life, if she added a third male. Third? Before she became consumed in her personal thoughts, Roxy flashed her smile, shrugged and went to William. "Just a little something, but hurry, the guys will be back soon."

"Then there's no time to waste. I love you." He wrapped his arms around her and connected their lips, not wasting any time in opening his mouth and slipping her the tongue.

Something was off, way off. What happened to the drop in the pit of her stomach any time he or Logan gave her a real kiss on camera? In fact, with the way Ryder practically shoved his tongue down her throat, she almost kneed him right in the groin. However, she didn't want to lose this take and gently pushed him back. "William."

"I want you so bad, why won't you let me get close to you?" Ryder pulled her in tighter.

"Where are you guys? We're late!" Logan's voice boomed from the other side of the wall.

"William." Again, she tried to push Ryder back. Thank God they made it through everything thus far, but now came Drew's line. Without moving a muscle, she held her breath. If he pulled out his line, she didn't want to be the reason for a retake.

Drew as Charles with all the prosthetics and padding attached to him, came around the corner, stopped, and backed up.

Erin said a silent prayer of thanks he didn't trip like last time.

She, actually Roxy, jumped away from Ryder, well, William.

Drew's character stared at her, gave a slight shake of his head and turned, hitting his mark perfectly and colliding with Logan.

"What gives?" Logan played the annoyed asshole all too well. "Are they here?"

Erin held her breath. Drew just needed to deliver the line and they were home free.

"Yeah, everyone's here, we're all here. Where else would we be? We are all stuck here." Again, his timing on point, he pushed passed Logan and headed for the BMW.

"Well, then let's get going." Logan winked, approached and took her arm. "Thank you for keeping her warm for me, I got it from here." He put his arm around her and led her off set.

She glanced back at Ryder and looked straight ahead, watching Drew who stood with his arms crossed waiting to find out the verdict.

"Cut!" The director called out and leaned over to the monitor.

Logan tightened his hold on her shoulder. They all wanted to be finished.

It seemed as if everyone on set froze.

"That's a wrap!" The director gave them a thumbs-up. "See you all tomorrow."

Everyone broke out into applause.

Everyone but Drew.

She watched him walk away, head hung low and his hands in his pockets.

Though she knew he hated her seeing him upset, she ran after him anyway.

Staying a few yards behind him, she watched while he disappeared into the wardrobe trailer, exiting quite a bit later in his street clothes and those damn prosthetics removed from his face and body and headed toward the tiny town.

In the distance, she heard Logan and Ryder laughing and creating a ruckus, if they spotted her she would get pulled into their world and she didn't want either one of them. Maybe it was hormones.

She chewed on her lip and tried to calculate her next move. If she just walked into town, she would create her own kind of ruckus. Only Drew had the luxury to walk around in public without getting noticed. Once he was out of his get up, it was hard to recognize him.

As fast as possible, she darted into the wardrobe trailer.

"There you are, let's get you out of that dress." The wardrobe mistress lunged for her.

"Wait!" She would never have time to fight with the lady, change, ditch the guys and catch up with Drew. "I need a jacket with a hood."

"Your wardrobe has nothing of the sort. Roxy would never wear that." The woman put her hands on her hips.

"Well, then you better go talk to Felix, he said he wanted one." Getting clothes from this person was like trying to get her mother to wake up before noon, but hell, she was an actress and could improvise with the best of them.

"Honestly." With a huff and a shake of her head, the woman stomped out of the trailer.

Seizing her opportunity, Erin ran over to the boys' wardrobe racks, rifled through the clothing and found the sought after piece of apparel. Before she lost Drew, she ran out of the trailer as she put on the jacket and pulled the hood over her head.

By the time she made it to the one street in the town, she could barely breathe and decided she really needed to take some sort of fitness class, or ask the studio to hire a rickshaw driver for her.

Thankfully, she spied Drew right as he disappeared into one of the stores. Without a second thought, she went after him, colliding with the door and then him while a stench of something horrid collided with her nose.

"Hey!" He tensed at her touch. "Excuse you."

"Excuse you too." She supposed her disguise was pretty good and lifted her face to him.

"What are you doing here?" He sighed. "What are you doing here in that?"

"I always wanted to come in this store." At last, she looked around, discovered the source of the stench and wrinkled her nose. "What is this store?"

"Hmm, let's think here." He took her arm and guided her to a row of cages. "I'm going to go with the reptile and fish store."

The sight of a huge snake separated from them by only a thin slab of glass caused her to jump and grab hold of Drew's arm. "Oh my god, I hope it doesn't bite us."

"I promise you're fine." With a shake of his head he walked down the aisle. "Snakes are just reptiles."

She took in each one of the snakes, each one appearing more ferocious than the next. "They better behave or we can take them back to Los Angeles and have a purse made out of them, although he does have his appeal."

"Come on, I think you may like a different aisle better." He led her down another row of cages.

"Turtles." Unable to stop a smile, she dragged him over to one of the displays of tiny turtles. "They are so cute."

From behind her, he let out a chuckle. "They're reptiles too."

"I know, but they're so sweet. Look at them, they look like they're wearing a turtleneck." Once she realized what she said, she burst into laughter and spun around to Drew.

He gave her one look and with a shake of his head joined her in cracking up.

"I'm just glad to see you laughing." She touched his cheek.

"It's fine." He motioned across the way to the lizards.

Preferring the sweet little turtles, she wrinkled her nose at the large scaly creature sitting on a piece of driftwood.

"They're reptiles too." He sighed and pointed to another cage.

This one was little and spotted with huge eyes. When they approached, the lizard turned to them and appeared as if it had a huge grin.

"Oh, this one is fabulous. Does it change colors?" The image of a color coordinated pet pleased her and she faced Drew.

"Sorry. That's a gecko, he just stays that color, but he's a reptile too." He raised his eyebrows.

Thus far, he had pointed out that everything in the reptile store was a reptile. Maybe they needed to go to the fish section or maybe there was something he was trying to tell her. "Is this a lesson on reptiles?"

"Actually, I was hoping you could educate me." He motioned all around him. "All of these are reptiles, so how come every woman likes the little turtles and the geckos, but they gloss over the big lizard that blends in with a rock, but would make an amazing pet. And though girls are scared of the snakes, they still have an appeal?"

Now she understood. Ryder and Logan obviously represented the geckos and snakes of the world, while her best friend was a loyal lizard who blended in with the surroundings.

It was only a matter of time before this came up. He had been more upset about the other two more than usual and she knew he had feelings for her. She swallowed. "Well, I think that maybe rather than always looking for the dangerous snakes and other reptiles that lure one in with their built-in shells and their smiles, sometimes a girl should learn to look at the obvious choice of the reptile who will protect her and stay with her, even hide her if need be."

"Why did you follow me here?" He stepped closer, looked down into her eyes and ran his hand down her arm.

Shivers ran through her, something she never experienced with him, a welcome yet terrifying sensation. If nothing else, she couldn't mess up with him, and chance ruining what they already had.

She chose to flash him a smile and pull the hood up over her head a little further. "There's a lot to be said for blending in."

"There's a marathon of that old 1970s show with the crazy family on. Will you be joining me tonight?" With a tilt of his head, he had led them out of the store.

Butterflies had taken over her stomach, but she nodded. "That's where I belong." She had wondered if reptiles ate butterflies.

Now, the same flutters took residence in her stomach, but she found her strength and lightly knocked on his door.

"Come in."

Before entering, she touched her hair and straightened her nightgown. At the moment, this was as good as she was going to look. She licked her lips and opened the door. "Aren't you going to ask who it is?"

"Call me clairvoyant." He lounged back in his bed in a pair of grey sweats and a black t-shirt and never even bothered glancing up from his book. "What do you need?"

"How do you know I need something?" She went inside and closed the door. Until now she hadn't entered his domain, and she took a moment to absorb the huge master bedroom some interior designer must have created to be fit for a Hollywood star or the owner of an important business. As if he were one perfect accessory to the oversized mahogany furniture, a fireplace and large flat screen television, Beaker lay at his master's feet.

"Again, my sixth sense is kicking in." He turned the page. "Out with it." His voice came out curt, almost snapping her. Too soon, he could tire of anger and head straight to silence.

"You know what I was thinking about?" Her heart beating loud enough for her to miss her cue, she tried to stop her voice from shaking.

"Enlighten me." He pushed a pair of reading glasses up on his nose.

"Remember all those bad old sitcoms we would watch together on location and we would literally laugh ourselves to sleep?"

"I do recall those nights." Still, he didn't bother with a glance.

"I also remember the night you spent combing my hair out after it got all tangled in that wind storm." She inched closer to the bed.

"I remember you yelling at me because you were sure I left you with a bald spot."

Stupid tears clouded the path to her goal. If all she left him with was bad memories, why did he bother coming back to her at all? "Then maybe you can remember the time I walked over a mile to a store to get some lotion from where your prosthetic cut into your skin, and I got us some forbidden treats." She held out her offering. "I'm sorry if I came on too strong today at your office."

At last, he took off his glasses and lifted his head. "What do you need, Erin?"

"My place." She pointed to the side of his bed. "Maybe a movie, maybe a laugh."

Without a word, he threw a remote to what she would always dub her spot and slid over.

She dashed forward, but Beaker went to her area. Not to be misplaced by her canine friend, she put her human treats on the nightstand, reached into the small breast pocket of her nightgown and revealed one of the biscuits she picked up when she got their snacks. "You know I was never allowed to have a pet, but I know if I was allowed one, I would have picked a beauty like you."

The dog sat down.

"I promise there is room enough for all of us, but can I be here?" She leaned way over and tossed the bone shaped cookie back at the foot of the bed.

Beaker lunged for his treat and lay back down, leaving the vacancy she was after.

"You know, he and I have had some amazing talks." She propped up the pillows. "I swear he understands English, or maybe he just understands Erin."

Drew shook his head.

While Beaker happily chomped away, she slipped in between the sheets. "What do you want to watch?"

"I don't care." He put his book aside. "Pick anything."

"Do you ever watch it?" She lifted the remote.

"Not for a long time. I suppose with the sequel now's a good a time as any." He motioned toward the large screen.

She glanced down at the buttons and wondered if he handed her a computer to make her look dumb.

"Get the snacks, this thing is annoying."

He took the multi-buttoned monstrosity back while she gathered up her goods, taking care to make his as she remembered he preferred, two pieces of chocolate with a thick layer of peanut butter in between.

The second the distinctive music from the film started and the lights dimmed, she paused to take in the magic. With the establishing shot of the four of them in high school, their names appeared, first hers, then Ryder and Logan, and finally Drew. She turned, gave him his food and sat back.

"How often do you watch it?"

"It's good background noise." She put the lid on the peanut butter and hugged the jar to her chest. Never would she admit how often she screened the film, she was a downright fan girl of her own work, one of those crazy people who watched the movie over and over again. Ivy might think she was an expert in the movie, but no one, absolutely no one topped her, she lived it.

"So, often." He could always call her bluff. Maybe he was clairvoyant, or magic. She preferred magic.

"When I'm alone I can turn it on and I don't even have to watch it, I just like to hear the voices." It was almost like they were together then. "You sound different, now."

"They put all that stuff in my mouth, I could barely breathe."

"It was a really long time since I heard you speak, so I had to take what I could get." She leaned back among the pillows and turned to him.

"Aren't you going to eat anything?" He took a bite of the confection she concocted.

"I shouldn't." Echoes of Brian's words about letting herself go filled her head, along with her talk with the casting agent, and she pulled up the blanket. Though she tried to be sexy, Drew barely noticed it at all, maybe out of sight was better.

"When are you going to realize that you are one of the most beautiful women out there?" He held out the other half of his treat.

She shook her head. "I'm out of shape."

"I like the curves."

Without thinking, she opened her mouth and allowed him to feed her the candy. His fingers brushed against her lips. One of the best combinations in the world filled her mouth, sweet and salty, creamy and decadent. There was only one thing on the planet bound to be better, and she longed to taste him. "Remember the night we watched that tearjerker in Phoenix?"

"For someone who claims they barely remember their name, you certainly remember a lot."

She stared into his face. "It was our last night and you went to kiss me." They might as well address it through express post rather than messenger pigeon.

He moved his face closer to her. "If my memory serves me correctly, you stopped me."

"I was so stupid. I told you I wanted to be with you, and then I didn't follow through." With her admission, she swallowed. "I wouldn't stop you now, never again."

"Then it's good to know that I can stop myself." He moved back, let his head fall against his pillows and scratched his hand through his hair.

"Drew, please." What did she have to do to make things better? "If I could go back, I would change things."

"Are you sure you wouldn't rather talk about work?" He huffed. "Before you walked into my office today I had a successful boutique lab. Now I'm a failure with no marketing department."

"You've always been one of the most incredible men I've known." She reached toward him, but stopped.

"Did you come in here to make sure I didn't forget to finish your contract?" He squeezed the bridge of his nose.

"I know you never forget anything."

He glanced over at her.

"You're not mad at me over marketing and contracts. Just say it. You showed up out of thin air to talk to me, just let it out already." She ground her teeth together to prevent herself from taking her words too far.

"When you said you wanted me and we would be together after we finished the movie shoot, did you mean it or not?"

"I know I was meant to be with you. I only realized it too late." One tear crept out of the corner of her eye.

"Are you going to realize it too late that you are laying in my bed and you came after me tonight?" He sat up and faced her. "I would ask the same thing about Hollywood Glow, but hell, we're going to have a contract. Don't think for one second I won't protect myself."

"I suppose, since the man I want to be in business with skipped out on me twenty years ago, I wanted to protect myself as well." She hugged a pillow to her chest. "Remember who you let in your bed even though you're furious. If you want me to leave, just tell me."

He didn't respond.

"Drew, tell me what you want." She wouldn't allow him to be docile.

"Let's watch the movie." He shook his head.

Not wanting to get him to a point where he did ask her to leave, she curled up on her side and watched herself, or the self she wished she was again.

WHEN DREW FIRST MORPHED into Isaac, he used to dream about Erin a lot. At times, his dreams were quite graphic, and he woke in an extremely uncomfortable state. Through the years his subconscious sightings of Erin lessened, happening only once in a while. Sometimes the visions were so vivid he felt strange the whole next day as if she really entered his thoughts to taunt him. Of course, with all the publicity of the 20th anniversary of the film, his movies of the mind involving one Erin Holland increased.

Stuck in that place between being awake and asleep, he swore another dream was upon him. They always started where they had a fight then somehow she materialized in his arms. Her back pressed up against him, she molded to his form perfectly. Her light breathing brushed against the hand she held. His erection swelled with unfulfilled need.

As always, he willed himself to stay asleep. Remain in this blissful place, finally get to the point where he actually made love to her rather than wake up in a compromising state.

Her soft coo echoed around him. A little indication she too wanted him. She moved, inched closer, hitting him in all the right places.

"Erin." He ground against her. His body throbbed, aching for the satisfaction always denied him.

"I'm here." She tightened her hold on his hand and intertwined their fingers. "I'm right here."

At her voice, he opened his eyes. For the first time ever, his dream wasn't a dream, it was reality. "Erin." The scene from earlier rewound in his head. What a nightmare.

"Damn it." He untangled his hand from hers and though his body protested, he went to pull away.

She caught his wrist and keeping hold of him and managed to turn over. "Drew, please."

By the position he woke up in, his sleeping self clearly sought her out and no doubt she clearly felt what was going on with his lower half. "I'm sorry, let me get up."

"Why are you sorry?" Her voice came out breathless.

"I just need to stand up." His situation wasn't getting any better.

"I think that's the last thing you need to do." She leaned in and kissed his neck.

He shut his eyes at the first time her lips touched him in anything other than a quick friendly peck. If it was possible, his erection worsened. "We all need to get to our respective beds."

"Do you really want me to go?" Once more she kissed him, this time opening her mouth, tasting him.

"Erin." He swallowed.

"Tell me what you want. I want you so bad, I'm likely to do anything." She grazed her lips over him, working up his jaw line then stopping. "Tell me, Drew."

He opened his eyes. The movie must have ended hours ago, but the television set off a glow, illuminating her features. There would never be a more beautiful woman and the lighting suited her to a tee. "You know what I want." Hell, if she didn't feel it, something was wrong with both of them.

She turned to her back. "Then why don't you take it?"

He stared down at her. How many times did he wish to be in this exact position?

"Please kiss me." She lifted her face to his.

"Damn it all." What was he supposed to do? What happened to making her beg? Would it always be her?

"God, I want you so bad, please." She pressed her palm to the side of his face. "No matter how much you hate me, I know you want me."

Just one kiss. He owed it to himself. Then when it wasn't any good he could return to normal. It had to be the not knowing that made him insane. "Always have." Unable to resist any more, he lowered his mouth to hers.

The second their lips touched he knew he was in trouble, deep, deep trouble, the kind of which no light would ever escape and he would vanish.

In a world where the most anticipated things disappointed, Erin's kiss not only lived up to his fantasy, it surpassed it because she was here.

As if they had been kissing forever, their mouths melded together, their tongues met, their movements practically synchronized. At last, he knew what she tasted like, how she felt, how she reacted. More importantly, she didn't stop him. In fact, she welcomed him, opening her mouth first, kissing him back.

Maybe she did want him as she claimed.

Maybe she did change.

Maybe the twenty years apart heightened every emotion.

With a jolt, he broke the kiss and pulled back.

She put her finger over his lips and kept her eyes on his as she peeled her nightgown off and tossed it over the edge of the bed.

The light bounced off her breasts showing off two perfect mounds with tight nipples ready and waiting for tasting.

She lay back on the bed and snaked her leg between his and over his more than obvious arousal.

Maybe the best thing for both of them was to capture the moment when they both wanted each other.

"God, you're beautiful." He tore his own shirt off, took her into his arms and crushed his lips to hers.

Their skin met. He cupped her breast taking note how it overflowed his hand, the way she gasped the moment his fingertip made contact with the sensitive tip. Giving in to his desires, his mouth followed the same path his hand made and he made sure to pay equal attention to each breast. Her sweet taste combined with whatever rose scented body wash she used, making him light headed.

She squirmed and ran her hands through his hair. Little moans escaped her throat.

His fingers traveled down her stomach. He took in the curve of her hip and tried to remember to slow down, imprint the moment in his mind. Still, he couldn't help but slip his hand inside her barely-there panties.

"Oh, God."

If her cry out wasn't enough to convince him she wanted him, the evidence of her arousal blatantly told him the truth as he slipped a finger inside her.

"Drew." Her breath hitched. She spread her legs wider and reached out to him.

He lifted his head and she kissed him, instantly opening her mouth and searching out his tongue with her own.

In an unexpected move, she broke their kiss, pushed him to his back, her hands and mouth setting off on their own set of explorations. Deep down he always pictured her to be the type of woman who wanted to be serviced. However, the way she slowly kissed him down his chest, rubbed her hands over him and at last reached into his pajama bottoms and grasped his erection proved him completely wrong.

No, she didn't demand to be taken care of, or simply lay there as if he were supposed to worship her. Instead, she took just as much time, if not more, tending to him with kisses and nips down his body and slow strokes up and down his already sensitized erection.

The world, their cat and mouse game, movies and laboratories all disappeared, while he simply relished in her touch and attention. At last it was his.

He twisted the sheets in his hand as she kissed down his chest, raked her nails lightly down his side, and used her tongue to trace a little pattern down his stomach. "Erin." With a fantasy coming true, he needed to be inside her soon, like now.

Her only acknowledgement of him speaking was a little chuckle as she continued.

She made her way to his hip and continued her downward path, her grip tightening, and he had no choice but to move with her. It would be so easy to let her take him over the edge.

"Erin!" He grabbed her arm and pulled her up flush against him before she had the chance to put her mouth on him. No doubt he wouldn't last more than a second.

"Are you okay?" She wrapped her arms around his neck and hooked one leg over his hip.

"Better than okay." Once more, he kissed her and took a breath. He needed a second to calm down. "Let me get a condom." If he didn't have one he was going to lose his mind. With his luck they were probably expired.

"I'm on the pill. Make love to me, with nothing in the way." She returned to her back and reached between them. "I've waited for this for too long."

"I want you. I can't remember not wanting you." He kissed her as she guided him inside her.

Again, he was faced with something much grander than what he could have ever envisioned. Not only the way her body accepted him with a tight, warm welcome, and not only the fact they were finally joined in the most primal basic nature, but how she sucked in her breath and held him as if she were experiencing the same extreme reaction.

"Oh." She coiled her legs around his waist.

"Erin." Her action only served to draw him further inside her with nothing separating them. They were truly joined. He was gone and he had no choice but to drive into her, hard long strokes to both alleviate and accentuate the building pressure.

"Yes." She moaned and slid her legs further up his back. "Don't hold back."

Even if she didn't give him permission, he couldn't restrain himself. In fact, he let go, doing as they both wanted and plunging into her. Everything seemed to happen at lightning speed, yet on another plane. He had waited a lifetime to be here.

She panted, held on tight and hid her face in the crook of his neck. "Oh, God, you feel good."

His body propelled forward in its quest for pleasure, pleasure only the woman beneath him could provide. His heart sped and his muscles tensed in preparation for his orgasm. "Erin." He could only manage to call out her name as he fought a losing battle with his own desire, but he desperately needed her to be there with him.

"Drew." She dug her nails into his back. "Drew!"

Never had his arousal taken over to this degree, control of any sort eluded him. He shook his head, but couldn't stop himself.

"I'm going to come." Erin yelled out and clenched her thighs. "Oh!"

Her cry was his undoing. The pressure finally demanded release and he slammed into her as he let go, his body wracked with all-consuming bursts of pure ecstasy. Immobilized by the intense pleasure overtaking him, he could only hold her as his orgasm crested. "Yes."

"Drew." Beneath him, Erin trembled. "Don't move." Her legs shook and the quivers of her climax washed over him.

Wanting to make sure she gleaned every last bit of satisfaction, he pushed his hips down and remained embedded inside her.

Somehow he managed to find the strength to turn his head and kiss her.

She pressed her hand to his cheek. "Stay inside me for a minute. Just hold me."

They simply lay together still connected, kissing and caressing the other.

Rather than simmering down, their kisses deepened. Under

his fingertips, her nipples remained tight and sensitive as evident in the way she gasped or shivered with his touch. He found himself grinding his hips to hers.

"Drew?" She moved with him.

"Yeah." Instead of basking in an afterglow, he was being overcome with a fresh wave of desire.

"If you don't stop I'm going to come again."

"I want you to come again." His grinds morphed into gentle thrusts.

"I can feel you getting hard inside me." She moaned. "That turns me on."

"You turn me on." As unbelievable as it seemed, he was as hard as before.

"I'm so glad." She pulled him in for a kiss.

Without the urgent need for release, he got to do as he always dreamed and actually made love to her. Now he took his opportunity to fondle and kiss her breasts and feel the backs of her legs as her muscles contracted with her increasing desire. He gradually built her need.

The two of them found their rhythm, hit that particular point in time where they rode the peak of their passion, the only sounds in the room those of their bodies meeting and the moans they were unable to restrain.

"Drew." She called out to him.

"Come. Let me feel it." He pushed himself up and gazed down at her.

"Kiss me." She tried to pull him down.

"I want to watch you." He kept his motions steady wanting to draw out her end.

"Drew." She twisted and squirmed. "Oh, God."

"That's right." He couldn't take his eyes off her and with his own finish nearing, fought the need to simply propel himself into her.

"Oh, oh." She squeezed her eyes shut, bit her lip, held her breath and at last gasped as her body went rigid, her orgasm rippling through both of them.

"You are so god-damned gorgeous when you're coming on me." With the words out he took his turn, lowering his head as he sped up and his climax crashing down on him. He burrowed deep inside her and let the exquisite waves of euphoria overtake him as he filled her a second time.

Once more he found himself holding her as they both came down. Exhaustion claiming him at last, he kissed her as he moved to her side and kept her in his arms.

She nuzzled up to him. After a few minutes of silence, she finally spoke. "Was it good?"

While he didn't want to admit it, he wouldn't lie to her or himself. "I've never experienced anything like that."

"I'm still throbbing from how hard I came." She tilted her head back. "I want us to always have this passion. We waited so long for each other we deserve it."

He glanced down at her. What did she mean always? When he found her at the anniversary gala part of him never expected them to get to the point where they would sleep together. He knew he wanted her, but didn't know what to do if he had her. Could he let go of the past and try to trust her?

"Drew?" She brushed her fingers over his lips. "Don't you think we deserve it?"

Maybe he showed her what she was missing, but now he didn't know what he had gotten himself into. "Yeah, we do." He held her a little tighter wondering what would have happened if they got together two decades ago.

HOLLYWOOD STARBURST

FADE IN:

INT. STEVEN'S GRANDPARENT'S HOME - GUEST
BEDROOM - DAY.

ROXY sits at the edge of the bed and stares at
the phone. She takes a deep breath and finally
lifts the receiver, and dials.

CUT TO: INT. INDIANAPOLIS - ROXY'S PARENTS'
KITCHEN - DAY.

Everything is cluttered, two children are
running around. There is a bubbling pot on the
stove.

ROXY'S MOTHER - WOMAN IN EARLY FORTIES,
DISHELVELED, HAIR MESSY, SMUDGE OF DIRT ON HER
FACE ANSWERS THE PHONE.

                    ROXY'S MOTHER
               (breathless)
               Hello?

A child screams in the background

CUT TO:

ROXY winces as the screech echoes through the
phone.

                    ROXY
               Mom?

CUT TO:
ROXY'S MOTHER

                    MOTHER
               (Yells)
               Quiet!

MOTHER puts phone between her shoulder and
cheek and waves the children pulling at her
away.

                    ROXY'S MOTHER
               Roxy.
               (voice lowers)
               How are you?

CUT TO:
ROXY

                         ROXY
               I'm okay. The last time
               I called you told me not
               to call again until I
               was on my way home.

CUT TO:
MOTHER, One of the children tugs at her, and
she lifts up a little girl. The girl starts
pulling her hair.

                    MOTHER
               (huffs)
               Are you on your way
               home? We need you here.
               The twins have been
               impossible, I can't do
               anything, go anywhere.
               You have commitments
               here.

CUT TO:
ROXY looks down at her lap.

                    ROXY
               If I come home can we
               figure out a way to
               afford college?

CUT TO: MOTHER

                    MOTHER
                We've been over this,
                your father and I can
                barely make ends meet
                now. We'll do our best,
                but trust me, college
                isn't everything, I went
                to college and all I do
                now is play maid. Funny,
                when I started my degree
                I just didn't want to
                end up pregnant with a
                bunch of kids running
                around. No one told me
                it would happen later,
                and I'd be stuck when
                I'm supposed to be
                putting my eldest
                through college. You
                need to get back here.

Another child runs through the background.

CUT TO:
ROXY puts her hand over her eyes.

                    ROXY
                I'm out of money.

CUT TO:
MOTHER

                    MOTHER
                Well, I'm not rolling in
                it or I would have some
                real help. You need to
                figure out how to get
                back. Your father said
                it would prove you can
                complete something.
                Plus, you're eighteen,
                you're an adult.

CUT TO:
ROXY

                         ROXY
               Remember when you told
               me I would always be
               your baby and you would
               always take care of me?

CUT TO:
MOTHER

MOTHER Shakes her head.

                         ROXY'S MOTHER
               Yeah, I think my mother
               said that before she ran
               off with that rodeo guy.
               (lets out snide laugh)
               Memories will kill you.
               Move on and take care
               of yourself and your
               responsibilities.

CUT TO:
ROXY

                         ROXY
               I have to go.

ROXY hangs up phone and lies down on the bed.

                    ROXY
          I have to take care of
          myself.

Chapter Eleven

IN HER UNPREDICTABILITY, Erin was nothing, if not predictable. One thing Drew could rely on no matter what was that his unexpected bedmate woke up at 5:00 AM no matter when she went to sleep or if she were sick or well. Yes, she might go back to sleep, but at 5:00 AM she opened her eyes. A useful fact he learned on set with *Hollywood Stardust*, and something he took advantage of to never be late. The woman was better than any alarm clock.

After making love to her once or twice, depending on how one counted, he longed to fall into a post-coital sound sleep, but instead he laid awake watching the clock and counting down the hours until five o'clock. Once the time hit, she would wake up and he would want to make love to her again. Even now he fought the urge to wake her.

In that stolen time while their bodies merged, the real Erin made an appearance, the woman he fell in love with too many years ago. No roles, no acting, no pretenses, just Erin, the person who could take anyone down one moment and then burst into tears if someone hurt her feelings. The world knew Erin Holland, the actress. Only a select few knew Erin Hollendanger, a beautiful woman who simply wanted someone to want her.

Well, he wanted her. As he said to her earlier, he always wanted her and now it looked like he could have her, or as she would say, she was his to lose.

Some said history repeated itself, and he wondered exactly how close to the original event the proverbial rewind would get.

There was another time he lay in almost this exact position and thought he had her, only to be proven completely wrong.

The movie had been due to wrap the next day, they had one last location shoot in Phoenix and he had waited in the hotel room for his bedmate. Terrified to sleep alone, she had taken to sneaking in with him early in the filming. Though they tried to get adjoining rooms, sometimes it wasn't possible, so it figured on the one night that mattered he had to wait for her to sneak down the hall.

Once more he'd checked his room, their room. Everything was planned to a tee. From the bottle of champagne he managed to get, though he was still underage, to the diamond pendant he made sure to purchase at one of the designer stores the other stars got their jewelry from. For a moment, he considered buying a ring, but it would cause undo publicity with the release of the movie. They would have to wait until all the craziness died down. The only thing that saved him while purchasing the pendant was that with some of the weight he lost and taking off all the crap they glued to his face, no one recognized him.

Just in case, he also purchased some condoms, but hell, they hadn't even kissed yet and the last thing he needed was to thrust his inexperienced body onto the woman he loved. Still, one never knew what could transpire. According to Ryder, Erin was an excellent teacher.

He swallowed the bile in the back of his throat at the thought of her and Ryder. Even worse was the image of her and Logan. Though his best friend never confirmed or denied any such encounter to his face, he knew the truth. However, he and Erin weren't together then, and he had no right to be upset.

Since she deemed them a couple two weeks before, she had calmed down and been happier. Though she came to his bed nearly every night, slept cuddled up to him and gave him little pecks on the cheek, she told him time and again they needed to wait and couldn't do anything to jeopardize the movie.

Then she promised they would make their coming out announcement after the wrap. Because she would have to fly home to see her mother, she let him know tonight would be special and allowed him to make plans for their future.

Though she normally had her timing down to the second, she was now a few minutes late and he paced the length of the room, wondering what could be keeping her, especially after he reminded her three times about tonight. Every time he mentioned it, she brushed him away, but he knew she had to keep up appearances. Thankfully, there would only be one more day spent in hiding.

At last, the long awaited light tapping on his door rang through the room.

His chest tightened and his throat constricted, but he managed to make it across the room and open the door.

"Let me in before anyone sees." Like a disheveled cyclone, she entered the room.

While he'd changed into street clothes after their day ended, apparently she decided to go a different route and rushed inside in her faded blue terry cloth robe with a bleach stain. She said it made her look like everyone else, but he just thought she liked it and didn't want to admit it.

"Are you all right?" He closed the door

She scurried through the room, pressing her hands to her cheeks and glancing in the mirror. Finally, she turned to him. "Yeah, I've just been doing a lot of thinking."

In a vain attempt to get rid of the knot in his stomach, he reminded himself to act like a man, a man worthy of Erin Holland. He joined her and pulled her in for a hug. "Tell me what you were thinking about."

For a moment she didn't move, in fact he thought she stiffened at his touch, but they had shared countless hugs together. He had to be reading into things. "Erin?"

Finally, she put her arms around him and patted his back. "Oh, Drew, why does everything have to be so hard?"

With her snuggled up to him most nights, he'd asked himself the same question. He kept hold of her and brought her to the bed.

As they always did, they lay down and he got the opportunity to look into her face. She seemed paler than usual.

He brushed her hair away from her face. "Tell me what's difficult, and I'll make it better."

"You're incredible." She pressed her palm to his cheek. "How did I get so lucky?"

"I was just asking myself the same question." At her words, his lungs inflated. He hooked his fingers under her chin and tilted her face up to his. "Why don't we make this night as special as we talked about?"

Though kissing wasn't his forte, he supposed he would figure it out and he closed his eyes and leaned in. "I do love you, Erin."

Before their lips connected, she put her fingertips to his mouth. "Drew." Her voice cracked.

She never echoed his words and he opened his eyes. "Tonight is our night," he said.

"I need to talk to you."

Every girl everywhere spoke about those six words and how they hated them. By the way he froze, yet broke out into a sweat he understood the dread. "What is it?"

"What do you see happening between us?" She didn't look him in the eye, instead focused beyond him as if she wanted to run for the exit.

"We've talked about this. You're going to act, I'm going to go to college, and we'll be together." He sat up.

"Do you want me or just the thought of me?" Her voice sounded far away and dare he say rehearsed.

"Erin." He got up off the bed and shoved his hands in his pockets. "I know the real you, not the one you play for the cameras. If neither of us ever took another role, it would be fine with me."

She shook her head and put her hand to her chest. "I have to act."

"That's fine, so what's the problem?"

"I want to be the woman you deserve, but I don't think I can be." A tear pooled in the corner of her eye.

"What does that mean?" Needing some support, he backed up and sat down in a chair across from the bed.

"I'm never going to be the woman you truly want. I tried for the last two weeks and it was all an act." Nothing but her mouth moved.

The last two weeks were the best of his life. "What do you mean you tried?"

"It would be so easy to be with you."

"What does that mean?" Now it was his turn to blur his vision and stare at the ugly peach wallpaper in the room.

"You would give me everything, and I would only hurt you in the end." At last, she moved and sat at the edge of the bed.

"You're hurting me now." He heard his voice, but didn't even realize he spoke.

"Drew, did you really think that tomorrow we were going to show up on set and be in love?"

He focused on her. Her skin remained pale, but the slight narrowing of her eyes told him she was annoyed. Did she want him to make this part easy for her too? "Actually, I did." Once more, he stood.

"When people are on set, it's like a wonderland, an island where no one can get in. Next week we are going to be back to our normal lives. We won't work there." She got up and went to him, standing just out of his reach.

"After spending every night with me, after confiding in me, after making plans with me and telling me you wanted to be with me, you're telling me it was nothing but some movie-making spell and poof tomorrow we'll be cured?"

She closed the distance between them. "You've changed so much these last few months."

"Obviously not enough." He practically growled the words.

"Drew, I do love you in my own way, but no one will ever believe the two of us could be together. In the real world we don't fit." Her tone turned maternal as if she were trying to console him.

As if she kicked him right in the balls, he backed up. He wasn't good enough, wasn't her type. He wasn't Logan with the bad boy swagger or Ryder whose smile made girls faint. He was only Andrew Fulton, the overweight, clumsy fool who'd been forced into the business by his parents when all he wanted was to study the stars rather than see them.

No, she knew Erin Holland could be the woman he wanted, what she didn't say was he could never be the guy she wanted.

Gathering any pride he had left, he went to the door and opened it. He would never beg for her again. Never. "Go."

"We have tonight." She ran to him and put her hands on his shoulders.

"You took tonight away. You took it all." He shook her off and jerked his head, telling her to get out.

Without another word, she scurried out of the room.

He slammed the door and vowed never to beg for her again.

After the movie wrapped, he almost broke his own vow. They didn't see each other for several months, but as the release of the film came closer, he knew he would at least have to be in the same room with her.

He got his contract for the sequel and before signing it, he discovered that not only were Erin, Logan and Ryder playing out their own bizarre love triangle in front of the camera and behind it, but she added their agent into the mix.

If this was what Hollywood had to offer, he didn't need to play any more roles. He wanted to disappear and start over, and though she was the one begging to talk to him, he vanished. A year later, right before he left, she had seen him at Brian's office, but he had taken the coward's way out and though she ran after him, he had driven away.

Erin let out a little coo and moved closer to him.

Jolted back to the present, he opened his eyes to find her still in his bed.

Twenty years later he knew she begged him. Of course, he also knew her career was in trouble. Hell, it didn't take a Ph.D. to figure that one out, or to deduce she had nowhere else to go. On top of that, he also knew now that sex wasn't the big deal it was back then.

At what point would she look at him with her big doe eyes and tell him that she really didn't expect them to be together?

He glanced at the clock. Within the hour she would wake up.

Refusing to beg her and resisting the need to make love to her, he snuck out of bed.

ERIN CINCHED THE SASH around her short, black, trench style coat, glanced at her reflection in the window to make sure her hair remained perfectly slicked back and licked her lips before throwing open the door to the lab's main entrance.

Without looking directly at Jennifer, the fan girl at the front desk, Erin held her head up and took strong, powerful strides toward Mr. Abram's office.

Her entrance produced the desired effect, by the time she reached her goal, a ton of his little worker bees gathered around his hive. She would show them all who was queen. Without knocking, she entered his office, slamming the door behind her.

Instantly, her mission hit a snag at the sight of him and his little protégée huddled together at his desk studying that damn computer monitor.

"Erin." Drew sat straight up.

Bambi only stared at her.

"I need to talk to you." She put her bag down on the chair by his desk.

"I need to finish up a few things." When he spoke, his mouth barely moved, as if he didn't want Bimbo to know they could engage in conversation.

"That's all right, I don't mind waiting." She motioned forward, telling them to continue.

As the two mumbled about that blasted road trip and the FDA and some new regulation, she untied her sash and let the coat fall open, revealing a quite lovely little red dress, and by little she meant short and low cut. When she sat and crossed her legs, the dress rode up a bit, and she leaned back to count the tiles in the ceiling. By her experience, she shouldn't get to ten.

Their chatter quieted down by the time she reached four.

At the count of six, Drew cleared his throat.

"Bambi, do you have it from here?" Drew didn't make it to eight. Good boy.

She didn't even flinch as she waited for her cue.

"Yes, I'll finish up and get you the final schedule for the trip." The little doe gathered up her items. "Let me go find that aspirin for you too."

Inside her mind, Erin shook her head. It was a road trip not a wedding and the woman needed to take an acting class and learn to enunciate.

"Thank you." Again, Drew cleared his throat.

By the time Bambi scampered out of the office, Erin had decided the laboratory had a truly ugly ceiling.

"Erin, you wanted something?"

She let Drew wait. After taking her time to inhale and exhale, she tilted her head at him. "If this morning is any indication, I can see why you haven't been in a serious relationship all these years."

"I've never been in a serious relationship." He countered with a bit of venom lacing his voice.

Fine, she deserved that, but she needed to continue. "Then let me tell you that leaving before a woman gets up, after you spend the night making love to her, is considered poor form."

"I didn't know there were rules."

At last, she looked at him. Though it always appeared as if he were a little disheveled in a cute, scientist sort of way, at the moment he looked like the Santa Ana wind attacked him and left him with yesterday's razor stubble. And people said appearances didn't matter. His told her everything she needed to know.

"Well, let me explain then." She stood and let the coat drip off her as she made her way over to him. Pushing his papers aside, she sat right down on his desk. "Normally when a man wakes up he has quite an incredible erection, and the naked woman in his bed is usually preferred over his own hand to alleviate the situation."

"Is that what you wanted?" He stared into her eyes.

"Of course that's what I wanted. Maybe I would have settled for a kiss and some kind words, but I'm not known for settling."

"Didn't you get what you had been after last night?"

"What does that mean?" Her jaw clenched, but she remained still as to not show too much emotion.

He answered with a lift of his eyebrows.

She leaned forward. "I don't need your pity screw."

"It wasn't me who gave the pity screw."

She took a second to absorb his words and once sure she had them right, she needed to say them aloud. "You think I gave you a pity screw?"

"Call it what you will. Don't worry, I won't say a word, no one would believe we were together anyway." He glared at her.

His words slammed into her. "That was twenty years ago."

"We landed on the moon over forty years ago, but it doesn't make it less true."

Her eyes heated, tears wanted to fall. He would never let her forget. No matter what they wanted, those words would haunt her forever. "Can you explain if I am so repulsed by you why I would even bother with a pity screw?"

He shrugged. "Who knows with you? Part pity, part conquest, part trying to pay your way?"

"Are you calling me a whore?" She ground her teeth together. How did the most important and special night of her entire life turn into an argument about her being a prostitute?

"Erin." He used the same condescending tone everyone did when they thought she didn't understand something perfectly simple.

"Do I have to pay you since I came?" She slid off his desk, knocking some papers to the ground in the process. "I mean if it is a job, I shouldn't have enjoyed it."

"Did you?" He sat back.

"Did I what?" Without taking her eyes off him, she swooped up the papers.

He pursed his lips.

"Oh, I get it, since it was my pity, conquest, pay for my keep screw, I must have faked it. I mean I'm an actress, right?" She walked across the room to retrieve her items. "Is that what you think?"

"I'm not going to go through the motions so you can feel better Erin."

"No, I agree. Apparently the words of an eighteen-year-old saying something stupid will drown out everything else." She crumpled his papers in her fist. "That same eighteen–year-old also has a scar on her hand from where she pounded on your car, begging for you to listen to me. Then, she was the twenty-two-year-old who lost a role because it was a comedy audition and she couldn't stop crying because it was your birthday. Forget the thirty-something-year-old who now has the reputation for being a lunatic because she's always searching for the one person who was missing from her life."

Without any reaction, he simply sat there staring at her performance. She practically expected him to clap. Logan thought he was typecast. Apparently he never auditioned for Drew then he would have no doubt. Willing him to say anything, she went to pick up her coat, but first glanced at the papers. A quick scan told her everything else she needed to know, and she dropped the documents to the floor. They were garbage anyway.

"You know, I'll give you one thing. Maybe you were a conquest. I waited for twenty years to be with you. I missed everything, I missed you earning your degree, I missed your success..." Once more, the tears threatened and she looked up. "I missed picking out the ceiling tiles in here."

At last, he stood.

Refusing to cry real tears in front of him, she exhaled. "A conquest only means you won, it doesn't mean you don't want to keep what you fought so hard for. I only wish you told me I wasn't in the running."

Refusing to hear anything he had to say, she clutched her purse to her chest and headed for the escape route. "Just so you know, I'm not that good of an actress. Maybe I was a bit over the top, but I was really turned on. You turned me on." She opened the door, but before leaving, turned to him. "If you were the gentleman you always pretend to be, maybe this morning you could have found out for yourself if my orgasms were real or not."

There would be no more relying on anyone else to save her. No one wanted her and no one cared. As always, she would rely on herself. She spun back around to find the drones standing there gawking, including little, sweet Bambi. Well, that was an unexpected conquest.

HOLLYWOOD STARBURST

FADE IN:

INT. INDIANAPOLIS- STEVEN'S FAMILY'S RESTAURANT
IN THE BACK BOOTH - DAY

>   CHARLES
>   If Roxy comes back
>   within the next two
>   weeks, she can still
>   graduate with summer
>   school. Anything after
>   that and she will have
>   to repeat the year.

>   STEVEN
>   (sarcastic)
>   She can always drop out.

STEVEN glances around the restaurant, nods at
one of the younger waitresses.

THE WAITRESS smiles and brushes his shoulder as
she walks by.

WILLIAM pounds his fist into the table.

>   WILLIAM
>   What the hell are you
>   doing?

STEVEN furrows his brow.

>   STEVEN
>   As if it's any business
>   of yours, I'm
>   appreciating the
>   scenery.

>   WILLIAM
>   What about Roxy?

STEVEN makes over exaggerated movements as he looks around.

> STEVEN
> Last time I checked she wasn't here. What do you care what I do? I would think you would welcome me stepping back. Or is it that you admit defeat?

WILLIAM leans over the table.

> WILLIAM
> I just don't want you messing with her. Maybe I care so much that I want her to be with the person she wants to be with no matter what, even if it isn't me.

> STEVEN
> Maybe you want to pawn her off.
> (Tilts head.)
> Actually, why do you want her anyway? What makes her so special that you are even willing to let me win so she is happy?

WILLIAM sits back and takes a sip of a drink.

                    WILLIAM
          I don't know. Something
          is missing from her and
          it needs to be filled.

                    STEVEN
          (Teasing tone)
          Did you discover that
          right about the time you
          got in touch with your
          inner feelings?

                    WILLIAM
          Well, for someone
          admiring the view of
          others, word on the
          street says you haven't
          been delving into the
          scenery lately. What's
          your reason?

STEVEN turns away

WILLIAM balls up a straw wrapper and tosses it
at Steven.

                    WILLIAM
          Come on, let's bare it
          all, get it out there.
          Did you just want
          another lay or is it
          something more?

STEVEN faces William once more.

                    STEVEN
          I just know I want her.

STEVEN looks down and fiddles with the straw
wrapper.

                    WILLIAM
          That's it?

                    STEVEN

Maybe there doesn't need
to be more.

          WILLIAM
So that's it?

          STEVEN
Maybe there doesn't have
to be more.

Chapter Twelve

DREW STARED DOWN HIS FRONT door. Inside was his stuff, his dog, and his fish. Also, over the threshold, he would find the woman he would call his nemesis and his obsession. Most of the time he was convinced they were two different people trapped in one luscious body. And now the obsession was even stronger since he knew exactly what he missed out on for twenty years.

Plus, she said she was turned on, really turned on. In fact, she said he turned her on. He groaned. All day he worked, planned for his upcoming trip and did his research, but the only thing he thought about was she told him about what she missed, and the way she said he turned her on. The image of her getting stitches after their encounter at Brian's office also haunted him.

With nowhere to go but inside, he lifted the box containing the various peace offerings he brought home and entered.

The aroma of spice and comfort greeted him, as did a bit of soft rock music playing lightly in the background. Only with Beaker's appearance did Drew overcome the urge to step outside and double-check he was in the right home. He greeted his dog then forged ahead to what appeared to be the source of the smells and the sounds and in the kitchen got the sights.

Erin stood at the stove, her back to him, and he took his opportunity to study his surroundings. Several different pots were lined up on the burners, she already set the small breakfast nook table with dishes and candles, and the entire place was completely pin perfect neat.

"Good evening, Mr. Fulton." She turned and smiled.

His breath caught. She changed from the plunging red dress with her slicked back hair into a sweet little black dress with her hair down soft and long. Either way, the woman was ravishing.

"Good evening. Something smells incredible." He prayed it wasn't the broth she wanted to boil his body parts in after she eviscerated him.

"I made dinner." One of her award-winning smiles graced her face. "I called Logan, and he walked me through a few things. I'll have you know, he and Ivy are having the same meal."

Well, at least she used her resources. He could tell she was trying, really trying, and he needed to make sure to do the same, be a gentleman, acknowledge her and make sure he noticed everything. With Erin, the details held the key. "You look lovely." Lovely?

The word must have worked because she struck a bit of a pose. "I thought you could open the wine and sit down, everything is out on the table, and I was just finishing the gravy." Like a good housewife, she spun back toward the stove.

Gravy. All he knew about gravy was it seemed difficult to make. Though he kept his eyes on her, watching for any sudden move, he put his box by his chair and did as she asked. He swore if the wine weren't corked he would be checking it for poison.

After he poured the drink and took his seat, Erin joined him with the aforementioned gravy in a little pitcher.

"I made pot roast." At her announcement she proceeded to lean over him and serve her meal.

Her breasts grazed his arm, her hair fell down, tickled his cheek, and the scent of her perfume melded with the food. By the time she put his plate together, including the grand finale of pouring the famous gravy over the meat, potatoes and vegetables, the last thing he was in the mood for was eating. Well, eating dinner.

"I thought we could talk," he said.

She scooted her chair closer to his, put her elbow on the table and stared at him. "How about you take a bite first?"

He glanced over at her empty plate. "Aren't you going to eat?"

"I made this for you. I'll eat later." She pushed his plate toward him.

"All right." He couldn't ignore the cooking. She actually cooked, with pans and pots and ingredients and gravy. As fast as he could without appearing as if he were rushing, he scooped up a representative sample of the meat, potato and other root vegetables.

The flavor of home-cooked goodness traveled through his mouth. Something simmered and tended for hours while the tastes melded together. The tender meat complemented the rest of the ingredients, and he almost thought it was a shame to swallow, but if he didn't he wouldn't be able to take another bite. "Wow, Erin."

"Do you like it?" With the back of her hand, she stroked his cheek.

"It's delicious." To prove his point, he took another bite and tried not to lean into her touch. The whole scenario pushed him into sensory overload.

"I'm glad. I always wanted to learn to cook. I had this vision about cooking for you the other day, so I wanted to live it out." As she talked she continued to caress him, her fingertips traveling across his jaw, down his shoulder and back up again.

Shivers consumed him. "You've always had talent for anything you set your mind to."

"That's why I've always loved you." Her voice came out more as a breath.

With his fork midair, he turned to her.

"I was really stupid. I am really stupid."

"You're not stupid, Erin. You were never stupid." He repeated the same mantra he used to tell her on set when he would find her crying behind a set piece.

She took a sip of the wine. "I've always been weak. If I wasn't, I would have been with you. Maybe I wouldn't have spent all this time waiting for you, and maybe once I got you back I would have done more than just make sure we made love at least once."

"Erin."

"How was the rest of your day?" She straightened up and smiled.

Unsure if she really wanted to know or simply wanted to change the subject, he went with it and answered. "I did some research on some new fruits and vegetables they are growing at this experimental farm."

"Wow, who knew they could make different fruits and

vegetables?" Almost like she developed some sort of food radar she added a bit more gravy to his plate, but managed to keep her focus on him.

He nodded. "They make hybrids with certain properties. Maybe something would be good for Hollywood Glow. I'm going to take a road trip to visit a few accounts and then go to that farm. That's part of what I wanted to talk to you about."

A smile danced on her lips. "You're going to do wonderful and Hollywood Glow is going to shine. I think I overstepped my boundaries enough in your work and personal life. When you have something for me to endorse, I'm only a phone call away." Once more, she touched his cheek and then stood.

"Erin?" He pushed back from the table.

"I did a lot of thinking today. After I went by the lab, I came back here and gave into my inner need to be something more to you than a needy woman who doles out pity screws. No matter what, those words I said that horrible night will never go away." She went to the sink and turned on the water. "Maybe some were true."

With his jaw clenched he went to her.

"Not the ones about no one believing we could ever be together, but when I told you I could never be the woman you wanted." She turned toward him. "I know Bambi is going on the trip. I don't want a pity invitation. I know at one point you were with her, and she's perfect for you."

"We are not together."

"Not now, but you should be." She shrugged. "So, I got to make love to you and I got to see you, and I even played house. I really thank you for giving me what I dreamed about, and though I wish it didn't end, I'm going to give you your home and your life back."

"You're going." He turned off the water. "Where are you going?"

"It doesn't matter, I never tried to find anywhere else, I wanted to be here." She wiped her hands on a dishtowel. "And you know I get what I want."

Left without words, he stood looking at nothing, a hole forming in his chest. Again, she used him, got what she needed and was on to better pastures.

"I didn't mean to make trouble for you. I don't know Isaac

Abrams. I only know Drew Fulton, and I really don't know him all too well. I only have a memory." In a rare case of her emotion getting the best of her, a tear fell down her cheek. A real tear, complete with pale skin and her nose and cheeks reddening, something she always hated because it betrayed her.

"Erin." Damn everything, what was he doing?

"We both know me living here isn't going to work. I'm going to leave before I'm asked to leave. You had to leave your own home in the middle of the night because you didn't want to see me this morning." She threw the dishtowel across the counter and walked away.

He pounded his fist into his leg and returned to his seat. "I'm not going after her."

For several minutes, he actually stayed put and continued to repeat his vow. He even gulped down his wine.

Yes, for a whole four minutes he did not go after her.

Then he leaned back and the box he brought home for her caught the corner of his eye. The words she spoke, both this afternoon and at the sink, echoed around him. Why was any of this even important when he lived without her for twenty years?

No, he existed for twenty years.

He took a swig directly out of the wine bottle, practically knocked over his chair getting up, and made his way upstairs after grabbing the blasted box.

At what was once his guest room, but now was her room, he knocked and opened the door.

"Drew." She sat at the edge of her bed, but turned away from him the second he entered.

If she planned on leaving, it wouldn't be any time soon. Her room was a disaster zone, with clothing and possessions strewn all over.

Rather than asking if he could talk to her, he sat down next to her, putting the box in front of him. "Remember when we were in the middle of filming somewhere in the middle of nowhere and none of us had a formal graduation from high school, so we made our own ceremony?"

Though she didn't look in his direction, she nodded.

"I remember you being upset because we didn't have a prom, but you were the only girl so our dates were limited."

At last, she turned. "I would have been too scared to go with who I wanted to anyway."

Well, at least she owned it. "I just wanted to disappear." He might as well own it as well, and he reached into the box and pulled out the oversized, ornate frame containing his degree. "So, after everything went down, I had to go. It was weird at first, like I was playing a role, but I liked Isaac because no one knew him. He had a clean slate, and he could try to be what Drew wanted to be, but instead became an actor." He pushed the diploma over to her lap.

She ran her fingers over his name.

"I legally changed my name and went abroad. Instead of studying astronomy, I went into biochemistry because maybe I was sick of stars and I wanted some answers to how the body works."

She sniffed and continued to stare at the diploma.

"I have to admit that I didn't want to leave school. It was safe, but then suddenly I was writing a dissertation on stabilizing polyphenols and I had my doctorate degree and maybe that's why I still like teaching."

"When you lecture at UCLA do your students call you Dr. Abrams?" she asked in a whisper.

"Yes, and it's really creepy." He gave her a light elbow. "Of course, now that it's out that I am in fact Drew Fulton, I think my classes may be a little more popular."

She let out a laugh.

"When I went to my graduation ceremony, and I was decked out in my doctoral gown and hood, one of the first thoughts I had was wondering what you'd think if you saw me like that." He bent down and handed her a picture of him in the outfit.

Rather than chuckling or smiling, she hugged the picture to her chest. "What was the second thought you had?"

"I wished you were there."

Still holding the picture, she laid her head on his shoulder.

"I decided to open the lab when I wanted to create my own formulations, and I got a few bites from some accounts I still have who wanted me to compound some solutions for them." He tried to give her a fast history of the last two decades and reached into the box once more. "What I lacked however, is someone with a flair for design."

He pulled out a sample ring of different ceiling tiles, deciding not to tell her he had half his staff tracking down any contractor to get this for her. "I was hoping you would make your mark."

She plucked the ring out of his hand and set it on her lap.

"You know? I was lucky because you let me watch you all these years."

She turned her face up to him.

"Yes." He stared down at her, taking her all in. "I got to watch your movies and I got to read about you in the paper and on the Internet. I now understand why so many people think they know celebrities. It's like your whole life is on display."

"It is." Like earlier, she touched his cheek.

"You let me live with you, even if you didn't know it, but I didn't do the same." Unable to resist, he took hold of her hand and kissed her wrist, spying the scar she spoke of, a little white raised jagged line on the side of her hand. He had no choice but to kiss the visible proof of her pain.

"Oh." She let out a little gasp, joy, surprise, delight?

He didn't know, but wanted to find out. First, he needed to make some things clear. "I don't want you to go. You need your chance to live with me."

Instead of answering, she wrapped her arm around his neck.

Before he gave in, he needed to know. "Erin, I want you to stay here and I want you to go on the road trip with me. Bambi understands the situation with us."

She put the items he gave her aside and pulled him closer. "Did you enjoy making love to me?" Her breath brushed against his lips.

"It was the experience of a lifetime." He stopped himself from kissing her. "Erin, answer my question."

"Make love to me now, please." She kept hold of him and leaned back on the bed. "Do it because you know I want you."

"Erin." Wise to her game, he tensed, resisted. It was all too easy to let go around her.

With a sigh, she shook her head. "We already took one road trip together and then I didn't see you for twenty years."

"It's always your way." He pushed back and managed to find his strength to get off the bed.

"I think that's hardly true. For twenty years, you called the shots." One leg bent, she remained reclined on the bed. No matter the situation, she struck a pose.

"And now I know why." Reminding himself not to take his eyes off her, he backed up.

"Don't go, Drew." She reached out for him.

"I'm Isaac, remember." He stopped at the threshold.

She simply gazed at him.

"I'm never going to beg you again." He went against his own vow. No wonder she always held the upper hand. Something was most definitely wrong with him.

"I was the one who came to you begging."

"I never saw this movie." Finally, he stepped into the hall.

"What movie?" she called after him.

"With whatever character you're playing tonight." He headed for his room. "You should have won an Oscar."

FADE IN:

INT. STEVEN'S GRANDPARENT'S HOME - DAY

ROXY is standing on a stepstool in the kitchen,
piles of dishes are all over the counter, and
she is scrubbing out the cabinets.

STEVEN'S GRANDMOTHER joins Roxy and puts a
plate of cookies and glass of milk on the
counter.

> STEVEN'S GRANDMOTHER
> Come take a break. How
> is everything going?

ROXY comes down off the stepstool and looks
between the cookies and Steven's Grandmother.

> ROXY
> I believe I have
> organized every nook,
> cranny, drawer and
> cabinet in your home.
> After I finish here,
> I'll start on the
> garage.

ROXY takes a cookie and with half-closed eyes
bites into it.

STEVEN'S GRANDMOTHER smiles and pushes the milk
closer to Roxy.

> STEVEN'S GRANDMOTHER
> Everything does feel
> exceptionally clean and
> tidy. You're a hard
> worker.

ROXY brushes her hair out of her eyes.

                    ROXY
          I feel accomplished.

          STEVEN'S GRANDMOTHER
             You are accomplished,
             and I love having you
             here, but I have to
             ask. Once you finish
             the garage what are you
             going to do?

ROXY looks down

          STEVEN'S GRANDMOTHER
             No matter where you end
             up, you have to go back
             to your roots. You may
             not end up there, you
             may take many twists and
             turns, but I think you
             need to make your trip
             full circle. Only then
             will you be able to move
             on.

ROXY nods and glances up at Steven's
Grandmother.

                    ROXY
          I'm scared.

          STEVEN'S GRANDMOTHER
             If you weren't there
             would be something wrong
             with you.

STEVEN'S GRANDMOTHER cups Roxy's cheek.

          STEVEN'S GRANDMOTHER
             You need to get back,
             and you need to do it on
             your own. You have the
             money you earned working
             here, and you have one
             more thing.

STEVEN'S GRANDMOTHER takes Roxy's hand and guides her though the kitchen and into the garage.

STEVEN'S GRANDFATHER, an older attractive and stylish man waves and steps back away from a huge vintage Lincoln sedan.

ROXY shakes her head.

                    ROXY
          I can't take that.

               STEVEN'S GRANDMOTHER
               (Laughs)
               This is part of your
               job. I need you take
               this car over to my son.
               Steven's father. I
               couldn't think of anyone
               I trust more to deliver
               the car.

ROXY turns to Steven's Grandmother and hugs her.

                    ROXY
               Part of me wants to stay
               here, part of me wants
               to run away.

STEVEN'S GRANDMOTHER pats Roxy's back.

               STEVEN'S GRANDMOTHER
               What does the biggest
               part say?

                    ROXY
               I have to work hard and
               see this through to the
               end.

Chapter Thirteen

ONCE UPON A TIME a six-year-old girl with brilliant blue eyes, blonde hair, and none of that awkward chubbiness showed up at a casting call. Without even having to wink and or smile won the coveted part as the smart ass daughter to a one-season sitcom about a family who lived in a department store and all the crazy antics.

Thankfully for one Erin Holland, and one Erin Holland's mother, her next role was right around the corner, another sitcom followed by a stint on a soap opera, and even a drama, all until her big break playing the role every teen girl coveted.

Life was good when she worked. Her mother couldn't find a pedestal high enough for her. Between roles when most child actors took a break, visited friends, went to school, her mother made them sit in the studio apartment in Hollywood and look for any way her talent could be sold.

Mr. Hollendanger, who preferred not going by his daughter's stage name of Holland, checked out right around the time her mother tried sleeping her daughter's way to the top. When he passed away seven years later, Erin had to threaten to cut her hair to be allowed to leave a location shoot to go to the funeral. Of course, when the former Mrs. Hollendanger did her the favor of leaving her worldly life behind, Erin decided she was too busy on set to do anything but send an arrangement of tasteful flowers. It seemed fitting.

If her mother could see her now sitting in an agent's office hoping to get a bite, she would die on the spot. Too bad the witch wasn't here.

There was only one person on the planet who understood. One person whose parents made her mother look like a Midwest homemaker. Exactly one person who she could tell these thoughts to, and two days ago, she crushed him by telling him she would leave, right? Who was she protecting?

The hole in her chest widened, and she slipped her hand into her bag to get her phone.

"The second I heard your name, I told my assistant someone had to be making a joke." Rick Southern, agent of many of her co-stars through the years, joined her in his office.

Playing the game, she didn't as much as glance in his direction. Instead, she crossed her legs, and waited with her hand still on her device. Part of her wanted to walk out and call Drew. They hadn't spoken since he walked out of her bedroom, and he would be leaving in a few of hours for his road trip with the blonde roadkill.

"I almost feel like asking you for an autograph." Rather than sitting across from her at his desk, he stood in front of her. The personification of an agent in a no-doubt gifted designer suit, slicked back hair, and features only suitable for a screen door, not the silver screen, he smiled down at her.

She let go of the phone, found her marker and whipped it out of her bag. "Do you want me to sign a body part or would you like an 8 by 10?"

"So, the rumors are true, you are a little vixen."

She'd been called worse. "Is that the word on the street?"

He crossed his arms. "No, the word on the street is the agent you've had since before your Stardust days dropped you like a burnt out starlet."

Trained for a lifetime to only show the emotions she chose, she sighed and glanced down at her manicure. "Funny, how the word on the street can be so very wrong, because I recall the story going something like I wouldn't give him *everything* he wanted and we chose to part ways." For pure effect and to make sure her point came across, she paused to look up at him. "But I am a vixen, so I guess you can never be too sure what is real and what is Hollywood."

Rick nodded.

If she could wrap this up, she might be able to see Drew before he left. "However, what is true is I don't like to put my own deals together."

"What are you saying, Ms. Holland?"

"I'm yours to lose." She brushed her hair back from her face.

"Do you have any deals now?" he asked. "Anything that needs to be negotiated?"

"I've worked since I was six years old, so I took a little break." At the moment she missed the lab and Hollywood Glow and Drew. The first time in a long while, she felt like she was worth something when she sat in Drew's office and spouted off some of the knowledge she knew about marketing.

"Of course I'll sign you, but I like my clients to do some footwork."

Before shooting back a snarky remark, she waited. Agents were supposed to get the work, not the actors.

"Oh, your silence tells me you're concerned." He walked around the desk, taking his chair. "Let me also tell you that your appearance here shows me that besides a falling out with an agent you've had over half your life, you're not getting the roles like you once were, you've gone a little soft and lost a little ground. Your social media is crap, are you not in this world?"

She pressed her lips together. "I email."

"You've totally disconnected from your fans." As if the whole situation were giving him a headache, he pressed his fingers to his temple. "In this day and age you can't be aloof—they want to know everything down to what you had for breakfast. No one uses email anymore unless they're over forty."

Her mouth fell open. She hadn't hit the big one yet.

"I would think with the *Hollywood Stardust* anniversary and the announcement of the sequel finally being made, roles and appearances should be plentiful." He strummed his fingers on the desk. "Look at your cast mates, Logan Alexander is all over now that he gave his beloved new bride the sequel as an engagement present. If the movie goes well, which it will, he will turn into one of those celebrity directors, and he had to overcome being the bad guy."

The fanfare on Logan's token of love to Ivy, and the buzz around casting would keep him in the press for months. A trickle of sweat traveled down her spine, but she refused to squirm.

"The buzz is that Ryder Scott may throw his hand into production with the movie, and he's made some late night talk show rounds while he continues to work on his never ending independent flick." Rick averted his eyes to his computer, clicked his mouse several times, and spun the monitor around to her. "And Drew Fulton or Isaac whatever? The man spoke one time at the Stardust party, but he is more relevant than you right now."

"He hasn't been seen in twenty years," she whispered. Of course everyone wanted to know what happened to him.

"If you're going to give me excuses, you probably should go down the street to my colleague, she loves has-beens."

For the second time in less than two weeks, someone suggested the third rate agent to her. Shelly Terry was famous for taking any old star and turning them into a second rate show piece. Once an actor ended up with her, it was the end. The black hole of existence left for only the most desperate, those stars left with barely any glow and no money. Truth be told, Rick Southern was only second rate, but he had some successes under his belt.

"Are you just going to sit there silent or are you going to tell me you need help?" He stared at her.

Heat built behind her eyes, and she didn't move, didn't speak.

"Tell me you'll do what it takes because you're Erin Holland."

Her muscles tensed in an instinct to run, get out of there.

She forced herself to inhale. If she faced her life, she would admit she didn't know how to do anything else but live in the land of make believe. "I came to you because I need to freshen up my career. Now, I'll do what it takes, the question is, will you?"

"All right then." His smile grew. He leaned back. "I have a thought."

"Are you going to keep it a secret?" She glanced at the clock. She had to see Drew before he left. Last time he left, she almost missed him, when she was too caught up with being Erin, the star of *Hollywood Stardust*. Playing stupid games with Ryder, Logan and Brian, she let the one person she wanted leave without asking where he was going or when he would be back until it was too late. Her heart sped.

"Reality TV is hot, it's an easy sell, good money and it gets you out there. People think they know you, can relate to you, and after being so silent for so long, it would be good." He nodded.

Dare she tell him that aside from acting she didn't do anything? Well, she worked in a lab for five minutes and then spent the last few days hiding from the one person she wanted to be with. "You think people want to see me go about my daily life?"

"Reality sort of has big quotations around it." He laughed. "They want to see a slice of your life. The interesting part, like the part where you're involved with the *Hollywood Stardust* sequel, the part where you're friends with the soon-to-be Mrs. Alexander, the part where you live your life, but the interesting part."

Maybe she could convince Logan to allow her some access to the making of *Hollywood Starburst*. Her wheels began turning. Ryder would definitely be on camera with her. If Drew allowed it, it would be amazing publicity for Hollywood Glow.

"What's your personal relationship status right now?"

She didn't dignify the question with an answer.

"We have to be straight with each other if we're going to turn this around." He rocked his chair back and forth.

Her teeth scraped together, hitting that right note to finally make her squirm. "Right now it's nothing." She squeezed her eyes shut.

"Well, since I know you're not living with Brian anymore, I need to know where you're staying." He prodded.

"I've been staying with Drew." She lowered her voice.

"And you think no one wants to watch you?" He rocked forward and grabbed the edge of his desk. "Go get me something with *Hollywood Starburst* and Drew and I'll make you a star on the small screen that will take you right back to the big screen."

"So what do we do, hire a crew?" Did the man think she had a show in her handbag?

He shook his head. "This is where you have to work. I need something to make this convincing. Everyone wants a program. Go get me some footage. It can be shot by you, but show me what you got. Give me something different."

She played around with cameras off and on, but would anyone allow her to film them? This wasn't Logan's wife and a crew. "What about a contract?"

"I'll give you a contract when you show me something to contract you for."

She stood and faced the door. When she called Rick, she practically expected him to have the contracts ready. What happened to her, her career, her life?

Wait.

He told her that her life was interesting. Well, could be interesting.

With new conviction, she turned back toward him. "I have an idea."

"Enlighten me." He held out his hand.

She swallowed. "What about a road trip with me and Drew building a nutraceutical line?"

Once more, he rocked his chair back. "I better get my cloth ready to polish up your star."

HOLLYWOOD STARBURST

FADE IN:

INT. ALBURQUERQUE, NM - INSIDE THE LINCOLN - Day.

With the music blaring and sipping a soda, Roxy speeds down interstate 40, she spots brake lights up ahead, and frowns when traffic comes to a stop.

Roxy tilts her head and leans way over trying to see the issue. She lifts up her map and looks out again.

Time passes as indicated by the setting sun. Roxy starts out relaxing and ends up with her hitting her steering wheel and cussing. Finally, a man in a uniform walks down the never ending row of cars, stopping at her window.

                    CONSTRUCTION WORKER
                 We had a bit of a delay
                 today. Things should
                 get moving here in the
                 next thirty to forty
                 minutes.

                    ROXY
                 Do you know how long
                 that is in car minutes?

CONSTRUCTION WORKER smiles.

                    CONSTRUCTION WORKER
                 I was supposed to be
                 getting off my shift
                 over an hour ago. The
                 delay was probably just
                 as long in overtime
                 minutes. Sorry. It
                 couldn't be avoided.

                    ROXY
          Maybe they shouldn't do
          construction in the
          middle of the day when
          it backs up everything.
          I have to stay on
          schedule.

          CONSTRUCTION WORKER
          Strange thing with
          schedules is everyone
          tries to keep them and
          they are really hard to
          hold on to.

CONSTRUCTION WORKER pats windowsill and moves
on.

Montage of Roxy doing things in the car to keep
busy. Folding paper, going through the glove
box, shifting in her seat as she realizes she
has to go to the bathroom.
At last the, traffic moves, slowly.

ROXY squeezes the steering wheel and shakes her
head as the cars crawl along the highway. In
the distance, lights flash and as she gets
closer, a fire truck and ambulance comes into
full view. The scowl on her face disappears,
she presses her lips together and she spies the
construction worker and though the road opens
up ahead of her, she stops.

CONSTRUCTION WORKER walks over and motions
ahead.

                    CONSTRUCTION WORKER
                      Maybe you can make up
                      some time.

ROXY watches as the paramedics wheel away a
stretcher with a body bag on it.

                          ROXY
                      Maybe I need to learn to
                      improvise.

CONSTRUCTION WORKER looks over his shoulder and
back at Roxy.

                    CONSTRUCTION WORKER
                      Guy was scheduled to go
                      home.

                          ROXY
                      I'm scheduled to go
                      home.
                      (Shakes her head.)
                      I'm so sorry.

                    CONSTRUCTION WORKER
                      Remember, be careful and
                      always make sure you
                      keep in touch with those
                      who matter. At least he
                      got to call his wife and
                      tell her he loved her at
                      lunch. We all made fun
                      of him but...
                      (Shrugs.)

Cars behind her start to honk.

                    ROXY
          I think I need to
          schedule a phone call.
          Again, I'm sorry.

CONSTRUCTION WORKER nods.

ROXY drives away and stops at nearest gas
station.

                    ROXY
          (speaks to self)
          I have some rescheduling
          to do.

ROXY finds a payphone and pulls her phone book
out of her purse. First, she turns to
William's number, then she bites her lip, turns
to Steven's page and puts some change in the
phone.

Chapter Fourteen

"I HAVE THE ENTIRE SCHEDULE printed out, but I also put it on the calendar that's downloaded into your computer and on your phone." Bambi opened the door to the SUV and put her notebook on the front seat.

Organized. Drew grabbed her one small piece of luggage and put it in the back. Yes, Bambi was organized. Almost to the point of exhaustion, but who was he to complain?

At least he wasn't starting his trip by stuffing Erin's suitcases into his vehicle and praying they fit, followed by managing his own schedule, and carrying every meeting while his former co-star tapped her foot and yawned waiting to go on to a place where she could be the center of attention.

Yes, Bambi was much better, a business associate who would take charge, knew her stuff, and understood his line of work. Bambi was a much better fit for him.

Of course, his business associate didn't lean back on the bed and tell him to make love to her because she wanted him to, nor did she occupy his thoughts for so long he couldn't remember not wanting her. Simply put, she wasn't Erin Holland. Though it wasn't Bambi's fault, it doomed them before they ever really got started.

Once he decided to take Erin, the road trip became much more than a business trip. In his mind they were supposed to take a real road trip together, a melding of both their worlds, but he was the only one who saw any significance in the act.

Hell, he hadn't seen her for the last two days. She only hit him with the fact she gave up and then hid.

Yes, he might disappear, but she hid anytime she felt threatened and then everyone was supposed to move heaven and earth to find her.

Back then he always went searching. As the filming of the movie went on, most times he hadn't liked what he found. The relationships between her and Logan, and between her and Ryder had seemed to intensify, often causing fights among them.

Then one day he had hit a jackpot, or so he thought.

Again filming in a new city, he glanced at the clock and waited for his bed partner's appearance. Things had been tense today. On the flight, he'd finally gathered enough courage to ask her if they were ever going to be more than friends. Actually, more like he'd stuttered the words. She didn't answer, simply stared at him with those huge eyes.

He must have dozed off because when he jolted awake the same clock read two hours later.

No Erin.

His heart racing, he shot up and darted to the door. Where was she? Only one other time did she miss their evening rendezvous, and he and Ryder hadn't spoken since.

He pounded his fist to the door, before throwing it open and stomping over to her room and calming down enough to muster a simple knock.

If she went running to one of her boys without the simple courtesy of telling him, he was going to have to stand up for himself no matter what it cost him.

With no answer, he searched the hallway, and then pressed his ear to the door. Though he welcomed the sound of her television, she left the thing on 24/7. He raised his fist, ready to tear the damn thing down when the door opened.

"Took you long enough." In a pair of men's style pajama's Erin put her hands on her hips and grinned.

What did he miss? She came to him. This was how they did it. "What?"

"I didn't think it would take you two hours. Did you fall asleep?" She giggled and backed up to let him in her room.

The reason they always went to his room was evident in all her belongings strewn all over the place, but among the dresses, shirts, pants and beauty supplies, there was one clean spot in the shape of the bed with a tray set up covered by a cloth.

"Yeah, I dozed off."

"Well, your timing is perfect. I want to welcome you to the Drew Fulton appreciation night." She took his arm, dragged him inside, and shut the door.

Wait. Hold on. What happened to walking in on an empty room or one where she was dressed to the nines ready to go out with one of his co-stars? What happened to her sad excuses or apologies and her running back to him in tears? "I don't understand."

"I know, but you will." She took his hand, led him to the bed and revealed the contents of the tray.

His mouth hanging open, he sat on the bed staring between her and her offering.

"This is my Drew Fulton appreciation kit." She adjusted the pillow behind him and lifted his legs on the bed. "First, we have the remote control. You may choose the movie tonight, even if it's an action one." With a bow, she lifted the device and handed it to him.

That alone made his night because he never got to choose the movie. He was the only male in America who didn't control the remote.

"I also have our snacks already prepared, as well as our drinks." Like a gorgeous game show model, she ran her hand over the tray.

He spied the peanut butter and chocolate coupled with some healthier choices. They would end up eating the peanut butter and chocolate.

"I also have one more thing for you." She pulled an envelope out from under one of the plates and took her seat next to him. "But before I give this to you I have something to say."

Holding his breath, he waited.

"Sometimes I just assume you will always be there for me. I always know you will rescue me no matter what, and that's what keeps me going." Tears glazed her eyes, and she held out the envelope. "You deserve an answer to your question, and I wrote it down so you can see instead of hear it."

After forcing himself to breathe and swallow, he took the envelope and opened it, pulling out a piece of her stationary.

Her note only had four words, but they were the most glorious words ever to exit from one of her purple pens, or maybe any pen on the planet.

Let's plan our future.

Once more, he glanced between her and the note. "What are you saying?"

"I think after this movie wraps and we have our lives back we should be together." She licked her lips. "If you still want me."

"Still want you?" He only managed to utter that one question until he was left with a loss for words. Not that it mattered. His heart grew to such a point where he wouldn't be able to speak anyway.

She shrugged.

Though he didn't want to break the spell, he had to ask the next question. "Do you want me?"

Through her lashes, she looked up at him. "You belong to me. I know I'm supposed to be with you. That's why I could never decide between the other two, I wanted you."

Unsure what to do when faced with getting what he wanted, he opened his arms to her.

Without hesitation, she went to him and curled up by his side.

They lay together, side by side, him playing with her hair, her holding on to him. Maybe this was why he was destined to do the movie, to find the rest of his life.

"I don't want this movie to taint what we have, I want us to wait until the movie wraps. Is that all right?" She ran her nail over the stitching on the sleeve of his t-shirt.

All that mattered was he had her. "We have the rest of our lives. A few more weeks won't change that."

"Do you want to pick a movie?" She had nuzzled down on his chest.

He had glanced down at the top of her head. "I'm happy just watching my star."

How did history repeat itself? How did he have her one second and the next was being told no one would believe they were together? How did he make love to her one night, only to have her want to leave?

He didn't know why he expected anything different. She played her roles like a pro. With a little too much force, he slammed the back hatch down in time to watch Erin's car skid into the driveway.

In a flurry only she could conjure, she jumped out of the car, and rushed toward him, her heels echoing a satisfying click on his stone driveway. The only break in her trek was a fleeting look at Bambi, but the presence of her foe didn't stop her.

"I'm sorry I'm late, but give me just a few and I'll be right down with my things." Her voice came out breathless.

He narrowed his eyes. "What are you talking about?"

"I just need to throw a few things into a bag and then we can start on our trip." Again, she glanced over at Bambi, but returned her focus to him.

"The last I heard you were leaving." Did he miss something? She stared at him.

"What are you doing?" He spoke through gritted teeth.

"Are you saying you don't want me to go with you?" Once more, she peeked over at the other woman.

"You can't do this." He crossed his arms and forced the words out. "You can't show up at my door and then leave when you want, you can't decline a trip and then come at the eleventh hour, you can't pull the same stunts you did twenty years ago and expect no repercussions. People have lives that you don't control."

"Then let me ask you this." She lifted her chin. "Where was my control when twenty years ago you vanished without ever letting me have a say? Where was my control when I begged to have any kind of contact with you and couldn't even send a letter? Where was my control when you decided the time was right for you to suddenly come out of hiding?"

At her accusations right back at him, his chest tightened. "Why do you want to go now?"

"This is our trip. I can feel it." She turned down to the ground. "Just me and you."

Damn him to hell, he wanted all her luggage, and her disorganization, and he wanted her to demand his attention after he did his work. He wanted it all, but still he had to give her one last test. "I can't ask her to leave now."

"Whatever." Erin shrugged. "Last time you left without me it cost me too many years. I don't care how you leave just that you don't leave without me."

"Do you need help packing?" He dug himself into his own hole and it caved in all around him.

"No, I'll only make you crazy." A slight smile flickered. She touched his cheek and rushed into the house.

He opened the back of the SUV and stared inside, quickly attempting to calculate the amount of room needed for Erin's items.

"What's going on?" Bambi came up behind him.

If anyone deserved the truth it was the woman speaking to him. He cleared his throat. "Erin sort of came back into my life, and I invited her to go with me. I was going to talk to you, but then she said she couldn't go. However, apparently we had a little mix up. She and I have communication issues."

"What do you want to do?" She leaned on the car. "Do you want me to leave?"

He was quite certain that Bambi didn't want the real answer to his question, and he pushed the image of Erin in nothing but a bedsheet in a hotel out of his mind. "I don't really know."

She made a clicking sound. "Maybe it's better if I'm there."

"You don't have to." He squeezed the bridge of his nose.

"This is my job, and I know you are not prepared for any of these meetings or your guest lecture. I've never seen you like this, so I'm going to go and take one for the Isaac Abram team." She patted his arm and returned to the front of the car, claiming shotgun.

The battle lines had been drawn.

While maybe it was better Bambi went with them, he also foresaw pending disaster. Yes, he could tell Erin not to go or insist Bambi not go, but instead he stared into the back of his SUV knowing he wasn't going to do either one.

"Drew!" Erin screamed his name.

He turned with enough time to watch her tear toward him while trying to keep hold of her rollaway, purse and two shoulder bags. The rollaway tumbled off the porch stairs and she gave up and dropped the two shoulder bags only keeping hold of her handbag as she collided with him.

"Drew." She took him by the shoulders and gasped for air.

"What's wrong?" Panic took over her face in the form of red splotches and wet eyes. "What happened?"

"Beaker's not in the house." A tear fell and she trembled. "I went to dress him and wanted to discuss what he wanted to bring, and he isn't there."

He knew he was in a bad way when rather than asking what conversation she was having with his dog or why she was dressing him, his heart swelled at the fact she seemed so distressed by his absence. "He's at the pet hotel."

She furrowed her brow. "Hotel?"

He nodded and allowed her time to process his explanation.

The red on her face faded. "Is it five-star?"

"I don't think they rate pet hotels that way, but they've helped me with Beaker since he's been a puppy." If she had decided to go when he asked her they could have taken the dog. It wasn't lost on him that the last two nights Beaker slept with her.

Her lower lip pursed out. "May I have the name of this hotel?"

Were they now sharing custody of his dog? They weren't even divorced. Well, they weren't even married. They were only sleeping together, sort of. "Sure."

"Thank you." She gave him a kiss on the cheek. "Thank you for letting me go with you too."

Where did this Erin go when the one who insisted she had to leave appeared? Now he had Bambi and her on a trip together. He definitely didn't play in this sandbox. "Let me get your things and lock up the house."

"Thank you. I want this one in the front seat with me." She treated him to another kiss then walked over to one of the bags and picked it up. "I have another suitcase in the house. Maybe if someone does something about our babysitter, he can see what's inside."

"Let me get it all." At least all her luggage provided him an excuse not to witness the front seat shenanigans. He wrangled everything up, locked down his house and turned toward the SUV.

Everything was way too quiet.

He tiptoed toward the vehicle and as he loaded the bags, or more accurately shoved the rest of the bags in the back, a shudder overtook his body at the sight inside the car.

Only by a miracle, the two females weren't arguing or even shooting each other looks and in a major plot twist Erin was not in the front seat. Instead, Bambi remained up front while Erin had set herself up in the back. With no blood splatters or dismembered limbs, he was going to consider the situation a win.

He got in the car and put the key in the ignition. No matter what happened now, he had to remember he'd brought it on himself.

"Drew." They didn't make it to the end of the driveway before Erin spoke.

He glanced at her in the rearview mirror and raised his eyebrows.

She scooted up behind his seat and put her hands on his shoulders, giving him a light massage. "Are we there yet?"

In a perfect world they would kiss, maybe decide to get on the road a little later and to back to the house. He could show her a different place to start her massage...with her mouth, or her boobs. The woman's touch was second to none and for one second he allowed himself to relish in a little muscle relief.

"Did you get it?" Erin asked.

He turned, caught sight of Bambi and exhaled. "Get what?"

"That's the line Roxy says right before they start off on their journey. We just watched the movie the other night." As if trying to speak a secret language, she gave his shoulders another squeeze.

Unfortunately, her words were all too easy to decipher, and Bambi shook her head.

"You better put your seatbelt on." He hoped she understood his underlying meaning.

"Do you think it's going to be a bumpy ride?" She chuckled and sat back.

He put his hands on the steering wheel. "I hope we fare better than our film characters."

"I hope we don't have a cliff hanger." She positioned herself in his rearview mirror, cleavage and all.

It would be a sin not to take in her chest. "Or fall over a cliff." He finally turned out of the driveway. Yes, he brought this on himself.

<u>HOLLYWOOD STARBURST</u>

DISSOLVE TO:

PAN OVER THE INDIANAPOLIS

ZOOM IN:
INT. INSIDE THE BMW.

The car is stopped in traffic.

STEVEN pounds on the steering wheel and turns
to William.

>   STEVEN
>   You know this whole
>   situation is bat shit
>   crazy, right?

WILLIAM hits his head back on the headrest.

>   WILLIAM
>   The fact we went to
>   Hollywood Stardust, the
>   fact you left, the fact
>   I left, the fact Roxy is
>   now driving across the
>   country by herself, it's
>   all bat shit crazy.

STEVEN tosses a paper at William.

>   STEVEN
>   What is even more bat
>   shit crazy is that we
>   actually had Charles
>   calculate a formula of
>   when we should pass Roxy
>   on the road and we
>   actually got in the car
>   and thought this would
>   work.

WILLIAM smooths out paper and tilts his head.

                    WILLIAM
          Charles would never give
          us a formula that
          wouldn't work. This
          whole thing was like one
          of those crazy math
          problems that no one can
          solve but Charles. If
          you have one car going
          one way at so many miles
          per hour and another
          going the other way at
          so many miles per hour
          it will take x amount of
          hours to meet in the
          middle.

STEVEN throws the car in park.

                    STEVEN
          Does anyone ever really
          meet in the middle?

WILLIAM puts the paper down.

                    WILLIAM
          Charles said we should
          meet in about twelve
          hours. We can be back
          by Sunday night and have
          her school situation
          fixed on Monday morning.

                    STEVEN
          Stop reading the paper
          and think. What does
          this problem really
          solve?

WILLIAM turns to Steven.

STEVEN faces William.

                    STEVEN

Are we solving any
problem by going after
her? She doesn't even
know we are on the
way. Does she even want
us to come?

                WILLIAM
          Meeting in the middle is
          not going to work.

WILLIAM crumples up the paper and tosses it
into the back seat.

STEVEN grabs the steering wheel and stares
straight ahead.

                STEVEN
          No one can ever really
          solve for x.

Chapter Fifteen

IN HER TWENTIES, ERIN played the love interest to some super hero whose power was being the smartest being in the universe. The movie wasn't a blockbuster, only because watching someone sit around and think while the other characters played out the action wasn't all that thrilling. However, there was one scene where they were both watching the villain on some larger than life screen and her character asked why he wasn't taking the evil energy sucker down yet.

The main character then looked at her, took her hand and told her that sometimes the first move in any battle began with sitting back, assessing your opponent, and making them believe you aren't nearly as dangerous as you are.

Rather than head in for an attack and thus making her the villain, Erin took the back seat without complaint and used the time not only to get her social media accounts in order, but to sit back and assess her opponent.

In the process, she discovered something extremely important about Bambi.

The woman was nothing if not boring. For the two hours they drove down the 15 Freeway she said absolutely nothing. Not only did she say nothing, she did nothing. She didn't read, didn't look out the window, and didn't point out anything. Never laughed, never smiled, and never moved from her position with her feet flat on the floor and her hands neatly folded in her lap. She didn't even cross her legs.

It was unnatural even for boring, and Erin knew boring. Most of being on a movie set was sitting around doing nothing, but this took the prize.

For a while, the nothing was welcomed. The quiet allowed Erin the chance to take a few establishing shots for what she decided would be known as a quasi-documentary for Hollywood Glow. It was easy enough to do with the silence.

What made matters worse was Drew. He did nothing as well. No wonder the great romance between Bambi and Drew didn't materialize, they had to be bored as hell.

Drew sat with his hands at ten and two on the steering wheel as if maneuvering down the straight, flat freeway took plenty of driving skill. She knew this road. Normally, the inhabitants of the vehicle would be buzzing with excitement as they drove to Vegas.

Wait.

The 15 Freeway only led to one place and that would be the city of lights, fun and sin. She sat up straighter and decided to take a sledgehammer to the silence. "Drew, are we going to Vegas?"

In what could be considered a miracle, Bambi moved in the form of shaking her head.

"Erin." Drew's voice took on the tone of a parent about to tell a child that instead of getting a pony for Christmas they would instead be getting a picture of a horse.

"Vegas?" She figured if she said the word with a bit of flair it might make it so.

"Bambi, do you want to go through the schedule with her since she wasn't privy to our meetings?" Drew wouldn't even look in Erin's direction.

"Yes, her attendance wasn't planned." Bambi pulled out her notebook.

Still in enemy observation mode, Erin dug her nails into her palm to stop from snapping.

"Tonight we will be staying in Mesquite, Nevada where we will have dinner at the little diner inside the hotel. Then tomorrow we will get an early start and after having our complimentary breakfast we will go to Payton Utah to Organic Oasis where we will do our presentation on custom formulations." Bambi inhaled.

Well, that whole thing was certainly a mouthful. Thus far, her diet would be amazing because there was no way she would eat some sugar laden Danish with day old coffee for breakfast. "Do we get to have lunch?"

"Lunch will be at the spa." Bambi turned the page in her notebook.

Spa? That spoke of potential. She kept her game face on.

"We will make our way to Colorado and the next day, go to Multimode Health." Bambi glanced over at her. "Dinner will be in the hotel along with breakfast."

She fought the urge to wrinkle her nose.

"After our meeting, we will be on the road, stopping early so Isaac can get some work done."

Well, after all that excitement, Drew may actually look forward to getting work done. Thus far she had nothing for a reality show, and she needed to make sure she didn't get Bambi, the wonder scheduler, in her shots.

"After dinner at the local restaurant, we will stay in the hotel and the next day drive to Albuquerque where Isaac will give his lecture at the University. Dinner is still undecided. Lastly, we will go to Las Cruces to the farm where Isaac wants to meet with the owner. The man can't meet for any meals, so we will find something on the road, and then we will go back home through Arizona." With a nod, Bambi closed her notebook.

"Well, that was extremely thorough." Maybe a second thought should have been in order before she bounded in the car with Drew and the human day planner, but with Drew and her career at stake she truly had no choice.

"If you would like, I will give you a copy of the agenda when we get to the hotel."

She swore Bambi flared her nostrils when she spoke and decided to fire a little ammunition just to get the chemist's attention. Sort of like a warning missile. "No, it's good, I got it. Mesquite, Peyton, Utah for the spa, Grand Junction for Multimode Health and work, Albuquerque and the lecture, Las Cruces, then home."

Bambi made a noise and turned to her.

"I memorize lines for a living." She graced her enemy with a sweetheart smile.

"Right." The woman spun back and pulled out yet another notebook. "So, Isaac, I reviewed some of your slides on antioxidant stabilization for your lecture. I wanted to ask you something about it." Bambi brought another notebook out from what seemed to be under the seat.

"All right." Drew punctuated his sentence by running his hand through his hair.

Erin held her breath, waiting for the woman to spit it out already. Along with being boring, this person taking her spot in the front seat was exceptionally detail oriented to the point of being annoyingly obnoxious. Erin bet at first most men found it charming, like Bambi was paying attention, then later they realized that the person they were now sleeping with was simply out of her ever loving mind.

"I changed the picture on the slide about liposome encapsulation. I hope that's all right." She held up a page.

Erin glanced over at the blob and shrugged. It looked like the same ball filled with gunk as other pictures she saw in Drew's office.

Drew quickly turned his head to look at the page. "What's the difference?"

Erin assumed brilliant minds thought alike.

"This one has a different color scheme." Bambi's tone took on one of annoyance, like she repainted a house and redid her hair and no one noticed. Though Erin had no doubt the walls in Bambi's home were white, a perfect, pristine white, and her hair, well, whatever.

"Oh, well, it's fine." He returned to concentrating on the road.

"Drew?" Erin saw an in to the constant chatter about what, she did not know or care, but now she could take center stage.

His eyes went to the rear view mirror. "Yes?"

Since he copped looks at her boobs through the whole trip, she slightly adjusted her pose to give him a better view. "What is liposome encapsulation?"

He opened his mouth.

"Wait!" She held her hand up, retrieved her video camera and focused to get Drew in the shot.

"You're going to film me?"

"I'm trying something for us and the lab is that all right?" She showed a little more boob and went in for the kill by pursing out her lower lip just like any good sweetheart.

"Good idea." He straightened up.

"Yay." She flashed him a smile and centered him in the viewfinder. "Now, as we are driving toward Not Las Vegas, Nevada on our road trip to get our Hollywood Glow on, please tell me what is liposome encapsulation?"

"Simply put, a liposome is like a little bubble or balloon. We can put certain ingredients inside to keep them stable and once the liposome arrives at its designated target inside the body, it will break and those ingredients, like antioxidants or such, can do their jobs."

She scooted up and, with some creative contorting, managed to get them both in the picture. "So what you are saying, Mr. Fulton, is that once the liposome is where it wants to be it will burst forth its goodness?" Her comedy was always a little racy.

With raised eyebrows, he turned to the camera and back to the road. "That is exactly right."

"Can we have the liposomes of which you speak of in Hollywood Glow?" She lowered her voice giving it a little growl.

"I think it's essential." The corner of his mouth raised in a smile.

"I think liposomes are sexy." Keeping the camera up, she gave him a little kiss on the cheek and hit stop. "This is going to be perfect."

"Maybe I should hire you as my marketing manager." He let out a laugh.

"I accept." Actually, the job sounded fun, but she didn't think he was serious. "Do you mind if I upload the picture I took my first day at the lab on my website and social media sites? I think it will be good publicity."

"That's fine." He nodded.

"How about if I start the lab a page?" Wanting to show Miss Changed-the-Color-Scheme how to truly be effective, Erin fired off another round and grabbed her computer.

"We can't have a social media page." Bambi piped in. "We have FDA regulations and proprietary formulations and other obligations."

And finally the little deer decided to take a shot at her, and all with words ending with *tion*. That made for truly bad script writing unless this was a parody and unfortunately it wasn't, but it did indicate the time for observation and warnings officially ended. "I counter your objection. Our competition has a page and though it's none of your concern, I will get Drew's validation before I post, and I'll even check my punctuation." Two could play the words ending in *tion* game, and she got a couple of extra ones in there.

Drew coughed, but she was sure he stifled a laugh.

"You can't post confidential information." Bambi continued.

"There's no need to have a conniption." She fought the urge to stick her tongue out at the woman. Score one more for her.

"Erin, maybe we should check with regulatory before jumping into the social media field," Drew interjected.

Bambi hooked her hair behind her ears and sat back.

No, the scientist wouldn't win only because Erin didn't have enough knowledge. What she lacked in the technical aspects, she gained in moxie. "Is Hollywood Glow confidential? I think it's crucial for marketing. Can that line have a page as long as I get your approval on posts?"

Bambi didn't move.

"That sounds fine." Drew tilted his head from one side to the other. "But let's be mindful of the industry."

Finally, the woman would learn who the victor would be, and with Drew being amiable, she decided to go in for the kill. Once more, she slid up behind him, but this time wrapped her arms around the seat and treated him to a massage. "Drew, are you tense?"

"It's been a long day." He moaned and leaned his head back on the seat.

"Oh my, I can feel the knots." She continued her ministrations. "Once we get to the hotel we will have to get you into a nice hot bath."

"Oh." Bambi scrambled for her notebook.

"Erin." Drew's voice came out a cross between a warning and begging.

"Don't worry, I'll take complete care of you once we stop." She ran the back of her hand against his cheek. "By the time I'm done with you, you will be happier than Beaker when he lies on that square on the floor where the sun shines in and he's all loose and sleepy."

"That reminds me, should I call the hotels and get more rooms?" Bambi interrupted their interlude.

"That won't be necessary. I don't stay in hotel rooms by myself." Erin cut the buzzkill off at the pass.

"Isaac?" Bambi stared down at her notebook.

In an instant, the knots she worked out seemed to reappear, and he shrugged her hands off him. "Since this is a business trip we should all have our own rooms."

Her cheeks heated. Drew should be making his stand. It would make everything easier down the road, pun intended.

"Let me call our first stop and get it set up." Bambi lifted her phone.

While the other woman dealt with the trivial pursuits, Erin inched over to Drew's far side and put her face as close as she could by his ear. "Don't worry I'll sneak in like old times."

"Erin this is my work." He spoke through gritted teeth. "You lost your chance for a romantic trip."

"Do you want me or not?"

"We can't do this now." He clenched his jaw. "Sit back."

She slumped in the seat and tried to think of her next plan of attack.

"Believe it or not there is some golfing tournament in Mesquite. We have the two rooms only." Bambi strummed her fingers on her notebook.

Drew audibly exhaled.

"It's fine. Erin and I can share a room." Bambi blurted out.

Whoa. She let her guard down for one minute and suddenly the innocent fawn took the offensive position. No way would she allow her to get the upper hand. "That's fine, it will give Bambi and I a chance to get to know each other better." She laughed. "Did you ever think you would be spending the night with a star?"

"The thought never occurred to me. I was never one to be starstruck." Bambi rifled through her pages.

So this was how it would be played. She needed to up her ante. "Would it throw off your plan if I told you I was starving?" Inside, her heart seized and her focus fell on the camera in the seat next to her. Though she really only wanted to be one person's sweetheart, she might have to settle on getting her job back as America's sweetheart. At least at the end of this sequence she would have something to work with.

❧

DON'T COMPLAIN, DON'T COMPLAIN, don't complain. Erin internally chanted her mantra from the moment she and Bambi stepped into the bland, sepia hotel room.

If she and Drew were together it wouldn't matter. The prints on the walls were older than *Hollywood Stardust* and the plain, rough sheets would only be things to laugh about, but here, trapped with Bambi, everything wrong screamed at her.

However, while their surroundings didn't make for a great environment, it would make for a wonderful segment on what had to be endured when on the road, and once more she got out her camera and took a surrounding shot of the room.

"What does this have to do with the making of Hollywood Glow?" Bambi hung up a tan business suit on one of the hangers made way too small for any normal pole for fear closet thieves may make out with it.

Erin had played in enough relationship movies to know everything she said would be relayed to Drew in some way, shape or form and thought before she spoke. "I think it will be entertaining to see everything that happens. You never know what shot will be the magic one, so the best thing to do is get everything."

"I suppose that sounds reasonable." The woman sat down at the little desk, reached into what was obviously her work briefcase, and pulled out a plastic bag full of little containers and liquids and things that looked like jewels.

"Oh, what's that?" Camera still in hand, she joined her nemesis.

"You can't film this!" Bambi grabbed the bag and clutched it to her chest.

"All right. You don't have to scream, just tell me." She put the camera aside and pointed to the treasure. "Are those for the meeting? I've seen them at the lab."

"They are for Oasis Orchard. It's prototypes of their custom products." The woman continued to hold the products as if protecting them from a kidnapper.

"Well, since I'll be in the meeting as well, may I see them?" She sat on the other chair in the room.

Bambi raised her chin. "I don't know if I should."

With a huff she held her hand out. "What do you think I'm going to do? Give it to all the competing labs I know? Seriously, I just want to take a look."

The woman pursed her lips and thrust the bag at her.

Though inside she boiled and wanted to pummel this person, she could mask just about any emotion, and with slow, calm movements opened the bag and removed the contents one by one. "Is this the only set?"

"No. Isaac has two more in his luggage." Bambi kept her voice low, but it trembled like it wanted to bubble over.

"May I?" She lifted a white bottle.

The woman shrugged.

They couldn't go through a week of this nightmare, or somehow she would end up being the one to blame. Right or wrong, she always ended up being the one at fault because she was emotional, a detriment to Drew and her career. "You know, I never got to go to normal school." She opened the first bottle. Inside were a bunch of capsules.

"Some would call you lucky."

"It's like being an only child. You don't know any other way, so you don't know what you miss. I got by because I'm an excellent memorizer." She put the bottle on her lap and went to the little baggie filled with what looked like jewels.

With a blank expression, Bambi stared at her. Dare she say the woman looked like a deer caught in the headlights?

"If I promise I will retain what you tell me, will you give me a quick lesson?" She held the baggie up.

For at least a minute the woman did nothing, but then finally gave her one nod. "Those are from the new ampoule machine. Isaac researched the antioxidants, vitamins and minerals in the fruit found at the orchard and put effective doses in the products and then combined it with extracts from the actual fruits from the orchard so their line would be completely unique."

"Oh, I love these." She opened the plastic bag and pulled out one of the pearlescent bright red little balls with a matching little stem. "They look like cherries."

"There are cherries at the orchard," Bambi added. "Inside is a serum, you just pull out the stem."

Serum? Impressive. "I love serums. These are perfect for travel. May I try one tonight?"

"I suppose."

Well, they weren't snapping at each other. That alone had to be a plus. She picked up a smaller bottle and glanced at the woman.

"That is a liquid with similar ingredients. The other one is a powder." Bambi then pointed to the other bottle on her lap. "That one is full of capsules."

"It's a whole system of products." Maybe their two worlds could come together, even if only for a moment. With a smile, she looked up at Bambi.

"Yes, the lab techs were running around like idiots once Isaac decided it had to be a line of products. What a waste of time. These deals are impossible to get anyway." Bambi retrieved her notebook. "Now I have to make a note on where those samples are."

"Then why bother if the deals are so hard to get?" She put everything back in the bigger bag.

"Because they are a good account and we don't want them to go elsewhere. So we make the products in hope they buy them, but especially so they keep what they already buy from us." Bambi shook her head. "Everyone wants to be a star."

"Yes, I know." She tried to stay cordial.

"So that's why we bother, to keep what we already have. Now we have you..." Bambi turned away.

Those were fighting words. "What does that mean?" She sat up, but still kept her cool.

With a noise of clear dissatisfaction, Bambi spun back and crossed her arms. "They are going to take one look at you and think that they can have everything, a custom line complete with a built in movie star, and they'll be really disappointed when they realize that's not the case. At best, these opportunities are for us to preserve business and everything you've done is only going to make it worse."

All she needed was for the little deer to tell Drew she would hurt his business, and he would never trust her again. "Did you see a movie with me in it and not like my character or something?"

Bambi narrowed her eyes. "I told you before I don't watch your movies."

"Then what is it that you hate about me?" Though she knew the truth, and people wondered why she didn't get along with other women. Everything stemmed from jealousy in one way or the other.

"You are distracting Isaac, his work is a mess and he's worse." Bambi pounded her leg. "The last time I saw him do anything that even smacked of work was make sure you had the right supplements. He even custom blended them himself. I bet you aren't even taking them regularly."

Honestly, she wasn't sure if she was sad or not to hear Drew was a mess. "I'm nothing if not fastidious, I take them exactly as he prescribed." To prove her point she reached over to her handbag and pulled out the little pouch where she stored her pills.

"What are you doing here really? Did you really pine away all those years for him, or are you studying for some role and using him as your research experiment?" The woman stood.

Still in character, Erin paused only to inhale. "Not that it's any of your business, but I'm here because I have to be, I have to know and I have to fix things." In order to even out the playing field, she stood as well. "Yes, there are some who say I went on with my life, but Drew was always there and yes, I pined away, maybe even waited for him."

"Something is off, and you are going to hurt Isaac and his work, I can feel it." Bambi hardened her jaw.

Some might say her filming for a reality show and not telling Drew would be the something, but in the end everyone would come to find she did it for him and so she could stand on her own. It would give him even more opportunities. She stepped toward the anti-Erin. "I think the real question is not why I am here, it's why are you here? While you may have the upper hand in the personnel department for now, you and I both know, I clearly hold the win in the personal department or I wouldn't be here at all."

"I'm here because someone has to take care of the business." Bambi turned positively red. "In fact, I have to ask Isaac something."

With her notebook in hand, the woman snatched up her room key and left before Erin ever had the chance to stop her.

"Damn it." Erin put her hand over her eyes. Unsure if she should follow and plead her case or not, she decided the best course of action was no action.

With nothing left to do but get ready for bed, she kept hold of the products for the spa and went into the bathroom. Apparently, Bambi had bested her. Every woman proved to be no different. A knot formed in her stomach. Somehow she would have to go to him alone without making matters worse and doing it in front of the too smart scientist. She should have never put her camera down. Without hard evidence, Drew would never believe she even tried.

HOLLYWOOD STARBURST

INT. SOMEWHERE MISSOURI, INTERIOR OF MOTEL
ROOM.

PANS AROUNDS A DINGY ROOM.

In her pajamas, Roxy sits crossed legged on the
bed organizing her items.

ROXY takes out two strips of photographs from
the road trip to Hollywood Stardust. One strip
is her and Steven, one is her and William. She
brushes a tear away from her eye and glances
over at the phone on the nightstand. She takes
a breath, swipes the receiver off the phone,
closes her eyes and dials.

CUT TO:

William in his bedroom, leaning back on the bed
with his school books.

> WILLIAM
> Hello?

> ROXY (O.S.)
> (Filtered)
> You made it home.

WILLIAM let's his head fall back on his
headboard.

> WILLIAM
> You didn't.

> ROXY (O.S.)
> (Filtered)
> I just wanted to see if
> you were okay.

CUT TO:

C.U. ROXY

               WILLIAM (O.S.)
               (Filtered)
               I'm not the one driving
               across the country by
               myself.

ROXY puts her hands over her eyes.

               WILLIAM (O.S.)
               (Filtered)
               What happens when you
               get home?

ROXY shakes her head.

                  ROXY
               I wish I knew.

CUT TO:

C.U. WILLIAM

Neither speak for a moment. William looks at
the receiver and then presses it back to his
ear.

               WILLIAM
               I want to be with you.

CUT TO:

C.U. ROXY

                         ROXY
                    (Sniffs)
                    Then why did you leave
                    me in Hollywood?

CUT TO:

C.U. WILLIAM

                              WILLIAM
                         Because I had to. Do you
                         even want me, Roxy, or
                         am I just a placeholder?

                         ROXY (O.S.)
                    (Filtered)
                    Sometimes I think I'm
                    the placeholder.

WILLIAM sits up and pounds his fist into the
bed.

                              WILLIAM
                         (Tough, powerful tone.)
                         Answer the question,
                         Roxy.

CUT TO:

ROXY sits straight up and looks straight ahead.

                              ROXY
                         Who wouldn't want you?
                         You're the one who took
                         me to see Hollywood
                         Stardust. You're the one
                         everyone admires. You're
                         the one who ruined his
                         school all to be with
                         me. Who wouldn't want
                         you?

                         WILLIAM (O.S.)
                    (Filtered)

But that's not what you
want.

     ROXY
It is. You are. It is.

ROXY POV camera pans over to Steven's strip of
pictures.

Chapter Sixteen

HOTELS, MOTELS, WHATEVER, came in three distinct categories. At the bottom tier were the motels, the roadside, dilapidated structures consisting of the smallest of rooms for those simply trying to make it through the night, or sneak through the night.

At the other end of the spectrum were the luxury hotels. Overpriced? Yes. Worth it? Yes. These resorts with their celebrity chef restaurants, little shops, and every amenity at one's fingertips weren't appropriate for a business trip. Well, a business trip with Bambi.

Between desperation and delicacies lay the doldrums in the form of the business traveler's hotel. These beehive-like institutions with Wi-Fi and cable TV doled out free breakfasts like honey.

Before Drew asked Erin on the trip, he made some of his own reservations at the tier three accommodations, but when she ditched him, he stayed with Bambi's original plan and now the three of them were in the land of rancid coffee and expense accounts.

With no normal channels on the television and a pit in his stomach, he laid on his bed staring up at the ceiling. Rather than check on them like he should, he remained in his self-imposed purgatory and prayed the women down the hall didn't kill each other. Erin could talk her way out of anything, and Bambi could perform miracles with chemicals, a truly bad combination.

At a knock at his door, he shot up. His chest tightened, and he glanced over at the clock, giving a nod to Erin for making it this long. He resisted rushing to the door and promised himself no matter what, he would send her back to her room. At least for tonight he had to prove a point and he couldn't hurt Bambi.

Inhaling and putting on a bit of swagger so she could go to bed thinking of him, he brushed his hair into his eyes and opened the door to Bambi.

Stop. Wait. Rewind.

Bambi?

He pushed his bangs back into place. "Bambi?"

"I'm sorry to bother you. I just needed to ask you a question." She didn't look directly at him.

"Sure, come in." Part of him wished he wanted her. It would make his life that much easier. "Is everything all right?" In truth, he knew the answer, but he sort of wanted to know if Erin was conscious or even there. What if she wasn't there? He stopped short of asking his chemist about Erin.

She stepped inside. "I was going through some notes for the meeting tomorrow. Erin saw the Oasis products and asked to see them. I stopped her from filming about them, but she insisted on knowing all about them and took them."

Erin left with his products. "Damn it!" At his outburst he turned his back to her.

"I'm sorry. I knew I shouldn't have given her the products. She said she wanted to learn about them, but then we had a disagreement, and I knew I shouldn't have shown her, let alone allow her to have them. So I came here leaving her to do God knows what with our ampoules." In what was supposed to be a comforting move, she put her hand on his back. "I'm sorry."

Wait, what did she say? "Where are the products now?"

"With Erin." A frustrated huff escaped Bambi's throat.

In a sudden surge of energy, he spun back around. "And where is Erin?"

"In the room." She wrinkled her nose.

The weakness of relief overtook him, and now he wanted to lie down. "I'm sorry, what is the issue?"

"Maybe if your first thought is that Erin left without a word to you, it's not me with the issue." She shook her head.

Bambi had a point, but she didn't have the history. "She doesn't leave." That title belonged to him.

"Everything she said was right, I don't know why I'm here." Without him having to say a word, she headed for the exit.

"What do you mean?" He dashed forward and opened the door for her. "Are you all right?"

She faced him once more. "I'm fine. I just want you to be fine."

"Tomorrow I will personally make sure you have your own room." He didn't know what else to say. "Did you need anything else?"

"No, you just told me everything I needed to know." She seemed to give him an extended look, and then without another word, left.

He peered down the hallway to ensure she got to her room and closed the door. With nothing else to do, he turned out the lights and flopped on the bed. The last thing he wanted was to hurt one of his good friends. Though she hid her motivations with concern for him, he knew she still thought there was a possibility between them. The fact was he hated how the pit in his stomach deepened when he opened the door to find the wrong woman on the other side.

For what seemed like forever, sleep eluded him. With every bump in the bed, noise in the hall, or one of his own horrid thoughts, his eyes opened. Over and over again he relived the last few days. His mind even went to a retrospective of the day he left his life and Erin and never turned back. Even after he drove away from her and got on the plane to England, she tried to contact him, yet he used Logan to play interference and ignored her, hoping his feelings would vanish.

Apparently, his strategy didn't work.

He turned over and hit the not fluffy pillow right as a light knock interrupted his analysis of how his life had become such a disaster.

There was no doubt who the next visitor would be, and he tensed. Yet, his instinct took over, and he found himself walking across the small cell to open the door.

In a floor-length sapphire blue robe, a towel draped over her head and holding a pillow, the right woman stood before him.

Was she the right woman?

"May I come in?" Her voice came out low with a bit of a sexy rasp.

He grabbed onto the doorjamb to stop from pulling her inside and throwing her on his bed. In the last ten hours everything around him turned to hell and it was all because of her. "You can't be here." He needed to keep his resolve.

"I'm not here to tattle on anyone, but if you're worried about the other woman, she's snoring in the bed by the bathroom and I tiptoed out. I have to say I was relieved she returned so quickly."

"This isn't working." He scratched his hand across his scalp.

"I agree." She looked up at him through her lashes. "I belong where you are."

Why did it have to always be her?

As if on automatic, he opened the door wider. She entered, and he shut the door.

In the bit of light from the window, she seemed to float across the room. She tossed the towel off her head and claimed what would always be her side of the bed with her pillow. Before sliding into bed, she slipped out of her robe and tossed it aside. The mere flash of her silhouette was enough to cause his body to react. In less than an instant he was hard and ready to indulge in something he didn't know if he could have again.

She stretched and arched her back.

He continued to stand there as she got in his bed.

"Drew, Mr. Abrams has an important meeting tomorrow and a long drive, come to bed." She threw back the sheets on his side and gave the mattress a pat. "I tried the products. You'll be brilliant tomorrow. I don't want to miss it."

Like a trained animal, or a trapped one, he joined her, and resumed his position staring up at the dark ceiling.

They lay in silence and he wasn't sure if she fell asleep until she spoke.

"Are you mad at me?" she whispered and inched closer.

"Yes." He shut his eyes.

"I deserve it." She cuddled up to his side. "I don't know how not to ruin your life."

He forced himself to keep breathing. "Well, I keep letting you."

"I'm sorry."

"You can't stay here." Even with Erin in his bed, his conversation with Bambi replayed once more. What would she do once she woke up and found Erin missing? This man wasn't him. He didn't hurt others to get what he wanted.

"Do you really want me to leave?" She took hold of his hand and intertwined their fingers. "I promise I'll get up early and sneak back to my jail cell, you know I never oversleep."

No, her leaving was what he feared, and he knew she feared the same with him. Not wanting to give in and tell her to stay, he didn't speak.

"Do you want me to go?"

"What do you want, Erin?" Someone had to have the answers.

"One day, I would like to get in bed with you and have you take me into your arms without me asking. One day, I want you to kiss me first, because you can't hold back." Before he could respond, she continued. "I know I could have had it once, I'm not trying to make you feel guilty, I'm the one who wrecked everything, but you asked what I wanted."

"So what if I don't ever do it?" He tried not to focus on how tight she held his hand. Since their reunion, she was always the first to initiate contact between them.

"Then I guess I'll take what I can get." She swallowed. "I promise. I'll leave first thing. I couldn't be in that other room thinking about you. I just want to lie here next to you, please."

No, he didn't want her to leave. Once more, silence overtook the room. Did the twenty years mature her, or was this about her needs that didn't include him?

"Do you like this hotel?" He didn't even know why he asked the question, especially since he knew the answer.

"It's okay. I don't mind it."

Fine, maybe he didn't know the answer. "You don't hate this place?"

"Once I changed rooms, it didn't matter where I was."

Unable to stop himself, he turned to his side. "Come here."

"Drew?" Her voice shook.

He let go of her hand and gathered her up into his arms. "Why couldn't you just come with me in the first place?"

"I told you. I can't stop ruining your life." She rested her face in the crook of his neck.

He stared off into nothing.

"You smell so good."

"It's just that little hotel soap." He didn't even know what he was saying anymore.

"It's just you." Her breath brushed against him in little puffs. "Someone really needs to tell people what they miss."

"What?" He leaned back.

She lifted her face up. "No one ever tells you that you're going to miss how a person smells, or how the air changes when they're near you, or what it's like to feel safe just by having someone you want hold you."

In the darkness, they stared at each other.

"Do I always have to ask you to kiss me?" Her lips grazed his.

He should kiss her, he wanted to kiss her, damn it, he needed to kiss her, but since he went back on everything else, he resisted. "Why don't you wait until I do it on my own since that's what you want?"

Rather than arguing or using some ploy to get her way, she nestled down in his arms. "Good night, Drew."

He tossed and turned for who knew how long, but now with her here, he could drift off. At least he knew where she was. "Good night, Erin." Between the two of them, they sent enough mixed messages to break an entire cellular network. No, he wasn't the man who hurt people, unless he counted crushing one of his true friends and leaving the woman he loved for twenty years.

INT. STEVEN'S PARENT'S RESTAURANT. - DAY.

Waitresses are scurrying about the busy
restaurant and the phone continues to ring in
the background. Finally, a waitress holding a
tray of dirty dishes picks up the receiver.

                    WAITRESS
              Delizio's. How can I
              help you?

WAITRESS holds phone between shoulder and chin
and nods.

                    WAITRESS
              Steven, phone!

Steven appears from around the corner. He
looks over the waitress and takes the
phone. The waitress smiles, but shakes her
head and returns to work.

STEVEN'S FATHER, an older attractive man in a
business suit, peeks head out from office.

                    STEVEN'S FATHER
              (Yells)
              How many times do I have
              to tell you not to take
              personal calls here?

STEVEN waves his father away, turns his back to
the rest of the restaurant and lifts phone to
his ear.

                    STEVEN
              What do you want?

                    ROXY (O.S)
          (Filtered)
           To talk to you.

STEVEN tilts head back and runs fingers through
his hair.

                    STEVEN
           Well, I'm here.

                    ROXY (O.S)
          (Filtered)
           How are you?

                    STEVEN
          (Sarcastic laugh)
           I'm totally fine,
           princess. Is that why
           you called?

                    ROXY (O.S.)
          (Filtered)
           I said I wanted to talk
           to you.

STEVEN leans forehead on the wall.

                    STEVEN
           Took you long enough.

                    ROXY (O.S.)
          (Filtered)
           Every time I tried to
           call, you either didn't
           answer or I chickened
           out.

                    STEVEN
          (Voice hardens)
           At least you had a
           number to try.

                    ROXY (O.S.)
          (Filtered)

                    Would you have called me
                    if you had a number?

                              STEVEN
                    I suppose that's
                    something we'll never
                    know.

                         ROXY (O.S.)
                    (Filtered)
                         I spoke to William.

STEVEN silently pounds fist into the wall.

                              STEVEN
                         And you're telling
                         me this because?

                         ROXY (O.S.)
                          (Filtered)
                    I don't know, maybe I
                    want you to be jealous.

STEVEN a smile creeps over his face.

                              STEVEN
                    Don't play your games
                    with me.

                         ROXY (O.S.)
                    (Filtered)
                    I wasn't playing games,
                    I was being honest.

                              STEVEN
                    Sometimes with you it's
                    hard to tell.

                         ROXY (O.S.)
                    (Filtered)
                    I guess I better go.

STEVEN presses lips together, balls hand into a
fist.

                    STEVEN
              Rox?

                 ROXY (O.S.)
              (Filtered, breathless)
              Yes?

                    STEVEN
              By Charles' calculation
              you should be home soon.

                 ROXY (O.S.)
              (Filtered)
              Yeah. Part of me
              pictured you and William
              intercepting me on the
              highway.

STEVEN shakes head.

                    STEVEN
              It would have been a
              long shot to find you.

                 ROXY (O.S.)
              (Filtered)
              Well, maybe I needed to
              do this myself.

STEVEN shrugs.

                    STEVEN
          Well, I guess you better
          go.

                    ROXY (O.S.)
          (Filtered)
          All right.

                    STEVEN
          Rox —

                    ROXY (O.S.)
           (Filtered)
          Yes.

                    STEVEN
          You may need to do this
          alone, but if you need
          help, you know where to
          call.

Chapter Seventeen

AT 4:55 ERIN'S EYES OPENED. Her timing must be off from nerves. Usually this happened on the first day of waking up on a new set, and in many ways, today could be considered the same thing.

Toasty, comfortable and still in Drew's arms, the last thing she wanted to do was move from the bed. Yes, she wanted Drew to hold her, kiss her, make love to her, but the simple act of waking up with him warmed her heart. Maybe if she proved she could be of use on the trip and show him the footage of them together, he would trust her and see where he belonged.

Above all else, she needed to start out right. Rather than staying where she wanted, she shimmied out of his embrace, brushed her lips against his and reluctantly slid out of bed. Until he kissed her on his own or told her to stop, she would continue on.

"Erin." His voice heavy with sleep, he held his hand out.

"I need to keep my promise to you." Her robe served as a poor excuse for his arms, but she wrapped the garment around her and bent down to kiss him one more time. "Go back to sleep."

He groaned, shook his head and turned over.

Like a sorority girl sneaking out of the frat house, she tiptoed out of the room. No sooner had his door clicked closed than she froze.

If her life were a movie, she would have the screenwriter edit in the hotel room key for her. She glanced between Drew's door and Bambi's. If she went to door number one, Drew would think she deliberately forgot the key. If she went to door number two, she would wake up the sickening little scientist and the woman needed every ounce of her beauty sleep. No way was door number three an option, returning to the front desk for a new key. If the tabloids were going to get a hold of their escapades, she would rather it be in a better place and with her makeup on. Technically, she wasn't even at this hotel.

After scanning her memory for anything that fit this stupid scenario, she stepped in front of door number two and lifted her hand to knock, right as the door opened.

Ms. Bambi didn't appear as if she slept much, actually she looked the same as always. If she put a white coat on, no one would know she had her pajamas on.

"You know, I always get up early and I thought it might be nice to get us some morning coffee, but they didn't have any." As Erin walked inside, she held her head up high and looked the deer right in the eye. Yes, eye contact was key. Of course, having a key would have been key as well.

Bambi closed the door and motioned toward the desk with a steaming Styrofoam cup. "In your bathrobe."

"It's designer." She went to the makeshift closet with only her clothes hanging on the rod and wondered if Bambi noticed her hanger for the Four Seasons. At least that hotel gave proper hanging devices. "Good luck drinking that. I actually went in search for a proper coffee house."

"Why didn't you just use the coffeemaker in Isaac's room?" Bambi's soft, sweet voice didn't mask the sour undertone.

Apparently, the woman thought she was stupid or could be tricked with the best of them, but the woman also didn't know what it was like to live her life in the industry. Every answer needed to be thought out before verbalizing. The other way around could land anyone in the tabloids or worse. "What's the dress code for today?"

"I'm going to be in jeans and a t-shirt, but you should probably dress up for Isaac's business meeting."

She turned to discover Bambi's suitcase open on the bed. "How come you get to dress down?"

"I did not come on this trip to manage a three-ring circus, and I'm not going to sit around while you and Isaac have sex all night after you put him under some sort of teenage crush spell." Bambi stomped into the bathroom and collected her few toiletries.

"Spell?" Erin turned and crossed her arms. "How did I manage to do that?"

"You know, I used to think Isaac was only a little off and slightly starstruck when he went to see all your movies or shows, and then suddenly Isaac wasn't Isaac, he was Drew, and he came complete with a psycho starlet who thinks she loves him, but will destroy him." Bambi rushed back to her luggage and threw her items inside.

Starstruck? She bit her lip to hold back a smile, and the little hint also told her why little Bambi didn't like her art. "May I ask you a question?" Since Bambi didn't speak, she continued. "Honestly, you had no idea he was someone other than Isaac?"

"No, he was Dr. Abrams, a chemist, a professor and the owner of Fluent Words Laboratory." Bambi grabbed her jeans and managed to get them on under her nightgown, an impressive feat for the non-experienced. "He was the man who learned how to stabilize the polyphenols in the willow berry, the man who has a doctorate, the man who knows how to make supplements that help people."

At recognizing the word polyphenol, Erin silently cheered herself, but let Bambi go on.

The woman barged over to her. "Isaac was never a two-bit actor in some overhyped movie."

"You do know that the overhyped movie of which you speak is considered to be genre changing?" Even with her jaw clenched, she managed to get the words out. "Also, I'm not quite sure you understand the talent that was lost when Drew decided to leave the industry. He was truly something special."

"What I do understand is that you're going to hurt him, and he's kind enough to let you, and I'm not going to sit here and watch you try to make him something he's not and then leave when you're through." Bambi returned to her suitcase, pulled off her nightgown and put on a t-shirt with some chemical symbol on it.

"How many relationships has he been in since you met him?" In an effort not to start screaming, she strolled to the edge of her bed and sat down.

Rather than answering, Bambi struggled with the zipper of her suitcase.

"How long did your relationship last? Did you end it or did he?"

Fists clenched along with her jaw, Bambi turned to her. "That's none of your business."

"You're making it my business."

The woman narrowed her eyes.

"I waited for twenty years for him. No one was ever him." Though she didn't need to justify her actions to this person, she would do it for Drew.

"You miss Drew and that man doesn't exist and once you figure that out, you are over and out. You miss the story you made up in your head, as simple as it may be." Bambi spun back to her luggage and resumed her zipper fight.

"Excuse me." The bimbo called her stupid. She jumped up. "If you want to twist this story around, I'll tell you that I think the man you know is merely a role he's playing, but it doesn't matter. Isaac, Drew, whoever he wants to be, that is who I want, and it's much more than fictional. For your information, I may not have a Ph.D., but I know more than you think."

"I think that if you hurt him that true villain of your story will get her comeuppance, but until my boss uses his massive brain, I refuse to sit here while he pants after you and you see what you can get." Bambi spat her threat out and gave her suitcase a tug. The bag fell to the floor with a loud thud and spilled its contents between the two beds.

Feminine instinct caused her to lunge toward the mess. "Let me help you."

"Stay away from me." Bambi swiped her hand out.

She fell, hit the nightstand, and knocked over a lamp and the clock. Pain radiated up her side where she made impact when she landed on the floor.

With her mouth wide open, Bambi stared at her.

Before she got the chance to scream for help, the door opened and Drew ran in. "Is everyone all right?"

Neither of them moved.

"What's going on?" Drew joined them, knelt down and looked between them, his focus settling on her, blaming her.

If she learned nothing else in her career, it was she or he who spoke first lost. It worked in contract negotiations, it worked when fighting for a character or a line, and it was a universal truth.

"Isaac, you know who you need to be on this trip with." Bambi spoke and therefore lost. "I'd like to go back to Los Angeles and get to work. I already researched the flights, and I can be back before one."

Drew pursed his lips and glanced over at her.

Erin ground her teeth together waiting for her turn.

"Nothing happened. I dropped my suitcase and Erin tried to help and tripped." She scooped up her belongings and once more struggled with the stupid zipper.

Drew wrangled the zipper. "I completely understand. Make sure you use the company card and expense everything. What do I need to do?"

Somehow, the same person Drew fawned over was the same person who called her stupid, and a fake and knocked her down.

"Nothing, all you need to do is do great on your meetings and lecture." Bambi stood, slipped on her shoes and grabbed the handle of her suitcase. "I already called a shuttle, so I'm just going to wait for them."

Well, wasn't Bambi productive this morning? Erin inhaled and waited for Bambi's grand exit. There were true celebrities who didn't need such fanfare to leave.

"Let me walk you down." Drew took the suitcase and turned back to Erin. "I'll be back. Do you need anything from Bambi?"

"Not a thing." Though she needed something from Drew.

"I put the schedule on the desk for you, just in case your memory fails." Her cheeks bright red, Bambi headed for the door with Drew in tow.

He turned back to her.

"I'm going to get ready." She wiggled her fingers at him and stood, her side still aching, then watched him go without even asking her side. Drew would have heard her, he always heard her. Maybe Bambi was right, she didn't know Isaac. Something told her that without speaking first or last, she lost.

WITHOUT A WORD, Drew took Bambi's suitcase and his chemist down the hallway and to the elevator. Once the doors parted, she stepped inside and held her hand out. "You don't have to do this. I'm capable of waiting for a shuttle."

"You're very capable, exceptionally capable, extremely capable." His entire body tight, he made his way inside the elevator. "I'm still going to wait with you."

She pressed the button and they only glanced at each other until the elevator reached the bottom floor and let them free in the lobby.

"Look, they're early." She motioned toward the green escape van and reached for her bag.

"Wait a second." He inhaled and rubbed his hand over his face. "I'm really praying I don't come back to the office and find a resignation letter on my desk."

"Thank you." She put her hand on his shoulder. "I don't plan on quitting, but it's nice to know you don't want me to."

"Never." He shook his head. "Are you okay? I mean with everything that happened in the room?" Of course she wasn't okay.

"Seriously, it was nothing."

With no choice but to believe her, he shifted his weight from one foot to the other. "Listen, I didn't sleep with her, well I did, but we didn't..."

"Isaac, it's none of my business." She patted him. "I learned something really important this whole time."

Maybe he could learn something. Right now he needed a Ph.D. in life. Hell, he needed the grammar school version. "What was that?"

"One day I want someone to worry about me leaving the way you did with Erin." She sighed.

"You deserve that." Not wanting to treat her any different than normal, he relinquished her suitcase handle and gave her a hug.

"I want you to have that too, Isaac." She hugged him back and looked up into his face. "You know I really don't see it."

"What?"

"Drew Fulton. I still see Isaac." She shrugged and backed up. "I really should go."

"Please feel free to burn up the company's expense report." He waved.

She gave him a thumbs-up and walked outside.

He waited until she got inside the vehicle and then retraced his steps back upstairs. Wanting to give Erin time to get ready without distraction, he passed her room and returned to theirs, or his, whatever.

His mind blank and reeling all at the same time, he jumped in the shower.

What on earth really happened between the two women? At the moment, he could only hope Erin did the same and took the high road with Bambi, but the fire in her eyes when he left told him he hadn't heard the end of it. What did he do now? Go back to his original plan with Erin and see if they could make it into more of a vacation or continue on with business?

He put on his suit, staring at himself in the mirror as he tied his tie. No matter what, he had to remember he needed to get his work done. Now without Bambi there for the meeting, he really needed to be on his game, but before anything, he had to make sure Erin knew certain rules like remembering to call him Isaac and not mentioning anything about Hollywood Glow to his accounts. Also, he didn't really want her to speak too much. She would already be a distraction. He shook his head. Why bring her if she didn't get to speak? He needed to finally admit he did want to show her off a little.

Maybe a lot.

A quick glance at the clock told him he better go hurry her along. They still needed to eat and get on the road. He finished packing and went right to her room.

Before he had a chance to even knock, she opened the door.

As every time he saw her, his breath quickened. She stood before him in a fitted white skirt suit with her hair and makeup done Hollywood style, her classic Erin Holland look. Something told him she did that all for him. "You look stunning."

"Thank you." She stared at him.

He glanced over her shoulder. Her multitude of bags was neatly lined up by the foot of the bed. "Are you ready?"

"It would appear that way, yes." She continued to stare.

"Why don't I see you to the car and then I'll come back up for you bags?" The sweet Erin who held his hand and cuddled up to him the night before was replaced by an Erin of few words. He hated to admit he hated that Erin.

"I appreciate the help. I can get a couple of them, and I don't think I should go traipsing through the main lobby." She gathered up her handbag and a shoulder bag.

"Good point." He retrieved her other bags and with her leading the way he found himself following yet another woman out of the hotel. Maybe it wasn't Erin who shouldn't make an appearance. He was the one creating the scandal.

After settling her and her items in the car, he took off his jacket and got in the driver's seat. Yes, he was at the wheel and Erin was by his side, the way this trip should have been. He turned and smiled at her. They could turn this thing around.

Rather than a smile in return or even yelling at him, she stared straight ahead and put on a pair of oversized sunglasses.

Yes, fine, she was upset. He needed to do a little groveling, all part of life with Erin. "Did I tell you how stunning you look?"

"Yes, and I thanked you for the compliment." She buckled her seat belt.

"Would you like something to eat?" He tried again.

"I had a bottle of water, the supplements you made me and a protein bar, but thank you for the offer." She opened her purse and peered inside. "I do have something for you."

He practically rubbed his hands together. "All right."

She pulled another protein bar out of her purse and tossed it onto his lap. "According to the schedule we have quite a little trek."

"Yes, we should get going." He started the car, set the navigation system and pulled away from Mesquite, Nevada.

She nodded.

Little did he know that was the last gesture of any kind he was going to get from her for ninety percent of the ride. After almost three hours on the road with only flat desert for scenery, no talk, no music, not even Erin's filming or manipulating her phone, he was one hundred percent sure he contracted a virulent case of cabin fever, even though they were in an SUV. While Bambi kept quiet on the first part of the trip, it was more of a passive silence. Erin's was definitely aggressive and rehearsed.

In a strange twist, he ended up the bad guy when he did absolutely nothing wrong. "Would you like to pick some music?" Unable to take it any longer, and still needing to talk to her about his business, he broke the seal.

"No, thank you." She continued to gaze out the window.

Okay. Now he had worse than silence, she returned to polite, translation pissed. He cleared his throat. "It always amazes me how you can remain so perfectly still for so many hours." She did have the uncanny knack for following direction perfectly, down to not moving if that was what the director was after. Maybe that was why she was such a hellion when not playing a role.

"One day I will make an amazing corpse."

Fine, a step worse from polite was sarcastic, translation, really pissed. He would counter bitch with charming. "I would rather not think of that."

"I beg to differ." She opened her handbag and pulled out a lipstick.

"What does that mean?" He kept his eyes on the road, but peeked over at her out of the corner of his eye. If he kept prodding, she would break.

"You like me quiet and docile, and are not at all interested in what I have to say. You only assume what you want about me." With a nod, she pulled down the sun visor to look in the mirror.

At least he didn't have to prod too much. "Your conversation has always been a highlight for me, but unless there is a large check and studio set, I don't think you have ever been quiet or docile in your life."

With her lipstick held up like a weapon, she turned toward him.

In preparation for the onslaught, he held the wheel tighter.

"You know, it doesn't matter." She returned her attention back to the mirror.

Yes, she goaded him. Yes, he took the bait. "I would like you to tell me what's the matter."

"Strange, it didn't matter to you this morning. What mattered was that your precious scientist didn't realize I was the one who spent the night with you." She took her time to apply the lipstick to her already perfect lips. "Is it only because we're nearing your client that you want to know, so I'll be picture perfect for you?"

"Bambi said nothing happened." While he knew she lied, he didn't want to make a huge deal about it.

"Lord knows if she says it, it must be true." She slammed the cap back on her makeup. "I mean, she's a scientist and gave you an objective opinion of something that is completely subjective, right? No doubt I would be too emotional or stretch the truth."

"That's a very well stated point." The second the words left his mouth he wanted them back, though her word choice impressed him.

"For the second time today, I've been called stupid. If I hit a third time do I win a prize or do I strike out?" She crossed her legs.

"I only called you stupid once." He winced and made the turn off the main highway toward the orchard and the spa. How did he return to the silent treatment? Meaning him being silent.

"And your little cohort did it earlier, but I know where she learned it from."

"I did not call you stupid. I mean I didn't mean it the way it sounded, and I cannot picture Bambi doing it either." He was glad he stopped himself from telling her maybe she didn't understand what Bambi meant.

"Even though you never asked for the other side of the story, I'll tell you that she told me that even my simple mind could realize that you're no longer Drew and apparently I'm only here because of some grand conquest." She threw the lipstick back in her bag and snapped it shut. "Of course, that was right around the same time she knocked me over when I tried to help with her suitcase, and called our film overrated."

After allowing for Erin's statement to sink in, he nodded. "What happened to make her say such things?"

She sat up. "Stop the car."

"What?" He glanced over to find her hand on the door handle.

"I said to stop the car." She opened the door.

He slammed on his brakes. "Erin!"

Without any pause, she got out of the car and shut the door.

His whole body tensed and all he wanted to do was to get out and force her back inside. Instead, he rolled the window down. "Erin get in the car, we're almost there. I don't want to be late."

"You won't be late." She motioned for him to go forward.

"You cannot leave."

"I'm not leaving, I'm walking." To prove her point, she started walking. "I'll meet you there."

"You're going to walk two miles to the orchard?"

"I'm aware of where we are. I'm not that stupid." She tapped her watch. "Better get a move on, don't want to be late for your curtain call."

"You're going to walk the two miles to the meeting?" He drove alongside her.

"Do you think our film is overrated?" She continued her trek.

"No, it's been called genre changing." The only thing he was thankful for was no one else was on the road to witness their exchange.

"Do you think I have a simple mind?" She shot another question at him.

"Absolutely not, and I apologize if I even inferred you were less than intelligent." Right now she had him trailing next to her in an SUV, who was the smart one there?

She stopped, turned toward the car, and put her hands on her hips.

His reaction time off, he hit the brakes a few feet past her and he backed up the car. "Would you like me to open the door for you?"

"Do you think that I'm only here as some conquest? Once I get what I want I'll be gone?"

He paused.

Yes, he paused.

Actually, he didn't answer, because he knew the answer and she knew the answer. Deep down, they both knew.

She pushed her sunglasses up. "You're going to be late for your meeting."

"Please get in the car."

"I need to think. I'll meet you there." She pointed down the road. "I will not get in the car with you right now."

"I'm going to drive away. I won't let you ruin this meeting."

"I agree, you should go to your meeting. According to you and Bambi, I won't be around long enough to even know the final outcome."

"You're probably right." He called her bluff and hit the gas. She could ruin every other woman for him, ruin his love life, ruin everything else, but he wouldn't allow her to ruin his business. They both knew how the story would end, yet they couldn't stop writing the script.

HOLLYWOOD STARBURST

EXT. BROKEN ARROW, OK, ON HIGHWAY 44 - DAY.

The Lincoln is pulled off the side of the road and Roxy is standing staring at the car with her hands on her hips.

> ROXY
> (Speaking to herself)
> This is why Charles kept
> calculating the gas.

ROXY puts her finger in her mouth and glances up and down the road.

> ROXY
> I can't even make it to
> Indianapolis without
> messing up.

Roxy spies a car off in the distance, the car comes closer and she straightens up and waves her hand. Rather than stopping, the carful of teenagers honks and speeds by her.

ROXY looks down and kicks at a rock, then lifts her head and spies two signs, one for a call box and one saying gas is two miles up the road.

> ROXY
> I need help.

ROXY bites her lip, takes a breath and walks up the road to the call box. She opens the door.

The camera pans over the four buttons. Red for emergency, blue for accident, green for major service, black for minor service.

ROXY -hovers her finger over each button.

> ROXY

> There's no call Steven
> or William button.
> (Pauses)
> He said I should call
> for help.

ROXY shrugs and hits the black button.

> DISPATCHER (O.S.)
> (Filtered)
> This is Highway Patrol,
> are you having an
> emergency?

> ROXY
> I ran out of gas.

> DISPATCHER (O.S.)
> (Filtered)
> Okay, I have noted your
> location we will have
> someone out to you as
> soon as possible.

> ROXY
> Ma'am?

> DISPATCHER (O.S.)
> (Filtered)
> Is there something else?

> ROXY
> Do you think a woman
> should be able to get
> her own gas?

                    DISPATCHER (O.S.)
                    (Filtered)
                    I'm sorry. I'm not sure
                    I understand.

                         ROXY
                    I mean you have a button
                    for true emergencies and
                    then like this sad
                    button for getting gas.
                    Someone should only call
                    for help if they truly
                    need it, right?

                    DISPATCHER (O.S.)
                    (Filtered)
                    Excuse me, is there some
                    sort of emergency?

                         ROXY
                    My first thought was to
                    call Steven or William
                    and sit back while they
                    fixed it. The call box
                    doesn't have a Steven or
                    William button.
                     (Looks up into the sky.)
                    I don't even know which
                    button I would choose
                    first.

                    DISPATCHER (O.S.)
                    (Filtered)
                    Miss, do you or do you
                    not need assistance?

                         ROXY
                    No, I'm fine, thank you.

ROXY hangs up the receiver, closes the call
box, returns to the car and gets her purse and
the gas can out of the trunk. Once more, she
walks down the highway passing the gas sign.

                         ROXY

I'm going to press the
Roxy button.

Chapter Eighteen

DREW DROVE AWAY.

Erin stood on the side of the road in the middle of absolute and utter nowhere and watched until his car disappeared.

He drove away and left her.

Every man knew to return. It was the rule, and she glanced at her watch and waited for what seemed like forever plus or minus several minutes for the sound of Drew's tires screeching against the pavement coming back for her.

The second peek at her watch revealed a mere four and half minutes went by. If he didn't turn around soon he would most definitely be late for his meeting.

Yes, any minute now his SUV should race toward her.

Except for the slight rustling from the wind, it was absolutely silent, not even the faint rumblings of any sort of motorized engine met her ears from any direction. Nothing but a vast ocean of trees and other growing things met her gaze. The only sign of any civilization was the road and the fence running the length of the road.

With her arms crossed, the sun blaring down on her and her foot tapping, she stood right at the point where Drew drove away and practiced remaining perfectly still like the time she had to play a statue that later came to life. The teenage girls loved that movie. Of course, she already practiced remaining perfectly still the entire ride here. She was an expert and didn't want to over rehearse. Finally, she let out a sigh.

Figuring only a minute or two passed, once more she looked at her watch.

Her stomach twisted.

Drew's meeting must have already begun.

He wasn't coming back for her.

Well, she would show him. She would just call a taxi and then decide which way her travels would take her. Hell, she could go back to Nevada and make her way to Vegas, or she could go to the orchard. Maybe she should show him what it was like to have someone vanish with unfinished business. The world was open to her, she could do anything, didn't need anyone. With her head held high she slipped her phone out of her purse, half expecting to see some apology from Drew.

Instead, she was thrust right into a post-apocalyptic movie when the words no connection flashed at the top of her screen.

Though a definite swell of nausea overtook her, she refused to have any reaction as she turned in the direction of the orchard and started walking. The click of her stilettos on the rough asphalt told her with every step she was ruining her heels.

After ten minutes of walking, the balls of her feet began to ache. After twenty, they started to burn.

Thirty minutes into her walk she remembered the time Drew taught her all about color and how black clothes absorb all the light rays and will make someone hotter if they wear black clothes in the sun, while white clothes will reflect the color and the heat. Well, once she saw the man who used to study the stars, she would inform him his lesson was quite wrong. Right after she tossed out her sweat soaked white suit.

He didn't think she could do it. He didn't think she would actually walk the two miles to the orchard and attend his meeting. She would show him, show everyone who only wanted to believe the worst in her. Why didn't anyone simply ask what she thought or what she wanted?

Well, Drew didn't care enough to ask, not this morning and not the twenty years he held her at bay.

In the silence, with nothing but her thoughts and no cell service, she needed to face the facts. He would say he drove off as to not be late for his meeting or to teach her a lesson, but if that were the case he would have figured out a way to come get her. In truth, he drove away because that's what he wanted to do.

No, he would never leave her out here stranded. If she didn't reappear by the time he was through, he would come get her, but part of him wanted his old life back, and wanted her gone. This action was merely him dipping his toe into the pool. He only reappeared the night of the 20th Anniversary Gala for the same reason, to know what it was like to be with her. Now he knew, and he didn't need her anymore.

Not really paying attention to where she walked, she tripped on a divot in the road, tried to catch herself, and only ended up face down in a bed of dirt.

Defeated, with her body aching from walking too long a distance in shoes only made for sitting, she shut her eyes. All she wanted to do was quit, throw up the white flag, or in her case the dirty white flag, and surrender.

Even with two decades behind them, they managed to keep hitting rewind on the same scene over and over again.

The day of filming had been hot, scorching, blistering, and any other synonym she could conjure for hot as they had filmed the scene where Steven's car broke down in the middle of nowhere. She had supposed the director and producer wanted to go for realism, because somehow they all found themselves on a two-lane road with nothing but dirt on either side. After technical issues, wardrobe issues, lighting issues and as strange as it seemed, car issues, they finally managed to do a couple of the necessary scenes.

"Cut, that's a print!" The director yelled. "Take ten."

Drenched from sweat and with makeup melting into her eyes stinging beyond belief, she literally crawled over Ryder to get out of the car, burning her thigh on the metal door in the process.

"Ouch!" She tripped, steadied herself by slapping her palm on the metal, and then recoiled from yet another burn.

"Erin, you okay?" Ryder kept his voice low.

"I'm fine." Her voice hitched, and she rushed toward the trailer and the promise of a little cool air.

Though every part of her seemed to be in some sort of pain, she managed to get inside the trailer after burning her hand once more on the hot handle. Air, at least a little cooler than outside, allowed her to catch a full breath, and she stumbled to the sink and turned on the water. She stuck her singed hand under the healing liquid and with her free hand, palmed some of the water and splashed her face.

"Now I'm going to have to redo your makeup."

The screech of the lady who assisted their main makeup person scratched through Erin's head. This person never liked her since Erin had to fix her makeup every time. The guys loved her because she was fast. Fast didn't equate to good. "Where's Bea?" She loved Bea. The woman was a true artist who had been in the industry for over forty years and taught Erin a ton about how to create makeup magic.

"She had to run into the main town. I was told to come in here and get you put back together." The woman pointed to the chair. "We need to stay on schedule."

"Why don't you go tend to the guys, and I'll take care of myself." She found a paper towel, wet it, and pressed it to her thigh.

"We need to stay on schedule." The woman crossed her arms.

So this was how the woman wanted to play it. "Then go keep it and I'll tell everyone I'll do my own makeup or wait for Bea to return."

"You think because you got Stacy fired and replaced her with Drew so he can't compete with you that you can just get rid of anyone you don't want around?" The second-rate artist put her hands on her hips.

"You know, I didn't get anyone fired. The powers that be just agreed that Stacy didn't have the right chemistry with the rest of us." The burn subsiding, she approached her nemesis. "Obviously, they wanted things to be right, or she would still be here."

"So the world revolves around your rules. Just remember I have plenty of my own connections. I wouldn't cross me."

There was not a chance in hell that Erin would allow this woman to touch her with any sort of makeup or anything else. She charged toward the door and flung it open right into Drew's, Logan's and the director's faces.

"Erin?" The director smiled at her. "Why aren't you getting your makeup touched up?"

Already there were stories in the tabloids about the feud between Stacy and her and how Erin played diva on the set, throwing in the star card to get the supporting actress fired. She didn't need more fuel to the fire. "I would rather wait for Bea."

"Actually, what Erin said is that if I didn't do her makeup perfectly, she would make sure she got me fired like Stacy." The woman charged forward.

"I never said that!" Her face heated. "Seriously."

"Erin." The director widened his eyes.

"You were the first one to agree that Stacy wasn't right." She put her hands on her hips. "If I tell you I didn't say it, then I didn't say it."

Logan rolled his eyes and pushed his way into the trailer.

"All right, Erin." The director shook his head and looked at the horrid woman. "Why don't you see to Ryder, Logan and Drew? Erin can tend to herself until Bea gets back. Don't worry about a thing, no one is getting fired."

He placated her. She ground her teeth together. "I told you I didn't say anything like that." Her eyes darted to Drew. If anyone would stand up for her, he would. Somehow he saw her as she wanted to be, as if his eyes had a filter.

"How's your hand?" He stepped forward and glanced down at her appendage.

"Really?" She wanted to say not as hurt as her heart, but had chosen to turn her back on them all, especially Drew, and went to one of the vanity tables with the makeup. No one had ever believed her or had believed in her. She had shut her eyes.

"Miss, miss!" A man screamed out, interrupting her thoughts. "Miss, are you okay?"

Still in the dirt, she opened her eyes and lifted her head to find an older man in dirty overalls running through the field toward her.

"Miss!" He caught up to her and climbed over the wooden fence. "Are you hurt? Can you move?"

"I think I'll live." She had to say she was impressed he managed such a feat.

"Here, let me help you." He held his hand out to her.

Only because he seemed honestly concerned did she put her hand in his and let him help her up. She brushed off her soiled suit and shook her head.

"I've been watching you for a while. What are you doing out here?" He seemed to check her over then reached in his pocket and handed her a handkerchief.

Well, she had been given a lot of things in her life to sign, but a handkerchief was new. Chivalry was dead and buried. "I'm trying to get to Organic Oasis. I have a meeting there and got separated from everyone." She opened her handbag, found her marker, and signed the little piece of cloth. "Here you go."

"That's another half mile up the road. I work here in the orchards." He stared down at his handkerchief, shrugged and shoved it back into his pocket. "I don't think you should be walking in those shoes."

"I am aware of that, but I can't quit. I have to make it. Everyone thinks I'm a quitter, or don't keep my commitments. No one believes in me." She smiled at the man. "I better keep going." No matter what, she would show up at this meeting. Then she would leave. Maybe she'd call Ryder to come get her in one of his snazzy cars, or one of his many benefactors' private planes and then demand Logan help her. If it wasn't for him, she would have much more money now.

Somehow, her entire life would always be centered around a few months when she was eighteen years old. In less time than it took to shoot a genre changing movie, she lost the one man she wanted, and she basically signed part of her life away. Everything narrowed down to the fact she was always fixated on appearing to be someone she wasn't.

Erin Hollendanger wanted Drew Fulton way back then and was too scared to admit it to herself or the world. That same girl wanted the world to view her as a darling little actress with the world at her feet. She wanted to shake off the role of Roxy and spread her wings. Wanted it so much, she spent twenty years bribing Logan Alexander to take the fall for her shortcomings and make sure the sequel to the film was cancelled.

Funny, now all she wanted was Drew Fulton and to be in the sequel.

Two things she couldn't have.

"Are the shoes already ruined?" He glanced down at her feet.

She didn't have to look to know her four figure shoes were no longer worth two cents. "As soon as I meet up with my luggage, I'm going to give them a proper send off."

"Come on then, I'll show you a short cut. It looks like you could use a walk through nature barefoot." He walked back toward the fence.

She glanced between the road and the fence. Maybe she needed a different path altogether. In a move she was even shocked at, she kicked off her shoes and followed the man, crawling through the fence slats and making her way onto softer ground. Most likely this would end with them hiring a search party for her to find her body in the middle of the rows of trees. However, there was something about being without cell service and being a little unsure of her location that was a bit thrilling and a lot freeing, especially with a man who had no idea who she was. "You know, I've been on a farm before."

"It was probably one of those city farms." He laughed and led her down a row of perfectly manicured trees.

In truth, his prediction was spot on. A complete city farm, or what people from the city assumed a farm to be, complete with a cow and a beat up pickup truck and a plow. It was during a film where she played one of those farm girls who wore wispy dresses and floppy hats. She quite liked the character, but not the director. The man made her stand in the sun in the middle of some cornstalks for over an hour while they waited for exactly the right shadow to cast behind her to get the shot he wanted. Then the damn scene ended up on the cutting room floor. Sort of like her life.

Shade cooled her while her guide led her through the rows and her feet squished into the dirt below her, a strange yet not unpleasant sensation. This would be perfect fodder for the reality show, and in a bizarre twist this was her reality. Once more, she reached into her bag and pulled out her video camera. "Hold on one second."

The man stopped.

She got a shot of her feet and shuddered, panned the area then shot up into the trees. "Oh, my god, there's fruit on the trees."

"Why don't you put the camera down a second and actually look at the trees?" He came up beside her.

For a moment she lowered the recording device and did as the man asked. There was something genuine and real about being here. "There's fruit on the trees."

"Have you ever had a ripe pear right off the tree?"

She shook her head. "Would you believe me if I told you that everything around me is designed to look perfect, but it's usually just a shell?"

"Yes, I would." He walked over to one of the trees and looked up, tilting his head from side to side. "Here's a perfect one."

"How do you know?" She had to get a shot of this and lifted the camera.

"Fruit is not unlike anything else. It takes time to grow and blossom. Just about the time you think you will never get a bounty, you look up into the tree and it's perfectly ripe and ready for picking and all the sweeter because you gave it time." With his poetic words, he reached up into the tree, plucked the fruit and gave it to her.

"Shouldn't we wash it off or something?" She gazed down at the pear.

"This is what nature made, just eat it because you want to."

She handed him her camera. As if he had a sixth sense, he continued recording and she took a bite. A juicy sweetness burst in her mouth, better than any high-end poached pear concoction she'd ever tasted, possibly even tastier than Logan's fiancée's diamond. "It's different than a store." Pear juice dribbled down her chin and damn if she didn't care.

He laughed. "Completely."

"Unbelievable." She wiped her chin with the back of her hand and took another bite.

"Some people say farmers are crazy. We are slaves to the weather and the right conditions and so many factors out of our control, but for the couple of times I got to hand a city girl a pear off a tree and see her face light up, it makes me feel like what I do matters."

Standing there in the middle of the orchard with her feet in the dirt and an overly juicy pear, she finally took a breath. "Thank you."

"Anytime." He held his hand out and she traded him the pear core for the camera.

"Okay, you need some city action, let me show you something." She hooked her arm in his and turned the camera around. "Do you have a family?"

"Yes, a son, his wife and two granddaughters. My son runs this place. I started the orchard with my father sixty years ago."

She centered them in the viewfinder. "Then when I get to my meeting I will make sure that your granddaughters get a copy of this. Tell them you had a selfie with the city girl and give them that handkerchief. Will you do that for me?"

"If that will make you happy." He kept hold of her arm as they walked.

"It's a start." Maybe rather than proving a point and leaving, or giving up, she needed to wait for things to ripen. The hurt between them went both ways. She could only pray Drew didn't want to leave her on the cutting room floor, and she could get him to believe in her.

"I WANT EVERYTHING my customers touch while at my spa to come from my family's orchard, and then I want them to go home with the supplements and products from these grounds. Everything must be exclusive and everything must be made with what you see in front of you." Allan Parker, owner of Organic Oasis, an exclusive retreat nestled in the self-proclaimed calming lands of Utah, held his arm out.

Drew studied the rows fruit trees in front of him and fought the urge to shake his head or roll his eyes. Everyone wanted their own custom blend until they realized the cost. He wasted more time quoting custom projects when he knew the customer would never go for the expense, because on the off chance one project went through, the money was astronomical. To date, only one was seen through to fruition for the hundreds he quoted, but a guy could dream. He always craved the unattainable.

Still, as a newer laboratory, he had to entertain every opportunity and hope at the end the customer would buy his brand. He had to say his own line of products were beginning to make a name for themselves and Hollywood Glow had a lot of potential if he didn't die trying to come out with it first. His celebrity clientele was on the upswing for sure.

The thought of celebrities made him focus on one star in particular. When he first wanted to take Erin on this road trip, he envisioned strolling among the bountiful orchard with Erin by his side, sneaking in a spa treatment for her, and possibly ending the day with a picnic among the pear trees, all while showing her exactly what he did for a living.

Instead, he left her over a mile away walking down a pretty desolate road in nowhere, Utah. He actually drove away and didn't even look in the rearview mirror. In an attempt to concentrate on his work, he scanned the orchard.

"Why don't you come show me and the girls what you concocted and give me the bottom line?" Allan came up beside him.

"Let's go talk shop." He nodded and followed his account. Aside from his concern over taking one of his top customers and pissing him off with the cost of custom blends, worry rose at where in the hell Erin could be? Did he not listen to Erin this morning because he didn't believe her, or because he didn't want to know the truth? He glanced at his watch and wondered how long it would take to walk here in a white suit with a short skirt and stilettos.

Allan led him back to the main building with the spa's other little luxuries and they entered a big conference room where the spa aestheticians would join them. He bent down to retrieve the samples he created.

"Oh, my god!" A woman's voice screeched through the room.

He shot up, expecting to find Erin.

Two of the women he recognized from his prior visits stood there pointing at him, one with her hand covering her mouth.

"Are you joining us for the meeting?" He resisted looking behind him.

The one with her hand over her mouth giggled, while the other tiptoed forward, bent down and stared at him. "I can't believe I never saw it."

"Is this that Hollywood thing again?" Allan shook his head.

"You don't understand. This is Drew Fulton." She held out her 20th Anniversary DVD of *Hollywood Stardust* and a marker. "Would you mind?"

"Well, you can call him what you want, but he is also Isaac Abrams, our chemist." Allan strummed his fingers on the table. "No wonder you hid, how can you get any work done?"

With one hand still over her mouth, and the other with a matching DVD, the second girl snuck up as well.

If the man only knew. Thus far he managed to stay out of the limelight and only answered questions to his staff and the few accounts that called. This was the first time he was confronted head on and he sort of wished Erin was here to see it. He took the marker and signed his name to the DVDs.

Both women hugged their prize and before he could return to the land of Isaac Abrams, a third woman came rushing inside the room. "You are never never never never going to guess who just arrived saying she is Isaac's or Drew's or whoever's Director of Marketing!" She pointed at him, jumped up and down and ran back down the hall.

Relief washed over him, and he put his samples in the middle of the table and stood. Part of him thought she might have walked the other direction and hitched a ride out of here. Once more she proved him wrong.

The other two girls dashed away.

"What is going on?" Allan leaned back in his chair and crossed his arms.

No explanation was necessary. A moment after Allan asked his question, the procession began, the two girls returned, one held a glass of water, the other carried a towel, a woman he didn't recognize from the original hubbub hurried in next and pulled out a chair, followed by the grand finale of the never never never never woman entering with her arm wrapped around his one time co-star and now Director of Marketing.

"Put her here." Chair lady patted the cushion and the other woman put the water at what was now dubbed Erin's seat. Erin's personal towel girl held out her offering and waited. He half expected her to kneel down and bow her head.

He winced and braced himself for the backlash. The white suit was now more of a grey and streaked with dirt, Erin's hair hung down around her face, and she limped as she took her seat and put her bag on the table. "I'm so sorry I'm late." She didn't as much look in his direction, but she held her hand out to Allan. "I'm Erin Holland, Drew's, I mean Isaac's Director of Marketing."

The man who seemed annoyed with all things Hollywood suddenly jumped out of his seat. "No introduction is necessary." He took her hand between his. "You *are* Erin Holland."

"I am." Her perfectly symmetrical signature smile grew across her face, albeit dirty face. "Who might you be?"

"I am Allan Parker, I own this holistic health center and orchard." Continuing to hold her hand, he leaned back on the table. "Do you mind if I ask what happened to you?"

Always one to know the importance of timing, Erin sipped her water, took the towel, dabbed her forehead and chest, and inhaled. "Well, truth be told Isaac and I got into quite a little tiff." Her voice came out innocent and light, a mere waif against the elements.

"What would he have to argue with you about?" Allan patted her hand.

Drew grabbed the edge of the table, but no matter how hard he squeezed there would be no stopping the freight train coming toward him. All he needed her to do along with mentioning their fight was let loose the Hollywood Glow information. His account wouldn't take too kindly to having Erin endorse what could essentially be the competition. If she would have stayed in the car so they could talk, he could have explained. In essence, he was screwed.

"As we drove here, I wanted to look at the grounds, they are so beautiful, and we were running late, I pouted and got out of the car and said I would meet him here." She pulled out her weapon of mass destruction and pursed her lower lip out.

"I'm so sorry. I should have never left you." Drew blurted out his apology. From day one, he was powerless against the lip.

All the women in the room gasped, one put her signed DVD down. Allan turned and glared at him. "You left her?"

"I left her." He turned his attention to her. More like he left her twenty years ago.

At last, she met his gaze. "Oh, don't be mad at him." Again, she cooed.

Everyone in the room returned to staring at their idol.

"I practically begged him to leave, he needed to get here. Us girls like it when the men make the money." She winked at Allan.

The girls let out a collective sigh and Allan nodded.

"I took a little tour of your orchard, I believe I met your father along the way and though I lost my shoes, I had the most scrumptious pear, the juice was dripping right off me."

Both he and Allan stared at her, no doubt both pictured juices dripping off her.

"Now I want you boys to get to your work." She slid her hand away from Allan's. "Do you mind if I do some filming? I'm doing a piece for Drew on the lab."

He noticed she didn't yell at him or mention Hollywood Glow...yet.

"We would be delighted." Allan motioned for the girls to join them and returned to his seat.

Drew gave everyone a moment to settle down. Out of the corner of his eye, he watched Erin take out her camera, set it up, sign the girls' DVDs and sit back with her water.

"Show us what you have." All smiles, Allan hit the table, and Drew swore he struck a pose for the camera.

"I went over the notes we made and I not only created some extracts from the samples we took from the orchard, but then I went to some raw material providers and got the actual pure ingredients that make each of these fruits so special and beneficial."

He motioned toward the samples. "I created some capsules, a drink, a powder that can be added to liquid, and some little ampules with the active ingredients. In essence, it's a system of products."

As always, everyone oohhed and ahhed over the custom blends and the girls assessed each product.

"So what are the numbers?" Allan kept his eye on the camera.

"As explained, any custom work is yours, and you will have your own run. Here are what the numbers look like." He handed Allan a spreadsheet and his chest tightened. Here's where the man would wonder how he could sell that amount, then the concern would turn into anger when he realized he would have to stay with the lab's brand because nothing would ever be as good as the unique product. Maybe he should mention Hollywood Glow.

The jolly smile on Allan's face vanished, his complexion paled. "I could buy a house for this amount. How am I supposed to sell all this?"

"That's why I recommended staying with the lab brand." Drew swore in some weird universe someone wrote this script and just changed the players every now and again.

"Look at these!" The girl who escorted Erin in the room lifted one of the little red ampules. "What do I do?"

"Oh, those are the ampules!" Erin reached forward, grabbed one and held it up letting it dangle from her fingertips. "Did you see how Drew made them look like the cherries you grow in the orchard with all the antioxidants?"

She knew cherries grew here?

"Don't touch those. Each one could buy a car." Allan tossed the paper back at him.

"Watch this." Erin ignored Allan and leaned way over the table.

Her disciples parroted her.

With her manicured fingernails, she twisted the top off the ampule. "This is one way to pop a cherry."

The girls laughed.

Drew squeezed his hand into a fist. A business meeting with real business people, not industry people, was no place for a joke with any innuendo.

Ever the show person, Erin slid her glass of water over, held the ampule up high and allowed a couple of droplets of his concentrated serum to fall in the liquid making a burgundy swirl.

Her audience all seemed to hold their collective breaths.

In an effort to interject, he lifted his finger. She needed to put the entire ampule into the water to get the proper dosage and taste.

"It makes your water taste great, but I discovered something else when I began working with the products." Rather than fielding his question, she squeezed the rest onto her fingertips and proceeded to rub his serum onto her face and chest.

The girls gasped as Erin ran her fingers over her own skin in an overtly sexy manner. If they were alone, he would definitely be aroused, and a quick glance over at Allan with his half-opened mouth revealed his client had the same thought.

"It absorbs right in, and look how hydrated my skin is after that long walk."

As if they'd joined a cult, all the girls nodded.

"But here is the best part." She licked her fingertips. "It's completely edible."

Like starving vultures, the girls descended upon the ampules, each taking their turn to taste the product and apply it to their skin and then to each other's skin. Erin didn't create a cult, she created an orgy.

"We can use these in our treatments!" one of the females exclaimed.

"I would be very impressed if I were in a facial and my aesthetician took out a custom ampule created from the fruits of the orchard surrounding the spa." Erin helped the girls apply the serum to the backs of their hands then opened one of the bottles of his customized, powdered antioxidant blend and sprinkled a bit on top. "It can be a scrub too." As if punctuating her sentence, once more she licked her finger, dipped it in the powder and put her finger in her mouth.

The room practically vibrated from the excitement as the one-time, calm, zen-like practitioners of holistic health turned into hedonistic madwomen rubbing and buffing their skin with only the finest ingredients.

If word got out about this display, he would never sell as much as a multi-vitamin again. His only saving grace was the fact that Allan wouldn't buy a thing.

"Oh, my god." The original one who asked for his autograph held her hands out stopping them all. "We can use the drink as a hydrating spray!"

"Your products literally will treat your customers from the inside out." Erin swooped in once more.

The squeals of delight caused Allan to wince.

"We have to have this." One of the women turned to Allan.

"I don't think you understand the cost." Allan pressed his hand to his temple.

"I don't think you understand the potential." In her bare feet, Erin stood and proceeded to do a complete hand treatment on his soon to be former account.

By the expression on Allan's face, Erin may just as well have given him a hand job.

"Now taste." She dabbed a bit of the serum on his lower lip.

As if caught in a spell, the man licked his lower lip. "The products are quite amazing."

Amazing? Drew forced his back against the chair. How did they know anything about the products? He never got the opportunity to say one word about anthocyanins, or polyphenols, or the special process he used to ensure the stability of the ingredients.

"I think amazing is an understatement." Erin sauntered back to her seat. "This orchard and spa are finally ripe, ready to go in for the kill. Your facility caters to a star clientele, so who better to create products for your customers than a star himself?"

The horrible scraping sound of his teeth grinding together in exactly the right way reverberated through his skull. He didn't want to be known as Drew Fulton, the casual chemist to the stars. He was Isaac Abrams, a serious scientist.

"The minimums are very high." Rather than speaking to him, Allan addressed his question to Erin.

She swiped the quotation paper off the table, giving it barely a glance before tossing it aside. "Once the media gets a hold of this, you'll be calling Drew in a panic to make more and we have a five-week lead time."

They did? He continued to watch the horror show.

Almost in slow motion, Allan reached over for the paper. "I don't know."

"You already have one celebrity spokesperson."

She was going to be his spokesperson? What happened to Hollywood Glow? He needed to speak. "Allan."

Erin cleared her throat. "She even created your regimen and is the spokesperson and Director of Marketing for the entire lab."

Somehow she dodged the Hollywood Glow bullet. Now if Allan saw her endorsing those products, it would make perfect sense.

"Daddy!" The second girl who asked for his autograph stomped over.

Daddy? Even if anyone had acknowledged Drew spoke, he wouldn't have any words left.

"Daddy." She put her hands on her hips. "I want these products and I want Erin Holland as my client and spokesperson. I did what you asked and instead of becoming an accountant stayed here with you and grandpa to run the business and these products made by these stars will be our legacy." The woman grabbed Erin's hand and pressed it to her chest.

An eerie silence overtook the room.

He had to stop the madness. "Allan."

Allan looked around the room, his gaze stopping at each person and then down to the products.

In what appeared to be a slow motion movement, Allan lifted his hand. "You said the deposit was fifty percent?"

The room went up in cheers and the women hugged each other and Erin.

"Erin, can we do a treatment on you now and practice?" Allan's daughter pulled her.

"I thought you would never ask." Erin got up out of the chair. "I'm quite exhausted after my workout."

The girls gathered around her and corralled her toward the exit.

"Thank you, Daddy!" The daughter called out.

"As long as you're happy, love bug. Take your time and work with her." Allan stood. "Why don't the two of you stay here at the spa as our guest tonight? Everything will be covered for you."

Erin looked over her shoulder at him. "Again, I thought you would never ask."

"Erin." It was his turn to stand, though his legs didn't seem to want to hold him up. "Our schedule."

Everyone turned to him. More like glared at him.

"Well, I'm staying here with my girls." Erin lifted her chin. "Go collect your deposit Drew. You have a lot of work to do."

The feminine whirlwind with Erin at the eye of the storm spun away. In its wake, it made a mockery of his business, but mostly of him.

How did he always end up in this position anytime Erin Holland entered his life?

HOLLYWOOD STARBURST

INT. OUTSIDE OF SPRINGFIELD, MO. IN A DINER –
DAY.

Roxy sits at a table with a cup of coffee and a
slice of pie. She stabs her fork at the pie
and shoves a piece in her mouth, repeating the
action.

WAITRESS comes over and tops off Roxy's coffee
and goes to turn.

ROXY swallows.

                    ROXY
              (coughs)
               Excuse me.

WAITRESS faces her.

                    WAITRESS
               Careful.

ROXY takes a sip of the coffee and licks her
fork.

                    ROXY
               May I have a piece of
               the chocolate cake?

ROXY uses her fork to point to the huge
chocolate cake on the counter.

WAITRESS nods, puts the coffee pot down, gets a
piece of the cake and serves it to Roxy.

                    WAITRESS
               So, what hole are you
               filling?

ROXY digs right into the cake and closes her
eyes as she chews. She puts one finger up,
finishes her bite and takes a sip of her
coffee.

                    ROXY
          Hole?

                    WAITRESS
          (chuckles)
          Do you have a hole in
          your stomach or hole in
          your heart?

ROXY takes another bite of cake and sits back.

                    ROXY
          I think I have a hole in
          my head.

WAITRESS lets out a real laugh.

                    ROXY
          You know a wise woman
          told me to always take a
          second helping of mashed
          potatoes, one day I'll
          regret not taking it.

                    WAITRESS
          So you decided rather
          than potatoes to have
          cake?

                    ROXY
          (Shrugs.)
          I decided to do what I
          want to do and not care
          about everyone else. I
          ran out of gas, got it
          myself, walked about 5
          miles there and back. I
          got the gas, set off
          again, and didn't make
          it two hours down the
          road when something went
          wrong with the car. The
          mechanic talked to me

                    like a baby, asked where
                    my dad was. I gave in
                    and called William, no
                    answer. I called Steven,
                    no answer.
                    (Hits the table)
                    I called Charles, no
                    answer! So you know
                    what I almost did?

WAITRESS leans on the booth and shakes her
head.

ROXY puts her elbow on the table and rests her
head in her hand.

                    ROXY
                    I almost called my
                    parents.

WAITRESS tilts her head

                    ROXY
                    But then I told the
                    mechanic to fix the car
                    and stomped over here
                    and decided that since I
                    can never decide between
                    cake and pie I would
                    have both.

                    WAITRESS
          Well, now it all makes
          sense.

                    ROXY
          You know what?

                    WAITRESS
          Tell me.

                    ROXY
            It's really good.

Chapter Nineteen

AFTER SHOWERING, SHAVING, moisturizing, shampooing, conditioning, blow drying, and taking one last look at the woman who sold a six-figure deal for her darling Drew, Erin fluffed up her hair and made her way into the main part of their suite at the spa.

She had to make a mental note that the accommodations were much better than the night before. A retreat for the "it" crowd to be pampered, this place provided for every amenity, down to gluten-free toothpaste.

In a replay of her other night with Drew, she found him in the overstuffed bed with a book in front of his face. Since he abandoned her on the side of the road they hadn't spent any time alone. After the meeting and her treatments, they ate a healthy meal in the spa restaurant. Once getting settled in their suite, they went their separate ways to their respective bathrooms. At least she didn't have to explain to the girls to put them in the same room, it all happened naturally.

Without a word, she walked the perimeter of the space turning off the lights until she reached the bed. The moment she untied the sash of the spa robe and tossed the garment aside revealing a light pink, form-fitting short nightgown, Drew turned to her.

In a need to torture the man a wee bit before allowing him to make everything up to her by having his way with her, she took her time stretching, picked up her fashion magazine and got in the bed.

For several moments he stared at her, but she continued to slowly turn the pages of her magazine. Instead of a smile of congratulations on her win, or groveling, he lifted his book once more.

"I just want you to know I forgive you." She continued to skim her magazine.

"For what?" His tone came out tight, as if ready to snap.

Who was playing hard to get here? She licked her lips, the tang of success and tart cherry lingering on her tongue. "You're the smartest man I know, so I'm sure I don't need to provide you a list."

"Maybe we can compare lists."

She tightened her hold on the magazine, crinkling the pages. "Does that list include you leaving me without a cell site?"

"Funny, my list has how you deliberately tried to make me late for an important meeting." He slammed the book shut.

"Well, mine has how you didn't listen to me, never asked my opinion, and took Barbie's word over mine." In an attempt to one up him, she threw her magazine off the edge of the bed.

"Bambi," he corrected.

They faced each other.

She narrowed her eyes. "What's the difference? They are both fictional characters." If he only knew.

"If there is any fictional character in my life, I'm looking at her." His voice came out low, vibrating through her and shaking her to her core.

The fire coursing through her, the same one ready for a fight, for the passion, for the explosion was snuffed out with his words. Before she gave into the tears, she turned out the light and laid down with her back to him.

They stayed in silence for only a couple of minutes, though it seemed like a few hours.

"Is that everything on your list?"

She shut her eyes. His voice didn't remotely resemble the teenager of twenty years ago. "Silly me, I thought we should be celebrating that nice fat check in your computer case."

"I'll pass on you making a mockery of my business."

"What? I walked two miles to get to the meeting, I made sure not to say anything about how you abandoned me, I showed the girls all the tricks with the products, what more did you want me to do? I can't make it for you too." She hit the bed. "Oh, excuse me, did I make a mistake and call you Drew instead of Isaac? I'm sorry I guess with everything my mind went on automatic."

"I didn't sell anything. For all they know that powder could be nothing but sugar and food coloring."

Even though he couldn't see her, she still shook her head.

"Not everything is about a check. You think my business is a joke, you think I'm a pushover. You always have, and when it comes to you, maybe I am, look where we are now." At last, his tone dropped some of its anger, but in its wake left hurt.

Once more she turned away. Once more silence encompassed the room. Once more they lay there further apart.

"You always think the worst of me." She toyed with the edge of her pillowcase. How long did she wait for her fruit to ripen? At what point did it get rotten?

He didn't respond, but the bed moved, and she knew he heard her.

"Not that you care about anything I have to say, but I had been using your products since you made mine, and I don't think I could have walked those two miles without them. I only saw the Orchard products yesterday, and when Bambi went to you I was so nervous I just started playing with them until she came back." She took a breath. "If I knew the science, I would have said something. You said these deals are impossible to get, I honestly wanted to help."

Her confession was met with nothing. He probably fell asleep.

"I walked along that road and I wanted to stomp into that meeting, slap you across the face and leave. Then I met with Allan's father who helped me reach my destination, and before I walked inside I promised I would show you what I could do, how we could be a team. Maybe a little flash of what life could be like down the road, but as usual, I was wrong." Tears heated her eyes. "You never believe in me."

Again, the bed shook and in what seemed to be out of nowhere, Drew put his arms around her. "You didn't even ask."

"Not like this." Refusing to turn him into a pushover or be an obligation, she shrugged him away.

With no argument, he turned back over.

For the first time since their reunion, she didn't feel the need to melt into his embrace and try to escape into the fictional world she created.

"MR. DREW FULTON, please tell us where we are on our way to now." Erin aimed her camera in his direction.

For the umpteenth time, Drew ground his teeth together and made a mental note to visit a dentist when they returned to Los Angeles.

Unlike how they went to bed, they woke face to face, their legs tangled, her lying on his arm, as if their subconscious pulled them together. Of course, his throbbing morning erection basically cried out for what it craved. More accurately, who it craved.

In the shower, though he thought he could quickly satisfy himself, he instead found himself reliving the entire trip thus far, ending his rewind with how Erin basically won the manufacturing job for him. Who was he kidding? There was no basically about it, he owed her a commission check and he also ran out of time to fix his personal problem.

While they got ready and loaded up the car, his situation waxed and waned. He could do with a bit more waning. More than that, how did he even talk to her?

"Oh, Mr. Drew Fulton." After an hour of silence on a barren highway, Erin finally spoke, basically calling her own type of truce. "Come on. Let's try to make the most of our trip."

At the moment, life held two choices for him, go with Erin's peace offering or... well there was no other choice. "Yes, Ms. Holland."

As if the games began, she bounced in her seat. "Tell your shotgun seat where we are going on this fine morning."

She gave him a reprieve from the apologies he owed her, and he played along. "Grand Junction Colorado to visit Multimode Health who specializes in using a variety of both eastern and western approaches to treating patients."

"Oh, that reminds me, I need to take my supplements." She attached the camera to the little mount on the windshield and proceeded to pull her bag of his creations out.

Out of the corner of his eye he watched her methodical process of reading each container and choosing the right capsules.

"This one is for energy, this one for mental clarity, you told me this one is especially for females, and this one is for stamina." She stared into her hand and tilted her head. "Interesting."

"What?" He recounted the pills in her palm.

"If I didn't know better, I would think you are trying to woo me with nutritional health."

Unsure of what she meant, he waited for her to continue.

"Drew." She held her hand out to him and crossed her legs. "Energy, female things, stamina and clarity. Are you trying to make me horny?"

He opened his mouth and glanced over at her and her leg. Nobody told him the dress code for the trip was short skirts and smooth thighs.

She gasped and pointed at him. "You're staring at my legs, you are trying to get me in the mood!"

"Those are a perfectly acceptable choice for any woman." He stared straight ahead.

"Is this the regimen you prescribe for any woman?" She inched toward him.

He sort of shrugged. Maybe he needed to be committed to the wayward home of passive aggressive men who couldn't let go of their first crush.

A low chuckle escaped her throat. She leaned way over, reached for his bottle of water, popped all the pills in her mouth and swallowed them down. "Did you take your vitamins today?"

The last minute he didn't hear a word she said, all he saw was her cleavage and he opted to shake his head.

"Let me help you then." Again, she retrieved her bag and took out a sampling of the capsules. "Clarity." She held up the pill to his lips. "Open wide, here come the supplements."

Beyond his control, he opened his mouth.

She doled out the first dose and repeated her actions. "Energy."

He forced himself to remain focused on the road.

"And the most important one of them all, stamina." Once more, she put the pill on his tongue and allowed her fingertips to graze his lips. "Maybe I should give you two."

Like earlier, his quote unquote situation waxed again, straining against his pants.

"You are most definitely not a contender for the female pill." She held the water up and gave him a drink.

The water cooled his throat, but nothing else.

"Drew." She placed her hand on his thigh and crooned in his ear. "I have another question."

If her question involved pulling off the side of the road and fixing the fit of his pants, he would get over being late. "All right."

"Do you think maybe you could learn to believe in me even a little, if I promise you that I don't think anything you do is a joke, and I think you're far from a pushover?" She brushed the back of her hand over his cheek.

Apparently, she decided to address last night. In all truth he had to admit he was more than surprised she not only showed up at the meeting with the spa, but only gave him an hour of the silent treatment. In many ways she proved she'd already changed. "I think that sounds like a plan."

"Me, too." She kissed his cheek.

He took a chance and held his hand out to her.

"The pills are working." Without any hesitation, she put her hand in his, intertwining their fingers. "I don't remember the last time holding someone's hand turned me on, yet here we are."

"If you only knew." He didn't mean to let the words slip, but his blood supply pooled elsewhere.

"How long does this meeting have to be and do you think you can adjust the couple of hours set aside for your work for something else?" She scratched her nails up and down his arm.

"We have to do the meeting right, because he's a long standing client of mine, but if you're a good girl, maybe we can forego the work and the corporate hotel and go stay at one of the B&B's by the wineries instead." Lord help him, they were planning their sex. He was never going to make it, but on a positive note, the trip he originally wanted with her seemed to be materializing. Actually, the life he wanted may be materializing. He tried not to go there.

"What do I have to do to be good?" She lifted his hand to her mouth and kissed his fingers, wrangling one in between her lips.

"Keep that thought until after the meeting." Not wanting to arrive at the meeting in his state, he needed to pull away, but lacked the strength.

"You want me to suck your fingers after the meeting?" Her voice taunted him.

"Erin." Heat consumed him.

"Maybe somewhere more fun. Is that what you're trying to tell me?" She laughed and pointed out the window. "Look."

At the moment he didn't possess enough faculties to do multiple things at one time. Driving and Erin were a questionable mix at best. Still, he glanced over at the sign that caught her attention. "Former site of Climax Uranium Mine."

"I think that's telling. I know I could go for a climax or three."

"If you only knew."

"I have an idea." She looked down at his lap.

"I told you to be good. I have to be able to walk."

"Oh, I like it when you take charge." She let go of his hand and slid over a few inches. "While you calm down, I better charge the camera for our meeting."

Camera. He forgot about the camera. "Erin."

With ease, she plugged in her cables. "You think it's safe to drink wine by that climax uranium thing, right?"

Everything with Erin came with two sides, black and white, yes or no. They were together or apart, on air or off, fake or real. The only trouble was he was never sure what side he stood on. "I suppose we'll either climax or explode."

HOLLYWOOD STARBURST

EXT. ROLLA, MO, AT A GAS STATION – DAY.

Roxy is on the payphone outside the station, the Lincoln is in the background by the gas pump.

> ROXY
> Well, one thing is certain, I am really sick of all these tiny towns. Right now Indianapolis is looking amazing. I am ready to see it.

CUT TO:

William in his bedroom.

> WILLIAM
> Are you ready to see anything else?

CUT TO:

ROXY bites her lip.

> ROXY
> I would be lying if I said I don't want to see you.

> WILLIAM (O.S.)
> (Filtered)
> I shouldn't have left you.

ROXY looks down.

                    ROXY
          I understand, I didn't
          give you much choice.
          The question is, will
          you be there when I get
          back.

CUT TO:

WILLIAM is sitting up.

                    WILLIAM
          Just say the word and
          I'm there.

               ROXY (O.S.)
          (Filtered)
          I'll be home tomorrow.
          It's only six more hours
          of driving.

                    WILLIAM
          How do you want to work
          it?

CUT TO:

ROXY takes a huge breath

                    ROXY
          I better talk to my
          parents then I'll call.

               WILLIAM (O.S.)
          (Filtered)
          I missed you. I'm glad
          you're almost here.

ROXY closes her eyes.

                    ROXY
          I'm going to find a
          hotel and see you
          tomorrow.

                    WILLIAM
              Be careful, I need you
              all in one piece.

ROXY hangs up the phone, runs her fingers down
the receiver and shakes her head. She turns
toward her car then back to the phone, then
lifts the receiver and shoves another coin in
the phone. She almost hangs up, but then
dials.

CUT TO:

STEVEN'S LIVING ROOM - DAY.

Steven sits, feet up on the table, television
blasting in the background. He rolls his eyes,
uses the remote to lower the volume on the
television and picks up the phone.

                    STEVEN
              What?

                    ROXY (O.S.)
                 (Filtered)
              Maybe you mean who?

STEVEN runs hand through his hair.

                    STEVEN
              Are you home?

                    ROXY (O.S.)
                 (Filtered)
              Do you care?

                    STEVEN
              That's why I asked,
              princess.

CUT TO:

ROXY'S hand is pressed against her chest.

                    ROXY
          Why do you call me
          princess?

            STEVEN (O.S.)
          (Filtered)
          Because if you ever let
          me, that's how I'd treat
          you.

ROXY shivers

                    ROXY
          Why did you drive away
          that day?

CUT TO:

STEVEN sitting with his head back staring at
the ceiling.

                  STEVEN
          Did you ever think I was
          waiting for you to run
          after me?

            ROXY (O.S.)
          (Filtered, her voice lowered)
            Is that what you wanted?

                    STEVEN
          Why do you think I said it?

CUT TO:

ROXY leaning on the building.

                    STEVEN (O.S.)
               (Filtered)
               When are you due home,
               princess?

                ROXY
                Tomorrow.

                    STEVEN (O.S.)
               (Filtered)
               Where are you going to
               run?

ROXY licks her lips.

                    ROXY
               Where do you want me to
               run?

                    STEVEN (O.S.)
               (Filtered)
               I didn't ask the
               question for nothing.

                    ROXY
               I better go.

                    STEVEN (O.S.)
               (Filtered)
               I'll be here.

ROXY hangs up the phone and presses her
forehead to the receiver.

Chapter Twenty

THE TINGLING THROUGH HER BODY, the smiles, the glances and the holding of hands. Somehow after one of the worst nights together, they captured the magic, found common ground and though they didn't actually say the words, the implication they wanted to be together was definitely out there.

Now as she watched Drew walk around the SUV, they shared another one of those looks, the kind that made her heart flutter, her stomach swirl, even made her want to giggle as her cheeks heated.

With his computer case and bag of products in hand, he opened her door and held his hand out. "Are you ready for your meeting, Miss Holland?"

"I'm ready for you, Mr. Fulton." She put her hand in his and managed to get out of the car without tripping on her own feet.

"You're going to be the end of me." His gaze traveled over her.

"You always knew that, but I promise you will love every hour."

"Erin?" He leaned in closer.

She held her breath, maybe now he would kiss her first and a little noise escaped her throat.

"Do you want to hold the samples when we walk in?" His tone teased her.

She exhaled and tried to determine if she was going to kick him in the shin or laugh. "Are you sure that's what you want me to do?"

"That is absolutely not what I want you to do, but it will have to suffice for now." He handed her the plastic bag.

At least he admitted it and at least their trip turned around. They couldn't go on when they focused on all the bad, they had to remember the fun, and that's what she tried to bring on the ride. "Well, then while we're in our meeting, I'll make mental notes so I make sure I live up to what you are imagining."

"I'm sure you'll have no problem." He held her hand and closed the car door. "May I introduce you as my Director of Marketing?"

"Anything you want." She liked the way he pulled her close to his side as they walked toward the big, red brick building. "I'll say that later too, just in case you were wondering."

They made it to the sliding glass doors and in an abrupt move he turned to her. "So will I."

While her insides flipped over, she gave him a smile and a nod and they made their way inside.

Unlike the spa that buzzed with excitement upon her arrival, Multimodal Health was completely different. The interior seemed to be more like a hospital or doctor's medical center instead of the hip yet serene surroundings of their first stop.

Instantly upon their entrance, the whispers and points started. While these things were now accepted every time she went out, she also knew enough to be able to discern the difference between the excited amped up actions of fans versus those who felt she was an intrusion. The energy in this facility was definitely the latter.

Before they ever reached the front desk with some dour woman in scrubs sitting behind a computer screen, a woman in an ugly brown suit appeared almost out of nowhere.

"Mr. Abrams, follow me. Mr. Trusdale is expecting you." She stared down at their hands and corralled them away from the lobby and into a hallway.

As they made their way through the tangled web of corridors, she held Drew's hand tighter. The woman didn't even acknowledge her, strange. Even if someone didn't like her, she always got a look or a comment.

The woman gave one knock on a dark wood door and opened it into an extremely plain office with white walls, a lot of bulletin boards, and dark wood furniture. Everything about this place was brown and dark.

A man who matched the office to perfection stood up from the desk. Honestly, Erin had no description for him. If he were an extra in a movie, he would simply be called a man in an office.

"Mr. Trusdale, good to see you again." Drew let go of her and with his hand out, approached the desk.

Mr. Trusdale? Was this man a teacher or something? She followed Drew, but stopped upon noticing there was only one chair opposite the desk.

"Isaac, have a seat." The man kept his lips tight, gave Drew a perfunctory handshake and shifted his focus to her.

"Mr. Trusdale, I am sure the woman beside me needs no introduction, but may I present Erin Holland?" With only what she would call a manufactured smile, Drew motioned toward her.

Maybe the man was nervous. It wasn't unusual. People either shied away from her or glommed on to her, and wanting to make Drew look good, she gave the man a statue-winning smile and held out her hand. "Hello Mr. Trusdale, what a pleasure it is to meet you."

He nodded and held his hand to hers though he didn't really shake it. "Have a seat."

The three of them seemed to collectively glance at the only chair.

"Erin." Drew took hold of the back of the chair.

"You go ahead, I don't mind standing after our drive." She kept her tone upbeat. After walking in heels yesterday, standing for a while wouldn't be an issue.

"Amy," Mr. Trusdale groaned. "Please find another chair."

The woman who guided them here huffed, disappeared for a moment and then returned, banging a beat up blue cushioned chair into the office.

Drew rushed forward, grabbed the piece of furniture and set it in front of her.

Well, one good thing this trip would do was an amazing job of thinning out her wardrobe. First the shoes yesterday, followed by the suit, and after she spied the stains on the cushion, this suit would follow. As she sat, she attempted to hide a grimace.

"Well, let's get down to business." Drew cleared his throat. "When we last spoke, we discussed bringing in some products for post-surgery, a post-natal vitamin and a supplement specifically for men. I brought some samples."

That was her cue. Playing the part of spokesperson, she jutted out her chest, held up her bag, and swiped her hand under it as if putting the products on display. Yesterday a few smiles and some creative play with products netted Drew a tidy sum indeed. This would be a piece of proverbial cake, or in lab terms, as easy as popping a capsule.

Mr. Trusdale pursed his lips and held out his hand for the bag.

Since the man didn't like the smile or the sweet Erin, she went with her other strength and stood, took her time walking around the desk and personally handed the bag to the man, leaning way down and basically putting her breasts in his face. If she allowed Allan at the orchard, he would have had lunch with her cleavage, and all men were the same. "Here you go, this all sounds promising."

"You think this sounds promising?" He took the bag and turned away.

Maybe the man blushed and couldn't look at her. Tonight his wife would benefit from the erection he was most likely starting to sprout now. "I think it sounds very promising." She sauntered back around the desk, sat down and crossed her legs. A little wink in the man's direction helped her get into character.

"As someone on the consumer side, I have to say that I would be impressed with the wide range of offerings. They meld different thoughts on medicine and the desire to take a proactive approach to patient care." Remembering how Drew wanted to talk about the science and what not, she nodded and took her camera out of her bag. This meeting would be perfect in contrast to the first one. "But I don't want to take over the meeting. Drew knows all the particulars I don't. I am here as the Director of Marketing and official lab spokeswoman, and I'm putting together a video." With elegance, she passed the baton to Drew and held up the camera.

Drew's account stared at her.

"Just go about your conversation." She gave him a little wave and adjusted the focus.

"Actually, I have a question for you." At last, the man acted as if she existed.

"All right." She handed the camera to Drew. "I'm all ears. Well, not all ears at least not the good parts."

Mr. Trusdale's face didn't change expression, and she was giving him some of her best work.

He put the bag of samples down. "What I want to know is since when have you ever been on the consumer side of anything to have an opinion of what is carried in this medical clinic?"

Out of the corner of her eye she saw Drew shift in his seat.

"Excuse me?" Before she ripped this man apart and then put his sorry ass on her new and improved social media, she wanted to make sure she heard him correctly.

"I'm asking my patients to come in here and buy products that are not covered by their insurance, therefore I want to know how you, as someone who gets paid to spew whatever the company doling out checks tells you to spew, know what the consumer wants."

The strange thing was the man's tone didn't change one iota. He might as well have been asking her to sign an autograph as he was insulting her.

In an effort to properly prime herself for her next batch of spewing words, she inhaled. Then she caught two things in her peripheral vision, the camera and Drew. Instead of snap, she decided to truly answer the man's question. "With all due respect, Mr. Trusdale, companies and sponsors of all sorts pay actors large sums of money because at the end of the day the public does listen to our opinion."

Drew audibly exhaled and the heat within her body lowered a few degrees.

"So then, as the lab's spokesperson, why don't you tell me about these products?" Mr. Trusdale slapped the bag on his desk and motioned toward it. "Let's hear it from the one who knows how to sell."

While she sort of knew the Orchard's products and her own supplements, she hadn't studied the entire portfolio the lab had to offer yet. All she knew was that it was part of the Fluency Physician Line.

"Mr. Trusdale." Drew held up his hand.

"Drew, I can answer the question." Improvisation was something she was taught when she was still a pre-teen. In fact, in more than one scene in *Hollywood Stardust* both she and

Ryder improvised lines. Logan and Drew preferred to stay exactly with the script.

Once more, she pushed herself up from her seat and took her time walking around the desk. With her mind working in the background she leaned back and picked up the bag of products.

The room took on an electric silence, the same kind a studio possessed right before the snap of the clapperboard.

She titled her head and began take one and only.

"Let me make the blanket statement that just the fact a medical office would recommend certain supplements to me would make it feel like it was a prescription and therefore something I should take for my health. I would be more than thrilled that they were offering something other than traditional prescription medications which we know many of my colleagues have issues with." She turned the bag around to read what Drew brought with him and glanced at both men. What a compliant captive audience.

"The post-surgery capsules are a no-brainer. Not only would I want to end my convalescence as soon as possible and replenish my body with the nutrients it no doubt lost while someone cut into me, but..." for effect, she moved closer to the man, her leg bumping his chair, "...anything that could help me look as perfect as possible is something I would pop in my mouth. Especially, if it helps with any unsightly bruising."

Mr. Trusdale looked down at her leg and up to her face.

"Smooth skin, no matter where it's at, is critical." She cupped her hand around her mouth. "No matter where."

Before anyone could have a chance to interject, she continued. "The post-partum one is crucial. Anything that I could swallow that would make me feel normal after a human being came shooting out of my nether regions is something to take without a doubt."

"In fact, speaking of swallowing." She stood and kneeled down by Mr. Trusdale's chair. The man had turned positively pale. "Let's talk about the men's supplement. Sell these to the wives in their late thirties and forties for their men. It seems to me certain urges peak for females, while the men may taper off. I'm sure you totally understand what I mean. I'm sure you've experienced it yourself."

"Erin." From behind her, Drew growled.

"Before I leave you and the smartest man I know to your real meeting, I will only impart to you one last bit of my vast marketing knowledge." With Drew's tone and her little ploy of tease and denial not making this man froth at the mouth, she knew when it was time to head off stage, and she tossed the bag onto Mr. Trusdale's lap. "While you may think you're doing something for the goodness of humankind here, remember at the end of the day you are marking Drew's little gems up and making a tidy profit. Everything in life barrels down to the sale."

Her final words out, she stood, stomped over to Drew, collected her purse and camera and held out her hand. "May I have the keys please?"

Without any hesitation, he surrendered what she wanted.

Though his jaw was set, his nostrils flared, she saw something else there, lingering in the background. Amusement? Understanding? Well, no matter, she already did the damage. "I'll meet you in the car, right after I create a ruckus walking through the lobby."

Like when she played a role, she saw nothing but her mark, as she did exactly what she promised, and stormed through the facility and out the sliding glass doors with her head held high. On the flip side, her performance was worse than any hack actor, over dramatized and done purely for shock value. She went right to the SUV, got inside and turned on some music.

The classic rock both she and Drew preferred filled the car and she shut her eyes and put her hand over her mouth. She wondered if Drew knew she really tried. Since the moment she entered Organic Oasis yesterday until she walked out of Drew's meeting just now, she tried.

When he looked at her, he struggled, unable to see anyone but the girl who broke his heart. Why couldn't he remember the fun too? How did he fall in love with her in the first place if she was only evil? Why were they even on this trip if he couldn't remember some of the good?

For all these years, those were the memories that kept her going.

She stared out the front window. This town had the same look and feel of where they shot the carnival scene in *Hollywood Stardust* and her favorite morning ever.

"Drew." The sky was just lighting up and she had pulled him to the opening she found in the chicken wire fence the day before. "Here it is."

"You do know this is called trespassing, right?" Shaking his head, he had held the little flap further apart, let her slip inside the fairgrounds and followed.

"How can it be trespassing? We're filming here." She grabbed his hand and dragged him onto one of the main thoroughfares. "I say we're getting into character."

"All right, whatever works for you." He yawned.

She turned around, absorbing all the grandeur that was the fair. "It's really cool here." All they had seen was the inside of the arcade, though she got to walk through a carnival a few times for some establishing shots.

"Typical carnival."

"I wouldn't know what's typical." From the time she was eight years old she created a spectacle everywhere she went. It was easier not to go.

They looked at each other.

Only with Drew could she have a whole conversation and never say a word.

"Come on." Now it was his turn to drag her. "Let's see what there is to see."

Hand in hand, he took her past the stands that in a few hours would sell really fattening food she wasn't allowed to have, the Ferris wheel and the games that were impossible to win until they came to a big long building.

"What's this?" She wrinkled her nose at what appeared to be nothing but a barn.

"You know, fairs are also places for exhibits." As if on a mission, he led her around the side to a door chained by a padlock.

She watched while he found a little tool in his pocket and used it to pick the lock. "Drew, what are you doing?"

"Get ready to run." The lock snapped open.

"Why?" She grabbed his arm.

"In case this is alarmed." He untangled the chain from the door and pushed it open.

Her heart beating at break neck speed, she gasped and jumped ready for sirens.

Only a big, black empty space greeted them.

Without a word, he guided her inside. He closed the door behind them enveloping them in pitch dark and fumbled along the wall.

"Drew." She kept tight hold of him.

"Hold on. I know it has to be here."

A click echoed around her and then suddenly the entire space was illuminated by huge hanging models of the planets. Against the black background it was almost like they were standing in the solar system. "Oh, my god!"

"Amazing, isn't it?" They walked to the center of the room. Little exhibits lined the walls all about space and astronomy.

"You knew this was here." Her co-star loved all things planetary.

"When you were filming the other day, I wandered over. I thought it would be perfect to show you." He pointed up at the sun.

"This is creepy cool." The place was impressive enough to be a movie set for sure.

"I knew you would understand."

Still looking up, they both walked among the humongous planets.

"You know what else would be creepy cool?" Electric excitement bubbled through her.

"Enlighten me."

"What if the planets were really this big in the sky, or what if we had multiple moons." Just the thought of the universe gave her shivers.

"Miss Holland, that would indeed fit the bill." He laughed.

"It would be cool, too, though don't you think?" She stopped and rather than continuing to stare at the planets studied him. Since they began filming he'd changed, turned into more of a man.

"Are you sure you never did a sci-fi film?" He winked.

"Nope, not my genre. I was turned down for a couple of roles though. I guess I'm not the galaxy explorer type, I'll leave that up to you." She poked him in the side.

He stifled a chuckle and swatted her hand away.

"You know what I want to do?" Hiding out with only the universe as their witness was most freeing, and she stood in front of him.

"Slide around the rings of Saturn?"

"Well, as fun as that would be, I think I may want to go to Jupiter where it rains diamonds." She stepped closer and held her arms out. "I want to dance."

"Well, then we'll have to do so with only the songs of the stars as our music." He bowed, put one arm around her waist and held her hand.

"Stars play a very important part in our life." She let him lead her in a little dance. "It will be our song."

"Deal." He had pulled her in a little tighter. "I wish everyone got to see this side of my favorite star."

"I reserve it only for you." The same feeling of safety she always felt around Drew had encompassed her.

The song on the car sound system changed, jolting her out of her reverie.

Everyone, absolutely everyone, had some sort of preconceived notion of her.

In the case of this meeting, she proved Drew right. She couldn't be trusted with his business or him. If she left, he might be able to claim his life as Isaac Abrams again, with her, Isaac was gone.

She bent over, sure she would be sick. Drew never even tried to defend her and for the first time she couldn't even be mad, because she didn't even give him a chance.

At a knock on the car window her heart seized and she shot up to find him standing at the driver's side.

She pressed her hand to her chest and unlocked the doors.

It seemed to take forever as he opened the back door, put his computer case away, closed the back door and got inside the vehicle.

He hit the button to turn off the music, put his hands on the steering wheel and stared out the windshield without starting the car.

"Drew." She had to say something.

In a slow move straight out of a suspense film, he turned to her. His eyes narrowed like a hunter zoning in on his prey.

"Are we still going to go to a Bed and Breakfast?" She tried to use a sing-song voice. "Maybe work out some of the aggression?"

His only answer was a blink.

"Drew?"

He continued to stare.

"Did he place an order?" She bit her lower lip.

He exhaled, more like huffed, and she sort of expected fire to come out of his nose.

"Drew?" At last she dropped the cutesy act. "I have something to tell you."

When she thought she saw a slight nod, she continued. "I was bad, really bad and I'm sorry."

With her apology his features seamed to soften.

"Maybe on our next stop we can dance. The songs of the stars will be our music." Tears heated her eyes. If he didn't acknowledge one of the best times of her life she didn't know what she would do.

He faced front once more and turned on the car, backing up out of the space, the tires screeching as he pulled away.

"Drew?" She bit her nail. "Where are we going?"

"To the Bed and Breakfast." At last he spoke. "Don't say another word until we are inside the room."

"Drew." She winced at having said his name.

He slammed on his breaks. "I'm not eighteen anymore. When I say do not talk, I mean do not talk. Do you understand?"

She nodded and sat back in the seat.

He hit the gas, and she prayed his idea of a bed and breakfast wasn't dumping her at the uranium mine with no climax and then vanishing again.

<u>HOLLYWOOD STARBURST</u>

EXT. POCAHONTAS, IL, HIGHWAY 70 - DAY.

Roxy is in the car, music blaring and speeding
down the highway. From behind a sign, a
policeman on a motorcycle emerges, turns on the
lights and sirens and pulls her over.

                    ROXY
               What?

ROXY hits the steering wheel and pulls the car
over to the side of the road. Out of her
rearview mirror she watches the officer come
over to her side of the car. Before she rolls
down the window, she tries to fluff her hair
and licks her lips.

OFFICER leans down into the window.

                    OFFICER
               License and registration.

ROXY tilts her head and smiles.

                    ROXY
               Is there something
               wrong?

OFFICER taps his pen against his clip board.

                    OFFICER
               You were going 85 in a
               65 mile per hour zone.
               The documents please.

ROXY gets her license out of her purse and the
registration out of the glove box and hands it
to the officer.

                    ROXY
               You know, honestly,
               there is no one on the

road. I guess I sort of
lost track of the speed.

OFFICER inspects documents and writes down
information.

>   OFFICER
>   The signs are clearly
>   posted.

ROXY purses her lips, but then forces a smile
on her face.

>   ROXY
>   Well, I definitely
>   learned my lesson. Do
>   you think I can get off
>   with a warning?

>   OFFICER
>   The ticket is the
>   warning. You can thank
>   me that I caught you
>   before we were scraping
>   you off the pavement.

OFFICER hands the clipboard to Roxy to sign.

ROXY lifts the pen, but doesn't sign. Instead,
she turns to the officer.

>   ROXY
>   You know the road is
>   really empty, nothing
>   was going to happen.

>   OFFICER
>   (Low, slow voice)
>   Miss, you will need to
>   sign the ticket, or I
>   will be forced to take
>   you into the station.

ROXY presses her lips together, signs her name on the ticket, and thrusts the clipboard back at the officer.

OFFICER tears ticket off the pad and hands it to her.

                    OFFICER
          Where are you going?

ROXY doesn't look in the officer's direction and tosses the paper on the passenger seat.

                    ROXY
          Home.

                    OFFICER
          Take it nice and slow
          and read the signs.

THE OFFICER leaves. Again ROXY watches in the rear view mirror as the officer gets on his bike and takes off.

                    ROXY
          Jerk!

ROXY flips off the officer as he drives away and gets out of the car.

                    ROXY
              (Screams)
          Jerk!

ROXY kicks the tire then yells out in pain and falls down, clutching her ankle. She leans over and starts crying.

                    ROXY
              (Whining)
          I just want someone to
          make it better for once.

Chapter Twenty One

"HURRY UP." Drew opened the door to their suite. Since Grand Junction didn't seem too fond of Drew Fulton, he donned a baseball cap and sunglasses. He checked into the promised Bed & Breakfast under Isaac Abrams and guest while the said guest waited in the car without speaking. If Drew Fulton proved to be too much, Erin Holland would be over the top.

However, at the moment, he didn't care who he was or who she was. He was a man, a successful man, but anytime he found himself in the vicinity of Erin Holland, he turned into a drippy nosed hormonal teenager. Especially once she mentioned the morning they spent at the fairgrounds. It had to stop now or he would personally put her on the next plane to LA LA Land.

Carrying the picnic basket the owner insisted on packing him, Erin rushed inside the suite, stopped and gasped. "Oh."

Aside from ensuring they had everything private, including an entrance and a bath, he also opted for the best suite, complete with a balcony and all the trappings a B&B offered, comprising overstuffed calico sofas, a fireplace, and what appeared to be a four-poster canopy bed in the bedroom. "I take it the accommodations are to your liking?" He dropped their bags in the entryway and crossed his arms.

"It's incredible." She darted around the suite, put the picnic basket on the coffee table and smiled up at him. "It looks like a movie set."

He willed himself not to be sucked into the black hole that was her pretty pink lips upturned as if she wanted to please him. "We don't live in a movie." If she didn't know this already, he needed to be the one to tell her. In fact, he needed to explain a lot of things.

"Would you like something to eat?" She peeked in the basket. "We have a bottle of wine."

He gave her a slight shrug and didn't move from his spot by the door. She might be the actress, but he would take on the part of director.

Playing her part to perfection, she remained silent while she set out the food, opened the wine, and poured them each a glass. Once finished, she sat on the couch and patted the cushion next to her.

Not in any lifetime would he go to her. Well, at least not now. The line had been drawn.

"Drew." She pursed out her superpower, the lower lip of death. "I really am sorry."

He decided not to tell her he got the order, and the fact Mr. Trusdale took notes on some of Erin's points. As a side note, he also chose to leave out the part about how the client was always a jerk.

"For the record, I think Allan is a much better account, especially since you're custom making his product."

"Did I or did I not tell you to be good?" Though the conversation seemed like it took place several years ago, he distinctly remembered uttering the words. "Is it possible you could have just remained quiet?"

"I told you I was bad." She took one of the glasses of wine, stood and approached him. "Why are we here, if I didn't earn my prize?"

"I wanted to be here. So we're here." He stared down his nemesis.

"Are we going to do what we came here for?" She kept eye contact and offered him the glass of wine. "I promise from now on when you tell me to be good I will be, starting right now. In fact, if you give me the chance, I'll be exceptional."

"You need to learn how to listen. Not everyone is taken with Hollywood and stars." As he gulped down the wine, he allowed her to lead him back to the couch. He sat and put the glass on the table.

She stood before him and unbuttoned her suit jacket, peeled

the garment off and tossed it on the floor. "The question is, Mr. Fulton, are you taken with Hollywood and stars?"

Her breasts overflowed from the cream-colored silk camisole she wore under her jacket and his body produced the requisite reaction. "Lately, both have been making my life extremely difficult."

"Maybe you should let the star make your life a little more pleasurable." She shimmied out of her skirt, kicking it in the opposite direction of the jacket.

"Maybe you should have thought of that before you shoved a camera in my account's face." His eyes went right to her legs.

"Oh, I was a bad girl, and I was trying so hard to be good." Still in her heels, she walked around the table, removing the camisole and her bra, leaving her only in a barely there thong. She got on the couch and crawled over to him, positioning herself face down over his lap. "Maybe I need to be punished."

The sight of her rounded bottom made his mouth water. Strange, even though she was a star and everyone commented on her beauty, he knew deep down she only saw what she perceived as her flaws. Since the day he met her, he only saw her, the person beneath the star. "You want me to punish you?"

"I think you need to punish me." She propped up on her elbows and turned back to him. "Maybe if someone did as he wanted and punished me, we could focus more on the good than the bad."

Point taken. He tilted his head and grazed his hand over her smooth skin, considering her offer. If anyone ever needed a punishment, it was the woman slung over his knees.

"I think you are dying to punish me." She wiggled her wares at him. Goaded him. Dared him.

For once in his life with Erin Holland, he called her bluff, raised his hand and spanked her. The snap of his flesh hitting hers echoed through the room, the sting radiated up through his palm and with it the overwhelming sensation of gratification surged through him.

"Drew!" With wide eyes, she stared at him.

A perfect red imprint of his hand appeared on her perfect white skin, the color deepening with each passing second, like a brand or mark. Visible proof she was his.

He glanced at her.

"Do it again." Now she bit her lip.

The time of her calling the shots was over. Twenty years ago he left in defeat. Today, he would take command. "Don't tell me what to do again." Without any warning he gave her another slap.

"Ah." She lowered her head.

A matching handprint appeared on the opposite cheek. Two handprints marred her skin.

His handprints.

His call.

His woman.

"Drew?" Her tone rang with disbelief. Well, it was time she took him seriously.

"I don't remember giving you permission to speak." He punctuated his sentence with his third spank.

She let out a little squeak, but didn't say a word.

"We need to get a few things straight. You need to understand why you're being punished." Above all else, she needed to learn her actions had consequences. She always had done better with structure. Hence the fact she always made it to set, knew her lines, had perfect timing. The second she was let loose, she faltered. He couldn't be free and easy, he needed to take command and both of them would flourish. "Do you agree?"

At first, she made a noise as if to talk, but stopped and nodded.

"Very good. You learn fast." Along with punishment came reward. He leaned over and gave her a kiss on her shoulder.

She let out a moan.

"Now, Ms. Holland. You will not ever create a ruckus in front of my accounts again." He sat up and doled out another sampling of discipline.

"Oh, God." Her bottom shook, but she didn't attempt to move away.

"No talking." An additional spank told her he would follow through.

Rather than responding, she panted.

"You will not shove cameras in anyone's face." Another spank.

"You will not make suggestive comments." Another.

"You will not make any more dramatic exits." Another.

She cried out and squirmed. Her writhing hit him in all the right places. His control and power coupled with her submission only edged him on.

"Erin." Once more he gave her a soothing rub over her skin, hot and red, and swollen.

She clutched the couch cushion, but continued to grind against him. His erection grew.

"Erin." He called out her name again and slipped his hand between her thighs. Someone else was also aroused.

A little noise escaped her throat, no words, but she spread her legs ever so slightly.

Rather than give in and allow her a small amount of relief, he skimmed his fingers along her, light touches meant to torment, not satisfy.

His attention only made her open her legs further, twist around to obtain relief. With none to be found, she hit her fist into the couch.

"Is someone complaining?" He jerked his hand away. His erection now throbbed. The first and only time they were together everything happened fast, but he vowed tonight to take it slow, draw out all the pleasure. Above all else, he promised to take control down to every last detail.

In a move of defeat, she covered her head with her hand and let out a whimper.

Before releasing her, he needed to get something off his chest. "Lastly, after you went to such lengths to be with me, I demand you do not lie to me, and you will be as reliable as when you are on set." He gave her one final slap. "Have you learned your lesson?"

Like a good girl she nodded and raised her hand.

"Speak." He never wanted her as bad as this moment.

"Don't leave me again." Her voice came out muffled by the couch, but her tone was absolutely serious.

"Is that a demand?" Though he longed to pull her into his arms, he refused to lose the ground he'd gained.

"No, it's a wish."

Her statement hit him right in the chest. "Come here."

She moved, sucked in her breath and put her hand over her backside, but without complaint, she got into his lap and stared into his face.

He took hold of her chin. Basically nude, with her makeup smeared and her hair a disaster, he had never seen her so raw or beautiful. "You're mine."

Her lips parted, but rather than speak, she nodded.

He curled one of his hands behind her neck and pulled her in, their lips almost touching.

"Oh." A gasp escaped her throat.

At last, he gave into a different one of her wishes and kissed her first. He chose when to connect their lips, he set the pace, he opened his mouth and he sought out her tongue with his own.

She melted into him and let him take the lead.

In a sudden move, he broke the kiss and pushed her back.

"Drew?" Her eyes widened.

He decided to test his newfound power, remembering to give her plenty of direction. "I want you to stand up, stand in front of me and take off your thong, then go to the bedroom and pull down the blankets on the bed and wait for me in there."

As if she had to decipher his code, she tilted her head. "What are you going to be doing?"

"What I'm doing doesn't matter." With his jaw squared, he kept his tone even, yet strong. "I want you to do what I told you to do, in the exact order I told you to do it."

"What if I don't?" She hooked her fingers on the side of her thong.

He caught her wrist. "There will be repercussions."

With her mouth open, she stared into his eyes.

"You have five things to do." He pointed in the direction he wanted her to take.

For only a moment she paused, but finally she got off his lap. Never taking her focus off him, she stood in front of him and pulled her thong off. Between two fingers she lifted the flimsy piece of fabric.

He rubbed his hand over the bulge in his pants. "Drop them."

In less than a second, the thong fell to the floor, and she took slow steps to the bedroom, stopping at the entrance. "Where do you want me once I pull the covers back?"

"Sit at the edge of the bed." Out of the corner of his eye he watched her disappear into the room.

He waited a little longer than necessary, but at last he stood. For the first time he felt in control of both him and her.

She needed to learn a lesson and needed guidance. Before joining her, he collected the wine and their glasses. He was already a professor, now he would become a director as well, and he would make sure she followed every one of his cues.

HER STOMACH FLUTTERING, her heart speeding and her body in a state of want, Erin straightened the blankets and sat at the edge of the bed, her legs together, hands neatly folded on her naked lap.

She would do whatever he wanted if he would just kiss her again exactly like he did before. The kiss that told her that he did indeed want her.

He kissed her first.

Not only did he kiss her, he took command of her and the situation, called her his, and for the first time in her whole life, she wanted to obey and give in. Truth be told, she wanted to relinquish control.

Now she knew why she didn't allow him to kiss her all those years ago.

Plain and simple, she wasn't ready. Wasn't ready for the passion that traveled through him into her body, wasn't ready to admit there wasn't anyone else for her. At eighteen years old she was terrified to admit he was the one and he would always be the one.

Finally, he entered the room. His form filled the doorway and she sat up, straightened her spine and continued to wait. He set the wine on the side table and stepped in front of her.

Her gaze traveled over him. Still in his suit, with his tie perfectly knotted, he appeared to be a strong, sexy businessman. His erection tented his pants and made her mouth water. She almost reached for him, but stopped, choosing to look up at him for his next instruction.

"Do it." His tone came out forceful, reminding her of being on set with a director who knew exactly what he wanted.

When given the right direction, she knew how to perform. She reached for his belt, unfastening the buckle and then his pants. She allowed his pants to drop to the floor, pulled down his blue boxer briefs and revealed her prize.

The one night he made love to her everything moved at such speed, she barely got the chance to notice anything except the fact she wanted him. Now she took him into her hands, slowed down and stroked him, studying his smooth length, rigid with the same need she possessed. Impressive wasn't quite the word she would use for him, maybe magnificent would fit him better.

At her attention, he let out a moan. She didn't need a written script to know what he wanted next, and without any hesitation encompassed him with her mouth.

"Like that." He loosened his tie and unbuttoned his shirt.

Rather than acknowledging he spoke, she tended to her man, swirling her tongue over him, sucking and kissing his length, savoring his taste, especially after waiting twenty years.

"Yes." He practically hissed the word and grabbed her hair.

For the first time with any man, she wanted to dole out pleasure and not simply as a means to an end. His reactions to her, from moving with her to caressing to the side of her face, had her pressing her thighs together and squirming in an effort to alleviate some of her need.

His breathing increased, he twisted her hair in his hand. If he wanted, she would take him to the end. The image of him letting go aroused her further, and she took him deep, until he skimmed the back of her throat.

"Erin." He growled and grabbed her shoulders. "Stop."

Yes, she purposely ignored him, instead choosing to find out how far down she could take him.

"Erin!" He pushed her back.

His erection popped out of her mouth and stood straight out, tense, throbbing and wanting relief. "What do you want, Drew?" She reached up and twisted his tie around her fingers, pulling it out from under his collar and dropping it as she scooted back on the bed.

"I want you to lie still." He tore off his shirt, kicked away his pants and joined her on the bed. In an instant, his lips were on hers, and he cupped her breast in his palm. His fingertips teased her nipples, and she shut her eyes, relishing in the way Drew both took command of her body and worshiped it.

With agonizing slowness, he trailed his lips down her body, kissing her breasts, her side and even her hips.

Desire flowed through her. She had to have him soon. "Drew."

At last, he made his way between her legs.

The anticipation building, she tensed, held her breath.

Feather light, his fingertips grazed over her.

"Drew." She gasped out his name and twisted on the bed.

"Stay still." His voice vibrated through her, and he kissed the tops of her thighs.

"Oh, God." In an effort to give him a little encouragement in the right direction, she spread her legs.

He lifted his head.

"Drew?" Her sensitized body demanded attention. She balled her hands into fists and leaned up on her elbows.

"Did you hear me before?" Once more, his fingertips made their way to her center where he traced a circle right where she needed it most. His light touch only served to tease and tempt, but nothing else.

"About what?" She bit her lip.

"I told you not to move." He moved between her legs, but stared at her face. "Now I'm adding that you may not orgasm without my permission."

"What happens if I do?" The sheer fact he mentioned it made her body twinge.

He answered by moving his hand.

"How do I stop it?" Without even thinking, she bucked her hips up, but just as fast lowered them back to the bed. "Drew?"

"I suppose you'll have to figure that out. Now do as I say." As if dismissing her, he spread her legs further apart. "Tell me you understand."

Were they doing some sort of kinky role play? She heard about this type of thing, but never thought Drew was the type, but hell, she was game. "I understand." Like a good girl, she laid back down.

Her compliance was rewarded when he lowered his mouth between her legs.

Oh, she couldn't remember the last time a man tended to her in this intimate way, and definitely didn't have any memory of a man performing like Drew. No millimeter of her went without him kissing, tasting and fondling her. He used his fingers to delve inside her, heating her to the core.

Throughout her entire body her arousal grew, her muscles tensed and she fought the urge to move with him for fear he would stop. "Drew. God." Her mind erased everything except how he lapped her up as if she were some great delicacy for the tasting.

The second he turned his focus to the one bundle of nerves designed to produce the orgasm she was supposed to control, she couldn't hold back. "Oh, I'm there." She arched her back. Her body teetered at the edge, ready to fall.

Then everything stopped.

"Ah!" As her body pulsed on nothing with no relief, she was left empty and wanting. She twisted the sheets in her fist. "Drew!"

Like a parent chastising a child, he shook his head.

"Drew!" The game wasn't fun anymore.

"You only listen when you want to. That's not acceptable anymore." A sly smile grew over the mouth that should be on her.

"Drew." She slapped the bed. "What are you doing? Make love to me."

"When you listen." He stood and walked over to the nightstand where he put the wine.

In pure and utter disbelief, she watched while he stroked his own erection, then poured some of the drink and sipped it down.

"Drew." She hugged her knees to her chest.

"Do you want some?" He held the glass up.

"Not of that." In an attempt to look sweet, she widened her eyes and gazed up at him.

"The wine is ever more delicious when combined with the taste of you." Barely giving her a glance, he continued to sample the beverage.

No, this wasn't a game. He wasn't giving in, and she would have to work for what she wanted. "I'll listen. Tell me what to do."

He took another sip of the wine and finally put the glass down. "Lie back."

In an instant, she did as he instructed.

With measured steps he returned to the bed. "Do you remember what I told you before?"

"Yes."

He positioned himself on top of her, giving her a deep kiss. "Then tell me."

His erection brushed against her and she swallowed. "Don't move and don't orgasm without your permission."

"You always did have an amazing talent for memorizing." Only his tip entered her. "Do you think you can comply?"

She whimpered. "I can."

"Good." He thrust into her.

At the sudden fullness, she cried out. Pleasure coupled with an insatiable craving consumed her, heightening with every stroke he gave her.

Though she longed to move with him, wrap her legs around him and grind away to her orgasm, she willed her mind and body to do as he demanded and stay still.

"Erin." He took hold of her chin and melded his mouth to hers. Once more his fingers found her breasts where he tweaked and teased her nipples. Every one of his actions was designed to bring her closer.

Needing to stave off the euphoria building inside her, she closed her eyes and used an old movie trick where she flipped her point of view. Rather than focusing on her end, she zeroed in on Drew using her body for his pleasure. After all, he told her not to move, not to come, and now he drove into her, his movements increasing, his breath hitching. Damn, this was worse. She wanted him to use her like this. "Oh, Drew. I can't..."

"Not yet." His tone warned her not to cross him. He hooked his arm under her leg and lifted it over his shoulder, burrowing himself deep inside her.

Her body took off on its own as his hard thrusts hit her in all the right places. "Drew, please."

"No." He panted.

"Help me." She prayed she could keep her word and had to show him she could do it, yet the tension built, stretched thin, any second she would have to snap. Before she gave in, broke her word, disappointed him, she tried anything to stop the inevitable, taking long breaths, thinking of everything but the way the man she waited for made love to her, contracting her muscles, then trying to relax them.

"I'm going to come." He plunged into her, tormenting her further. "God, I'm there."

"Drew." Did he forget about her? She would never make it once he came, she would have to join him. Still, she restrained herself. Her body broke out into a heated sweat as she held back and trembled. "Please."

"Now." He kissed her.

With his permission, she let go. At last, she reached the end she sought, her body caught up in those euphoric pulses that matched her mates. "Yes." She relished in the ecstasy, and in the way the heat of his passion radiated inside her.

The pulses slowed and turned into ripples, and her body went weak from the exertion.

The way he panted and lowered himself on top of her told her he felt the same. "Baby." He wiped her hair out of her face and kissed her once more.

"Drew?" Her voice came out breathless, and she wanted to drift away.

"Yes." He kissed the back of her hand.

"May I touch you?"

"Absolutely." He gently moved to one side, but gathered her up in his arms.

At last, she opened her eyes, smiling at the way he looked down at her. She pressed her palm to his face. "Drew."

"Yes." He covered them up and held her tighter.

The bigger picture, everything that just happened, came into focus. "I'm going to listen, and I'm going to keep my promises."

"Erin."

She watched the way his lips moved when he said her name. "Yes."

"I'm going to be your man."

Tears surfaced in her eyes, but she didn't try to stop them. Instead, she wrapped her arms around him, kissed him and then hid her face in his chest.

"What's wrong?"

She looked up at him. "I just wish I learned twenty years ago." Her chest ached every time she thought about all those years. "I wasn't ready for what I felt for you.'

"We have now." He swept his lips over hers. "All right?"

She nodded and held on hoping now meant the future as well.

<u>HOLLYWOOD STARBURST</u>

EXT. POCAHONTAS, IL, PHONE BOOTH - DAY.

ROXY is sitting in a phone booth, her foot up
and crying.

>   CHARLES (O.S.)
>   (Filtered)
>   Is your ankle swollen?

>   ROXY
>   (sniffs)
>   Yes and now it's turning
>   purple.

CUT TO:

CHARLES' bedroom.

CHARLES is reading a first aid book.

>   CHARLES
>   The best thing to do is
>   elevate your ankle and
>   put ice on it. You also
>   need to stay off your
>   foot.

>   ROXY (O.S.)
>   (Filtered)
>   How can I stay off my
>   foot? I have to get home
>   tonight. I'm almost out
>   of money, I have to try
>   and salvage anything
>   with school, William,
>   Steven, my life! I
>   can't drive like this.

                    CHARLES
          Calm down, Roxy. Why
          didn't you call William
          or Steven?

CUT TO: ROXY

ROXY wipes her nose and shrugs.

                    ROXY
          They said to call if I
          needed help, but I can't
          call them.

                CHARLES (O.S.)
          (Filtered)
          Why not?

ROXY shakes her head.

                    ROXY
          I didn't know who to
          call first.

                CHARLES (O.S.)
          (Filtered)
          Too bad you didn't
          figure that out before
          you arrived home.

                    ROXY
          I thought once I saw
          them I would know.

Silence takes over the phone.

                    ROXY
          Charles?

CUT TO: CHARLES

CHARLES is still reading the first aid book.

                    CHARLES
          You really shouldn't put
          pressure on that ankle.

               ROXY (O.S.)
          (Filtered)
          Will you help me?

CHARLES wipes his hand over his face.

                    CHARLES
          I'll have to get them,
          both of them. I'm not
          going to make this
          decision for you. Is
          that what you want?

               ROXY (O.S.)
          (Filtered)
          I think so.

                    CHARLES
          You need to know,
          Roxy. You can't keep
          doing this.

CUT TO: ROXY

ROXY leans against the phone booth wall with
her eyes closed.

                    ROXY
          What would you do?

                    CHARLES (O.S.)
                  (Filtered)
                  It doesn't matter what I
                  would do. What matters
                  is you and William and
                  Steven and ending this.

ROXY mumbles something to herself.

                    CHARLES (O.S.)
                  (Filtered)
                  What did you say?

                        ROXY
                  There's already too much
                  pressure, I shouldn't
                  put any on my foot.

                    CHARLES (O.S.)
                   (Filtered)
                  Tell me exactly where
                  you are and we will get
                  you.

                        ROXY
                  I'm at the Lost Trail
                  diner in Pocahontas.

                    CHARLES (O.S.)
                  (Filtered)
                  All right. Stay there,
                  see if they'll give you
                  some ice and let you put
                  your foot up.

                        ROXY
                  Okay, you're coming too,
                  right?

                    CHARLES (O.S.)
                (Filtered)
                 Someone has to be the
                 brain.

                         ROXY
                (Let's out a little laugh)
                 Thank you.

                    CHARLES (O.S.)
                (Filtered)
                 I have a lot of work to
                 do. Stay put and we'll
                 be there.

CLICK OF PHONE HANGING UP.

ROXY looks at the receiver.

                         ROXY
                 I said why can't it be
                 you?

Chapter Twenty-Two

WORK. FOCUS. CONCENTRATE. Drew stared at his computer screen, but nothing he read sunk in. After a night and morning of making love to Erin, he was toasted, a perfect happy golden brown with just the right amount of melted butter. He would never view his morning erection the same way again, and he better start getting up when Erin did or he would be late to work every day.

"Drew, I put some butter and jam on your toast." Picture perfect in his white button down, panties and nothing else, Erin sashayed into the room holding a plate.

Speaking of buttery toast. His mind cleared as he watched her come over. Only minutes before she'd presented him with a mug of coffee. Apparently, the owner of the bed & breakfast liked sending baskets of food to rooms.

"Do you mind if I join you?" She eyed the cushion with his pad of paper on the couch next to him.

"I would love it if you joined me." In a flash, he swept away the unused office supplies.

Her smile shone and with her plate in hand, she cuddled up on his side and lifted a triangle of toast to him. "They have blackberry jam, your favorite."

He took a bite, the creamy butter, the tangy sweet jam, the bread with a bit of crunch all fed to him by one gorgeous star with bare legs who was to be much more tasty than the delicacy she created.

"Oh you have a little butter on your lip." She leaned up on her knees and kissed him.

The only strength he possessed was enough to let out a moan, but even after making love to her twice this morning, a spark of arousal ran though him with her attention.

"Is it all right if I watch you work?" She fed him another bite and put her head on his shoulder.

Yes, work. He was working. The schedule blocked out time for his work. "Sure, I'm just answering some emails."

"I checked my email before. Is that all right?" She rubbed her fingers over his jaw.

"You need to do whatever you need to do." Before delving into the emails he needed a little fortification and he turned and kissed her. More than a peck, less than something that would wind up with them in the horizontal position.

"Do you still want to walk around the town today?"

The way she gazed up at him made him forget his name, an easy task since he answered to two now. "I thought before we get on the road we could walk around the antique mall down the street." They probably needed to do something other than make love and work. Well, they needed to do something other than work. Truth be told, he wasn't working, he was staring at a screen until he had the chance to stare at her. "In fact, why don't we get going?" No sooner were the words out of his mouth than his phone rang.

Erin swooped over scooped up his phone and handed it to him. "I'll go finish getting ready sir, and you take your phone call."

"All right." He hit the button on his phone and watched her leave. As she sauntered back into the bedroom, she slipped his shirt off leaving her completely nude. "This is Drew."

"Cool, but can I have your other personality and speak to Isaac?" His production manager, James, laughed into the phone.

"Yes, as soon as I switch brains." Somehow he had to get his act together. He forced himself up and rifled through his briefcase until he found his supplements. With all his activity he had to be depleted. "What's going on?"

"We went backorder on five different SKU's and we are getting phone calls from retailers wanting to carry Hollywood Glow."

"How is any of that possible?" Before he left, he checked the stock levels personally and Hollywood Glow didn't exist yet. He piled up the capsules in his hand. Maybe double wasn't good enough.

"Our marketing department posted a picture of you and her on her social media. The photo went viral. It has been the top story on chargge.com for a day and a half. Where have you been?"

Drew shoved the capsules in his mouth and backed up, peeking in the bedroom to spy Erin getting ready. He supposed telling James that he was sleeping with the marketing department would not be an appropriate response. "Well, now we know social media works. Send me an email with what we're out of and get it into production, and let's start a waiting list for Hollywood Glow."

"How are the formulations going? Every day we don't have something on stability testing is another day we don't have a product to sell for the line."

Drew wondered if maybe he needed to get James a black cloak and a sickle. Stability testing would take three months, and that was after they had a product they wanted to produce. At best these projects took six months to a year. "Get me the emails and let's try to stay in stock on what we have on our shelves. Call me if there are any more issues."

"Aye, Aye." James hung up.

Drew's mind spun as he considered what happened. Though selling well and fast was incredible, amazing, backorders could ultimately hurt business, not to mention people wanting a product that wouldn't be available for quite some time. His chest tightened. What if they couldn't fill the demand? What if his current accounts bccamc angry? What about their production schedule?

The damage had already been done, so now he needed help and without a thought he ran into the bedroom. "Erin!"

"Drew!" Now in a form fitting pink sheath dress, Erin ran out from the bathroom. "Are you all right?"

He stopped and took her in. Every time she entered a room, the world changed.

"Oh, my God." She pressed her hand to chest. "Is this outfit all right? Did you want to choose something?"

"You're gorgeous. The dress is gorgeous." He held his arms out.

Without any hesitation, she went to him and wrapped her arms around his neck. "What's going on in that brilliant mind of yours? Is work all right?"

"The lab is busy. We have some items that went on back order and nearing backorder and we didn't plan for it." The simple act of telling her only amped up the ulcer that wanted to start. What if he made a mistake and couldn't provide for her?

"Well, isn't that wonderful." She stood up on her tiptoes and gave him two kisses on his lips.

"You think it's wonderful?" Though he stared into her eyes, he allowed his hand to travel down her waist to the delicious swell of her backside.

"Yes, as wonderful as the way you're copping a feel." In what had become her signature move, she brushed the back of her hand against his cheek. "As wonderful as the fact that we're finally here with each other."

Her words tempered the anxiety a small amount. Needing time to clear his mind and to be with Erin, he didn't want to change their plans. "Let's go walk over to that antique mall."

"I'm ready." She donned a large pair of sunglasses.

Following her lead, he also put on some sunglasses, grabbed her hand, and for the first time they went out in public truly together.

The crisp, sunny day welcomed them. Grand Junction was a nice little ski town. He guided them up the street to the antique mall and opened the door for her. "We also have people calling for Hollywood Glow."

"Now that is fantastic news." She kept hold of him as they made their way inside.

"We don't have a product line yet." Maybe he needed to remind her.

"Which direction should we take?" She took her sunglasses off then reached up and removed his, putting both pairs in her purse.

"I like your idea of having a system of products and having the film theme throughout, but we aren't even in development yet." Once more, he felt panic coming on, and he swallowed. "It takes months to make a product and then stability testing. You haven't even picked containers yet." He broke out into a sweat. "We're selling to empty shelves. We don't have product."

"Drew." She stood in front of him.

He stared down at her, but all he saw was his failure. Along the way he got caught up in Hollywood, fame and his business complications. Now he would pay. Every rule he put in place he threw to the wayside to get his second chance.

"Do you give me permission to offer a suggestion?" Her big gorgeous blue eyes widened.

"It's our line." The voice coming out of his mouth didn't even sound like him. Not wanting to appear as a lunatic, he led her over to one of the booths with antique appliances.

"Do you have some products that haven't been released, but are ready now and not spoken for? Then we can come out with some big hero products when *Hollywood Starburst* releases." The simple question left her mouth while she studied a vintage toaster. "Look Drew, this is like the toaster on that commercial for bagels. It would look perfect on the counter."

Everything around him blurred as a solution focused. "Erin."

"Oh, no!" She spun toward him. "Am I not supposed to put things on the counter?"

"What?" Where did her panic come from? He quickly texted James and Bambi for the information he needed. "Do you understand what you've done?"

"Did I break the rules? I thought it would be romantic to have something we bought together in the house, your house." She pressed her lips together and her eyes glossed over.

"No." He cupped her glorious face in his hands. "I think you saved my business."

She furrowed her brow. "I did?"

"I have some formulations and you can choose what you like. At least it will give us something to launch with." He kissed her. "Together, you and I can work on the star products just like you said."

"So you're not mad about the toaster?"

"Mad?" Unsure where she got that idea, but wanting to prove he was anything but mad, he grabbed the toaster. "Erin, you and I need to have this toaster. It'll be our toaster for our toast."

Her patented smile lit up her face. "I hope I can make toast as good as the lady at the bed and breakfast."

"I have no doubt." With a new conviction and new ideas running through him, he put his arm around her waist and continued their trek through the mall. "I'll call the lab and have James send a list of what we have and we can start choosing products. Hopefully, when we visit the farm in New Mexico we'll find something there too."

"This is so exciting. I can hardly wait." She pointed across the way. "Drew, may we look over there?"

"If that's what you'd like." Still giddy and with his thoughts wandering in a million different directions, he simply motioned forward.

"What would you like?" She brought him over to a rack of different bandanas and gazed up at him.

In an effort to keep the sexy going, he raised his eyebrows.

The smile never left her face and she stood up on her tiptoes and kissed his cheek. "I'm sure we'll have time before we have to get back on the road." She put her fingertip to his lips. "If that is indeed what you want?"

"You never have to worry about me wanting that." While Erin shopped, he took his opportunity to finally glance around the large antique mall with the little booths set up for each individual vendor. He also noticed that even though the place was pretty barren for the late morning on a workday, a few of the people milling about glanced over at them, pointing and whispering.

He supposed between his choice in women and the choice to reveal his identity, he needed to get used to it. Still, he pulled Erin closer in an attempt to shield her. They should be allowed to buy a toaster and some doodads without an audience.

"Do you think we should get one that says Colorado on it, so he has a souvenir?" Erin chose a bandana with pictures of mountains and the name of the state.

"Souvenir?" He glanced at the bandana but continued to watch the people watching them. More seemed to congregate.

"Then again, blue is his color. Maybe we should get them both? I think he'd like that." She chose a second strip of fabric. "Is that all right?"

"Who are we buying what for?" Along the way they became a we. With all those eyes on them, he stopped from bending down and kissing her, choosing instead to reposition them once more. The way the two of them were huddled together there was no doubt they were together.

"Beaker." She held each of her selections up to him.

No matter which direction he looked, it seemed as if there were strangers staring at them. More like gawking. In fact, a woman even pointed at them.

"I called the dog hotel and they let me talk to him. I hope you don't mind, but I asked them to make sure that he got an extra cookie cause I wanted one to be from me. The people there are very nice and told me they would play some of my movies for him so he hears my voice."

"Get whatever you want, Erin. Maybe we should go." No matter where he looked there seemed to be strangers staring at them.

"Drew. I'm sorry. I didn't mean to call the dog hotel without your permission. I've been doing it every day to check on him. I'm sorry."

One of the onlookers lifted their phone, the typical stance for someone taking a picture.

"Stop!" On automatic, he pushed Erin aside and rushed across the space to the woman and held up his hand.

"Drew!" Erin ran after him.

The woman gasped and put her hand down. "I'm sorry."

He opened his mouth, but Erin collided with him, wrangled his arm once more and faced the lady. "Did you want a picture?"

As if she were about ready to burst into tears, the woman's lower lip shook, but she managed a nod. "I'm a huge fan, and I couldn't believe when I saw the two of you together."

It seemed as if the entire population of Grand Junction, Colorado gathered to watch the display.

"Well, we thank you, but as you see Drew isn't quite used to being in the public eye anymore, however, I'm sure we could give you a little photo op." Keeping hold of him, she began signing autographs from the pens and papers that seemed to materialize out of thin air.

When she elbowed him, he took his cue and also signed the papers, nearly putting Isaac down a few times.

"All right." Like a pro, Erin got the entire situation under control, answering questions, and joking with the crowd. For a finale, she wrapped her arms around him. "It's picture time."

No less than fifteen people lifted their phones and snapped their image.

At last, he was the guy, the one by Erin's side. Through the years he watched various men take this position, hating each one of them for standing where he should be. Now with the title his, he didn't know what to do, how to handle it. Sweat broke out over him, and after a couple of minutes he leaned down to her ear. "We need to go, now."

Erin held her hand up. "Thank you all. We have to go now."

Without bothering to glance at the price tag on the toaster or the bandanas, he pulled out some bills from his wallet, and handed them to the first woman as they left the building.

They didn't speak as they returned to the bed and breakfast. Once inside, Erin glanced at him, put her hand over her mouth and ran into the bedroom.

"Damn it." While she fixed his career, he must have ruined hers. He set down their purchases, rubbed his hand over his face and followed her, finding her in the bathroom sitting at the edge of the tub with her face hidden in her hands.

He took his place next to her. Was it his place? "Erin."

She sniffed and looked up, but not at him. "I'm so sorry Drew."

"For what?" Though he longed to take her in his arms, he resisted. Instead, he grabbed the edge of the cool porcelain. After having their pictures taken and being with him in public, he was ready for her to drop the bomb.

"I don't know what I'm doing." She wiped her eyes.

How did he end up in a rewind of twenty years ago? Before he had a chance to tell her to stop, he didn't need to hear this again, she continued.

"I insisted on the toaster, I just assumed I could decorate your house, I called the dog hotel multiple times, and each time I made sure Beaker had something special. Then with that whole photo situation, I took control when I should have let you do what you wanted. I just didn't want you or me or the lab getting a bad name." With her outburst, she grabbed onto him and burst into tears.

As he tried to digest her words, he took her into his arms and shook his head. Did the picture upset her? What had he done to cause her to be sobbing in his arms? "I want you to decorate the house and call the dog hotel and think about me and the lab."

She wiped her face on his shirt and lifted her face up to his.

"I didn't want them taking our picture and then having you see it somewhere and think no one would believe we are together." His jaw tightened.

"Can't we let it go ever? I thought we were together, finally." The tears continued to stream out of her eyes. "I want the world to know."

He pulled her in and connected their mouths, her lips salty from her crying, but still delicious.

"Do you want me?" Her voice came out barely a whisper.

"That's all I've ever wanted." He answered the question, though she always knew he wanted her. With his fingertips, he wiped her eyes.

"Tell me what I need to do." The tears welled up again.

"Start by explaining why you keep asking for my permission on everything." Between backorders, product lines, pictures and still coming down from simply being with her, he didn't have time to focus on her strange behavior until now.

"After yesterday I thought that's what you wanted, but I don't know if I'm any good at this outside the bedroom." She bit her lip. "Don't you want me to be docile and have you make all the decisions?"

The proverbial light bulb flashed on and he exhaled. What he needed he gained yesterday. He needed to be a man, take control and draw the lines. If he wanted Erin, he had to know how to keep them both happy and that included a definite direction. "I want Erin. I don't want Erin playing a role. I do want the Erin who thinks enough about me and the lab to take over and make sure I don't ruin publicity. I told you yesterday what I wanted."

Once more she grabbed his shirt and wiped her nose. "I do have to admit I sort of wanted to know how naughty I had to be in order to get another spanking."

A jolt ran through him at her admission. "I think ruining one of my favorite shirts would be cause for a little discipline." Needing to make her smile, he leaned up and fished a dollar bill out of his wallet.

She slid to his side and watched him create his intricate folds.

He finished off the little piece of art and held it out to her.

"I still have the flower you made me in my wallet." At last, the tears stopped. She took the little folded heart and pressed it to her chest. "I guess we just have to get used to us again."

"Yes, we do." With her in his arms, he stood up. They still had a lot of work to do to be together, even if neither of them wanted to admit it.

INT. TERRA HAUTE, IN, INSIDE THE BMW – LATE
AFTERNOON.

Steven is driving, Charles is in the passenger
seat with a map, William is in the back.

WILLIAM leans up and sticks his head in between
the seats.

>   WILLIAM
>   So how much longer until
>   we get there?

>   STEVEN
>   What are you five years
>   old?

>   WILLIAM
>   No, I'm worried about
>   Roxy. I wish she
>   would've called me to
>   tell me she was hurt.
>   Last I spoke to her she
>   sounded amazing, and we—

WILLAM cuts himself off and moves back into his
seat.

STEVEN adjusts the rearview mirror.

>   STEVEN
>   And we what?

CHARLES lifts the map.

>   CHARLES
>   We should be there in
>   just over an hour.

>   STEVEN
>   STEVEN

                    Quiet Chuck, William was
                    enlightening us.

WILLIAM puts his hands behind his head.

                         WILLIAM
                    When she returned I was
                    going to go see her.

                         STEVEN
                    (Smiles)
                    Interesting.

WILLIAM puts his hands down.

                         WILLIAM
                    What is?

                         CHARLES
                    I'm glad I stopped for
                    some first aid supplies.
                    Depending on the
                    swelling, it will be
                    good to get a bandage on
                    that ankle.

                         WILLIAM
                    What - is - interesting?

                         STEVEN
                    Well, you may have been
                    going to see her, but
                    last I spoke to her she
                    was going to come see me
                    when she arrived home.

Silence takes over the car. Steven and William
glare at each other.

                         CHARLES
                    Last I spoke to her, she
                    was injured and didn't

want to call either one
of you for help.

    STEVEN
Gee, I wonder why she
couldn't call one of
us? I mean if she was
going to come to me, and
William was going to go
to her, why on earth
wouldn't she call one of
us?

    WILLIAM
(Lowers voice)
She doesn't know what to
do.

STEVEN puts his hands at ten and two on the
steering wheel and shakes his head.

    STEVEN
Maybe she knows exactly
what she is doing.

Chapter Twenty-Three

"YOU KNOW, IF PEOPLE COMPLAIN about it being too crowded in the city, they should just drive from Grand Junction to New Mexico and see the wilderness." Erin stared at the perfect blue sky, the pristine mountains and the greenery. It seemed as if they were traveling through an extremely long movie set painted to look like the outdoors. "Isn't it weird that there's all this vast space? Why did no one ever settle right here? What made them decide a city should be somewhere else? What was it like when they built the road? Did no one ever think maybe hey let's put a building here?"

"Are we waxing philosophical now?" Drew held his hand out.

"Drew." Thankful they finally reached the point where he wanted to hold her hand. She slid over in the seat and took his offering. "Why do you think they never built anything here? Don't you think it's strange?"

"Maybe we shouldn't have watched that horror movie last night." He let out a laugh.

"You weren't complaining when I hid my face in your chest." With a little knowing chuckle of her own, she slid closer. "Then again, you weren't complaining when I moved lower either."

"You're a bad girl." He quickly glanced at her.

"What do you plan on doing about it?" Since their little discipline session, Drew had changed. Yes, he was the Drew she wanted and needed, but now ramped up. He was still the man who would watch an old-fashioned movie with her and get a little misty eyed, but then he would be the man who would carry her into the bedroom and take full control while he made love to her. She loved seeing the side of him that took no prisoners and told her what to do. The whole thing was sexy.

A smile took over his face. "If I were you, I would be good."

"Ohh. I will try." Her body tingled at the thought of later tonight in the hotel.

"You will do more than try, you will do it." His tone lowered and he faced her.

"Don't look at me like that. We'll be late to your lecture and I would never, ever want to make you late, boss." She bit her lip.

"You are naughty." He leaned his head back on the headrest. "Behave, I'm trying to get into the mindset of talking about stabilizing polyphenols."

"Oh, are you stressed? Maybe I can help in my own naughty way." A thought on how they could pass the time entered her own mind and she reached down and massaged his thigh. "There's no one around for miles and I can take care of my man so he will be all relaxed by the time he has to step in front of those eager young college students."

"You know you are every man's fantasy." He rolled the seat back a little.

"I only want to be your fantasy." Her own body heated with the way his erection grew, tenting his suit pants.

"The entire time you're talking, I want you to picture how hot you make me every time I get to taste you." She ran her hand over him, leaned down and unfastened his belt buckle.

A bump in the road jostled her hand, but she kept her focus and pulled down his zipper.

"Oh shit," Drew growled.

For a split second she thought something unfortunate happened in Drew's pants. Hell, she wouldn't make him feel bad if that's how much she turned him on, but with no evidence and the car pulling over to the side of the road, she lifted her head. "Drew!" Her chest tightened and she grabbed his arm. "What's wrong?"

"Looks like a little engine trouble." His voice came out even and unconcerned. He turned the car off and tried turning it on again.

Nothing happened.

Twice more, he repeated his actions to no result.

Everything in the car seemed to have stopped. "Drew!" Her breath came short. This wasn't being two miles away from a spa. They were literally in the middle of nowhere. There wasn't even a telephone pole. Did they even still have telephone poles? In any case, there was nothing. "We're stranded!"

"We're going to be fine. I promise." He zipped up his pants, fastened his belt, kissed her, and opened the door.

"Wait!" Adrenaline and panic surging through her, she managed to catch his arm and pull him back.

"I need to check the car." The vision of calm and collected, he gave her another kiss.

"Don't leave me." She held on tight. "There's a reason there's no civilization here."

"I'm just going to look at the engine." After one more kiss, he untangled himself from her and got out of the car.

She watched him do the man thing where he opened the hood, shielding him from her. Again, she glanced around. There really was nothing here. Not even a bird. Without even thinking, she grabbed her phone out of her purse and decided to check her email.

A bit of bile rose in the back of her throat when she saw an email that came in the day before from Rick Southern, the slimy agent, with the subject *Things are warming up*.

With Drew still diagnosing the car, she opened the email.

> *Well, well Ms. Holland, seems as if your star still wants to shine. Social media is looking good, and from the looks of the latest Internet gossip, you and Drew are doing well. I took the liberty of hinting at your project and already have some bites. Come back with something amazing and your star won't only shine, it will blaze you back to the top.*
> *Give me an update and let's meet when you return from your road trip.*
> *Rick*

Her first instinct was to go tell Drew. They were an amazing team, sharing ideas. If they banded together in both their businesses, they would be unstoppable. Once their reality show came to fruition, Hollywood Glow would quite literally go super nova. Look what happened with just a couple of social media posts.

She hit her leg. No way could she take the chance and mention this to him. They were too new and had too much baggage. In the antique mall, he still seemed skittish about being recognized, not to mention he first turned down a tiny role in *Hollywood Starburst*. When she revealed her project, he would see how they would benefit and work together and be together.

Wanting to see what Rick referred to before Drew saw, she tried to go to the web browser on her phone, her heart seizing at the error message indicating no cellular connection.

"Drew." Though she went to scream, her cry came out more of a garbled squeak. A flash of every horror movie she had ever starred in, or seen. went through her mind. Before stepping outside to join Drew, she retrieved her camera. Documentation of any strange occurrences was vital both for posterity and their show.

One day she would remember not to wear heels in these situations and she tiptoed around the car, breathing a sigh of relief at the sight of her man hunched over the car. Focused on his unintentional sexy pose, she hit record.

"Are you okay?" Drew's voice came out strained as he reached inside the engine.

"We don't have any internet or cellular connection. I think this trip is determined to make us live off the grid." She stood by him. "Do you know what's wrong?"

"I hope we have a flashlight." He pushed back from the car. "You're filming this?"

"I like watching you work. It will make for good b-roll for my video." Though the truth, she still wished she could tell him everything. "Here, I think I can help and get the shot at the same time." With a quick flip of a switch the light shone on the front of the camera.

He pointed to where he wanted the light. "How is this part of a video for the lab?"

Ad-lib. Her mind worked fast. "Well, you already came out as an actor, so I think showing your many facets may be an excellent addition to my cinematic masterpiece." She nodded to herself. "Also, maybe it will be for my private collection."

He chuckled. "Maybe we should add to the private collection."

"Anything you say." She slid against his side.

"Keep that thought and aim right here." He motioned to some doodad.

For quite some time, he fiddled with the engine parts, returned to the inside car and tried to start it, and then resumed his fiddling.

"Drew." Not that she knew anything about inner car workings, but it seemed as if he wasn't truly doing anything.

"Yeah, baby." He unscrewed some thingamajig.

"How do you know how to work on cars?" Wanting to capture how he looked when deep in thought, she moved the camera.

"Light." He tapped the thingamajig.

In a flash, she moved the light back. "How did you learn to work on cars?"

"I don't know. Some from Logan, some from just having to make do when I lived in the United Kingdom, definitely not from my family."

At the mention of his family, she decided to simply hold the light steady. His parents forced him into acting. She always thought his adolescent weight problem was his way of trying to make himself unmarketable. Of all of them, he never seemed thrilled to be on set, never possessed the excitement. "Drew."

"Hold on." He pushed back and went back inside the car and tried to turn it on.

Again, nothing happened.

She filmed him stomping back to the front.

"Erin, put that godforsaken thing to good use and aim the light where my hands are." His tone came out a bit more gruff.

Still thinking about his family, she did as he asked and stared off at nothing. The couple of times his parents came to the set, he had become withdrawn and upset. Of course, the one time she called his parents to find out if they knew his whereabouts, they hung up on her. "How are your parents?"

"I get a card on my birthday if I'm unlucky. Maybe they're on a cruise or making someone else miserable." Once more, he went inside the car and attempted to start it to no avail.

She stood perfectly still and her cheeks heated. Apparently, he disengaged from people who hurt him. One day would he disappear on her again?

He returned to the engine and motioned toward the part of the engine the light already illuminated. "Aim the light right here!"

"Drew," she whispered.

"What!" He jiggled a wire and a whatnot.

"What if we have to call a tow truck, we don't have a cell site?" After letting out the words, she winced.

"I'm not calling any tow truck and I am not going to be late for my lecture and I will make sure that I am not stranded out where there is only a road and nothing else!"

At his outburst and his lack of the word "we," she bit the inside of her mouth and held the stupid light.

"There it is!" He slapped the side of the car. "Stupid ignition wire." Without giving her a second glance, he went to the back of the SUV, joining her and her light a few minutes later with a roll of black tape and a couple of tools.

Without any direction from the lone dictator, she managed to illuminate the space enough for him not to bark at her. She tried not to take in the cute way he tore the tape with his teeth or the way his fingers deftly repaired the wire.

Once through with his patch up job, he again returned to the front seat of the car. This time the car started. He turned the car off and on a couple of times and then came out, slammed the hood and turned to her with a huge grin. "Our chariot awaits."

"Don't you mean your chariot awaits?" She pushed past him and let herself in the car.

He got in the driver's seat. "Erin?"

Not wanting to get into it, she lowered the visor and looked at her image in the mirror. "Shouldn't you get going? I wouldn't want you to be late."

"Tell me what's wrong." He strummed his fingers on the steering wheel.

"I believe I just did."

"I'm sorry if I was short tempered. We're on a tight schedule." Like earlier, he offered her his hand.

"Now it's we?" Rather than take his gesture, she crossed her legs.

"What does that mean?" He faced her.

Pressure built behind her nose and her eyes heated. "Out there you kept saying I not we. If something happens, are you going to disappear again?" She crossed her arms and looked out the window.

"I was just upset with the car." He put his hand on her shoulder. "Honestly, my first thought was if we had to go walking how was I going to carry you the entire time?"

"What? You weren't just going to leave me here and walk off? Not that it matters, it's not like we have a commitment or anything." A sick sensation took over her stomach at her own words.

"I would've never done that." He brushed her hair aside. "Look at me, please."

Though she wanted to resist, she glanced over at him.

"I promise, no matter whatever happens, I will never disappear again." He took her hand, kissed the back and held it tight. "Do you hear me?"

She answered with a shrug.

"Erin, I think you know I was committed to you practically from the day I met you. We both tried to make it work with others and still we ended up here. Just the two of us on this road." His voice lowered and he pulled her in, brushing his lips against hers.

"Maybe the road is here to lead us to our next destination." She had no choice but to hold on tight and try to rid her mind of the horror films she saw. Though she knew they weren't real. Of course, no one said the romance ones were either.

"Right now I really need the road to take us to my lecture. I've had this scheduled for months." He gave her one more kiss and started the car.

Yes, he had his life scheduled for months, even years before he even thought about returning to her or being in a movie or Hollywood Glow.

She glanced down at the camera still in her lap and still filming. Before she told him about their project they needed to reach their destination together.

HOLLYWOOD STARBURST

INT. POCOHONTAS, IL, INSIDE A DINER - EARLY
EVENING.

Roxy is sitting with her ankle up on the booth.
The door to the diner opens. CHARLES, WILLIAM
and STEVEN enter and ROXY sits up straighter.

                    ROXY
               (Breathless)
               You really came.

CHARLES rushes over and inspects Roxy's leg.

WILLIAM comes over to the booth.

                    WILLIAM
               When Charles told us you
               were injured and asked
               for us, what did you
               expect us to do?

ROXY winces when Charles touches her ankle, but
manages to smile up at William and glances over
at Steven.

WILLIAM slides into the booth next to Roxy.

                    WILLIAM
               Why didn't you call us
               yourself?

ROXY looks between William and Steven.

STEVEN, hands in his pockets, saunters over and
stares down at her.

                    STEVEN
          Perhaps it's because she
          couldn't decide who to
          call?

                    CHARLES
          Steven, leave it.

                    STEVEN
          Why should I leave it?
          It's what's on
          everyone's mind. Right?

ROXY opens her mouth and turns to William.

                    WILLIAM
          Don't look at me. I have
          the same question.

ROXY turns to Steven, back to William and then
at Charles.

CHARLES shakes his head.

ROXY stares at the table.

                    ROXY
          I...

STEVEN crosses his arms and taps his foot.

                    STEVEN
          With your ankle, I got
          my answer. I don't think
          you'll be coming by any
          time soon.

STEVEN turns and walks out the door.

                    ROXY
          (Whispers)
          William

                    WILLIAM
          Seems like I'm always
          the one running to you.

WILLIAM slides out of the booth and follows
Steven.

CHARLES finishes bandaging Roxy's ankle.

                    CHARLES
          I was afraid this would
          happen.

                    ROXY
          There was no other way
          this could happen.

CHARLES glances out the window and watches the
BMW drive away.

                    CHARLES
          Well, I will play your
          chauffeur.

CHARLES gets out of the booth and helps Roxy
hobble out of the diner and looks down at her
feet.

                    CHARLES
          Well, something tells me
          you got what you wanted.

                    ROXY
          (gasps)
          What?

CHARLES points down at her ankle.

                    CHARLES
          You could have driven,
          and you would have been
          home by now. It's your
          other foot.

                    ROXY
Maybe I wanted it to
happen or maybe I was
trying to get a miracle.

Chapter Twenty-four

ABOUT THIRTY MINUTES AWAY from the University of New Mexico, Drew realized he didn't really know much about his lecture except that Bambi changed the color of the liposome slide. Lucky for him, he had given this lecture many times. However, it would help if he knew some minor details. "Erin, would you mind looking in that folder and telling me what building the lecture is in?"

"Oh, I can play assistant." Erin opened the folder. "I wish I had a pair of horn rimmed glasses. That would be perfect."

While he wanted to smile, or play along, they really needed to get to the lecture.

"We need to go to the science lecture hall." She tapped the page.

"All right. That's what I assumed." Without the car trouble, they would have arrived with enough time to check into the hotel and take a breath, but now they would glide in with only minutes to spare.

"So what else can I do to help you?" Erin checked her makeup in the mirror and did some minor touchups.

Yes, Erin. Ms. Erin Holland. Star of both the big and small screen. He pursed his lips. If they were on time, and they didn't have a talk about commitments and him disappearing, he might have suggested she take a nice long bath in the soaking tub at the hotel and have room service waiting for him when he returned.

That plan would have worked perfectly, but as they said, the best of plans.

He strummed his fingers on the steering wheel. While he may be able to temper the Drew Fulton reveal to the few biochem students who showed up, the appearance of the one and only Erin Holland would create a definite distraction.

"Drew?"

He needed a solution right now. Like any good scientist, he started by looking at his environment and spied the camera on the seat. "I think I have the teaching part covered. Why don't you do some filming?"

"That works." She checked her camera. "I'll keep it low key for you, Mr. Fulton, or should I say Dr. Abrams? I'll be good."

"I'll make it up to you later." Ways he could make it up to her ran through his mind.

"I'm looking forward to hearing you speak." She moved a lock of hair out of his face. "How many people will be there?"

"No more than fifty or so. The Department Head of Chemistry and Biochemistry is a friend of mine." At last, they came to the campus and he navigated his way around to faculty parking lot stopping at the attendant's booth. He rolled down the window. "Hello, I'm Doctor Abrams—"

"You are Drew Fulton!" The guard pointed at him and bent down peering inside the car. "No way! That's Erin Holland." He clapped and pointed. "Charles and Roxy!"

Erin giggled.

"I have a lecture?" At least Isaac Abrams needed to do a lecture.

"We moved the lecture to the theatre." The man took out a map and circled the location and then took out a pad of paper. "Do you mind?"

A quick glance at the clock told him he needed to get a move on. He scribbled his name on the paper, held it for Erin who did the same and handed it back. Finally, the man let them through the gates.

"Sounds like it's going to be more than fifty people." Erin sat up.

He followed the signs to the theatre, making his way around to where two uniformed officers with white gloves motioned for him to drive forward. "What the hell is going on?"

"Drew!" Erin gasped.

Well, he didn't need to wonder any longer why they moved his lecture. A mass of people were lined up at the theatre, more accurately, they were lined up around the theatre. "Something tells me these students aren't interested in polyphenols." Damn, he was all prepared for polyphenols.

"I think I'll be able to call you Drew after all." Erin cleared her throat. "I wonder if this has anything to do with the pictures we took yesterday."

"Or my new Director of Marketing." He stopped the car where directed and swore he saw a film crew from the local television station. Under the guise he still might discuss something remotely related to chemistry, he grabbed his laptop case, got out of the car and came around to let Erin out.

She laced her fingers in his. Before he had a chance to figure out how to handle the situation, his colleague, Dr. Warren, came sprinting toward him along with several other faculty members.

"Dr. Abrams." Dr. Warren held his hand out, but stared at Erin.

Drew shook the man's hand and pulled Erin a little closer. "I take it we had a slight change in plans?"

"The students obviously made the connection to your entertainment past. That, coupled with the pictures of you and Ms. Holland exploding all over the Internet, caused more than the normal number of students to sign up to learn about stabilizing polyphenols."

Strange how people now recognized him. Three weeks ago he could go anywhere and no one gave him a second thought. In an instant everything changed, maybe as much if not more than the day he decided to put Drew Fulton away for twenty years. Would anyone remember Isaac? "Well then, I think we should show them a little something about chemistry. Lead the way."

Dr. Warren motioned forward and keeping Erin close, he followed.

"We're very happy to have you here. Both of you." A woman in a cream colored business suit rushed alongside them. "I'm Chancellor Harvey and I'm a huge fan of your work."

Erin nodded and smiled, shook hands and kept a tight hold on him.

As they walked toward the theatre, the rumblings of the students grew louder. Once they spotted him and Erin, the low roar turned into cheers. Some even held up signs with *Hollywood Stardust* written on it and Charles and Roxy's names.

"We need to sign some autographs," Erin whispered in his ear.

"I need to give a lecture." The part of him that remained Isaac needed to stay grounded in his work, but his Drew side surged with some pride at the gathering.

"The press is here. If our toaster run got on the Internet, this will get on broadcast television. We have to be gracious to the fans. Trust me." She squeezed his hand. "I have a career and it will be good for the lab."

Damn if he didn't want to go greet his public. He gave Erin a nod and she pressed a pen into his palm.

While the university members continued toward the auditorium entrance, he veered and walked to the middle of the line of people.

"We love you!" A group of girls jumped up and down and held out their papers for signatures. "*Hollywood Stardust* is my mom's favorite movie! I grew up watching you drive across the country!"

They both began the age-old ritual of signing their names to various scraps of paper and made their way down the line. People truly loved the movie and had even handed it down to the next generation. For the first time he allowed himself to experience the fans like his co-stars.

"We always wanted Charles and Roxy to end up together!" A group of girls gathered around them and took selfies.

Erin hugged those girls.

"You're even prettier in person." One of the same girls in that group handed Erin a flower, then turned to him. "I always knew Charles would grow up to be hot and smart."

Unsure if he should thank the girl or not, he let Erin guide him to some more fans. He supposed the transformation was dramatic, especially after two decades.

Erin let go of his hand and immersed herself in another group of women.

"If I knew you were a professor, I would have definitely gone to UCLA." A particularly buxom brunette jutted out her breasts and pulled her form fitting white t-shirt out.

He stopped. The outline of the woman's nipples clearly showed through the thin fabric. Fine, he gawked a moment, he was still a male after all, and at last signed his name. "Are you a fan of the film?"

"I'm a fan of you." The woman winked at him. "That tickled."

Erin glanced over at him.

"Thank you." His instinct told him to move along.

Two more scantily clad co-eds gathered around him and took the same stance as the first. "You ended up to be the hottest of all of them." One girl simply stood there, her enormous chest needed no further introduction.

Caught between staring at this person's more than obvious wares and wanting to tell her to go put on a bra, he opted to sign the shirt and smile.

Erin narrowed one eye at him.

Though he might not be the ladies' man his other male co-stars were, he knew enough about Erin and women to know her expression was the universal sign for knock it off or you will never have sex again.

He attempted to move past the group, but the last one jumped in front of him.

"Don't forget me." She put her hands on her hips and stood on her tiptoes as if her boobs weren't right in his eye line anyway.

A flash of watching Logan and Ryder in similar positions went through his mind. Stuck with all the prosthetics on his face and forced to stay in character, he always tended to lag a few paces behind the other guys. The limelight was finally his. What he missed out on was here for the taking. Once more, he signed his name. For twenty years he'd signed a different name and it was never across anyone's breasts.

"Drew." Erin faced him. "The local station wants to interview us."

Stardom was more powerful than any drug, stronger than anything he could put in a capsule, powder or drink. A quick snap of a photo and his products went backorder. A mention on social media and customers called requesting a line he hadn't created yet. Hell, they wanted him.

Erin held her hand out to him.

At the end of the day, the most important person wanted him. Ignoring everyone else, he went to the one woman who mattered and put his arm around her.

The crowd clapped.

She leaned against him and posed for some pictures. The spot he always coveted belonged to him.

The reporter approached them. "So, Drew Fulton, what's it like returning to stardom after being an unknown chemist?"

He glanced between Erin, the fans, and the faculty waiting for him to enter the auditorium. Though he wanted Drew and lord help him, all the trappings that came along with being Drew, he wasn't ready to abandon his invented alter-ego. Would Erin be happy with Isaac?

"SO, IN CONCLUSION, if you protect the polyphenols with the proper stabilization technique, the polyphenols will protect you." Drew flicked off his laser pointer.

The lights in the packed auditorium illuminated and the crowd, most of whom Erin assumed were not chemistry students, clapped and cheered. If these students didn't know what a polyphenol was or why it had to be stabilized before Drew's lecture, they sure as hell would now. She would never look at antioxidants and their benefits to the body the same way again.

In truth, Dr. Abrams was a brilliant professor. If she ever attended college, he would have been the exact type of teacher she wanted. His passion radiated through his words, and his background in acting gave him a smooth interesting edge that had his students enamored no matter what the subject.

"Now, are there any questions?" Drew put his hands in his pockets and sauntered around the auditorium stage.

The entire room seemed to raise their hands.

"Are there any questions about polyphenols?" He chuckled.

From her seat over at the edge of the stage, Erin continued to film and watched about half the hands lower.

"All right." Drew pointed. "Third row, female, green shirt."

A girl who looked as if she wasn't old enough to watch a PG-13 movie or sit through a college chemistry lecture jumped up.

Erin nodded. If Drew chose one of those tight t-shirt girls, he would be hard pressed for any other boobs tonight, namely hers.

"I was wondering what Charles' and Roxy's favorite sources of polyphenols would be?" The girl hugged herself.

Drew crossed his arms. "All right, all right. I see how this is going to be played. I'll offer ten minutes of questions as long as we keep it calm and I can bring my co-star out with me."

Waiting for her cue, she turned off the camera and sat up straighter in the chair.

Once more, the audience applauded. Drew turned toward her and held his hand out.

In an instant, she stood and went to him, taking his hand and holding it tight.

"You've been in a ton of movies, and even in the theatre, but have you ever been in front of a class?" He winked at her.

"I was never the teacher type. I leave that to you." She leaned closer to speak into the microphone clipped to his tie.

The crowd let out a low chuckle.

"So, the girl in the green shirt wants to know what are Charles' and Roxy's favorite sources of polyphenols?" He put his arm around her.

"I think you're testing me to see if I was listening." She laughed and scanned her memory banks. "I think Roxy would have to say strawberries, blueberries and cherries."

"Very good." He gave her a little squeeze. "What about Charles?"

Not wanting to have a chemistry test and wanting to redirect the questions to what the audience wanted to hear, she tried for a different answer. "I'd say anything that would get him home in time for his test."

The audience clapped and they looked at each other.

"Let's take another question." He motioned toward the other side of the theatre. "Fifth row yellow dress."

"I have a question for Erin." The girl waved to her. "What is your favorite part of *Hollywood Stardust*?"

Erin returned the gesture and took a breath. Too many images materialized in her head. For twenty years she didn't answer a question about the movie, at last she had her opportunity. "I love that it's a journey both literally and figuratively. I love how each character had their own story, but they all intertwined. I think my favorite part is how Roxy changed through the movie and became a woman." The story centered on Roxy, the new girl who wanted to return to California to see the Hollywood Stardust theatre before it was torn down. Logan and Ryder played Steven and William, the two points of her love triangle while Drew played Charles, the misfit best friend who got dragged along for the ride. Strange, how life did indeed mimic art.

"We have time for two more questions." Drew lifted his chin. "Way back, man in the blue suit."

"If I go get my doctorate in chemistry will I be able to appear out of nowhere and end up with the MILF of the year?" The man, more like boy, clapped at his own question.

"Not by asking questions like that." Drew barked into the microphone.

The crowd roared with laughter.

She froze at the person's description of her. MILF? She wasn't even a mother, but she could be one. In fact, a quick scan of the room told her that she had the potential to be a parent to most of the audience members. These weren't even the people who watched *Hollywood Stardust* during its first run. No wonder Logan wouldn't let her play her role, no wonder Drew gawked at those young girls, no wonder she didn't get the roles she went after.

Somewhere along the line she'd changed, the world changed, but damn it, she didn't feel any different.

"Last question." Drew pointed right in front of him to a younger woman, who reminded Erin of the female version of Charles. A bit awkward, a bit disheveled, a bit of a standout.

"This is for Erin." The girl spoke in a voice barely above a whisper. "After twenty years, are you finally going to tell us who you were with behind the scenes?"

Twenty years.

Two decades.

Two hundred and forty months.

As it all came into perspective, a chill took over her body and she shuddered.

"Do you want the truth?" Her voice sounded as if a ventriloquist was speaking for her.

Drew didn't as much as tighten his hold on her as he dug his fingers into her side.

The entire auditorium became utterly silent.

"I wanted to be with Drew, and I should have been with him, and now I am with him." She inhaled and, wanting to end the interrogation, bowed her head.

For the umpteenth time that night, the room roared with applause.

While her thoughts went elsewhere, Drew said his goodbyes, collected his things, and shook his colleague's hand. She played the role of dutiful significant other, shook hands, smiled, signed a couple more autographs and then thankfully Drew led her back to the car and let her inside.

They may have spent twenty years apart, but he still knew her. Instead of talking or asking questions, he simply kissed her, turned on some music, and drove straight to the hotel, more like a resort. Of course, he didn't mention what she said. Maybe when faced with her in reality she wasn't nearly as grand. After all she could be a mother.

She meant the words she said in the auditorium. All those years ago she should have been with Drew. It was what they both wanted. She never put on a better performance than she did that night when they were supposed to make it official. Every day since, she paid for her stupid mistake.

What would have happened if she'd allowed them to be together twenty years ago? Would they now have a child or two in high school or college, a little combination of the two of them who watched his or her parents in that quote unquote genre changing movie and laughed?

Would they have even made it or would their hearts have been broken in a whole different way if they couldn't stay together? The pit in her stomach deepened.

Unlike their other stops, she didn't hide. Instead, she chose to go with Drew as he checked them in, and they followed the bellman to their suite just like a couple.

The room was nothing if not glorious. Decorated in a Southwestern flair, a huge bed overlooked a picture window of the New Mexico landscape and off to one side she spied an oversized bathtub in an even larger bathroom with every amenity.

After tipping the bellman and locking the door, Drew came up behind her and put his arms around her. "Let me tell you what we're going to do next."

Still caught in her reverie, she looked up backward at him. Maybe they needed to talk about what happened at the University.

"I'm going to order us some room service and you are going to go get in that bathtub." He kissed her nose. "I booked this room specifically for that bathtub."

"Is that it?" Really, he wasn't going to say a word?

"I just need a few minutes to decompress." After another kiss on the nose he patted her bottom as if shooing her away.

With her only choice to do as he requested, she turned her back to him and lifted her hair. "Would you mind?"

"I never mind." His fingertips skimmed the back of her neck before he pulled the zipper down.

She shivered at his touch and walked toward the bathroom, stopping at one of her suitcases along the way and giving him one last chance to say something.

"I got everything, go relax." Drew loosened his tie.

She pressed her lips together, stopping any argument on her part and went into the bathroom and closed the door. For a minute she simply stood there and then finally summoned her courage to look in the mirror.

Roxy, at least the Roxy who existed two decades ago didn't exist anymore. Who did Drew see when he looked at her? The Erin who played Roxy, the Erin in her heyday he watched from afar, or the Erin who was nearing her fourth decade with a few more curves and a little less career?

She started the water in the tub and poured in the bubbles especially left on a shelf with other potions and lotions and then took off her clothes.

At one time in her life she wouldn't have cared who Drew wanted because she got what she was after. She lived that way for years with Brian. With Drew she wouldn't settle.

She needed him to want this Erin.

At last, she stepped into the tub.

Maybe it was time Roxy finally grew up.

FRUIT, CHEESE, BREAD, finger sandwiches, and a great bottle of wine provided the perfect meal to eat in a bathtub built for two. Drew rubbed his hands together and pushed the room service cart toward the bathroom door.

One could say his lecture took many unexpected turns. Scores of fans, a change in venue and a film crew completely changed the entire event. However nothing, absolutely nothing, compared to Erin acknowledging their relationship to the world. It was a wish two decades in the making. On the ride to the hotel she stayed mostly quiet as if lost in her own thoughts. He could only hope she didn't simply say the first thing that came to her mind when faced with a question about her past relationships.

"No." When she finally said the words aloud, he vowed then and there to stop focusing on the old Erin, do as she asked and focus on other things. If they were going to build anything, they had to move forward, he had to move forward.

Right before he made it to the bathroom door, the dual vibrations of both his and Erin's cell phones reverberated through the room. Though he wanted to ignore it, the fact both their phones went off at the same time gave him cause for concern, and he backtracked, pulled his phone out of his suit jacket pocket thrown over the chair and read the text from Logan.

> *Hey all. We are going to start casting calls for Hollywood Starburst, we want you there to pick your twenty year ago self. Don't worry, you will all be getting paid. We think this is not only for the good of the movie, but publicity. We are starting at the end of the week.*

It seemed as if anytime he was ready to let go of the past, it came barreling toward him. The last thing he wanted was to interrupt his and Erin's time with talk of Hollywood Star-anything. Erin was right, they needed to focus on the good and some of his best times were when she wasn't being a star, she was just being her. He smiled as one of the better times flashed into his mind.

The door joining their two hotel rooms had shot open. "Drew!" In a pair of leggings and a pink t-shirt that almost reached her knees, Erin had rushed into the room, looked around as if she were being chased and with a look of pure mischief had backed up against the wall with her hands behind her back.

He shot up from the small desk in the room and faced her, loving when she took off all the makeup and was just natural. She was an absolute beauty. "Why does it look as if you've been bad?"

"Don't you want to see what I have?" She raised her eyebrows.

If she only knew. Rather than tell her what he really wanted to see, he tried to play it cool and slowly strutted toward her. "What do you think?"

"Okay, you asked for it." With a bit of flourish, she pulled a video game cartridge from behind her back.

"Fire Fury Deluxe?" Okay fine, while he would still rate seeing Erin with less clothing at the top, the game was a cool second place. "How did you get that?"

"The director got it, and I begged him for it, and now I shall show you who is the crown princess of the fire planet." Cartridge in hand, she darted around him to the couch and rubbed her hands together.

He followed and pulled over the game console he brought with him. Working in unison, they set up the game, and with an over exaggerated movement, she put the game into the slot.

In less than five minutes, they were entranced in their quest to take over the fire planet.

"I got you!" The competitor in Erin emerged, and she stood as she manipulated the controls.

"Oh, yeah." He managed to get around a huge barricade and slid down on the floor.

"Oh, my god, here come the flame throwers." She reclaimed her seat on the couch, but slid closer to him.

If someone would have asked him of all the stars of the movie who would end up to be his video game partner, he would have never guessed Erin. Yet, he caught her one day, and they had been the perfect pair ever since.

They both warded off the flame throwers coming in his direction, and he managed to make his way around a fire pit, taking her from behind and delivering a fatal blow.

"You got me!" As if she were shot, Erin slapped her hand over her chest and fell back on the couch.

He wished. With a laugh, he turned back to her. "You okay over there?"

"I'm recharging my fuel tanks so I can take you on again." She combed her nails through his hair.

"Anytime." Hey, he had to give her a little innuendo. "You know when we met, I never pictured you a closet gamer."

"There are some benefits to being girl number three in the first version of this video game console five years ago." She slid down onto the floor next to him, lifted her control device, and widened her eyes. "Look, the images are so lifelike it's like I'm actually in the game."

At her performance, he clapped. "Very convincing. If I didn't already play, I would want to now."

She elbowed him. "Part of my pay was the game. I felt normal playing it."

"Well, I for one adore plain old Erin, the gamer."

"What about Erin the actress?"

"I'm a fan, what can I say?" He restarted the game.

"I'm a fan of Drew Fulton, actor and future astronomer." She punctuated her statement with a kiss on the cheek. "Let's play."

While he was enamored with Erin the actress, he was in love with plain old Erin. Rather than dwell on it, he went head to head with the fire throwers once more. He had nicknamed them Logan and Ryder, and he had taken them down, at least in the oh so lifelike video world.

The memory faded and once more he looked at his phone and the message from Logan. No, not tonight. Tonight was for quests of a different nature. He exhaled and returned his phone to his pocket. The two of them were on the cusp of something. He knocked on the door.

"Enter at your own risk." Erin called out. Her quiet from earlier was replaced with her low sexy tone.

Well, their relationship had advanced from video games. He opened the door to one of the most magnificent sites ever to grace his vision. If nothing else, Erin Holland knew how to set the stage.

She followed his instructions and lay in the oversized bathtub with her hair pulled up in a bun and her face scrubbed clean of her makeup. Great mounds of bubbles overtook the tub, strategically covering key body parts with only her smooth leg peeking out.

"Is something the matter?" She held a sponge up and washed her gorgeous appendage.

"Only the fact that I'm not the one with the sponge in my hand." Already his body reacted.

"I can think of way better things to put in your hands if you would join me." She turned away and paid attention to her leg.

Preferring to savor rather than dive in, he poured the wine, made a plate of some of the morsels from the tray, and took off his clothes. "I did want to clean up." He handed her a glass of wine.

She took the drink and sat up, giving him room to join her. "Funny, from the looks of things it seems as if you want to get dirty."

Yes, his erection was already thickening. "I can't help myself when I'm around you." He stepped into the tub, on the opposite end to face her. Her slick legs slid against his, electrifying his skin.

"Really?" She tapped her glass against his and took a sip.

Strange. Normally Erin didn't ask for reassurance. Maybe this had to do with those t-shirt girls. "You never need to ask. I just glance in your direction and I want you." He drank and put his glass aside, choosing instead to run his hands up her one submerged leg.

A smile struggled on her lips. "When you look at me, who do you see?"

Anyone else would balk at her question, but as a former actor and someone who changed his identity, he understood completely. "I see you, Erin."

"Which Erin?" The water splashed as she put her glass with his and slid closer to him.

"The one who showed up at my house the night of the gala because I willed her there." His hands traveled up to her hips.

"I felt it."

"The one who would flop around on any hotel couch and play video games with me."

"You remembered." She pressed her palm to his cheek.

He grabbed her waist and pulled her to him. "I see the woman who I wanted twenty years ago, but back then I don't think either of us was ready."

She shook her head.

"But at the end of the day, I see the Erin who gave me a gift tonight that only she would understand when she decided to tell the world what she wanted." Unable to resist, he wrapped his arms around her. "I'm not sure how you got more beautiful, but it happened."

"I meant every word." She leaned into him, her lips caressing his as she spoke.

"So did I." Acting as one, they kissed. A deep, slow, lingering kiss with no rushing, only perfect unison.

She curled her legs around him and pressed her body to his, her nipples already hard with arousal. "God, Drew."

He ran his fingertips over her breasts and kissed down her neck, lapping up the water droplets lingering on her skin.

A low growl escaped her throat and she reached between them, stroking his enflamed erection.

"Um." The way she touched him always set him off. He couldn't get enough of her, her mouth, her hands, her body.

Once more, he found her lips and their mouths connected.

Without a word, she braced against his shoulder, raised herself up, and with almost torturous slowness, guided him inside her.

"Yes." In need of the pressure, he pushed her down further.

She pulled back and stared into his eyes, his erection embedded in her, they spoke a silent, erotic language only lovers understood. Her tightness coupled with the slight knowing smile on her face caused him to twitch inside her. The more he had her, the more he craved her, and he was damn well certain he would make up for the years without her.

Rather than lunging down on him, she ground her hips in a circle, a languishing tease. His entire body became sensitized, and he fought the need to move and allowed her the chance to take the lead.

"Do you really think I'm more beautiful now?" She arched her back, giving him a full view of her magnificent breasts that she cupped in her palms.

"You know I do." Lord help him, was she going to treat him to a private show? The moment she licked her fingertips and touched her nipples, he bucked his hips.

"You like watching me?" She reached behind her, pulled her hair out of her bun, her blonde locks falling down her back and over her shoulders.

Overcome with the urge to thrust, he nodded. "Erin."

His sharp tone must have told her what he wanted. In one fluid motion, she slid up his shaft and down again. "I love how you feel inside me."

Keeping the same rhythm, she repeated her action over and over again. His desire built, but it wasn't enough to satisfy, only tease.

She ran her hands over her own body, her face, down her neck and once more over her breasts before making her way to her hips and finally her center. "Feels so good."

"This is mine." He swiped her hand away, rubbing the one spot where she required more attention.

"All yours." She leaned back, braced herself on his knees and sped up. As she neared her end, her smooth strokes turned into hard plunges.

"Don't forget that." At last, he took his opportunity to drive up into her, his own release coming on hard and fast. Each time their skin met, the water splashed, but nothing mattered except reaching the crest of the wave. "Come Erin!"

"I'm there." She clutched the edge of the tub. "Drew!"

Under his fingers and through his body, delicious throbs signified once again she'd reached the ultimate pleasure with him. At watching her throw her head back and gasp as her orgasm flooded her and feeling the way her body drew him further inside, he had no choice but to succumb to his own climax.

Right as she bore down, writhing against him, he gave her a final deep thrust and let go. Perfectly timed pulses radiated through every inch of his body, lasting longer than he expected.

"Yes." Like earlier, he grabbed her hips and kept her pressed down to him as the last few vibrations ebbed away.

She collapsed against him, laying her head on his shoulder and kissing his neck. "I need you, Drew."

"I'm right here." An undeniable and complete exhaustion coming over him, he embraced her and shut his eyes

"I don't want this road trip to end." Her voice cracked. "I just want to be here with you."

Yes, the road trip offered them a definite respite, an oasis away from everything they didn't want to face. "Well, we still need to go visit the farm, so the trip isn't over." He braced himself for this next part. "But we'll have a lot to do at home. We have the Hollywood Glow line. Also, Logan texted us, they're casting for the movie and want us there at the end of the week."

At first, she didn't move. When she finally did, she simply held him tighter. "When did you find out?"

"Before joining you in here." He combed his fingers through her hair.

"I'm not Roxy anymore." The pain dripped out of her mouth with her words. "I ran from her, and when I wanted her back I couldn't have her."

While he didn't need to relive Charles, he understood her need to keep hold of Roxy. They all ran from their roles in different ways, only to find the road lead right back to them. "I think it's your duty to choose the best predecessor you can, someone who will do the role justice."

"When you saw those students tonight, what did you think?"

Not sure what her question meant, he shrugged. "I don't know. They were a group of college students."

"Their parents watched us." A shudder ran through her. "Any one of those girls in the auditorium could play Roxy now."

Well, when she put it that way he wondered if he needed to go get them a matching set of rocking chairs. "I'm their professor." He wrinkled his nose.

With a laugh, she lifted her head. "What happens when we get home?"

"We'll hand over the batons and go live our lives." In an attempt to tell her how it was going to be, he leaned in and kissed her.

"I know I have some more roles in me." Once more, she kissed him and lowered her head.

He looked up at the ceiling. Though he tried not to doubt her, he couldn't help questioning his own role when she got a new role and Hollywood crept into their lives.

INT. INDIANAPOLIS, IN - INSIDE THE BMW - NIGHT.

The traffic crawls on the highway. STEVEN hits the steering wheel and then hits William's shoulder.

> STEVEN
> You know, it figures we would hit traffic when we're fifteen minutes away from the end of the trip from hell. I would have rather been studying.

> WILLIAM
> So now after over three hours you decide you're talking?

> STEVEN
> I didn't have anything to say until right now.

> WILLIAM
> You mean with finding out Roxy is playing both of us down to the point where she couldn't look us in the eye. So, you had nothing to say until we hit traffic a few minutes from home?

WILLIAM hits Steven's shoulder

> WILLIAM
> You are the biggest asshole.

STEVEN lifts his chin.

> STEVEN

          Hey, spread your legs
          there.

WILLIAM sneers at Steven.

              STEVEN
          (Leans over to William.)
          So it's about time you
          got rid of your pussy
          and grew a set.

              WILLIAM
          You know, at least she
          was going to go to you.
          I was the one running
          after her.

STEVEN shrugs.

              STEVEN
          Just another way of
          running after her
          without saying it.

They both glance at each other.

WILLIAM shifts in his seat.

              WILLIAM
          I guess we both saw
          something different in
          her.

                    STEVEN
          I think what matters is
          at the end, we saw the
          same thing.

WILLIAM holds his hand out.

                    WILLIAM
          Well, we've been friends
          since third grade.

STEVEN pauses and then shakes his hand.

                    STEVEN
          So since you are the
          sensitive one of the two
          of us, now what do we
          do?

WILLIAM purses his lips.

                    WILLIAM
          We are assholes.

                    STEVEN
          Then we were perfect for
          her.

                    WILLIAM
          I think sometimes you
          have to know when to
          drive away.

                    STEVEN
          Well, this time we did
          it together.

                    WILLIAM
          I think I'd rather fight
          you for her than know
          what I know.

                    STEVEN

Yeah, it's better
when they're
princesses.

Chapter Twenty-Five

ERIN OPENED HER EYES, wondering who in the world put a heavy electric blanket on them, and turned it up to swelter. Though she didn't need to, she glanced at the clock, 5:00 on the dot and way too early to be in a hot box. Before heating Drew up, she decided to cool things down in here and went to get out of bed, touching Drew's arm to shimmy out from under it without waking him.

She turned over at discovering the source of the heat. "Drew?"

Nothing. He didn't move, didn't react.

Before deciding on her next course of action, she pressed her palm to his forehead and then to hers. With her being overheated she had to make sure, and remembering something from one of her movie roles, she pressed her lips to him. Sure enough, her lips proved to be a more accurate gauge. Heat coursed through him and with her heart racing, she jumped out of the bed and headed for the bathroom.

After rinsing a washcloth in cold water she dashed back to Drew. He still lay on his side and she swore his breathing sounded raspy. "Drew?"

He let out a moan when she managed to turn him onto his back. "Erin?"

"Are you all right?" She gently placed the cool cloth on his forehead and pressed the back of her hand to his cheek. "You're burning up."

As he swallowed, he winced. "Erin."

"Let me get you some aspirin." Once more she jumped up, this time dumping her toiletry bag out until she found the sought after medicine and grabbed a bottle of water on her rush back to Drew. She doled out two tablets. "Just take this."

Pain flashed across his face as he sat up and downed the medicine. "Give me a little bit, I'll take care of you." He moaned, sunk back down in the pillow and closed his eyes. "We have to get on the road."

"Try to rest." She brushed his bangs to one side. No matter what, he wanted to take care of her. For a few minutes she watched him. After the cool washcloth and the aspirin, she used up everything she knew about taking care of someone that didn't involve sex. She bit her nail. Honestly, she didn't know anything about taking care of anyone or anything, and she was pretty sure she just gave Drew her hangover remedy. Luckily, it happened to work for fever as well.

If this were the other way around, no doubt Drew would have something more up his sleeve. Already he was back to sleep. Even if he woke up with enough time for them to get on the road, by the looks of things, there wasn't a chance he could sit in a car or do a meeting.

The responsibility to take care of him fell on her and she stood. All this time she still knew he held back from her, kept his heart at bay, but maybe if she could prove she could take care of him in times of sickness, he would let her all the way in. Yes, she could do this.

First things first, she needed to provide sustenance. Her mind instantly went to orange juice and toast. Careful not to wake Drew, she went into the bathroom to use the phone. She lifted the receiver, looked in the mirror and narrowed her eyes. Her whole life she stayed in hotels and knew the quality of their toast and juice.

Under her watch, Drew would not have juice from a carton, and he would not take a bite of soggy lukewarm toast. With her plan in place, she pointed at her image and dialed room service.

"Room service how can I help you?" A pleasant sounding woman answered.

"Hello, this is Erin Holland." She stood up straighter.

"I was told you were at the hotel." The woman let out a little giggle. "Ms. Holland, what can I do for you?"

"I need something extremely specific and if you produce it for me in the next thirty minutes, I promise that before I leave the hotel I'll autograph something special just for you."

"Ms. Holland, I will have whatever you need. I'm waiting."

Erin smiled, not only at her image, but her good little soldier. "I need an electric juicer, two pounds of fresh, organic oranges, a toaster, your best wheat bread and all the condiments that toast requires, as well as some coffee and a banana." Of course, she could use the toaster she and Drew bought together, but it was all wrapped up in the car and it felt like they should use it at home. Well, his home.

When the woman didn't respond, Erin tapped her foot, but forced herself to smile before she spoke. Everyone could hear a smile. "Are you still there?"

"Yes, Ms. Holland, and I'll produce everything that you need. I was taking notes. I apologize for the delay."

"Well?"

"Set your timer. I'll be there in thirty minutes with everything."

Erin could practically see the woman salute. "What's your first name?"

"Martha."

"I'll see you then, Martha. Don't knock. I'll open the door in a half hour. Go." With conviction, she hung up the phone and again glanced in the mirror. Along with nourishment, Drew must have something beautiful to look at. That would surely be healing.

While she could take hours getting ready, she also had the uncanny knack to look nothing if not presentable in exactly twenty-five minutes. She didn't spend her life on a set for nothing. Every makeup and wardrobe person came with their own set of tips and in record time, she cleaned up, did her hair and makeup then tiptoed out and put on a pair of black leggings and one of Drew's white shirts she tied at the waist. The white was a nursing color for sure.

Before answering the door, she found one of her 8x10 glossies in her luggage, signed her name, added Martha's name in huge letters, and right at the thirty minute mark opened the door.

Sure enough, sometimes star power worked for good. An older round lady in a hotel uniform silently clapped. "You are Erin Holland."

"And you must be Martha." She held out the photo.

"I brought everything, including some organic honey too." Martha wheeled the room service cart into the main room of the suite and took the present. "I can't thank you enough."

"Right back at you." Erin checked over the contents of the cart, signed the receipt and nodded. "Here's one more signature for you."

Martha clutched the little folder the receipt came in to her chest. "It was an honor."

In a need to give the lady the full show, Erin bowed. "Thank you." She motioned toward the door, and Martha backed out closing the door behind her.

Before starting in, she tiptoed back to the bedroom and peeked in on her patient. He'd moved to his side, his arm outstretched as if he were looking for her. Though she longed to crawl in bed beside him, she had a mission. A mission of health, so with her head held high, she spun on her heel and returned to the main room. She proceeded to set up her workstation, starting with pouring herself a cup of coffee and taking a quick sip of the brew that wasn't nearly as good as the French press Drew dispensed in the morning.

A brief inventory told her she indeed received everything she requested. She plugged in the citrus juicer, assessed all its parts and components, and put a glass by the spout and sighed. Seemed to her that a juicer should be built that held the juice, it would be easy to forget the glass especially if one wasn't a morning person. Maybe she and Drew could invent something like that. Juicing was definitely part of nutraceuticals.

Since they didn't provide her with a cutting board, she moved the basket of oranges off a plate, selected a fruit and a knife and proceeded to slice the orange along the equator. The two halves fell apart and she smiled at having cut the orange the correct way.

She sipped her coffee once more and took another fruit. With a bit more flourish, she sliced through the skin, her skin, not orange skin. "Oh!" She dropped the knife and gazed down at the gash along the side of her hand, right over the scar she gave herself the last time she saw Drew after she told him no one would ever believe they could be together.

Her career had hit a high. The cancellation of the sequel allowed her to take the role she wanted in an edgy suspense film where she played the young ingénue who the hero has to save and ended up falling in love with her. At last, Roxy was memory.

Finished with a day of filming on her latest movie, she had driven to Brian's office to review a couple of offers and go to dinner at that new restaurant at the west end of Sunset. All the paparazzi gathered there and she would pretend she didn't like her photograph taken. Maybe she would call Rye and have him tag along. Until the end of time they would be linked through their contract with Logan, they might as well make the most of it.

Not wanting to run into some second rate wannabe star, she let herself in the back of Brian's office. As she snuck past the file room and the screening room, she unfastened the top three buttons of her shirt and messed up her hair, giving her a little bit of the just got out of a bed and ready to get back in it look Brian loved, and tiptoed toward his office.

No sooner had she put her hand on the doorknob then she heard him. Even muffled through the door she knew the voice like she knew her name.

No, not Brian.

Drew.

Her stomach bottomed out and suddenly all the air left her lungs. Since that horrible night, she had seen him only when absolutely necessary for the *Hollywood Stardust* premiere. Though she tried to talk to him each and every time, he only held his hand up and walked away from her.

Well, now she had him cornered and on her turf and she flung the door open.

"Erin!" Brian jumped up out of the chair from behind his desk.

Drew spun toward her.

"You're early." Brian's voice came out low as if he were trying to tell her a secret when he had been the one keeping it all along. How many times had she asked him to get Drew for her? She would deal with him later. All Brian did was cite the damn contract with Logan and Ryder stating she wouldn't go to any lengths to contact Drew. Well, no one could account for chance meetings.

"I think I'm exactly on time." Heeding what she learned on set, she blocked the doorway, preventing any escape and focused on Drew. It had been too long since she saw him without the prosthetics and padding they piled on him.

They stared at each other. At least he finally looked at her. Maybe it was a start. "Drew, may I speak to you please?"

For a moment he paused, his gaze traveled over her, and he opened his mouth.

She held her breath.

In a flash, he turned back to Brian. "Is our business done?"

Her agent and lover nodded and didn't bother glancing in her direction.

With her blocking the exit, Drew approached her and her shaking intensified. She held out her hand. "Please, Drew."

"Let me go." He stared into her eyes. The double meaning of his words was not lost on her.

She stood her ground.

Brian joined them, took her by the shoulders, and pried her away from the door. "Come on Erin."

The second there was enough room to pass, Drew left. No, he didn't run, but he wasn't slow about it either.

"Damn you." The tears started, real tears, the same ones she cried every time she saw him since that stupid night.

"Just leave him be." Brian pulled her in tighter.

"Leave me alone!" If nothing else she needed to have her say. She didn't go to any lengths to find him, he simply appeared, and she had to take her chance. Gathering her strength, she shrugged Brian off and dashed out the back of the office.

She scanned the small parking lot behind Brian's building to find him sitting in a blue sedan. "Drew!" Not caring if every photographer in Hollywood showed up out of the woodwork, she ran toward the car and knocked on the window. "Drew!"

He didn't look at her, only sat there shaking his head.

"Drew!" She continued to pound on the window. "Please, let me just say something, then you can leave."

Though he didn't face her, he rolled down the window a crack.

Breathless, she knew she better get the words out that she promised she'd say if she ever had the chance. "I love you, Drew." At hearing her confession, she gasped.

Time stood still. She balled her hand into a fist and waited for his response, a reaction, anything.

The window slid up, closing her out, and the engine of the car rumbled.

She simply stood there as he backed out of the parking spot and left.

Expecting some Hollywood magic she didn't move, anticipating him returning, opening the car door, saying he loved her as well, and then them driving off into the sunset. She refused to budge until he came back.

"Erin, you've been standing there for an hour. Come inside now." Brian called to her.

An hour? She inhaled, spun on her heel and charged back toward the building, where she stopped and turned back one more time. Refusing to cry, she channeled any heroine she knew to remain strong. The energy built up within her and she had punched the wall. The side of her hand had caught a small nail. Instantly, blood had gushed from the wound, dripping down onto the cement.

Back in the present in their hotel room, she blinked, inhaled and watched a much smaller amount of blood trickle onto the napkin. At least this wound wouldn't require stitches and a trip to a doctor who wouldn't talk to the tabloids. Once the bleeding stopped, she finished juicing the oranges and with her glass of liquid health in tow, tiptoed into the bedroom.

"Erin?" Drew's voice came out ragged like it had been ridden hard and put away wet.

Before turning to him, she cleared her throat and took a breath to rid her mind of those old images churning in her head. They were different now. He promised he wouldn't shut her out and she wasn't afraid of her feelings. Right?

At her core, she was still an actress, and she faced him, knowing the smile she wore was convincing. "How's my patient?"

"I don't remember the last time I felt worse." He draped his arm over his eyes, but held his other hand out to her.

"I made you some juice." She sat at the edge of the bed.

"You made juice?" From beneath his arm he peeked at her. "You mean you made it by ordering room service?"

"No. Room service brought me a juicer and oranges and I made juice." Just to make sure he knew she spoke the truth she waved the glass in front of him.

"Fresh juice from your hands?" With a grunt, he forced himself into a seated position. He took the glass, sampled her beverage and licked his lips. "As delicious as the woman who made it."

She swore her cheeks heated with his compliment, and still trying to put her memories on the back burner, she glanced around the room, stopping when it reached her video camera thrown on the chair. Perhaps she should have documented her juice making extravaganza, but her focus on Drew made her forget her other job. There was also still the matter of getting to Logan's casting.

"Hey." He rubbed her shoulder. "Are you okay?"

She turned back. "I just want you to concentrate on getting well. In a little bit I'll call Las Cruces Agricultural Sciences and reschedule. Then I'll call Logan to double check the time of the casting, and as a grand finale I'll make you some toast with the toaster and fresh bread I had room service bring. I thought it would be easy on your stomach."

He stared at her, really and truly stared as if he never saw her before.

"What is it?" Though used to having people look at her, gawk even, when Drew did it, the experience was completely different.

Rather than answer, he took hold of her hand, his fingers grazing against her wound.

She gasped and tried to pull away. "Oh."

He inspected the damage. "How did this happen?"

"It's just a little cut. One of the oranges didn't want to stay put, nothing important." She tried to laugh it off. "I just wanted to take care of you."

Again, their eyes met. He knew the origin of the original scar.

Keeping his focus on her, he brought her hand to his lips.

She held her breath and wondered if he remembered that day, what she said, what he didn't say.

Once more, he leaned back on the pillows. "Well, I not only have the most delicious nurse in the world, but the most gorgeous one as well."

Her stomach twisted at the compliment, but not the right words. A sudden feeling of exhaustion took over her. "Why don't you rest? I think I might join you."

He lifted the blankets and she curled up in bed next to him, holding back the tears when he spooned her and kissed the back of her head. "If this isn't healing, nothing is."

When he remembered that day, he likely remembered wanting to be done with her, while she remembered chasing after him. In truth, what she remembered most was wishing he would say he loved her too. Something told her they needed more healing than a glass of orange juice.

EXT. EFFINGHAM, IL - OFF THE SIDE OF THE ROAD.
- NIGHT.

Charles and Roxy lean against the Lincoln
sipping a drink looking out over a field.

>   ROXY
>   It's the last stop
>   before home.

>   CHARLES
>   (Nodding.)
>   You ready to face the
>   world?

>   ROXY
>   Not really. But I'm
>   also not ready to hide
>   anymore either.

CHARLES takes a gulp of his drink.

>   CHARLES
>   You know, when I first
>   met Steven I was so
>   terrified of him I'd
>   hide around corners so
>   he would pass me in the
>   hall. Then one day I
>   was running late for
>   class.

ROXY smiles and turns to Charles.

>   ROXY
>   You were late?

                    CHARLES
          (Frowns.)
          I was in elementary
          school and had to rely
          on my mother for
          transportation.

                    ROXY
          Poor baby.

                    CHARLES
          Anyway, so I was late
          and ran down the hall
          and there he was.

                    ROXY
          What did you do?

                    CHARLES
          I faced him head on. I
          just figured I was
          already late and I may
          as well get it over
          with.

ROXY leans in.

                    CHARLES
          So, you know what he
          did?

ROXY shakes her head

                    CHARLES
          He thrust his backpack
          at me, put his arm
          around my shoulders and
          told me how to get a new
          slab of clay from the
          teacher so we didn't
          have to use the old clay
          with all the crud stuck
          in it.

ROXY bursts out laughing

                    CHARLES
          So, after that day, I
          carried his crap and did
          his stuff, and he always
          took care of me in his
          own special and slightly
          twisted way.

                    ROXY
          Well then, as the
          smartest person in the
          group, what advice do
          you have for the girl
          who broke everything
          including my foot?

                    CHARLES
          It's merely a sprain.

CHARLES holds out his arm and escorts Roxy back
around to the passenger side of the car.

                    CHARLES
          You really need to
          decide what you want,
          and I'm not talking
          about William and
          Steven. What do you
          really want?

ROXY stares at Charles

                    ROXY
          All I know is that I
          don't want this to be
          the last stop. There
          has to be something
          more.

                    CHARLES
          There's a lot more, you
          just have to find it.

ROXY gives Charles a kiss on the cheek, then
gets inside the car.

                    ROXY
          I hope so.

Chapter Twenty-Six

THE TIRES ON DREW'S SUV ground against the gravel as he and Erin made their way down the long driveway leading to LCAS or Las Cruces Agricultural Sciences. Part farm part laboratory, the facility was known for specialty agriculture.

"Are you feeling all right?" Erin leaned over and grazed her hand against his cheek.

After parking the car, Drew turned to her and couldn't help but pull her in for a quick kiss. The woman proved to be an amazing nurse. Hell, she proved to be amazing period. No one could take care of him like Erin, and it wasn't only fresh squeezed juice. While he rested, she fixed their schedule, fed him, entertained him and just stayed with him. Any residual doubts about her and about them finally faded. "I feel much better." Thankfully, whatever feverish illness that overtook him only delayed them two days.

"It must be all the vitamins." As she spoke, her lips brushed against his.

"I think I can attribute my miraculous recovery to something else." He took her hand. For the first time since their bed and breakfast stay they didn't make love in the morning, or the middle of the night, or...well, they didn't make love. His need returned with his strength. He kissed her once more, a little deeper. "Actually, I feel incredible."

"Is incredible your new word for horny?" Her giggle vibrated through him.

"Very good deduction, I'll turn you into a scientist yet." He forced himself to pull back.

"Well, right now I'm going to play secretary and tell you we better not be late. We have ingredients to choose for Hollywood Glow and then we can pick a product from your finished ones to start with." She wiped his bottom lip. "Later, for our last night on our road trip, I'll play the role of demure damsel and you can have your way with me."

The last night of their road trip. His chest tightened. Would they do as well in the real world? Again, he pushed the thoughts away. "Then I'll play gentleman and open the door for you." Before he ravaged her in the front seat of his SUV, he gathered his laptop bag, got out of the vehicle and went around to retrieve her.

"Thank you, kind sir." She put her hand in his.

He helped her down and gave her the once over twice. Hell he could do it all day long. Rather than wearing something over the top, she chose a pair of jeans with a tight pink sweater and boots. Gorgeous.

"What is it?" She slid her sunglasses down over her eyes.

"It's our first meeting as..." Realizing what he almost blurted out, and not wanting to sound like some jerk, he led her away. "You're right, we need to go inside."

She pulled her hand away. "I'm not going anywhere until you tell me what first this is."

Instead of answering right away, he took two deliberate steps toward her, stopping less than an inch in front of her. "This is our first meeting where we are a couple, and I'm telling you right now my damsel, unless you want to be in distress, you will be good." As any good director would say, everything was in the delivery.

A slow smile overtook her face. "I'll be good Dr. Fulton." She reclaimed his hand, stood on her tiptoes, and gave him a long kiss complete with some tongue action.

In order to ensure she knew the effect she had on him, he pushed his body to hers and ran his hand over her backside. "Hold that thought." They both turned toward the entrance and standing right there in jeans, cowboy boots and a Stetson, was his colleague, Dr. Costa. Well, he couldn't blame this on her, only his overactive libido.

"Well, I guess I'll get that spanking after all," she whispered and without warning, charged forward.

Though he tried to catch her, she proved to be too fast.

"Dr. Costa. I'm Erin Holland." She held her hand out. "Thank you for being so flexible with our schedule."

She thanked him.

Not only did Erin thank him, she called him by the proper title and the woman who needed no introduction, introduced herself. Drew slowed down, took a breath and waited for the response. Fine, he said a silent prayer this meeting would turn out well and it all depended on the man's response. Please let him be a fan of some sort.

Dr. Costa shook her hand then stood back and crossed his arms.

Drew held his breath, more like choked.

"So, you're that fancy Hollywood actress who Dr. Abrams brought with him. One day he's a chemist, the next a one hit wonder teen in some dated movie, and I'm supposed to be impressed?"

Erin opened her mouth.

A surge of adrenaline caused Drew to rush forward. He grabbed Erin by the shoulders and pulled her to him. "Dr. Costa, no offense, but I will not allow you to speak to Miss Holland this way. There are many other sources for what I need."

With her mouth still open, Erin gazed up at him.

"There may be many other sources for what your *lab* needs, but I think there's only one source for what you need." Dr. Costa burst into a round of laughter and pointed at Erin. "I heard she was a fiery one, and I just wanted to see what she would do, but I must say the look on your face and your actions were priceless."

As if she might pass out, Erin leaned against him.

Once the man's words processed through his mind, Drew smiled.

"To tell you the truth, I'm a huge fan of your work. Both of you." Dr. Costa held his hand out.

Erin held her finger up. "Drew, for the record, I was going to be nice."

Since there was no point in refraining from his actions, he bent down and gave her a light kiss. "I believe you."

"But for the record, thank you for defending me." One of her true, gorgeous smiles lit up not only her face, but the world around them. She finally faced the man who made this moment possible and shook his hand. "Dr. Costa, I believe we would like to see some peppers now."

"Call me Adan." He gave Erin a hearty shake.

"Call me relieved." Drew also shook his hand and they all entered the facility. The fact she had to thank him for defending her left a sour taste in his mouth. While she tended to him during his sickness and fought for them every step of the way, he had simply sat back and reacted to her, and he was never on her side.

The greenhouse almost looked like a movie set with rows and rows of different vegetation in various colors and shapes gracing the massive space.

"This is like having the best of the outdoors, indoors." Erin slipped her camera out of her bag and held it up. "Adan, do you mind if I take some shots?"

"Only if you get my good side." Adan straightened up and began playing tour guide, pointing out different hybrids of vegetables and fruits.

They stopped in the area devoted to all different types of peppers and chilies.

"You said this was for a new product?" Adan corralled them around a bright red pepper.

"We're doing an entire product line." Erin panned the area and put the camera down. "Hollywood Glow."

"This one is a hybrid of a cayenne pepper, higher levels of capsaicin and once concentrated, it has good levels of vitamin A." Adan picked the vegetable off the vine and held it out.

Drew leaned in for a closer look and glanced over at Erin. Her wrinkled nose told him she wasn't impressed. "Capsaicin..." Before he even finished the sentence, Erin piped in.

"I know, it has a lot of health benefits, mostly under exploited. It can help blood pressure, lower cholesterol, and some say it's even an aphrodisiac." She rested her hand on her hip. "I thought it would be cool to use the pepper in a drink for cleansing. People do it all the time with cayenne."

Well, at least she did her research and had a plan. "So why do you hate it?"

"Because it looks like just a pepper, who cares?" As if she couldn't stomach the sight of the pepper, she turned away.

"It's a unique hybrid." His eyes crinkled up with amusement, Adan stepped toward her. "No one has used it yet."

"Because it's boring." She shrugged. "I don't want some hybrid cast off. I need to have a marketing story to tell. I want an amazing pepper, one that looks different, is different, is worthy to be on my ingredient deck."

Drew was pretty sure he was becoming aroused not only by Erin's marketing prowess, but her use of the proper terms. "Do you have something different?"

No sooner did Adan point, than Erin turned and walked down the row.

"This one." She stopped in front of a red pepper with orange stripes in the shape of a spiral.

"The levels of Capsaicin are not as high in this one." Adan joined her.

Erin lifted her chin toward him.

"We can concentrate it." Drew approached the pepper. If nothing else, it was unique.

"It's fragile. It's very perishable." Adan shook his head.

"Drew can stabilize anything." Like an unwanted gnat in a greenhouse, Erin brushed Adan away.

When Adan glanced back at him, Drew let out a low chuckle. "I trained her well."

"No one else is using it?" She ran her fingertips over the shiny skin of the fruit.

"Not at triple the price." His colleague tapped his foot.

"Well, maybe you're more like double the price." Erin spoke to the pepper, raising her voice as if it were her pet. "But you are definitely a prestige brand pepper for a prestige brand product line. Of course at double the price, we want the exclusive for at least five years."

"At triple the price, the exclusive will be for two years." Adan crossed his arms.

Before continuing, she peeked over at him, a slight widening of her eyes asked him for permission and Drew winked, giving her the go ahead. They always spoke a silent language.

The corners of her mouth twitched, but she hid her emotion before she spun on her heel and faced Adan. "You want to sell me some pepper that will rot under normal circumstances, and you want Drew to have to work extra to fix your little hybrid mess, and you want me to pay triple and not have an exclusive?"

"I thought you were an actress." Adan lifted his hands like he wanted to surrender.

"For your intents and purposes I am the marketing director for Fluent Words Laboratory." With slow steps, she stalked toward Adan. "I make sure that what is created can actually be sold, and I don't think this or anything else here will be viable without a five-year exclusive and a small premium over your loser pepper down the aisle."

"Double the price, five-year exclusive and a custom autograph for my wife." Adan held out his hand.

"Shake with the man in charge, and show me something bursting with polyphenols. Drew is known for his work with polyphenols. Hollywood Glow must have his DNA." Lifting her camera once more, Erin walked away.

Both of them watched her go.

Adan gave him a playful punch in the arm and joined her.

His mind wandering, Drew followed them. Here he thought when Bambi left he would have to carry every meeting, but his and Erin's combination was even more powerful. Bambi would have opted for the more suitable pepper. Erin based her choice on her gut instinct for sales, marketing and him. God, he loved her.

He stopped.

Yes, he loved her. Always had, always would. The time apart, the trials, the tribulations, the drama, nothing changed the simple fact he loved her. From the day she basically adopted him at his screen test, he loved her. Just because he wouldn't admit it until this second didn't make it less true.

"Drew!" Erin's yell echoed through the greenhouse.

Instinct or a homing device he sprinted toward her, finding her and Adan in the part of the facility that housed the berries. "What is it?"

With a sexy saunter she approached. "Open your mouth."

He obeyed, and she placed a large round purple berry on his tongue. The moment he bit down, a familiar yet not familiar sweetness, mixed with a perfect tang took over his mouth and he nodded.

Staring right into his eyes, she put another one in her mouth, then one more.

"I take it you're either hungry or you like the berries?" He had no choice but to smile at the way the purple stained her lips.

"Drew. This is a mix of three berries. They took a hybrid of two berries and then made a hybrid with another berry, isn't that amazing?" She turned her attention to the perfectly plump spheres cradled in her palm. "They have the highest level of polyphenols and though I think berries have been done, I think with the connection to you, these purple pearls would be perfect."

"I love you, Erin." The words seemed to burst out of his mouth.

"Oh." She dropped the rest of her berries and they rolled across the floor. Tears instantly welled up in her eyes. "Did you really just say that?"

A flash of the first time he tried to tell her twenty years ago ran through his mind, but he kicked it away like unwanted trash best forgotten. They were here now, and he loved her. "I love you."

"I love you. Never think I went one day of our time apart without loving you and wishing for this second." Her tears fell and she flung herself into his arms.

He put his arms around her and gave a quick glance to his colleague.

"I'm going to get you some research papers and samples to take back with you. I'll draw up the paperwork and email it." Adan saluted him and backed away.

"Thanks." Not wanting to let go of the woman who finally said she loved him, he raised his chin to the man and ran his fingers through Erin's hair.

She tilted her face up to him. "Say it again."

Before giving in to her, he leaned down and brushed his lips against hers. "I love you." For the second time in his life, he lost a significant amount a weight, this time in the form of the weight on his chest at having let his feelings out and having them returned.

"Tell me we'll never be apart again." As if she were afraid he would vanish, she held him tight. "Promise me."

"I promise." Once more, he kissed her. The past finally managed to go back to where it came from. They had a new beginning built on a lot more than the first time around.

"How about we grab some berries and check into the hotel?" She pulled back and gazed right into his eyes. "Now you can really make love to me."

"We're going to have it all, Erin." Visions of them working together in the lab floated through his head. "We're going to work together, be together. You're brilliant in marketing."

"Maybe we can even get cast in a film together as a real couple." She jumped a little and hugged him. "Just promise me that when I go on location you'll come with me."

His body tensed. Her career tore them apart before. He wanted college, she wanted to act, and no one would believe they were together. Without even realizing it, his thoughts jettisoned back to twenty years ago.

"Drew?" Though she only said one word, her tone dripped with worry.

Somehow they had to break the cycle, and he needed to be the one to start.

He held her out at arms' length. "I'll never leave your side."

"I love you." She crushed her lips to him.

This time he got the kiss.

This time was different.

"BEAKER, LET'S GO into the kitchen and while I make your meal we can have a quick chat." Dog leash in one hand, the love of her life's arm in the other hand, life was good, maybe better than good. The last few days on the road were straight out of a romantic comedy where everything was tied up with a nice little bow, all punctuated with them getting their pet before they entered their house together.

Drew slid the key into the lock. "What do the two of you chat about?"

When life was good, it also meant it could rapidly become un-good. "Drew, don't go inside!" Erin pulled both her males back away from the door to Drew's house.

"What's wrong?" He wrapped is arm around her.

Beaker stood in front her, a sentry protecting her. They should just stay right here.

"Babe, what's wrong?" Drew tried again.

Though she broke out into a sweat, she swallowed, took a breath and let it out. "What if we step in there and things change?"

"How so?" He went from holding her to rubbing her shoulder.

"Maybe we need to live a life on the road. We found ourselves out there, you told me you loved me out there, you and I became us out there." Her mind running off in a million different directions, she fought the urge to run back to the SUV in hopes Drew would follow.

"You know what I learned?" Drew coaxed her closer to the door.

"What goes up must come down?" A tear streamed down her cheek. Inside, all that waited for them was casting calls, reality shows, commitments and things that wanted to separate them.

"I think we already lived that part." He kissed her temple. "Maybe rather than Isaac Newton, we should go with something Leonardo Da Vinci said."

She stared up at him waiting for this revelation.

"In rivers, the water that you touch is the last of what has passed and the first of that which comes; so with present time." His voice lowered and sounded almost ethereal.

Drew's words, actually Leonardo Da Vinci's words, washed over her and she allowed herself to inhale.

"Of course, we could always go with something Drew Fulton has to say." He leaned down to her ear.

His breath on her skin caused shivers, and she shuddered. "What does he say?"

"In this house, we need to have a guest room again." Again, he gave her a kiss.

Fine, she couldn't stop a smile and a jolt ran through her. "I don't quite understand."

A sly chuckle escaped his throat. "The man and the woman of the house should sleep in the same room and intermingle their possessions. That is the first step on the path of a fresh beginning."

Woman of the house. She relished her new title, pressed her palm to his cheek and kissed him. "Then I say that the man and the woman of the house should intermingle everything."

"I think we need to do that post haste." At last, he opened the door. "Go have your chat with Beaker, and meet me upstairs."

"All right." Like the day she first arrived, she looked down as she stepped over the threshold. She unclipped Beaker's leash and he ran over to his dishes in the kitchen and as if he instinctively knew she was indeed the woman of the house, turned, looked back at her and swatted his bowl with his paw.

"I think someone knows I have a surprise for him." Before spoiling the pet of the house, she glanced behind her. Drew was lugging their luggage upstairs and she took her opportunity to reach into her bag and pull out a gourmet dog cookie she couldn't help buying when they picked up Beaker at the dog hotel. "I know it's before dinner, don't tell your daddy."

Beaker sat like a gentleman, and she fed him the treat.

"Part of your conversation with Beaker should include how he shouldn't have cookies before his dinner." Drew laughed and dashed down the stairs and outside for the rest of the bags.

At being discovered, she pursed her lips.

As if he understood, Beaker cocked his head.

"Anyway, I also got you a little something to wear." She found one of the bandanas she bought him, kneeled down and tied it around his neck. "That is definitely a smart look for you. Now pose."

Beaker stood up and lifted his nose in her direction.

"Well, you certainly know how to vogue." She gave the dog a little pose in return, and using her best strut walked over to the dog food canister she scooped up his serving and got a bottle of water out of the fridge.

Once more she looked around for Drew. With him nowhere in sight, she sat right on the floor. "Don't tell Daddy I hand feed you." She poured some kibble into her hand and held her palm out.

Like a true gentleman, Beaker scooped up a few pieces and crunched away.

"Do you mind if I live here with you full time?" She let him continue his meal.

Beaker looked into her eyes. He actually paused and stared at her.

She held perfectly still waiting for the verdict.

The dog leaned over and gave her a lick on the nose.

She giggled and wiped off the wet kiss. "I have to say I love your kisses almost as much as I love your daddy's."

He returned to taking some kibble out of her hand.

"Thank you for letting me share your house." Unable to resist, she wrapped her arms around the canine. "I always wanted your daddy, but you are a major bonus."

The dog pulled back and glanced over at his empty water bowl.

"Well, I must say you have me well trained." She pulled Beaker's water bowl over and poured him some of her bottled beverage. "You may not want to tell your daddy about the water either."

"Erin, come up here!" Drew's yell echoed through the quiet house.

House.

A simple call from the upstairs made her heart swell. It was just a simple act, but one that felt homey and cozy and she didn't remember the last time she felt like she belonged anywhere. "Coming." She finished giving Beaker his food and water, kissed the dog on the top of his head, and dashed up the stairs to Drew's, or the master bedroom.

The sight of the room coupled with the already warm sensation running through her and a burst of something she would identify as happiness.

Apparently, Drew took it upon himself to destroy the room. Clothes, both his and hers were strewn all over the place. Drawers were taken out of the dressers and the contents of all their suitcases were either spilled on the bed or on the floor. "Looks great."

"As great as you feeding Beaker out of your hand and giving him that bottled water." With a sneer, he glanced over at her.

"He deserves the best." How did he know? She furrowed her brow. "What happened?"

"Well, I started by moving my stuff out of the drawers and then I was looking for something and then the rest just sort of exploded." He scratched his hand through his hair.

"Do you want some help?" She headed straight into the eye of the storm and stood by his side.

"Yeah, hence me screaming for you." He pointed toward the dresser. "Can you do me a huge favor and figure out what's in that bottom drawer?"

"Sure." She stepped over some debris and pulled the handle on the one and only drawer Drew didn't take out of the piece of furniture.

Inside was only one thing. A long red jewelry box from a designer she knew all too well. Her cheeks heated. Hell, her whole body heated. She took a breath and tried to shake away the tremble that overtook her. Drew had a life before her. They had twenty years of living and no doubt this was some remnant of another time.

"What's inside that has you so silent?" He joined her. "Oh, I see."

Though she wanted to stomp her foot and point at the box and demand an explanation, or even better burst into tears and fling herself crying on the bed until he bought her a piece of jewelry, for once in her life she chose the high road. "I'm going to go collect some hangers from the other room, and we'll get his place cleaned back up."

Before she left, he caught her wrist. "Don't you want to see what's in the box?"

Somehow she knew things wouldn't last beyond a road trip. In some odd way their movie seemed to tell the future. "Drew, I really don't want to see something you purchased for someone else." Why was he torturing her after he said he loved her?

"Well, in my mind the person I bought this for and the person receiving it seem like two different people, but technically they are one and the same." He pressed the box into her hand. "Open it."

Not understanding his riddle, she huffed and flipped the lid of the box open. The jewelry piece was perfectly Drew and the designer, simple and elegant. A tri colored gold chain scattered with diamonds. She knew the line this particular necklace came from and always admired it.

"I bought this quite some time ago for the woman I loved." He extracted the piece of art from its velvet bed.

She ground her teeth together waiting for him to get to the point.

"I had to wait twenty years for her to say the words to me." He looped the jewelry around her neck and fastened it. "So many times I went to throw it away or sell it, but I couldn't. I suppose I waited, hoping one day the rightful owner would claim it. I knew I stashed it in here and had to find it. Sorry about the mess."

She didn't even realize tears were streaming down her eyes until she tried to look at Drew and he was nothing but a blur. "You bought it for me?"

"Of course. There was always only you." With his thumbs, he wiped her tears away.

"I love you." She pressed her lips to his and closed her eyes when he wrapped his arms around her. The same feeling of safety and belonging encompassed her anytime he held her.

They were up so high right now, she only prayed it didn't come down.

INT. INDIANAPOLIS, IN – AT SCHOOL IN THE
PRINCIPAL'S OFFICE - DAY.

Roxy, her parents and the principal are having
a meeting. The principal is going through a
file.

ROXY sits with her hands folded on her lap and
glances over at her mother.

>   ROXY'S MOTHER
>   (Speaks through her
>   teeth)
>   It's not like I don't
>   have enough work at
>   home, now we have to go
>   through this.

PRINCIPAL glances over at them and then back to
the papers.

>   ROXY'S MOTHER (CON'T)
>   I'll never understand
>   why you made this
>   pilgrimage anyway. What
>   a waste of time.

ROXY'S MOTHER shifts in her seat and shakes her
head.

>   ROXY
>   I know you don't
>   understand, and I don't
>   really care.

ROXY'S FATHER raises his head for the first
time and looks over at Roxy and her mother.

PRINCIPAL closes file.

>   PRINCIPAL
>   Well, even though
>   Roxanne has not been at

this school very long,
her past record as an
excellent student does
speak for itself. I
believe the move coupled
with many other life
changes did affect her
judgment, and we are
prepared to offer her
the same solution as we
did the other student
who went with her though
she was gone longer.

                    ROXY
          So, I'll be able to
          graduate and make it up
          in summer school?

                    PRINCIPAL
          Yes, and you'll be able
          to go on to college just
          fine. Have you chosen a
          school?

ROXY opens her mouth

                    ROXY'S MOTHER
          Unless she's getting a
          full scholarship down to
          the cost of her shampoo,
          this one here is getting
          a job not an education.

ROXY looks down at her lap.

PRINCIPAL leans back in his chair.

                    PRINCIPAL
          There are a lot of
          programs to consider
          before we rule college
          out.

ROXY'S MOTHER stands.

> ROXY'S MOTHER
> Well, I'm not going into
> any more debt for any of
> my children. This is
> something we need to
> discuss ourselves. I
> don't need any rhetoric
> about the virtues of
> going to college.

ROXY'S MOTHER stomps out of the office.

ROXY'S FATHER looks around and follows Roxy's
mother.

> PRINCIPAL
> Roxanne, what is it you
> want?

ROXY stands.

> ROXY
> That seems to be the
> question of the hour,
> and once I'm sure, I'll
> tell you. All I know
> right now is I need to
> let go of certain
> things, hold on to
> others, and make a huge
> change.

Chapter Twenty-Seven

"LOGAN SAID THEY ALREADY narrowed down the selections. We're just seeing the tapes to give our input." Erin wrung her hands and shifted in her seat.

The movie. The blasted movie. Since last night when Erin realized the casting was the next day, she turned into a one-person disaster zone. Drew grabbed her hand. "Baby, you're shaking." It seemed as if anytime the quote unquote industry entered their lives, Erin fell apart. Not this time.

"This is it. Once I give my opinion, I won't be Roxy anymore. I'll just be an extra." She clutched his hand.

"You will always be the original Roxy and you will always be Erin." He pulled into the studio gates, nodded at the guard at the booth, and without question was guided to the studio back lot.

Yes, he visited the studio the night he burst in on the 20th Anniversary party, but it was a different experience entirely to be welcomed in like a regular on a workday. No wonder people were addicted. Once spying Logan's car, he pulled into the spot next to it.

"Drew." Erin's voice came out cracked, fractured, as if it wanted to break into a million little pieces. "I don't know if I want to do this or not."

It was his job to make this better, his job to fix it. Maybe once they got through this they could move on. Yes, part of him wanted to come back to parts of this, but not at the expense of his love. "Listen, let's do this and then we'll go grab Beaker and drive down to the beach for a bite and pick some products for Hollywood Glow."

Rather than speaking, she nodded and touched her necklace.

With no other choice, he got out of the car, retrieved Erin and guided led her into one of the studio buildings to the small theatre they sometimes used for screenings. Normally, this level of casting was done screening footage on tablets in a restaurant. Leave it to Logan to make it an event. Logan, Ivy, Ryder and some woman were already there.

"There is the last of our group." With wide eyes, Logan stomped toward them, leaving Ivy to talk to the other woman. "You're late."

Ryder strutted over and joined them.

"Ten minutes." Drew shot him a look right back. "That's early by LA standards."

"The studio sent someone to check up on us." Logan spoke through clenched teeth. "They didn't see the need for such fanfare in casting, but I hold creative control."

"Who is she?" Drew glanced over at the woman who was most obviously an executive with her precision haircut and perfectly tailored suit.

Ryder shook his head. "That's Cora Caine, the CEO of chargge.com. She's worth a pretty penny."

"Figures you would know that." Erin mumbled under her breath.

Ryder narrowed his eyes at her. "Of course I know, maybe she wants to invest in another movie."

"Make your movie already and stop talking about it." Erin snapped. "Leave that poor girl out of it."

Once more, Drew took Cora in. She seemed a bit young for the position, but he shrugged. Whatever.

"Well, apparently our project wouldn't have been green lighted without her or her money, so we have to play nice." Logan's eyes went right to Erin.

"It's not like I run with scissors." Erin barked at him.

"Your track record with women isn't so great," Logan countered.

"Log, leave it." Drew needed to step in. His best friend didn't care or realize what Erin was going through.

"Just cause she has a vagina doesn't mean I can't speak civilly. Look at me and Ivy, we are practically best friends." Erin lifted her chin. No matter what the circumstance, his girl would hold her own.

Both Logan and Ryder stared at Erin as if she spoke a foreign language.

Out of the corner of his eye he saw the newcomer turn their way and approach. Before he could let out a warning, she came to the edge of their little circle.

"I hate the phrase time is money, but in this case it's absolutely true." She glanced at each one of them. "I know we don't need any introductions, so to use another tired phrase, let's get this show on the road."

Her words out, Cora Caine spun on her heel and took a seat in the third row of chairs.

Again, Logan gave him a look. Ryder smiled and Erin rolled her eyes.

"Well, let's do this." Drew figured they had no choice but to comply.

They all took their seats around the tiny theatre, Logan and Ivy in the first row, Ryder off to one side and he and Erin in the second row behind the three of them.

"Well, after screen testing quite a few teens, we narrowed it down. They're all reading a scene from *Hollywood Stardust* so we can relate," Logan announced. "Because this movie holds such a personal place for all of us, I thought it only be right that we choose our successor. I will start by showing who will be the new Steven."

The lights lowered and the screen lit up with a blond teen, ponytail and all. If Drew squinted he could almost mistake the kid for Logan, down to some of the inflections in his voice. However, it wasn't Logan. Unless they could time travel and get Logan back, this was the absolute best they were going to do.

The segment ended. Everyone but Erin clapped. She simply stared straight at the screen.

Logan turned back to Erin. "What do you think?"

She gave him a nod.

"Now, here are the two candidates for William." Once more, Logan faced forward and they were treated to watching two Ryder lookalikes read a scene of William discussing why they needed to see Hollywood Stardust before the theatre was torn down. The first one definitely had more of a swagger than the second.

Erin fidgeted in her seat.

Drew wrapped his arm around her and kept his focus glued on this bizarre experience.

The lights came up and everyone turned to Ryder.

For a man so at peace with himself, even their leading man seemed confused. He rubbed his face and cleared his throat. "Where did you find these people?"

In truth, Drew had been wondering the same thing.

"We work in the industry. A huge studio is backing us. Where would you think we'd find the people?" Logan faced him.

"They look like me, but they're not me." Ryder inhaled deeply and looked up at the ceiling. "It's like a ripple in the universe."

"Well, which ripple speaks to you, Mr. Scott?" their money woman barked across the theatre.

Ryder turned back to Erin. "Which one speaks to you, Miss Holland?"

As if caught in an unexpected spotlight, Erin didn't move.

"Babe, speak to me." Ryder snapped his fingers in her direction.

At Ryder's term of endearment, Drew jutted his jaw out. "Leave her alone."

"Just because you finally stepped up to the plate, doesn't mean you own her." Ryder leaned over the back of the seat and stared him down.

"Listen to me. I'll do what's best for Erin no matter what." He moved forward. "And you calling her babe and asking her to choose for you clearly isn't what's in her best interest."

"I suppose it was best when you left her then." Ryder faced the screen.

Before he could take hold of his woman and drag them out of there, she spoke. "Choose the second one. He reminds me of you when you first arrived on set," Erin whispered.

"The second one." Ryder hit Logan on the shoulder.

Wait, wasn't she going to say anything else? He tensed.

"I hope the new cast has less drama than what's going on in this room. Can we get on with it or should we have just had Miss

Holland screen all the tapes and saved a lot of anguish?" the bitch in the back called out through the small space.

"Let's get to Charles." Logan lifted some remote and the screen illuminated.

In a flash, he was staring at someone who dressed and looked like the Drew of twenty years ago, but as Ryder said, it wasn't him. Still, it was like a window in time.

This whole experience was like a window in time. The way Erin was acting, sparring with Ryder, being at the studio and everything, in less than a second, his mind transported right back to that time.

Even with her notes saying she had wanted to be with him, there were times it was hard to believe her words, especially on those days after shooting and she had disappeared, an occurrence that seemed to have happened more and more as they neared the end of their film.

However, they had finally returned to Los Angeles after being on location and he wanted to take her out that night. Yes, he knew she wanted to wait until they wrapped to make them official, but it wouldn't be odd for them to be seen together. No matter, with all the crap they glued on his face and padding they kept adding as he lost weight, he was rarely identified in public. They needed to do something other than lie in a hotel room bed together. Well, not really, but they did need to add to their repertoire of activities in many, many ways.

Though part of him expected to find her waiting for him after he finished a quick retake with Logan, the other part wasn't surprised she was nowhere near the set. Without bothering to change out of his wardrobe, he went in search of her in the studio back lot.

He walked among the rows of big buildings that could contain anything from a set done to look like someone's living room to an entire other world. He kept his eyes and ears out for his missing soon to be better half. Already they were planning for their future. Yes, late at night when the movie world had finally went to bed and faded enough for them to be alone, he would hold her and they would whisper about their plans.

God, he just needed for this movie to end so they could start their lives.

He reached the end of the buildings and turned toward the façade the studio made for the Hollywood Stardust theatre, a set piece he would never be filmed in front of because his character was already on the way back home by the time the other three reached their destination.

Only a few days ago, the four of them met in back of the façade and signed their names in a secret spot in the back. The action seemed fitting. It also fit that Erin might go here while she waited for him.

About ten yards away from his goal, he heard the laughter. First, the giggle he had come to know and love followed by one he despised.

Every muscle in his body tensed as he approached. He knew what he expected to find on the other side, yet nothing prepared him for it either.

"There he is. I told you he would find me!" Lying slumped over with a bottle of vodka, an ashtray and other paraphernalia surrounding her, Erin held her hand up to him. Just as fast, her hand fell, and she stared straight up into the sky. "Drew always finds me." Her voice trailed off.

His blood raced and he surged toward her. "Erin, are you all right!"

"Calm down. Let her be. Turn off the homing device for half a minute and let Erin be Erin." Ryder took a long drag of a joint and shook his head. "Are you a pigeon, Drew? Can you fly?"

Ignoring Ryder, he kneeled down next to her. While he knew Erin had been sneaking drinks, he hadn't been privy to the more illegal substances. What else was she hiding from him? Her actions and his thoughts chilled him. "Erin, look at me."

It took her several seconds too long to shift her red-rimmed eyes to him. "I think you're going to fly one day, and then you're going to leave me."

"I'm not leaving you, I came to get you." His prosthetics suffocated him and he broke out into a sweat. "Let's go."

"Drew." Her voice came out slurred and slow. "Instead of me going with you, why don't you sit down? You're too high strung all the time. You need to have some fun."

From behind him, Ryder let out a low chuckle.

He twisted around and faced his enemy. "What have you done to her? Look at her!"

"Dude." Ryder held the joint out to him. "Take a load off. You and I never really got the chance to get to know each other."

He swiped Ryder's arm away from him and the joint went flying, landing a few feet away.

"Now you're wasting good weed. You're a waste." With an exaggerated movement, Ryder reached into his shirt pocket and pulled out another joint, taking his time to light it and inhale on the makeshift cigarette.

"I'm getting you out of here." While his co-stars might be smoking, he was ready to spontaneously combust. He returned his attention to Erin and attempted to gather her up in his arms, but with her body limp, she was nearly impossible to move.

"I suppose the two of us won't make a Hollywood exit." She laughed and shook her head. "I'll be fine. I just want to relax and feel good. I'm always so anxious."

"Erin, if you are caught like this, it could ruin your career. I want you to come with me now." He wiped her hair out of her face. Did she need a doctor? What did they do? She would be horrified if the media caught wind of this. Hating his own thoughts and not doing the right thing to start with, he went to lift her gain.

"You are such a buzz kill." Ryder crawled over and joined them. "Go do some good somewhere else. We don't need you here."

Refusing to acknowledge the one who was supposed to be the good boy, he kept his focus squarely on the woman who supposedly was going to be with him. Well, she needed to make a choice right now. "Erin."

"I'm fine, Drew, I want to stay here." Somehow, she found the strength to push him away.

He decided to give her one more chance. "Erin, come on."

Instead of words, she took the joint out of Ryder's fingers and inhaled.

Well, apparently this wasn't the first time she'd indulged, and he sat there worried about her. This would definitely explain her wandering off.

"I'm not going to stay here and watch you do this." Before he had a chance to second-guess his decision, he stood and turned away from her, Ryder, and the situation. How did he save the two of them? What else could she be hiding?

"Drew?" Erin's hand on his arm jolted him back into the studio twenty years later with the woman he wanted finally by his side.

"What?" Exactly like that day way back when behind the façade, she didn't defend them, didn't say a word against Ryder.

"Which one?" she whispered.

He stared at the still frame comparing the two selections. "Are they wearing prosthetics?"

"Yes, they were fashioned to look exactly like the originals." Logan twisted around in his chair.

Poor guys. What they thought was cool now, would end up cutting into their skin, inhibiting their ability to breathe, depriving them of being recognized and loved like the other three. Still, whomever they chose wanted the part, or at least he hoped they wanted to act. "Erin, pick one." Fine, he took the escape route.

"The first one. It has to be him." Her voice broke. "I remember the day I first saw you with all that stuff glued to your face. I don't know. I just feel it has to be the first one, there's something deeper there."

"Does it matter?" Ryder asked. "Once you paste all that crap on the character, anyone could play the role."

Before his mind could even formulate a comeback, Erin slapped Ryder upside the head. "All they need for you is some pretty boy with a smirk, right babe?"

"Hey!" Ryder swiped his hair back into place. "Keep your hands to yourself if you please and don't call me babe."

"Right back at you." Erin pushed her back into the seat and curled her arm through his.

Damn it, he wanted to be mad and that whole plan had been thwarted. He glanced over at Logan, held up one finger and said a silent prayer that this Charles had an Erin behind the scenes to take care of him.

Logan nodded and faced forward. "Well, now for the grand finale, our Roxy."

Erin dug her nails into his arm.

That day in the studio with the drugs, he couldn't think of a solution. Yes, he did go stomping back and forced her to go with him, but it didn't stop her, and he later left for good.

Today in the studio, he would give her the support she deserved. "No matter who's up there, no one will ever be you." He leaned over and kissed her temple. "Let's just watch."

She gave him one lone nod and the tape started.

As they watched, her trembling returned. Roxy's lines about being alone when all she wanted to do was return to California and see Hollywood Stardust filled the room.

The first Roxy had the lines down and the look. Whoever the young actress was, she obviously studied Erin down to certain mannerisms like the way she held her hands, widened her eyes. Almost too perfect. Too Roxy.

Erin, the original, stared at the screen with only what could be described as a look of confusion with her brow furrowed, nose wrinkled, mouth half opened as if she needed to say something but the words left her.

In truth, neither of them would ever find a suitable Roxy. The role was hers, she owned it, and he was in love with the woman who played her. He was closer to Roxy than Charles who, for over half his life, Drew tried to distance himself from at all costs.

The scene ended and the second Roxy started. This actress wasn't a carbon copy of Erin, but rather had more of Erin's nuance. Where the first one seemed to want to just duplicate what Erin brought to the table, this one took Roxy and added a bit of her own inflection and an innocence he felt the character always possessed. Hell, who else would drive across country with three guys she just met in school?

The tape ended and everyone in the room turned to the first actress to grace the role.

Where she could pick everyone else's character in less than a second, she returned to simply staring at the screen, tears glistening in her eyes.

She glanced around to everyone in the screening room, but her gaze settled on him. "I can't do this. How do I choose?"

Reclaiming his girl and his life also meant knowing when he had to protect them. "Sometimes you have to say goodbye to something to open the way to the future."

She pressed her palm to his cheek. "We finally have our future."

"We do, and we waited a long time for it."

"The second one is the one who will take my place." A tear fell as she bid farewell to the role she fought to get away from and fought to take back.

"I agree, but no one will do you justice." With his thumb, he brushed her tear away.

She shrugged, but touched her necklace and smiled.

"How about we get out of here?" He took her hand and stood.

Without a question, she followed him, holding up two fingers to Logan as they made their way out.

Before exiting, he looked back to the screening room. The movie ended at the Hollywood Stardust theatre. In reality, it was nothing but a façade. As he led her out and away from the movie and all the drama, his goal was to take her to something real.

HOLLYWOOD STARBURST

EXT. INDIANAPOLIS, IN - ROXY'S FRONT YARD, EARLY EVENING.

Roxy is sitting outside on the porch steps watching her younger siblings play. William drives up and gets out of the car.

ROXY straightens up.

WILLIAM high fives the smaller kids and goes to Roxy.

>   WILLIAM
>   Hey.

ROXY pats the step next to her.

WILLIAM sits down and groans.

ROXY turns to him

>   ROXY
>   What's the matter?

>   WILLIAM
>   When Steven and I came
>   home I promised I
>   wouldn't come here. When
>   Charles dropped off the
>   Lincoln at Steven's
>   house, I promised I
>   wouldn't come here. When
>   I saw you and your
>   parents at school I
>   promised I wouldn't come
>   here.

                    ROXY
          But you're here.

ROXY touches his cheek.

                    WILLIAM
          Give me a reason to
          stay.

ROXY stares into his eyes.

WILLIAM leans in to kiss her.

ROXY backs up and puts her fingers to his lips.

                    ROXY
          Is that what you really
          want?

WILLIAM moves her hand away

                    WILLIAM
          It's what I've wanted
          since I met you, and I
          want it now. Give me
          something to go on.

ROXY closes her eyes and kisses him.

WILLIAM wraps his arms around her and tries to
deepen the kiss.

ROXY pushes William back.

                    ROXY
          William.

                    WILLIAM
          Come on Roxy, you know
          it's supposed to be you
          and me.

                    ROXY
          I want it to be.

                    WILLIAM
          But that's not all you
          want.

ROXY shrugs.

                    ROXY
          I need to clean up some
          loose ends.

WILLIAM stands.

                    WILLIAM
          Then get to it or you're
          going to lose it all.

Chapter Twenty-Eight

"MISS HOLLAND, MR. SOUTHERN is waiting for you." A frazzled woman jumped up from behind her desk.

"I have no doubt." Done up in full Hollywood regalia, including the slicked back hair, red lips and sunglasses, Erin headed straight for the door of her agent's office. The fact she and Rick didn't yet have a contract was but a mere formality. Her contract was safely nestled away in her tote bag in the form of hours of footage of her and Drew on the road.

The woman practically tripped running ahead of her to open the door.

Rather than playing the waiting game like last time, Rick sat behind his desk playing the role of the nonchalant businessman. He needed to take a better acting class. The fact he shot up from his chair the second she entered told her what she already knew.

"You look radiant. The trip did you well." With his hand outstretched and a huge smile, Rick approached.

"Yes, it was amazing." She glanced down at his hand. No doubt he wanted her. Well, the man was going to have to work now. Her social media was off the rails, the product line she was an integral part of was selling before it was created, and the movie she made famous was in the headlines. Drew loved her. Everything else was gravy. She passed him and took her seat.

"So, I see we're dispensing with the niceties." He sat across the desk from her. "I take it we're getting right down to business."

"I have to get to Drew's lab. I have a job, you know." Now that she reclaimed her position of power, she leaned back in the chair and bided her time.

"Actually, I do know." He lifted some bound papers.

A contract. The coveted document people in her position craved. She tried not to focus on the prize.

"But before I lay all my cards on the table, I'll tell you that I have someone who wants to produce your show and has the money to back it. Before you and I make it official and I make a nice chunk of change for saving your career, before all of that, I want to make sure you have the goods."

"I gave you plenty of previews." Though she forced her voice to remain even, she wanted to lunge for that contract and make sure the dollar signs were there. Once she could provide for herself again, she and Drew could be together without any more doubts. Yes, she still needed to tell him about the show, but with the movie and the product line, he would see this would all be positive.

However, before she told her love, she needed to show her agent the goods. She slid her tablet out. Since they returned from their trip the previous week, life had been a whirlwind and she'd only had enough time to string her video clips together without really watching them. However, she wouldn't leave this man with any raw footage until she was sure of the deal. "I believe this is what you want to see." She scooted her chair closer to the desk, held up her little portable screen and hit play.

Suddenly, she and Drew were in the car headed for Nevada talking about liposomes. It was the first leg of their trip, and they were both still so unsure about everything. Hell, even Bambi was with them.

It seemed forever ago.

That was the last night she ever snuck into his room.

Rick nodded.

She skipped ahead to her in the orchard eating the pear.

"That's perfect." Rick laughed.

The video cut to the meeting with Allan where she won the contract manufacturing deal and her chest tightened at two things. First, at hearing herself from the vantage point of a spectator, more accurately, Drew. That night he accused her of not taking him seriously, and as she went off on her unplanned dissertation on how to use his products as skin care, she maybe understood why he felt that way. The whole presentation smacked of an act.

Second, was the fact that she was showing Rick Southern a confidential business meeting with Drew's clients.

Her heart seized, but she managed to slide her finger along the bottom bar and fast-forwarded over the rest of the meeting.

"I was really enjoying that. You were brilliant." Rick rocked his chair back. "Let's see some more."

The further they got into the footage, the larger the lump in her chest grew and her eyes misted over. Somehow, she not only filmed a road trip, she filmed them discovering each other, falling in love.

She shook her head at that one meeting they at had Holistic Health, blushed at the images of their little hidden Bed and Breakfast in Grand Junction, and smiled at the footage she'd captured of Drew in front of all those college students lecturing about polyphenols when they only wanted to ask about *Hollywood Stardust*.

The last little segment was of them as they headed back into California. They had stopped and had a little picnic in the car. She set up the camera on the dash mount and sat next to him. The sunset made the interior of the car glow and Drew put his arm around her.

"Ready to go home, Miss Holland?"

She shook her head. "Maybe our life was meant to be on the road."

"I think our life was meant to start now, no matter where it is." Drew leaned in and kissed her.

"Say it again." She whispered into his open mouth.

"I love you, Erin."

She smiled and the light hit her face in just the right way, or maybe she was just glowing. "I love you too, Drew."

The film ended, freezing on her and Drew in a kiss.

"Well, one can tell you grew up in Hollywood." Rick clapped.

The tear welling in her eye finally fell.

"You did excellent, completely perfect, and you shall be rewarded for your work."

Before she faced Rick, she wiped the sign of her emotion away and cleared her throat. "Let's see the deal."

"Not so fast. There's one small glitch." Rick rocked his chair back and forth and tented his fingers.

Her teeth ground together. Right now she wished Drew was here to deal with all the legal nonsense. "There is one request."

"Well, there's mine and the money's." He leaned forward. "It would be better for everyone involved if we could get Drew to sign on the dotted line as well."

Her cheeks heated, but she froze. "What?" Though she swore she heard what Rick said, she needed to make sure.

"We want Drew. Trust me it will make it better."

"I wanted an agent. What kind of deal is this?" She clutched the arm of the chair.

"This, my dear, is how deals are done now." As if he were telling her any other mundane fact, his tone came out casual.

"I want to go back to making movies. What? Are they going to require Drew there as well?" Actually, that wouldn't be such a bad thing, but still.

"You came to me asking for help. Here it is." He swiped his hand over his desk. "What deals do you have now?"

Every part of her wanted to jump up and yell she was the Marketing Director for one of the best boutique laboratories in the world, but it wasn't officially her title. Where did Erin Holland the movie star go? She didn't know how to be anyone else.

"In truth, I'm surprised Drew didn't come with you today. The two of you put on quite a little performance. Seems to me he would be on board all the way." Rick tilted his head. "Wait, does he not know? Was that whole thing actually real?"

As if she'd been slapped, she flinched and pressed her back into the seat.

"Well, my suggestion is to go find this man who loves you and get him to sign. If all goes well, he can buy some more vitamins." He tossed a stack of papers at her. "One set is for you, the other for your man. Use your manipulation techniques, he'll be powerless."

With a bad metallic taste forming in her mouth, she swiped up the documents. She didn't know or understand this Hollywood, but she knew no other life. Somehow, someway, she had to get Drew to agree to this. She heard him say part of him wanted his life back, but in truth, the man first said no to even having a bit part in *Hollywood Starburst* and didn't even want to go to the casting. If only she could convince him, they could have everything, the lab and their film career. In time, he would see this was the best on all counts.

She headed toward the exit.

Rick ran ahead and opened the door for her. "I expect to see you both tomorrow. Never leave money on the table."

Without a word she left. It was one thing to have a part in a movie, another thing to do a reality show, but she could make Drew see this was the answer. He would do it for her.

HOLLYWOOD STARBURST

INT. INDIANAPOLIS, IN - STEVEN'S HOUSE. DAY.

Steven is reclining on the sofa, books around
him, music on.
At a knock on the door, Steven tosses his book
aside, gets up and opens the door to Roxy.

STEVEN leans against the doorjamb.

                    STEVEN
               I don't remember needing
               another delivery from
               you.

ROXY puts her hands on her hips.

                    STEVEN
               Okay, I get it. Somehow
               you're mad at me for the
               sins you committed.
               Interesting role you
               have cast yourself in.

ROXY raises her chin.

STEVEN steps back and opens the door.

ROXY keeps her eyes on him as she walks inside.

STEVEN closes the door.

                    STEVEN
               Would you like a snack,
               a drink, perhaps you
               want one of our cars to
               drive away?

ROXY walks right to Steven and kisses him.

STEVEN takes over the kiss, bends her back and
then just as suddenly pushes her away.

ROXY puts her hands over her eyes.

                    STEVEN
          What, you're not getting
          what you wanted? You're
          the one who came here.

STEVEN backs up and goes and resumes his seat
on the couch.

ROXY lowers her hand and glares at Steven.

                    ROXY
          I got what I wanted.

                    STEVEN
          And what was that,
          princess? Enlighten me.

                    ROXY
          I'm cleaning up loose
          ends.

                    STEVEN
          If that's what I am,
          sugar, turn around and
          walk out the door now.

ROXY presses her lips together, but doesn't
move.

STEVEN sits up

                    STEVEN
            Are you sure you got
            what you came for?

ROXY stomps across the room, goes to Steven on
the couch, straddles him and kisses him once
more.

STEVEN pulls her in, tangling his hands in her
hair.

ROXY makes a noise and pulls away. Breathless,
she stands up.

STEVEN leans his head back on the couch and
runs his hand through his hair.

                    STEVEN
            So, is this how we're
            going to play it?

ROXY backs up to the door and puts her hand on
the knob.

                    STEVEN
            So, I guess you figured
            it out?

                    ROXY
            Actually, I have more
            loose ends than ever.

Chapter Twenty-Nine

BEFORE ENTERING THE DOORS of Fluent Word Laboratory, Erin ran her fingers over the letters on the tinted glass door and stopped. "Wait." She studied the letters and shook her head. Part of Drew always wanted to be found. The name of his laboratory was an anagram of his real name. Too bad she wasn't looking here.

A newfound conviction engulfed her, and her mind went over the case for them to do the reality show together once more. She hoisted her tote bag up on her shoulder and swung the door open.

"Miss Holland." Jennifer giggled and jumped up. "Isaac is waiting for you in the lab."

"Oh, well, I have a meeting with Drew, Isaac will have to wait." Erin gave the woman a wink and charged forward.

On her way through the building she now knew by heart, she waved at the shipping people and smiled at James, the production manager.

"Are you going to pick me some glowing products?" James gave her a thumbs-up.

"That's the plan." In truth, the thought of choosing the first product in the Hollywood Glow line outshined the reality show, contracts and especially telling Drew about the whole thing.

"Good, then I'll get ready to go, and I'll have a product on my desk in the morning." James gave her a salute.

As she continued toward the back of the building, she realized there was one major lab player not accounted for in the form of one little doe who she last saw leaving a business hotel in Nevada.

With the normal business day coming to a close, Erin could only hope the deer went home or got stuck in a piece of machinery, or just went somewhere far away and played around with her chemicals.

As she thought of different places Bambi could go that didn't involve anywhere near Drew or her, she rounded the corner to the actual laboratory and winced at the flash of natural blonde hair.

This chick seriously needed to find her own forest.

Thankfully, both Bambi and Erin's stud were facing away and she had a chance to compose herself. Along with getting Drew to agree to their show, she could probably get him to open up hunting season. Then she shook her head. No matter where she was, a movie set or a laboratory, there would always be co-workers who didn't get along. There was no getting rid of them because someone would take their place. The only time it worked was when they handed her Drew. It was one in a million, and she didn't want to hedge her bets.

Rather than insist Bambi go and make life hell for her man, Erin squared her shoulders. She already aced the game so now it was time to be a gracious winner. At last, she stepped inside and cleared her throat.

Both scientists turned around and she waited to discover how Drew would treat her.

"There you are." Without any hesitation on his part, he came right for her and kissed her on the lips.

Perfect.

"Well, you told me to be here by 4:45 and I know how to listen." She wiped a bit of lipstick off of his lower lip and smiled. "You're wearing a white coat and everything."

"I thought I would dress the part for you today." He tilted his head.

Excellent, he wanted to play a role. She had just the project for him. "You look amazing."

"I know the two of you have a lot of work to do, so I'll get going." Bambi clutched her notebook to her chest. "We were just finishing pulling samples so you can work."

"Thank you for that." Erin swallowed. Why did the world have to be full of confrontations?

Bambi rubbed her lips together and looked into her eyes. "I heard what happened at Organic Oasis. It's a huge project. I wanted to say congratulations. Marketing is very important."

Perhaps she and Bambi read from the same script. "Before I can market it, someone has to make it, so congratulations as well."

They stared at one another.

"Well then, I look forward to helping make your vision come to life with the new ingredients you found." The tiniest of smiles flickered across Bambi's face.

"Maybe we could go on a little outing, have lunch and study the competition." If they had a prop of an olive branch, theirs would have taken over the lab. Erin wondered if an olive branch had any ingredients they could use, perhaps something calming.

"Lunch with Erin Holland." Bambi glanced over at Drew.

Drew let out a laugh. "She does eat."

Bambi's cheeks took on a bright red hue. Since everything seemed to be going so well, Erin resisted calling her Bambi, the red-cheeked deer.

"I suppose I have to get used to working around stars."

"Ha!" With a little jump, Erin pointed at her. "I knew you were a fan."

"Let's not go crazy." Bambi held her hand out. "I've seen a few movies, that's all."

Erin took the offering and pulled her in closer. "Do you want an autograph?"

Out of the corners of their eyes they peeked at each other.

"Yes, on the paperwork so we can get your line going."

They both busted out laughing. One of the many anvils on Erin's chest lifted. It wasn't unheard of for her to have a female she didn't try to murder. Look at her and Ivy, they were basically besties.

"Now I'm going to go so I can have that autograph." Bambi squeezed her hand, patted Drew on the shoulder and left, closing the door behind her.

"Erin." Drew took her by the shoulders and stood in front of her.

Oh, here it came, the talk about not taking Bambi to lunch for fear she would do something to her. As if. It would end up all over the tabloids or worse. "Yes?"

"I love you, baby." He leaned in and kissed her.

Again, she was taken off guard. She snuck her arms under his white coat and returned the kiss, but a little deeper.

A small moan escaped his throat and he pulled back. "So, do you want to see what you have to choose from?"

"No, I'm happy with what's right in front of me." Sometimes it was still hard to believe they managed to find each other.

"You make it impossible for me to think." He wrapped his arm around her waist and guided her toward a long counter with a multitude of different capsules set up.

"That's my job." She scanned all the different colors and combinations. "It's like looking at a rainbow of health."

"Now before we get into the particulars of each formulation, let me tell you that we can't change anything except the label."

While Drew continued to expound on FDA regulations and so on, she assessed each one, her eye going right to a black and clear capsule. On the clear side one could see little white balls inside.

"You can have full control over any box except for the copy that must be there, and we have to pass compliance." Drew continued.

She lifted one of the capsules between her fingers, spied a bottle of water with Drew's name on it, popped the pill in her mouth, swallowed it down with some water and nodded. "This one's perfect. We'll call it a white tie affair and the box can have an image of a red carpet. I want the kind of box that has a lift off top like it's a high-end watch. You have to want to keep the box. It's like a present." Her decision made, she put her bag down and slid out her camera. "May I capture this moment?"

"You don't even know what's in it." His voice hardened. "Also you just took something you had no idea what it was."

"Drew." She spun toward him and faced him head on. "Let me assure you I know what's in it."

"How is that possible?" One of his brows lifted.

"Simple. First, you would never have put anything in front of me that wasn't appropriate for the Hollywood Glow project." A bit of attitude lacing her voice, she put her hand on her hip. "Second, you would never put anything in front of me that I couldn't put in my mouth. I just wanted to make sure it was easy to swallow."

He stared into her eyes.

Apparently, the word swallow diverted his attention elsewhere. "Can't you be the sexy scientist and feed me the information, so I can be the starlet and branding expert?"

After a pause, he gave her a slow nod.

"Now, I need some knowledge." She lifted her camera and turned it on. "Tell me about the first item in the Hollywood Glow line." The best way to get him used to the idea of being in front of a camera again would be by putting him there.

In less than an instant he straightened up, flicked his bangs out of is eyes and cleared his throat. "The formula for White Tie Affair is a proprietary blend of antioxidants for the skin including Vitamin C, Vitamin A and a complex of B Vitamins with the addition of collagen."

"So what we put in our creams can also be good to ingest. Beauty is outside in and inside out." She stalked up alongside him.

"That's exactly what I'm saying, but as my marketing director you know how to put it much more eloquently."

"So tell me Mr. Fulton, why bring me to the lab rather than your office?" Just as she knew Drew wouldn't put anything for her fit for their line or her consumption, she also knew he brought her here for a reason.

"Well, I thought it was time I show you a few things." He motioned her over.

"I'm always up for a private showing. How do you make one of these wonderful supplements anyway?"

"Well, we start by doing some initial research and look at studies and respond to the market place. As you know, we work with raw material providers and specialty raw ingredient manufacturers. Once we play with a formula for a while, we will make some test batches and choose the container. When that's ready, we conduct an FDA stability test, which is why once a formula is complete we can't change it or the container because we would have to do the test again, and it's costly." He took her arm and guided her over to a machine. "This is the HPLC."

"English would work here." Though unsure what the big computery looking machine with keypads and tubes was, she filmed it anyway. Drew seemed excited about it and he looked really cute telling her all these things.

"High-performance liquid chromatographer." He caressed his hand over the top of the monitor. "Once we get the raw materials in, they are quarantined and checked to make sure they are not contaminated, then we bring samples back here and check them. We run the raws through this machine, and it will tell us the purity of the product, or in some cases, the relative amounts of different compounds."

The way he gazed at the thing almost made her jealous. There were definite hearts coming out of his eyes.

"Do you want to see it work?" While he spoke to her, he kept his eyes affixed on his baby.

Erin swore she felt the plot to a bad sci-fi fic coming on. The love triangle between man, woman and HPLC. "Sure." Maybe they needed to have a ménage, but she didn't want to share Drew.

The man practically jumped as he turned on the machine and got everything all set up.

"So we put the sample in here, and it runs through the sensors and it'll tell us what is in the sample. Here I have a solution I created for one of our supplements." Using a syringe, he injected some fluid into the machine, hit a few buttons on the attached computer, and stood back, putting his arm around her waist.

While he stared at the screen, she stared up at him.

"What the machine produces is called a chromatograph." He pointed toward the monitor.

"Oh." Out of the corner of her eye she watched the little graph come up on the screen, but continued to gaze at him, his eyes narrowed in intensity, his jaw set. Unable to stop herself, she traced his chin with one finger.

"You're not watching." He turned to her.

"You're sexy when you're all scientific." She raised her eyebrows at him.

"Don't you want me to decipher the chromatograph for you?" His hand slid down to her bottom.

"Absolutely." She curled her leg around his. "I think all your science is perfect for my film."

"Oh, yeah?" Now his hand cupped her backside. "This is pretty perfect."

"You know what else is perfect?" Their electricity seemed to spark on a moment's notice.

"Enlighten me." His voice lowered.

"The erection growing in your pants. Your lab coat can't hide that." She lowered the camera, looked down at his bulge and back up into his eyes. "I just have to wonder if you always get hard when a chromatograph graces your monitor."

"I get hard when you grace my vision." A growl accentuating his words, he turned her and pressed his body to hers.

Wanting to remind him of the magic of the screen, as well as in need of some endorphins, she asked her next question. "In all the years we were apart, did you ever watch me and get hard from the vision on your screen?"

Rather than answer, he widened his eyes.

"Do you know how many nights I used to lay in bed, close my eyes and picture you there with me?" She put the camera on the counter near the magic machine. "You're so much more satisfying in person than anything I made up in my head and anything my fingers could do."

He snaked his other hand around her and clutched her other cheek. "There are a few scenes from your more recent movies that may or may not have been relegated into my own personal collection."

She brushed her lips against his. "How many times did you come thinking about me?"

"Too many times." He ground his hips to hers and kissed her, a quick yet hard one, accentuated with a flick of his tongue. "Maybe not enough, because I always wanted you."

As if sharing one thought, they grabbed each other, their mouths connected, their hands roamed. Maybe it was the time they spent together, or possibly the time they spent apart, but Drew seemed to instinctively know exactly how to touch her to make her body ache with need.

"God, I want you all the time." Drew's slid his hands under her dress.

"Tell me what you imagined when you watched my films alone in your bedroom and maybe I'll act it out for you." She nuzzled his neck and worked her way up to his ear where she took his lobe between her teeth.

"Ummm." He moaned as he peeled her silk panties down and kneaded her backside. "Would you believe me if I told you it involved this room?"

"Did you want to conduct experiments on me?" The thought jolted through her. "What would you do to me?"

"We would start like this." Without delay, he slipped her dress up over her head leaving her standing in front of him in nothing but partially pulled down panties and her bra.

Instantly going into her role, she put one hand up to her lips and pressed her knees together. "Dr. Fulton, are you sure this is part of the experiment?"

"In order for everything to react as it should, we have to take things step by step." He rubbed his hand over the ever-tightening front of his pants and pulled off his lab coat, holding it out to her. "First, you need to be only in this."

"Only that?" The fact he instantly went into character made her body flood even more. As if she were shocked by the prospect, she widened her eyes.

"Wasn't my instruction clear, Miss Holland?" His voice took on the same dominating quality as the day at the bed and breakfast. "Do you want to ruin my hard work?"

"I'm so sorry, Dr. Fulton." Without delay, she removed her bra and with her eyes on his, dropped it to the floor, then she pulled her panties down, kicked them off the end of her shoe, and put the lab coat on. "Oh." She wrapped the piece of clothing around her and pursed out her lower lip.

"What seems to be the trouble, Miss Holland?" He took one step toward her and unbuttoned his shirt.

"The fabric is rough against my skin, especially here." Using her best damsel in distress high-pitched voice, she showed him the source of the trouble, circling her fingers over her nipples.

"I believe I should inspect this unexpected issue further." Before approaching, he unbuckled his belt, allowing the ends to fall open and bounce with his footsteps.

First, she pulled the collar tight around her, feigning the shy heroine.

"Let me see." Now he stood less than two inches from her.

"Yes, Dr. Fulton." After a pause, she finally turned away and opened the coat, exposing her breasts to him.

"I see the issue." His fingers brushed over her breasts.

"What is it? I don't want to destroy the experiment."

"In any experiment, you must be prepared to deal with any contingency." He gave each one of her tight peaks a light pinch. "Your nipples are hard and sensitive and must be dealt with."

His touch shot thorough her and she sucked in her breath. "Oh, yes, I felt that everywhere. It's very distracting. What can we do?"

"In order to treat you, I need to do a little further research." He lowered his head and guided one of her nipples into his mouth, grazing the sensitized nub between his teeth.

"That's only making it worse." At least she didn't lie. "Now it seems to be spreading." She clenched her thighs together.

"A vexing problem, indeed. I believe this requires me to look for something specific to determine my next course of action." Once more, he stared into her eyes. "Are you ready for what I must do?"

Lord, he was going to be her undoing. She loved role-play, did it for a living. No other partner she had would ever indulge her. "As long as the situation is alleviated. I'm beginning to ache."

"All right, be prepared." He ran his hand down her side and snuck his fingers between her thighs. "Relax Miss Holland, I promise I'll make it better."

After a brief pause, she parted her legs.

He slid his fingers over her, a soft stroke, but one that served to ignite her senses anyway and she let out a little coo.

"This is what I expected. You are wet and too stimulated to be of use to me. We must take care of this at once. " Though his touch was light, his words came out hard and strong. "There's only one solution, but I assure you it will work."

"What is it? What do I have to do?" She put her hand over his. "Are you sure you know what you're doing?"

In a flash, he stood up straight and took her shoulders. "Are you questioning my vast knowledge, Miss Holland?"

"Oh, no. I would never doubt you." She shook her head. "Just tell me what to do."

"Turn around, put your hands on the counter and bend over."

Without question, she complied, facing the machine Drew loved. Well, she won, so there.

The distinctive sound of a zipper lowering echoed through the air, and her stomach coiled with anticipation.

"Very good." He came up behind her and slid the lab coat up to her waist.

Right before she shut her eyes, she spied the flashing red light on her camera. Her muscles tensed. Should she say something or not? She didn't mean to record this, but the thought thrilled her. However, would he believe her?

Even if it ruined their interlude, she had to say something, she simply needed to do it without breaking the moment. His reaction would give her a good indication of how he would take the contract and the reality show.

"Well, do I get good marks for documenting everything we've done tonight?" Just to make sure he knew what happened, she adjusted the camera.

He grabbed her hips. "You recorded this?" The playfulness left his voice.

"Consider it for posterity sake." She wiggled her backside at him. "I also think it's something you and I should revisit in the future if we ever find ourselves in this position again."

He didn't say anything only tightened his hold on her.

"I think this needs to remain part of our private research, but I also think it's damn hot. If you don't take care of me soon, I may have to do it myself." In an effort to entice him, she bent over further. "I want to see what I look like the second you enter me."

"You look gorgeous." With the words out, he entered her.

At his unexpected action and the sudden, welcomed fullness where she needed it most, she gasped and clutched the edge of the counter. "I'm not seeing how this is helping." Thankful he went with it, she went immediately back into character.

"Give it time." He took his time pulling back, and just as slowly reentered her.

She shut her eyes, concentrating on the way he felt inside her. How he was a part of her. "Perhaps I need more."

"I agree." His thrusts sped, came at her with ever increasing power and hitting her in exactly the right way.

"Dr. Fulton." She pushed back, meeting him every time he embedded himself deep within her. "I'm not sure this is helping. I feel a strange pressure growing within me."

"It gets worse before it gets better." He leaned over her, kissing the back of her neck. "I am experiencing the same build up."

She turned back and he captured her lips, a quick peck that ended when he slammed into her.

"Miss Holland." Again, he reached his hand to her center, rubbing her most sensitive spot.

"Oh, Dr. Fulton." Pleasure shot though her. He prodded her closer and closer to her end and she hit the counter. "I'm going to explode!"

"Yes, that's what we want. That's the end goal," he panted. "Let go, Miss Holland, now."

The way he stayed in character, the way he went with his passion and made love to her right in his lab, the way he always made sure to take care of her, all served to push her over the edge. In a sudden burst, her entire being was wracked with relieving throbs of pleasure that rippled throughout her, only growing stronger. "Dr. Fulton, it feels so good!"

"Yes, that's right, just like that." Now he drove into her faster and then stiffened. "Ride it out."

As the euphoria subsided, her knees weakened and she found just as much satisfaction in the flood of warmth at Drew's release.

"Damn." He pressed himself deeper inside her and kissed her shoulder.

For a couple of minutes they remained in that position. The only movement Drew made was kissing her shoulder and curling his arm around her waist.

"Dr. Fulton, do we have to get to the experiment now?" She kissed his arm.

"Miss Holland, that was the experiment."

"Did it turn out the way you planned?"

"It definitely proved the theory of every action has an equal and opposite reaction." He chuckled. "I love you."

They both winced as they separated. She wrapped the lab coat around her and turned toward him. "I love you, Dr. Fulton. We make a pretty good pair if I do say so myself."

"I would have to agree with you, Miss Holland." He gave her a soft kiss. "Speaking of which, there was something I wanted to talk to you about."

For the first time in her life, a man said he needed to speak to her, and she didn't crumble. With Drew there was safety, and she knew it had to be something good. "I do as well, but this time I'll let the gentleman go first."

"I've been thinking a lot about this. I want us to work together. Really make it official." He took her hand and kissed the back. "Actually, we need to make a lot of things official, but let's start by really giving you the title of Marketing Director."

Her heart swelled, especially when she read between the lines and realized what he was really telling her. "I accept your offer, and I'll raise it. I want us to work together here and on some film projects as well." Everything was playing out perfectly. Her anxiety at telling him her news melted away.

He ran a trail of kisses along her jaw line. "We will do Logan's film, but I think the industry has changed a lot. I watch you struggle, and I watch the effect it all has on you. Why don't we focus on the lab? You'll always be the star here and there will be plenty of media opportunities."

Wait. The knot of nerves came back full force and she pushed him up. "Do you think I don't have what it takes anymore?"

"Of course not. I just want our lives to be less in the public eye. I don't want everything dictated by an industry that tore us apart before." His jaw jutted out.

"I was sort of planning on us living a bit more in the public eye." She bit the inside of her mouth.

"What aren't you telling me?" He backed up. "What's going on?"

Her body still weak and recovering from their lovemaking and now her heart speeding at his spot-on accusations, she walked over to her purse and pulled out the contracts. "Look at the opportunity we have." Her voice shook.

He swiped the papers away from her and read the top page. "Erin, what have you done?"

His gaze burned through her. "Reality show?"

"It's for us, the lab, for you." Her throat dried out and she forced herself to swallow, praying he heard her words.

He tossed the papers to the floor. "Just admit you did it for yourself."

She froze.

"Admit it!" With his outburst, he kicked the contracts. "You did it for you. It's always been for you."

In a move of desperation, she reached out for him.

Scratching his hands through his hair, he turned away.

No. This wasn't happening. It started by turning away and then walking away and then driving away. She forced herself to go to him and put her hand on his back. "Maybe it started for me, but that's not how it is now."

"It's how it will always be." He shrugged her away. "I should have known better."

She shut her eyes. Things were up. She needed to defy physics and figure out a way for them not to come down.

<u>HOLLYWOOD STARBURST</u>

INT. INDIANAPOLIS, IN - SCHOOL LIBRARY. DAY.

Charles enters the library, looks around and
then goes and joins Roxy at a table in the
back. Roxy has a book shielding her face.

> CHARLES
> Hey, ready for some
> studying?

ROXY doesn't lower the book or speak. She
sniffs.

> CHARLES
> Roxy?

CHARLES moves to the chair next to her.

> CHARLES
> Why are you crying?

ROXY hands Charles a newspaper clipping from
her notebook.

> CHARLES
> They tore down Hollywood
> Stardust today.

ROXY sniffs and nods.

CHARLES pats her shoulder.

> CHARLES
> Well, at least you got
> to see it before they
> destroyed it.

                    ROXY
          I'm not sure what's
          worse, seeing it and
          knowing how beautiful it
          was, or not knowing at
          all.

                    CHARLES
          I think you have to look
          at it as a great memory.
          Wouldn't you have rather
          seen it before they
          boarded it up and
          destroyed it? Now you
          have a memory.

ROXY rests her head on Charles' shoulder.

                    ROXY
          I think it's too soon
          for it to all be a
          memory, but I suppose
          one day I'll be
          grateful.

                    CHARLES
          I think maybe rather
          than looking at the past
          it's time to look at the
          future.

CHARLES reaches in his bag and hands her some
pamphlets to colleges.

ROXY rifles through the papers and hugs them to
her chest.

                    ROXY
          I don't know.

                    CHARLES
          Just think about it.

                    ROXY

                    (Nods.)
          I'm going to look
          forward to a lot of
          things being a memory.

                    CHARLES
          Use your memories to
          create your future.

ROXY looks up at Charles.

                    ROXY
          How do you know these
          things?

                    CHARLES
          Maybe I have a lot of
          memories.

                    ROXY
          I think of anyone, you
          have the most amazing
          future.

                    CHARLES
          (Smiles.)
          No matter what, remember
          this is just a moment in
          time.

Chapter Thirty

HIS BODY NUMB, HIS MIND reeling, Drew stared at the monitor on the HPLC machine. On the screen were all the peaks and valleys which indicated what components were in the formula. Good thing he wasn't showing her a proprietary formula. For all he knew, it would have ended up in some reality show. When he showed his love the piece of equipment he never expected anything in this room would be on anything other than the film she continued to record for the lab.

The film for the lab.

His focus went to the camera still on the counter.

The film for the lab.

Once more, his mind rewound the words, his chest tightened and the room around him seemed to spin. "Erin."

"Drew." Again, she put her hand on him. "Please, we have to learn to work through these things."

Before he assumed the worst, he faced her. From the day she stepped into his screen test he had never laid eyes on a more beautiful woman. She had changed, had proved it over and over again. "I want to ask you a question and I want you to answer me honestly."

"Of course." A tear dripped down her cheek, and he fought the urge to take her into his arms and kiss it away.

"All the filming you've done since the beginning of the road trip. Was it really for a promotional video for the lab?" In an effort to stop his shaking, he balled his hand in a fist.

Her lower lip quivered. "Not in the way I portrayed it."

Every time she picked up that damn camera he knew. Deep down, he knew. His gut instinct was always right on except when it came to the woman in front of him. "So when you came tearing over to my house wanting to go on the road trip after you decided to leave me, you only came because you needed material for this show?"

"No." She shook her head. "You don't understand. I was at the agent and he told me what to do, but the whole time I wanted to leave and get to you."

"Would you have gone on the trip with me had it not been for the fact you needed an unwilling supporting actor?" He slammed his fist into the lab counter. The entire trip, her support, everything was a lie.

She wrapped her arms around her shoulders and stepped back. "I don't know. We weren't in a good place, but it gave me an excuse to be with you."

"You used me, you used my business, you used everything! For what?" He looked up at the ceiling, praying an answer would come to him. "You did the same thing twenty years ago. I must be crazy!"

"I couldn't watch you drive away from me again." Multiple tears fell. "Part of me used it as an excuse."

"What did the other part did you use me for?" With no divine answer to be found, he shut his eyes.

"I needed a job, Drew." Her voice lowered. "I needed a job."

"I thought you had one." He opened his eyes to his reality.

"I'm an actress." All the color had left her features, but honestly, he wasn't sure if she was upset because of him or because she was found out.

"I know." At the end of the day he knew what she was, but he still dreamed of something else.

"I love you, Drew. I waited twenty years to be with you. I won't do the show if that's what it means." Her voice broke. "Please."

"What? And have you miserable, always wondering if you could have reignited your career with some two-bit show?" Sweat broke out all over his body, and he wiped his face. "Reality show? Have you sunk that low?"

"The agent I spoke to said it was on trend, it would help. I thought we could do it together and show the world Hollywood Glow being born. Look at what happened with a few little appearances we had together. The business would explode." As if she could fix everything with the promise of money and fame, she held her hand out to him.

"Then why didn't you tell me before you ever turned the camera on?" He stared into her eyes.

Silence cloaked the already oppressive room, answering the question for them.

"What happens now?" She lowered her hand.

"We always seem to want different things out of life." Twenty years ago she wanted to be a star, and he wanted to be a scientist. Some things never changed.

"Don't say that." Her tears continued to fall in a steady stream. "Please, don't say that."

"It's the truth. Not saying it doesn't make it less true." He swore he would be able to pinpoint the moment his heart didn't break, but withered away. "How can we be together once the joy of being reunited wears off, and we make the other person miserable?"

"Why did you come back?" She turned away and hid her face in her hands.

"I wanted my life back." Where there was silence, her sobs now filled the room. His heart begged him to play the role he'd been handed years ago and take her into his arms, tell her they would work it out, but his mind asked what stunt she would pull next. "I never expected it to be filmed and sold."

"I think you wanted payback." With her back still toward him, she nodded. "You got it. I was shattered the day you left me and I don't think I'll recover from this one."

Another round of silence took over the space. He couldn't deny he maybe wanted some payback, or he wouldn't have toyed with her at the beginning.

Suddenly, she spun back toward him. Her tears stopped, her hands were on her hips. "You know, you were right. We always want different things."

He lifted his chin. The way she said his words smacked of her telling him no one would believe they were together.

"Somehow, I thought this time we would learn to compromise." She slid off his lab coat and let it fall to the floor then walked around and redressed. "Maybe we were only together to finish the story. Let us know what it was like for us to be together, and now we know. We know it was glorious, and we know it won't work."

He watched her collect her papers and shove then back into her bag. Where was she going? "Erin."

"You know, I understand why you can't trust me ever again, I get it." She headed toward the door, bent down and picked up her panties. "It's just like how I'll never get over the fear that you'll disappear on me. Well, this time I'll make it easy for you."

"How so?" Nothing with Erin was easy. They couldn't do this anymore.

"I'm going to leave this time." Without another glance back at him, she dropped her panties into the nearest garbage can and walked out the door.

The door slammed shut on the woman he loved, and he simply stood there with his pants still around his ankles, just like the Poindexter he tried to fight his whole life.

RUN AFTER ME.
Erin ran out of the lab and collided with her car, her hands slapping against the unforgiving cold metal.

"You have to follow me." Tears streaming out of her eyes, but she focused on the doors. Any second Drew would run after her, find her here, insist they talk it out. They worked too hard to be together.

Nothing. Not even the shadow of someone in the office looking to make sure she made it through the dark parking lot all right.

"Why did you come for me?" This time she asked the question to nothing but the wind. The answer was the same, and she pounded her fist into the roof of her car. "Why!"

Her scream scratched her throat, and she put her hand up to her neck, touching her necklace. He held on to a damn piece of jewelry for twenty years, and he couldn't even run after her. She coiled her fingers around the gold and yanked, the chain making a sickening pop as she broke it and it fell limply to the ground.

Twenty years it waited for her, and she didn't get to have it for a month.

"He's not coming." The same sensation as the time she went

under anesthesia took over her. She didn't even feel as if she were in her own body.

Last time he left her, she ended up in the back office of a doctor having her hand stitched up. She didn't think any doctor could repair what was wrong with her now. When she went to get her keys, she dropped her bag, the contents spilling all over.

"Come out here and help me." She dropped to her knees. The rough asphalt dug into her skin, and her nails scraped against the ground as she corralled what she could. Not caring about anything anymore, she opened the door, threw the bag, the crumpled papers and her wallet on the seat and forced herself inside.

Only by luck did she manage to get the key in the ignition and start her vehicle. Once more, she turned toward the lab. What was he doing now? Sitting there relieved? Playing with that insane machine?

One thing was certain, he wasn't running after her and declaring he couldn't live without her. He did it before, and he would do it again. She would have to do the same.

She drove out of the Fluent Words Laboratory parking lot. The name was an anagram for Drew Fulton. He was right under her nose the whole time, and she never knew. If she did, she would have gone running.

Her hands on ten and two, she took off to see where her car took her. Last time, it took her to Drew. She had no other place in this world she wanted to be, and she couldn't go there.

Her driving took on almost a hypnotic state, but all roads always led her to one place. Hollywood. She supposed her and Roxy were the same person after all.

Through her tears, the lights on Hollywood Boulevard blurred into streaks, and she could barely see. Her car crawled down the famous street. More than once, people honked at her and flipped her off, never knowing who she was besides some woman in a car she couldn't afford.

As someone who could walk into just about any venue in the country, or the world, and be recognized, Erin had never been more alone in her life.

There was a reason she kept people at a distance, turned them away with a glance and a sneer.

No matter how she looked at it, she always ended up with nothing to show for her life.

However, with the way Drew returned, they got reacquainted and the way their lives merged, everything had meaning. She wished she would have known her life had been in a holding pattern while she waited for the love of her life to reclaim her. Deep down in her heart, she knew he would always come for her.

At a stoplight, she lowered her head to her steering wheel, her tears dripping onto her legs. After everything, he couldn't trust her, didn't believe she wanted him. If she had any advice to impart to anyone on this planet, it would be to watch what you say. One sentence she said twenty years ago ruined her life.

The second the words were out of her mouth that night, she wanted them back. She wanted everything back. The games she played with Drew, the way she put him off, the stupidity. For the first time in many, many years, she allowed herself to relive the moment where she destroyed herself.

"What do you see happening between us?" She had known it was the night. The film had been wrapping and now was the moment to lay it all on the line. Could she do it? He was going to want to make love to her, tell the world. What would happen when he realized she was nothing but a whore in actress's clothing?

"We've talked about this. You're going to act, I'm going to go to college, and we'll be together." Hopeful, his eyes sparkling at getting what he fought so hard for, he sat up.

"Do you want me or just the thought of me?" Too many men, Logan, Ryder and Brian included, only wanted her for how she looked, who she became, not because they wanted her. It had to be different with Drew.

"Erin." He got up off the bed and shoved his hands in his pockets. "I know the real you, not the one you play for the cameras. If neither of us ever took another role, it would be fine with me."

"I have to act." She pressed her hand to his chest, not sure if she was trying to push him away on purpose. In truth, she didn't know how to do anything but act. Maybe that was the problem.

"That's fine, so what's the problem?"

"I want to be the woman you deserve, but I don't think I can be." Her eyes clouded with tears. Drew deserved someone who would be home and take care of him. He needed a woman who would make dinner and take care of the laundry and do all those things she wanted to do, but never learned.

"What does that mean?" He sat down in a chair across the small hotel room.

"I'm never going to be the woman you truly want. I tried for the last two weeks, and it was all an act." She wanted to go out, experience life. Yet when she was partying with Ryder or Logan, she longed to be back with Drew. Everything about her was an act. She didn't even know who she was. Neither of them deserved that.

"What do you mean you tried?"

She stared off at nothing, trying to visualize her life with Drew, without him. Was she ready for what he wanted? Already offers were starting to come in for her. If they were together, it would be forever, and she would have no room to do what she wanted without feeling guilty all the time. "It would be so easy to be with you."

"What does that mean?" His tone hardened.

"You would give me everything, but I would only hurt you in the end." All day she'd toggled on what she needed to do. At making her decision, her body felt weak, and she sat at the edge of the bed.

"You're hurting me now."

"Drew, did you really think that tomorrow we were going to show up on set and be in love?" She had to do this for both of them. They were destined for disaster with her leading the pack. Now she just wanted to get out of there.

"Actually, I did." Again, he stood.

Of course he did, why shouldn't he? It was easy for him. "When people are on set, it's like a wonderland, an island where no one can get in. Next week we're going to be back to our normal lives. We won't work there." She got up and went to him, but stopped.

"After spending every night with me, after confiding in me, after making plans with me and telling me you wanted to be with me, you're now telling me it was nothing but some movie making spell and poof, tomorrow we'll be cured?"

She stepped closer. "You've changed so much these last few months." They would both change, but would they change together? What happened if she became a has-been? Would he want her then?

"Obviously not enough." He tensed.

"Drew, I do love you in my own way, but no one will ever believe the two of us could be together. In the real world we don't fit." She swallowed back a gasp at her words, but she had to break it off or forever be caught in the safe haven of one Drew Fulton. They would stifle each other and it would end in nothing but pain.

He stomped to the door and opened it. "Go."

Wait. Her body heated. She didn't mean it. Actually, she didn't know what she meant. Maybe they just need to take a breath and see what happened. "We have tonight." She ran to him and put her hands on his shoulders.

"You took tonight away. You took it all." He shook her off him and jerked his head to one side, telling her to get out.

He gave her permission to leave. Before she had a chance to chicken out, she rushed out of the room.

The door slammed behind her, and she jumped then wrapped her arms around herself. She had to go back, beg for him. The hurt she caused him was evident in his eyes. Could she do this? Maybe she just needed some time to sort it all out.

Again, she had looked back at the door. Everything good was on the other side. Safety, her best friend, the man she loved, more accurately, the man she fought not to fall in love with.

They just needed some time. In tears, she had run back to her room.

A horn honking jolted though her. She blinked and hit the accelerator.

What had they done to each other? Would it have been better if they would have just left the scarred over wounds remain, never opening them to find out what was on the inside?

Again, tears wracked her body, and she was overcome with exhaustion. Her whole life consisted of being with Drew or waiting for Drew. Now she was nothing.

Knowing she needed to stop driving around with no destination, she forced herself into survival mode. Her mind reeled, and she considered her options. Her go-to mop, Brian, was out of the question, as well as her sort-of new agent. If she could find Ryder, they would only end up in bed and the thought of sleeping with someone else caused her stomach to churn.

In search of her phone, she dug through her few possessions. The communication device was nowhere to be found. On auto pilot, she headed to her only other option in this world, and drove into the back lot of Logan's brother's bar.

Most likely, her next move would land her both in a psychiatric ward and the tabloids. Maybe her new agent would think it was great for publicity. Either way, she forced herself out of her vehicle, walked the few yards to the back door and knocked.

The door opened.

"Erin? What's wrong?"

The backlight didn't allow her to see him, but she knew that voice. It was the voice of the man who fixed things. Only this time she didn't have anything to offer him in return. Still, she collapsed into Logan's arms and burst into tears. So much for Hollywood endings, she could only hope this whole part of her life would end up on the cutting room floor.

INT. INDIANAPOLIS, IN – SCHOOL HALLWAY - DAY.

Students scurry to their respective classes.
Books clutched to her chest, Roxy stops dead in
her tracks when she sees William and Steven
coming her way.

Roxy glances around, but the hallway clears out
leaving the three of them alone as the final
bell rings.

STEVEN elbows William.

                    STEVEN
          I told you Roxy still
          went to our school.

WILLIAM crosses his arms.

                    WILLIAM
          I wasn't sure, since she
          left so many loose ends
          all over the place.

ROXY takes a step back.

                    ROXY
          Sometimes loose ends are
          hard to tie up. Things
          continue to become
          unraveled.

                    WILLIAM
          Well, I suppose it's
          better than getting
          everyone involved tied
          up in knots.

STEVEN steps forward.

                    STEVEN

                    Did you ever find what
                    you were looking for?
                    I'm happy to be of
                    service anytime you need
                    to conduct more
                    research.

ROXY lowers her head.

                         ROXY
                    Would it help at all if
                    I said I was sorry?

No one speaks and Roxy raises her head.

                         ROXY
                    You know, the two of you
                    came into my life when I
                    needed you most. We all
                    made mistakes, I made
                    the most mistakes,
                    especially the mistake
                    of thinking I could
                    somehow have you both.

William uncrosses his arms and Steven steps
back.

                         ROXY
                    How do you choose?

ROXY motions between them.

                         ROXY
                    How do you choose?

                        STEVEN
                    Did you ever think it
                    shouldn't have come down
                    to that?

                       WILLIAM

                    I think you just wanted
                    it all.

The three of them stare at each other.

                         ROXY
                    Yeah, I wanted it all.

ROXY runs down the hall.

Chapter Thirty-One

A BOTTLE OF PORT, a broken necklace, a broken phone, a lipstick, a pair of panties and a video camera.

Drew's life consisted of these six items.

He took a gulp of the port then lifted the necklace, taking in the damaged links. After downing another glass of his elixir, he put down the jewelry in its designated spot on the coffee table and picked up the phone. Though the screen was cracked, it still illuminated. Last night, he did what no person should do and entered the password on her phone and looked at her texts, hoping to find some incriminating evidence on Erin. All he discovered was the last text she sent was to him saying she loved him with a kiss face emoticon. He answered with a heart. Everything else was talking about Hollywood Glow or him. Oh, her password to get into her phone was her birthday and on everything else it was still *Hollywood Stardust*.

The lipstick was her favorite shade. A classic designer red she wore since the Hollywood Stardust days, and he ran his fingers over the black case then took in the next piece in his sad collection, the panties. He tried not to think about the panties and how they ended up with him and not on her person. How they christened his lab in the most amazing way. No, he didn't need to think about it because he had it all documented on the camera she left behind when she ran out.

As if asking where the mistress of the house was, Beaker came over and looked between him, the front door and the stairs.

Drew ran his hand through his hair and gazed over the remnants of their night once more.

Where was she?

With no phone, no panties, and no lipstick, her options were limited. He tried calling Logan, but he didn't answer yet. After driving around aimlessly, he chose to wait at the house. Eventually, she would need her possessions.

Last night, when he finally came home, he half expected to find her either in their bed under the covers asleep or in the guest room hiding.

She never came back, and he deserved the fact he stayed up all night waiting for her. Then again, she filmed them with the intention of selling them and never said a word, a violation in every way.

When she ran out, he knew his job was to follow. One wasn't with an actress such as Erin and not know the plot to the movie in her mind.

This was the second time he ruined her script. The first time was the day she found him at Brian's office.

Logan taking the rap for Erin and Ryder's indiscretions had been the end. Drew had applied to Oxford and got in, and he was going across the pond to get away from all of it. He was done with astronomy, no more stars for him, instead, he was going to major in chemistry, create actions, reactions and a brand new name for himself.

They were just about through tying up all the loose ends, and he leaned in to collect his papers when he heard Brian utter her name.

"Erin!" Brian jumped up out of the chair from behind his desk.

Drew turned toward the door. There she was. His weak point was personified in the form of the most beautiful woman on the planet. Would he ever be able to look at her and not react?

"You're early," Brian growled.

"I think I'm exactly on time." Rather than looking at their agent, Erin kept her focus squarely on him.

They stared at each other.

"Drew, may I speak to you please?"

For a moment he paused, his gaze traveled over her, and he opened his mouth. He knew she continued to ask about him. Both Logan and Brian told him she wouldn't let it go. Could she truly care, or did she want something else? He didn't even want to know the answer.

No, he couldn't know the answer. Again, she would ruin his plans, and he didn't have time for a do-over. He spun back around to Brian. "Is our business done?"

His now ex-agent nodded.

Though she still blocked his exit route, he refused to react to her or let her suck him in as he approached.

She held out her hand. "Please, Drew."

"Let me go." He stared into her eyes hoping she heard the not too subtle message in his words. She was right, no one would believe they could have ever been together, he didn't even believe it anymore.

Erin didn't move. She just stood there with her big beautiful eyes glossing over and begging him.

Brian joined them, took her by the shoulders and corralled her away from the door. "Come on Erin."

The second there was enough room to pass, he shimmied by her and rushed out.

As he left, he heard her yell and start crying, setting off every one of his alarm bells. Still, he forced himself forward toward freedom and sanity.

He got into his car and shook his head. All he had to do was make it through the next forty-eight hours and he was off. Away from her, away from acting, away from Drew Fulton. He needed to pull away. Just go and be done. She didn't return his feelings. No, he was nothing but a warm blanket for her. He never even got a kiss while everyone else slept with her.

Suddenly, she appeared, and knocked at his window. He half expected it. Hell, he'd had time to pull away.

"Drew!" She pounded on the window. "Drew!"

He didn't look at her. One look would be his downfall, but somehow he was unable to leave.

"Drew!" She continued to pound on the window. "Please, let me just say something, then you can leave."

No, he never had any resistance when it came to her. Almost beyond his control, he rolled the window down a crack.

"I love you, Drew." She sucked in her breath.

For one brief second, the world stopped. She finally said the words he dreamed about hearing come from her lips.

He allowed himself an extra moment to relish in her confession. Not sure if it was an act or not, or if she even knew the answer, he didn't want to hear anything else from her.

In his final role as an actor, he rolled up the window and drove away.

Yes, he ruined the grand ending of her story, but for him it was perfect, and now he could leave.

As he had driven away from the woman who would always represent his heart, he bid a final farewell to Drew Fulton. Too many times he had asked why it had to be her, but it was and he had known he would never love anyone like that again.

A knock on the door reverberated through his home, just like her knock on the window that day. "Erin?" Would he roll down the window today?

He stood and glanced out the peephole, grinding his teeth together before opening the door.

"I expected you to look less like crap, but I was wrong." Holding a large brown paper bag, Ryder let himself in.

"Where is she?" Drew watched the man make himself at home, first by taking a dog bone out of the bag, and handing it to Beaker, then by sitting slap-dab in the middle of the couch, legs spread, taking up as much room as humanly possible.

Ryder held up his hand. "Don't worry, I brought you a present too." Once more, he reached in his bag, this time revealing two bottles. "Some excellent scotch and a bottle of alkaline water."

"Why?" Drew crossed his arms and leaned back on the door. The man deliberately didn't answer his question. Though technically he didn't have any say in the matter, but if Erin went running to Ryder, it would be the ultimate betrayal.

"I'm figuring you need the scotch, especially since I pictured you downing that syrup that thinks it's wine. The water is because whenever you get good and drunk, you should really rehydrate." Ryder took two of the empty port glasses on the table, opened the scotch and poured them each a glass and pushed one toward him.

"Where is she?" He refused to move until Ryder answered, though in his gut he knew.

"For someone who broke up with her last night, I don't know why you care." Ryder sat back and spread his arms out wide over the back of the couch.

Wait. For the first time, he didn't have to play nice with Ryder. There wasn't a movie, there wasn't Erin, and he didn't have one tie to this shyster. The anger, frustration and irritation about everything finally bubbled to the top and burst. In a surge of energy, he ran across the room and grabbed Ryder by the collar. "Get out of my house."

Beaker barked and ran to his side.

Rather than fight or comply, Ryder smiled. The bastard smiled.

Drew pulled back his fist. The urge to ruin Ryder's perfect Hollywood smile overwhelmed him. "I told you to get out of my house."

"She didn't come running to me last night. I haven't even seen her. I received a message from your best friend asking me to pick up some things for her since he doesn't want her wearing Ivy's clothes, and in the process, I'm now privy to all that happened." Ryder pushed him aside and reached over to the table, picking up Erin's panties. "I assume she showed up to Wilson's with not much."

Drew loosened his grip a little. She went to Logan, not Ryder. However, not too long ago, Logan was here and Drew played the part of support system. How did he end up with Ryder? The man wasn't even second best, he was beyond the bottom of the barrel, he was under the barrel. "Put those down."

"She never wore anything this racy with me." With a tilt of his head, Ryder dropped the drawers and lifted the camera. "I take it this was the weapon of choice?"

Drew ground his teeth together.

Ryder looked up at him. "Listen, I know I'm not Logan swooping in with my cape and making everything better. But he's tied up with someone much more high maintenance than you are, so why don't you let go of me, sit down and take a sip of your alcohol like a good boy."

At last, Drew let go of his once co-star, sat down on the side chair, and swiped his glass off the table. For a finale, he chugged down the drink, nearly choking as the burning liquid slithered down to his empty stomach.

"And cheers to you as well." Ryder poured Drew some more, then lifted his own glass, took a sip, and fiddled with the camera.

The best course of action was probably to get drunk, and Drew chugged the glass down, right as his and Erin's moans filled the room. He dropped the glass and lunged for the camera, inhaling to get out a warning, but an errant droplet of booze got stuck in his throat, choking him and he broke out into coughs.

With a huge grin, Ryder held the camera out of his reach. "Nice move, I didn't know you had it in you."

Drew managed to clear his throat and take a deep breath. "Give that to me."

"Hold on, I just want to see how it ends." Ryder glanced over at him. "I have a feeling." He switched the camera off and put it back on the table. "I have to say the movie I'm making is not as predicable."

If nothing else, now Drew could put a nice helping of mortification on top of his self-loathing sundae. Of anyone who could have revealed the video, he never thought it would be him. This is how these things went viral. He returned to his seat and put his head in his hand. What the hell happened to his life?

"Do you love her?" Ryder patted his leg.

Beaker trotted over to the man who gave him the treat. Traitor.

"What kind of question is that? I've always loved her." He watched as Ryder scratched his dog behind the ear. Erin loved Beaker, Beaker loved her, and in fact he kept looking for her. There was a huge hole Drew somehow fell into with no way out.

"Normally, a man who loves a woman doesn't leave them for twenty years, seems like that man would do anything to stay with her." Ryder gave him a glance and then returned his attention to Beaker.

"You don't know anything about what happened." Not only did he not owe this man an explanation, but as a person who collected women for sport, Ryder wouldn't understand.

"Yeah, I do." Ryder gave Beaker another pat and leaned forward. "Remember, while you went off for twenty years, I stuck around. Do you think in all those years and all the crying and all the what ifs she didn't confide in me in what happened?"

An overwhelming heat took over his body. Now Erin was telling personal business?

"Dude, she never thought she would see you again, but she

always held the torch. Don't blame her for needing a confidante." Ryder narrowed his eyes. "I know she put you off, I know she said she would be with you, and I know she chickened out at the last minute and said some truly terrible things."

He sat back and stared off into the yard at the lemon tree he planted for Erin even when she wasn't part of his life.

"You got her back and then some. I think the universe is even. I think you needed the time apart because you weren't ready for each other."

Ryder's words echoed around him, but if the man was going to pass judgment, then he needed to know the whole thing. "She filmed us for a reality show without telling me."

"Right." Ryder nodded. "Because she was afraid of this."

"Don't you understand? She violated everything we built." Drew focused on the man he saw as his rival since the day he met him.

"Right because she was afraid of this."

"I thought she wanted to be with me, but all she did was use me to get her footage." It was a mistake to even tell him. "She lied, again."

"First. She never lied, she backed out on you. Maybe she's not the most truthful person, but she didn't lie. What she did is withhold the truth, and can you blame her?" Ryder shrugged. "I'm not saying what she did was right, and I'd be pissed too, but flip it and see her side. You know, when anyone faces fear, the best thing to do is ask—what is the worst that can happen, but no one expects it to happen? Well, in Erin's world, this was the worst, and then it happened."

He stared at Ryder. This was the most they ever spoke unless it was scripted. "I didn't come back to be put on display."

"Who's the liar now?" Once more, Ryder stretched out and put his hands behind his head. "Dude, you came back in a really public way, you took a part in the sequel to the only movie you made, and you set your sights on a woman who is very visible. You crave the limelight just like anyone else, only you're too much of a pussy to admit it."

Yes, he wanted his life back, but he wanted it on his own terms. Drew balled his hand in a fist. If he was part of a couple, it couldn't be only on his terms.

After an over exaggerated stretch, Ryder stood. "I'm going to collect a few of Erin's things, only enough to fill this bag." He lifted the paper bag. "The rest the two of you will have to work out."

"End of the week we're having a media event at the *Hollywood Stardust* façade." Ryder laid that on him and headed toward the stairs. "I suppose I better give you a warning since you're so camera shy, though it didn't look so from all those social media updates on your trip."

No one would go through Erin's things without him, especially Ryder. He stood as well and the room spun. Port, scotch and the realization he was going to help collect her items made him light headed. Was this his acceptance of the end?

Ryder stopped just short of the first stair and turned back to him. "I ask you again, why do you love her?"

He stared at Ryder. How did he tell him? There were so many reasons. Maybe not enough or maybe too many.

"You both have a lot of pain. I think before you do anything else you better be able to pinpoint it, or you don't belong with her." Ryder bounded up the stairs.

Damn everything. Maybe his sworn enemy was right, or maybe the guy was only here to mess with him. If there was any truth in his life, it was that Ryder Scott only cared about Ryder Scott. Still, Drew needed to figure it out, or he needed to leave her again.

"'ROXY LOOKS BETWEEN the three of them and puts her nail in her mouth.'" Her heart racing, Erin turned to the last page of the *Hollywood Starburst* script and hugged the script before continuing. At long last, she would know who her alter ego ended up with.

In truth, this was her moment, it didn't belong to some other actress who didn't do the first movie, but with no choice, she spent the last two days up in the living quarters above Wilson's bar reading to herself and acting out all the parts.

Tears clouded her eyes. The *Starburst* script held the same magic as *Stardust*, the same raw realness, the same situation that made her already battered and bruised heart ache.

"I can do this." Erin went to the mirror and nodded to her reflection. Well, she couldn't do anything else, so she may as well read the last line.

At last, she gazed down at the page.

"What?" Her breath caught. She had to have read it wrong. "Wait." After taking a long breath, she read the line again. "Logan!" Clutching the script in a death grip, she collided with the door. She swung the door open as if she were the heroine in that natural disaster movie she once did, she went careening down the stairs into the kitchen. "Logan!"

"She read the end." At the sight of her, Ivy put her hand over her mouth.

Spoon in hand, Logan turned away from the stove. "But she's out of bed and dressed."

Erin set her sights on her prey and charged, hitting Logan with the script. "How could you do this?" She hit him again. "Are Roxy and I destined to be tortured for eternity?" At her own words, she burst into tears, spun around, and flung herself into her best friend's arms.

Ivy patted her. "I warned you that you may not want to read the script at this moment in your life."

Erin caught her breath and pulled back, holding Ivy at arms' length. "Ivy, as my best friend and an expert in this particular film, I demand that you fix this travesty."

"Well, the script was written this way. Logan and I discussed it with the studio, and we really feel doing it any other way would not do the story justice." Ivy widened her eyes.

"What happened to the Hollywood ending?" Roxy had to have a Hollywood ending, because one of them had to have it.

"It's not that kind of story." Ivy pulled her in for another hug. "It's a poignant film."

"I made you your yogurt." Logan tried plying her with breakfast.

"It will probably win a ton of awards, but the public will hate it." Her head hung low, she let go of Ivy and dragged herself to the stainless steel table in the middle of the kitchen.

"It's going to be okay." Ivy's tone was one of a big sister.

Erin slapped the script down and opened it up to the last page. "'I'm going to take all my memories with me and see what happens. Roxy smiles and turns. Fade to black.'" The tears restarted, and she hugged the script to her chest. "This is why I couldn't play Roxy."

Logan came over, dropped a bowl in front of her, and with an oversized spoon, plopped some yogurt in the dish. "*Bon appetite.*"

Ivy sat across from her. "What makes you say that?"

"If Roxy were my age, she could make a decision. If Roxy were my age, she would know what she wanted." She shook her head. "I know what I want." Even if she couldn't have him, she knew what she wanted, actually who she wanted.

"Do you?" Logan put a plate of pancakes in front of Ivy and sat down with one of his own. Somehow, the two of them found the true "it" factor, the one where they could eat and create and be together.

Only last week, she was in this position with Drew. She made an omelet and they sat together with Beaker and talked about their line of products.

Beaker. She couldn't even go there.

"Do I what?" She stared at the pancakes, and her mouth watered. Logan's pancakes were famous, well at least in her circle, even Ryder would eat them.

"Lord, help me." Logan stood and made another plate and set it down in front of her. "Do you know what you want?"

She looked around her place setting, lifted her napkin and her plate, and then put her head in her hand.

"Erin?" Ivy reached over to her.

"I want my supplements." For the millionth time since she walked out of the lab, her eyes heated. What would happen to Hollywood Glow now?

"Anything else?" Logan strummed his fingers on the table.

"I don't want to always worry about the next role. I want to make pot roast and products, and I don't want to feel like I have to add more controversy to something if I don't want to, and if I accept a part, I don't want it to feel like the last line of *Hollywood Starburst*." She wanted everything she couldn't have. Through all the tears came a moment of clarity and once more she stood. "I don't want to do this reality show. I have to get out of it." No matter her money situation, she wouldn't take a job out of desperation.

"Are you going to let me help?" Logan hit the table.

The job of her helpmate didn't belong to Logan. It belonged to someone else, but since he didn't want the job, it belonged to her. "No. It's not your responsibility. Never was." Along with everything else, she wanted or didn't want, she knew beyond a shadow of a doubt, she didn't want Rick Southern as an agent. "I'm going to go talk to Brian." With no phone and some groveling to do, she would just go to his office and wait like every other actor. It was better to be a star who faded gracefully than one who turned into a black hole. She sort of forgot that along the way.

Finally with a purpose other than self-doubt and mourning what could have been with the man she loved, she shoved down a pancake and darted back up the stairs. Rather than focusing on looking picture perfect, she collected her items, threw on a pair of sunglasses, and ran back down. After she made a quick pit stop to put another pancake in her mouth, she waved at Logan and Ivy and opened the back door to Brian.

"Ah!" She jumped back, dropped her bag, and put her hand to her chest. "What are you doing here?" Without a doubt, she was going to have a heart attack, or some sort of cardiac event.

"I helped anyway." Logan patted her on the back. "Ivy and I have some things to do for the media event. Take as much time as you need."

Originally, she was going to have a drive to think about what to say to him, but with that option taken off the table, she was forced to improvise. She picked up her bag and straightened up. In a suit and tie and with his sunglasses on, the man could have been a movie star himself, only he always said he couldn't act his way out of a designer bag. "I was just on my way to see you."

"You look different." He touched her shoulder and made his way inside.

"As you said, I let myself go." She shut the door and returned to the table.

"Actually, I meant you looked beautiful." He took the seat across from her.

They stared at one another.

Brian, being Brian, finally spoke. "Logan told me what happened."

"Well, I think we both know I had to go with my heart, or I would have always wondered and always held the torch." Life would have been easier if she could have loved Brian the way he deserved.

"Why do you think I made you go? You didn't need me complicating your life, besides I kept you as long as I could." He shrugged.

"It was time." She reached her hand across the table. "For what it's worth, I'm sorry."

"For what it's worth, so am I." He took her hand and squeezed. "Now will you let me reprise my role and let me see what horror show you got yourself into?"

"It's a reality show." Exhaling, she handed him her entire bag.

"What is the one thing I always taught you about this business?" After taking a moment to peek around in her purse, he excavated the contract.

"I don't know just one, you taught me everything." She poked her fork into the remaining pancake on her plate. "Never take a part because there's nothing else out there."

With raised eyebrows, he glanced over at her.

"I don't have any money." Lest even a fly heard, she whispered.

"You don't check your bank accounts, Miss Holland." He got a pair of reading glasses out of his suit jacket and began reading the contract.

Her bank accounts? "What do you mean? You gave me my check register."

"Love, you are nothing if not predicable. Go online. You have several savings accounts and investment accounts. I didn't say anything because I didn't want you shopping when upset." He furrowed his brow and turned the page.

She had money? Really? "Why did you say anything now? I'm still not happy!"

"But look what you did." He thumbed through the last couple of pages and put the contract down. "You went out there, you got a job, and you could have survived if you needed to. I'm really quite impressed, even if you went with an agent you have no business being with."

"I was scared."

"I'm just surprised he didn't sign you on the spot. What a fool." Brian pulled his cell phone out of his pocket.

Truth be told, she thought the same thing. "Can you fix it?"

"No, but you can." He pushed the contract back at her, pointed to one of the paragraphs and gave her his phone.

"I can't fix anything."

"That's because you don't know what you want." He countered.

What she wanted seemed to be the theme of the morning. She and Roxy were one and the same, neither of them knew what they wanted, but damn if she wasn't determined to figure it out.

"What do you want? You're a woman who fights for what you want, you proved it right here." Brian tapped the contract. "Tell me what you want."

"I don't want to go through my life scared someone will disappear." Unable to look him in the eye, she read the paragraph he pointed out on the contract.

"He didn't disappear this time." Brian lowered his voice.

Her chest took on that familiar ache. "But he didn't run after me either."

"Maybe he's waiting to find out if you know what you want."

"I only know I don't want to be worried all the time, and I don't want any stupid poignant ending." She dialed the phone.

EXT. INDIANAPOLIS, IN - SCHOOL FIELD - DAY.

Rehearsal for graduation just ended.

ROXY picks up her bags and looks out at the
bleachers.

CHARLES comes up behind her.

                    CHARLES
              Hey, how's it going?

ROXY gives Charles a hug. She lets go when
William and Steven join them.

                    ROXY
                 (Whispers)
                 Hi.

STEVEN waves.

WILLIAM lifts his chin.

                    WILLIAM
              We were hoping to find
              you here.

ROXY hides slightly behind Charles.

                    ROXY
              I meant it when I said I
              was sorry.

                    STEVEN
              Well, then I need to add
              my apology to yours.

ROXY moves further behind Charles.

                    ROXY
              Why?

                    STEVEN
          I didn't realize I
          wanted a princess until
          I put all the games in
          motion.

ROXY cries, a tear falls down her cheek, and
she gives Steven a hug.

WILLIAM goes to her side.

                    WILLIAM
          I should have stood up
          for what I wanted. I
          made it too easy for you
          to waiver.

ROXY lets go of Steven and hugs William, then
steps back to Charles.

                    WILLIAM
          Maybe loose ends are
          better.

                    STEVEN
          And ending the games.

                    CHARLES
          Maybe it's time for all
          of us to look forward.

ROXY pulls a college pamphlet out of her pocket
and hands it Charles.

                    ROXY
          That's exactly what I'm
          doing.

                    WILLIAM
          Wait, you're leaving?

                    STEVEN
          We have the summer to
          figure it out.

ROXY looks between the three of them and puts
her nail in her mouth.

                    ROXY
          I'm going to take all my
          memories with me and see
          what happens.

ROXY smiles and turns.

FADE TO BLACK

Chapter Thirty-Two

WHEN DREW DECIDED to find Erin and reenter his life, he snuck onto this exact studio and into a set decorated to look like the never seen interior of the Hollywood Stardust theatre.

In search of Erin once more, he walked toward the famous façade of the Hollywood Stardust theatre. For the first time, he would be photographed in front of the intricate set piece. This was the scene of the finale of the movie, the location where Logan proposed to Ivy the first time, and the place where they were now having yet another media event to announce the new cast. Pass the baton, so to speak.

No matter what, he promised himself he would talk to her today. Good or bad, they had a movie to get through. They had to talk, be adult, and not make a scene. Yes, they needed to be mature and have a conversation. He wasn't the man who made these huge gestures, ran on high emotion, she knew this. They had to be civil and figure out what to do about their relationship.

Hell, he just needed to talk to her... or see her. At least see her. A glimpse.

Once he made his appearance, the gathered crowd of select spectators and media applauded. At last, he was recognizable, due wholly to Erin's social media efforts. If he didn't want to be in the limelight, he should have told her she couldn't post their pictures.

"Drew." Logan flagged him over behind the set.

Was Erin back there or was she lurking about, avoiding the confrontation? Not sure which option he wanted, his heart sped. He gave the public another wave and went behind the set only to be met with Logan, Ivy and Ryder, a couple of studio executives and that one bitch, Cora Caine. Where was Erin?

"Look, do you remember this?" Logan took his arm and dragged him over to the hidden panel they once scrawled their names on and wrote their future occupations, thinking it was this grand gesture.

Drew quickly glanced down the list. First came Ryder who wrote rock star next to his name. The man had enough bravado to pull it off. Erin went next, and his chest tightened at her big bubbly script. She put actress. Drew was next in line back when he wanted to be an astronomer. Lastly, Logan signed his name and chose director as his chosen line of work. In many ways, the man succeeded except in the traditional sense.

"I would have made an awesome rock star." Ryder hit him in the arm.

Drew continued to stare at Erin's name. She was the only one who called her own future. She was always an actress, always would be an actress. She knew it and so did he. Then why did he want to change her? He knew what he got when it came to her.

"What do you think?" Logan elbowed him.

Before he had a chance to come up with an answer other than what he really thought, the low mumble of the crowd amplified. Applause vibrated around them.

He turned with enough time to watch Erin approach.

Like every time he saw her, his breath caught. The jewel among the three of them, she swooped in wearing a form-fitting white dress, her hair curled and bouncing with her every step, and bright red lips curled up in her signature smile. She was Hollywood personified.

"I'm sorry I'm late. I had some things to attend to." Her perfume wafted around him, but without a pause, she bypassed him and walked right to Logan. "Should we get started? There is quite a crowd."

"Yes, I think the time for reminiscing and lollygagging has passed, let's get started." The crone of a woman, Cora Caine, turned on one heel and walked away, leaving the two studio people rushing to catch up with her.

"Lollygagging?" Ryder shook his head. "That woman needs a gag all right."

"We better do this." Logan gave them a thumbs-up. "A quick press conference, some Q and A, and an announcement of the new cast. We have not only the traditional media here, but chargge.com is covering this and some other notable bloggers as well."

Taking Ivy's hand, Logan went forward and Ryder followed. Now was his chance. Before she had a chance to scurry away from him, Drew caught her arm. "Erin."

She gasped and stopped. "Drew."

"We need to talk." He didn't let go of her.

"Right now?" Her voice shook.

"Yes, we need to talk, right now."

"Between our last night together and this moment, the only time you have to talk to me is right now, before a press conference?"

"You walked out of the lab." He lifted his chin.

"I believe you practically chased me out and then locked the door behind me." She raised his lifted chin by jutting out her jaw.

"Come on!" Logan yelled for them.

"I actually can't believe you're here. Are you going to be all right? There are big scary video cameras out there." With her shot fired, she flipped her hair and headed to the front of the *Hollywood Stardust* set.

A fire blazed through him like never before, and he rushed after the rest of them, but as luck would have it, Ryder ended up between him and Erin.

"I want to welcome everyone here today." Logan began his speech. "This movie has waited twenty years to be made, and we're very proud to be the ones helming the ship."

Drew shifted his weight from one foot to the other. Though he vowed they would not make a scene, he also promised he would talk to her. What he had to say could not wait. He reached around Ryder and tapped her.

"What are you doing?" She leaned back and spoke through clenched teeth.

"At least the cameras here I know about." There, he said it and he punctuated his statement with a snide chuckle.

"Shhhh." She hissed. "What I did, I did for us."

No one was going to tell him to be quiet. "If there was an *us* in that sentence then I should have known about it." Why was this so hard for her to understand? In case she didn't hear the emphasis he put on the most important word, he spoke a little louder while still remaining under the radar.

"Calm down, buddy." Ryder patted him.

"*Hollywood Starburst* is filled with the magic that made *Hollywood Stardust* the film of a generation." With narrowed eyes, Logan glanced over at Drew.

"The media is here." Erin shook her head and looked out on the crowd once more.

All right, maybe he didn't exactly remain under the radar, but he was definitely a minor blip. A blip who would not be stifled by the media. "So, now who's afraid of the camera?"

"What?" She spun toward him. "Why are you even here? Don't you have a disappearing act to pull off?"

Logan cleared his throat into the microphone and spoke louder. "We felt it only right that the originators of the roles that made them famous, help choose their predecessors."

"You go get him, Wren." Ryder chuckled.

"I told you I would never leave again." His efforts to keep his voice lowered were failing miserable. "I was young, and what you said killed me."

"Killed you!" Erin shoved Ryder out of the way.

It seemed as if the entire audience let out a collective gasp.

"Erin?" Logan barked her name into the microphone.

"Go on with your speech already!" Without even bothering to look back at him, Erin waved Logan away.

She slowly inched toward Drew. "How many times do I have to pay for the stupid things I did? Was waiting for you for twenty years not enough? Or maybe it was how every day since you came back into my life, I've been afraid you were going to leave it. I'm terrified one day I'm going to wake up and you'll be gone again and even twenty years won't bring you back. That's why I didn't tell you, because I'm afraid that poof, you'll be gone." She snapped her fingers.

He flinched as if she slapped him.

"You were my strength and my safety and you made me feel smart. With you, I feel like I'm a part of something and not just a decoration. Maybe I did what I did because I wanted the world to see that, or maybe I was a has-been and was searching for anything so you and the world wouldn't see me as a failure and not want to be with me." Tears freely streaming down her cheeks, she stomped over to him. "I don't think you ever loved me."

Through the gasps and rumble of the audience, he only heard her admission. On automatic, he reached out for her. "How can you say that to me? I spent my life loving you. I loved you even when I hated you."

As if protecting herself, she wrapped her arms around her shoulders.

Not caring that the entire event stopped to focus solely on them and their display, he decided to make his own confession. She deserved it. "You make me feel like a man, and every morning when I wake up and see you there I can't believe you're with me. You make me laugh, and believe it or not, I crave the dramatics you bring with you. We are the most incredible team and maybe I wanted to keep you all to myself and be selfish." He put his hands on her shoulders and stared into her eyes. "I have always loved you. Always. No matter what happens, I will never leave you again."

"I love you." She wrapped her arms around his neck. "You belong to me."

The crowd burst into applause.

"Always." He bent her back in a picture perfect kiss, making sure the photographers got their best angle.

"MAY I HAVE MY OFFICIAL job as Marketing Director back?" Erin wiped the lipstick off of Drew's lips, but then went in and kissed him again only tinting his lips once more. They now stood off to one side of the Hollywood Stardust façade, but she didn't care where they were, or if the cameras were rolling, or what tabloid she ended up on, she had her life back.

"Of course, but since this will be playing out in front of the world on our reality show, I think a name change may be in order." With his thumbs he wiped the last remnants of her tears away. "I know you have to go by Erin Holland, but do you think you may want to hyphenate that to say Erin Holland-Fulton?"

Her heart swelled and along with her tears, the anxiety that traveled with her as an unwelcome companion left as well. "Well, there's only one little problem."

Drew's eyes narrowed and he tensed. "What might that be?"

"I turned down the reality show. If a part comes along that is spectacular like Roxy, we'll talk, but other than that, I'd rather just have the role of Mrs. Fulton. No hyphen required." Once more, she kissed him.

"We may be able to pull that Roxy role off." Logan said as he and Ivy joined them.

"Is the press conference over?" Drew never took his eyes off her.

"I'm not sure it ever started. I didn't even get to say half of what I wanted." Logan shook his head.

"What were you saying about Roxy?" Erin gave Logan a quick glance and then kissed Drew once more.

"There will be a third movie." Rather than Logan, that nasty woman, Cora or Coral or whoever, intruded into their circle.

"That was what I wanted to say." Logan groaned, and Ivy patted him.

She tightened her hold on Drew. "What?"

"After hearing your critique of *Starburst*, we had a meeting. There will be a third movie, *Hollywood Stardom*. It'll take place twenty years after *Hollywood Starburst* ends." At last Logan smiled the smile that got him the role of Steven in the first place. "We're all going to have our roles back."

"Make no mistake. The shenanigans you all played out the first time will not be tolerated this time. The studio is putting a lot of money behind you." Cora encroached into their circle further and then pointed at her and Drew. "Also, the two of you should make a reality show. All of you should. You have that exact right dose of crazy. I may just write it into your contracts."

"If you own a website, why are you involved with us?" Ryder was the only one of them brave enough or stupid enough to confront the battle-axe.

"I am CEO of a multi-faceted media company. Do your research better, Mr. Scott." She leaned in to him and just as abruptly pushed passed them.

They all seemed to hold their collective breath while they watched the woman storm away.

Ryder shrugged. "I'll do my research all right."

"Do I really get to finish Roxy's story?" Still reeling from the news of getting her role returned to her, Erin's knees went weak, but Drew was there to hold her up.

"We all get to finish their story." Drew pulled her in for a hug. "This is a role I will be honored to reprise with you."

She melted into the man she waited twenty years for, a small amount of time compared to what they had ahead of them. "I got my Hollywood ending." Now it was time to give Roxy hers.

The End

Dear Reader,

Thank you for reading!

I hope you enjoyed this look in to the world of Hollywood Stardust. If you would be so kind as to remember to rate and review the book, it would be more than appreciated.

If you would like to keep on top of the latest news and releases by signing up for my newsletter here, www.kimcarmichaelnovels.com you will also receive a free short story right in your inbox!

Kim Carmichael

Sneak Peeks!

Typecast

A HOLLYWOOD STARDUST NOVEL

What's Your Fantasy?

Twenty years ago, the movie *Hollywood Stardust* defined a generation of teens and changed the four actors' lives forever.

Typecast as the villain both in front and behind the silver screen, Logan Alexander has purposely allowed his star to fade. Now with the 20th Anniversary of the movie on the horizon, he is the only one fit to step into the spotlight, deal with the unwanted publicity, and make sure that things meant to be left on the cutting room floor remain there.

Ivy Vermont has always longed to be a leading lady, yet her paralyzing stage fright has relegated her to stay behind the scenes as a fact checker for Chargge.com's entertainment webcasts. However, when her one-time poster-boy crush walks in to the studio demanding only she be in charge of his story, she knows she must take advantage of her big break.

Now, Logan tightropes between old loyalties and new love, while Ivy struggles to stay in reality with her ultimate fantasy.

An Excerpt

"There is absolutely no way I am going out there and interviewing some B-list has-been bad boy." Julia Davis, the lead entertainment reporter for Chargge.com crossed her arms. "Your little fact finder screwed up again. Seriously, Craig, how can I be expected to work this way?"

Heat encompassed Ivy Vermont, but she met Julia's crossed arms with a set of her own and glanced between Craig Stockton, her boss, and Julia. "Technically, Logan Alexander is not a B-lister. He doesn't even act anymore."

"Your ridiculous details mean nothing." Julia's nostrils flared.

"Ivy, what happened to getting Ryder Scott or Erin Holland from *Hollywood Stardust*?" Shaking his head, Craig approached. "It's a little hard to do a story on the twentieth anniversary of the movie without one of the stars. You told me everything was set."

With facts, rather than stature on her side, Ivy stood up straighter and lifted her chin. "Logan Alexander was as much a star in the movie as the other two of them, well three."

"Last week, rather than getting that little boy in the hot dog commercial with the catchy line, you brought me the dog." Julia stared her down. "How can I interview a dog?"

"The trainer was there. Some say dogs have the mentality of a two-year-old, and it did tricks." No one ever saw the potential. If she could talk as eloquently in front of the camera as behind, she would be the reporter. Actually, she would have been an actress and the interviewee. Even the camera on her phone terrified her, not a flattering trait coming from a family of actors. "A few fetches and atta boys would have been perfect for your report."

"I am not doing this interview." The click of Julia's heels on the wood floor of the conference room grew louder as she approached. "What? Are you scared to face me?"

Though she tried not to look directly at her, Ivy gave in,

swallowing back any mention of the tiny mascara smear above her left eye. Julia should meet Mr. Alexander with such an imperfection. "The agent promised me Ryder or Erin. Only, two hours ago, he called to say Logan would be here instead."

"He was one of the major stars." Craig wiped his brow.

"Stop defending your personal pet." Julia turned her back to him.

Ivy held out the note cards she made for the wicked reporter. "Logan Alexander is an excellent person to interview. The villain is always the most interesting. Even after all the scandals, *Hollywood Stardust* is one of the most beloved teen movies ever made, and changed the genre forever."

"I don't need your details. Did you spend your life studying this movie?" Julia grabbed the cards out of her hand and tossed them to the floor. "He was arrested and personally responsible for getting the sequel canceled. He is as bad in real life as he was in the movie."

"Don't forget that I ran off innocent Drew Fulton and no one has ever heard from him again."

At the unexpected male voice, Ivy turned. Her breath caught as her ultimate teen fantasy stood before her.

The heat in the room intensified, but she froze. Mr. Logan Alexander leaned in the doorway—more like filled up the doorway. He lifted a cigarette, twirled it between his fingers, and placed it in his mouth.

Unlike someone who lived the hard-knock life of a disgraced actor, time had kissed him, leaving him looking much like his teen dream self, only a little more rugged. While his other two male costars from the movie possessed more of the good and wholesome image, Logan Alexander personified the conniving character. He was the one who lured people with looks that could only be described as remarkable.

As if this whole thing were nothing but a bother, he pushed away from doorjamb and entered the room, glanced at Julia, turned his back to Craig, and faced Ivy. "So, you think the villain is the most interesting?" The cigarette bounced between his lips.

Interesting? Interesting as in the way he pulled his dark blond hair into a ponytail that hit the nape of his neck leaving one long strand to hang down the side of his face? Maybe interesting in the way his light blue eyes seemed almost translucent, half-closed, and definitely naughty? Of course, also interesting in how the slight bit of stubble highlighted the angles of his face, and the way he managed to keep his cigarette balanced. Then the answer was yes, he, or the villain, was the most interesting.

"The villain always needs to go under the most transformation." She managed to squeak out the words and pointed to his cigarette, unsure if she needed to tell him about the no smoking rule. Did fantasies follow rules?

"Don't worry. I'm not going to light it." His gaze scanned down to her shoes and back up to her face.

Interesting. She licked her lips. The man was more glorious in person than on the silver screen.

"What if the villain hasn't undergone a transformation?" Julia tapped her foot.

Ivy ground her teeth together. If anyone needed to change, it was Julia.

"I suppose I'll get more hard-hitting questions than asking a dog trainer if Rover, the hot dog hunter, is potty trained. You sure know how to dig deep." Though he answered Julia, he continued to look at Ivy. "I liked the dog, a much better choice than the obnoxious little boy."

Transfixed, she continued to stare at him.

"Just because the villain can change, doesn't mean they will." Julia moved over as if trying to get his attention.

He exhaled, but the cigarette stayed in place. "How can I do an interview with you when I know you are team Ryder all the way?"

"*Hollywood Stardust* was the typical love triangle." Julia raised her chin. "Today's teen movies are better developed than movies decades ago."

"Oh, that reference to my age really does pain me." He pressed his hand to his chest. "Tell me, did the villains of your era wear pompadours and leather jackets, or perhaps suits of armor?"

In an effort to stifle a laugh, Ivy bit the side of her mouth. There was something to be said for the villain getting their comeuppance, and she didn't mean Mr. Alexander.

Julia narrowed her eyes and spun toward Craig. "I am not

playing her game of bait and switch. If Miss Details loves villains so much, Miss Details can do the interview. Call me when you get a real star." She stormed out.

"Well, that is one thing your runaway hostess and I agree on." Mr. Alexander's smile revealed a perfect set of Hollywood teeth.

"What would that be?" Craig wiped his brow.

"Miss Details should do the interview." In a swoon-worthy move, Mr. Alexander bowed to her.

The spotlight shined down on her and the same stage fright she battled every second of her life took a strong hold over her body, made worse by being presented with her teen idol in the flesh. "Craig." How she managed to utter even one word was beyond her, but she took it as a good sign.

"Oh, no. No, that won't do at all." Craig shook his head. The first and only time she was on camera at Chargge.com, she ended up running off set and throwing up in a trash can. "I am sure Julia will be right back."

"Don't bring her back on my account. I'm Team Details all the way." Logan raised his fist as if he were about to begin cheering and, with a wink, lifted his chin in her direction. "She is clearly an expert on the movie and knows story structure."

His gesture, though probably insignificant to him, served to ignite her courage as well as her body. She chose to ignore them both. All she needed was to throw up on one of the *Hollywood Stardust* stars.

Craig cupped his hand over his mouth. "She is an expert on every movie."

Yes, fine, but she was mostly an expert on *Hollywood Stardust*. She remained silent.

"I refuse to be interviewed by anyone who is not an expert in cinema." Mr. Alexander picked up one of her note cards, gave it a quick scan, and sauntered over to her. Yes, it was a total saunter. His walk may have also included a bit of a swagger as well. "Miss Details is the only one for me. It seems she has found something to talk about other than drugs, Drew, and sequels, since I won't answer those questions anyway."

She fought the need to hug her prepubescent crush, bury her face in his chest, and breathe in what could only be the smell of cologne and cookies. Later, they could go back to her apartment, and she would confess she used to write his name in her notebook and practice kissing him on the back of her hand. In her dreams, she could interview him and then they'd conquer the world together. In reality, she knew he was only playing a role and she would never be able to utter a sentence. Dumb reality.

"Either she interviews me or you can call the company that owns not only *Hollywood Stardust*, but your website as well, and tell them the video blog they expect to make waves won't air today. I'll be in the lounge not lighting my cigarette." He handed her the card and walked out the door.

She leaned forward, bracing herself on her knees. "Oh God, I want to do this."

Her boss paced across the floor. "You would be the perfect person if you could just learn to calm down. It's what we hired you for."

Though Craig never admitted it, she was the bane of his existence. He hired her as a favor to her father, and they gave her the job as a reporter. Technically, her current job as fact-checker and scheduler didn't even exist. The reporters were supposed to do their own research, but Julia sort of snatched her up as a personal assistant. Both her parents who possessed multiple acting awards between them, looked at her with wide eyes and pity every time they discussed her career. Even they weren't good enough actors to hide their disappointment.

She crumpled the note card in her fist and straightened up. "I'll do it. I will interview Logan Alexander." Part of her expected a spotlight to shine down on her signifying her strength of conviction. The other part was thrilled she didn't live in a world where spotlights randomly illuminated at key life-changing moments. She would end up living in the bathroom with the lights off, shaking.

Craig shook his head. His skin had turned the most unusual shade of red.

"This is the movie of a generation, the one that spoke to that specific time. The story should be told by someone who truly loves everything it represents." For once, she needed to be her own spotlight. "This is the movie that pushed the boundaries, didn't rely on the happily ever after, asked the questions." Maybe the movie that meant the world to her could also cure

her.

"We need this story, Ivy." He crossed his arms. "Seriously, we need the story. Other sites are competing with us. We need something to go viral. The advertising dollars are not coming in as they should, and you know what that means."

Yes, it meant cuts, starting with the person who technically didn't have a title. She might as well go big or go home, literally.

"Do the interview, but make sure you ask about Drew Fulton and the arrest and the sequel."

"He said he wouldn't answer those questions." The swirl of anxiety circled around her stomach.

"Ivy." He rubbed his hand over his face. "You can do this. You were made for this. Go to wardrobe, ask them for something more contemporary and fashionable, and ask the questions. We need you."

For once she wouldn't disappoint. She stopped herself from saluting and gave him a strong nod. "I got this." As she walked out, she made a mental note to have a trash can put near the set.

HOLLYWOOD STARDUST
Supporting Roles – Giselle & Wilson –

Some girls only want to have fun.

Giselle Abromowitz lives her life with two simple rules. 1. Have fun. 2. Defer to rule number one. She does what she wants when she wants, and when things get too complicated she moves on to happier, more casual pastures.

As the older brother to Hollywood star, Logan Alexander, Wilson Alexander has played the role of pacifier, parent and protector. With the opening of his club it is his time to step in to the spotlight and make his own life.

When Giselle stumbles into Wilson's regimented life and takes over, Wilson knows he found the missing piece of his life, now he only needs to convince his lady love that fun and love can coexist.

An Excerpt

"What are you doing here?" Ivy Vermont pressed her back to the building and put her hand over her eyes.

Giselle Abromowitz wrinkled her nose. Apparently, her best friend needed a recap of their last several hours, even though they'd been together the entire day. "We're stalking Logan Alexander, the actor you've loved since you were twelve and the guy you're supposed to be working with, but ditched you. Now we're standing outside his brother's bar." She shielded her eyes as she looked up at the sign. "It's not open though, and I could use a drink."

Ivy groaned. "I meant what are you doing here with me stalking actors when you are supposed to be at work?"

Rather than answer, Giselle tiptoed over to one of the windows and attempted to peer inside.

"Giselle. What happened to your job?" Ivy joined her and stood on her tiptoes to look in the blackened windows. "This was supposed to be the one."

With Ivy in her full quirky vintage business regalia, Giselle resisted the urge to lift her fun sized friend. "I don't think I want to be an assistant."

"You said you wanted to work in an office." Ivy pressed her forehead to the glass.

"It has too much paper, my hands got dry from touching all of it, and I got a paper cut." She held out her hands and studied them and swore she still saw the faint remnant of the cut. "Look."

"Offices have paper." Ivy shook her head.

"Not if they're green." One day she would best her best friend in the battle of wits.

Ivy huffed.

"Why don't we take care of your job and stop worrying about mine." Giselle stomped over to the front door and knocked.

Ivy rushed over and grabbed her arm. "What are you doing?"

"Getting you in the door, that's the job I'm best at." Ever since her best friend took on the assignment of reporting on the anniversary of her favorite movie, *Hollywood Stardust*, she had been unlivable. Once Ivy's crush, Logan Alexander entered the picture and became her co-reporter, she went from unlivable to not fun. Now it had to be fixed. Giselle struck a pose, boobs out, butt popped, hand on hip and waited. The pose hadn't failed her yet.

Finally, the door opened. At the sight of the man, hot man, really hot man, before her, Giselle added at little lip pout to her guy wrangling stance.

In less than an instant, a smile took over the man's face. "Please tell me you're the delivery I'm waiting for."

She stepped forward and leaned on the doorjamb. "I'm the delivery you're waiting for."

The man raised his eyebrows, making his already friendly and fluid features even more likable. He reminded her of the guy in a movie who stood in the background, but every time the camera panned over to him one kept thinking how cute he was, how his blue eyes would steal the show and his smile could make the lead in the movie do almost anything.

"So you're the person delivering the glass washer and hooking it up to the existing plumbing?" He tilted his head.

"Do I not look like a plumber?" She turned back to Ivy and nodded, she had this guy, but good.

Ivy put her hand over her eyes.

"Well, considering the person on the way is named Harvey, and last time I saw him he was about quadruple your size and with a lot less hair, I'm going to go with no." As if waiting for her to confess her deception, he crossed his arms.

"All right, you caught me." She played along and pressed her hand to her chest. "Actually, I'm here on behalf of my poor friend, Ivy. I have reason to believe one Mr. Logan Alexander may be inside, and she needs him desperately."

The man raised his eyebrows.

"And by desperate, I mean her work is relying on him, although the poster she had of him on her ceiling when she was thirteen, so she could go to bed looking at him, may speak of a different kind of desperation." Giselle thought she should lay it all on the table.

The man glanced between the two of them. "So, you're Ivy. I'm not surprised that you're here." He opened the door and stepped back.

Ivy looked up at the man.

"Come on, I got you in." Giselle motioned for her best friend and trotted inside. The whole place smelled like remodeling, and she smiled at the way the interior was done up to look like a 1920s speakeasy with art deco finishes and dark booths. There was no place in Hollywood like it. "This is cool."

Gazing up at the man with a slight bit of hope, Ivy followed. "Is he here?"

"I think I may be able to conjure him. Stay right here and check the place out." He put his hand out and leaned forward. "I'm Wilson by the way, Wilson Alexander."

"Alexander. As in Logan Alexander." Rather than shake his hand, Giselle hooked her arms in his.

Ivy took his hand. "I really do need to talk to him for even a second."

"Well, as fun as this all is, I will retrieve my baby brother for you." He glanced down at Giselle, took his time untangling their appendages, and with one last glance in her direction, left and disappeared behind a swinging door. "Logan!"

"See? I told you it would all work out." Giselle put her arm around her friend.

"I wish I could live my life like you do." Ivy patted her and moved away, pacing around the space.

"What do you mean?" Giselle shrugged and took a seat on one of the bar stools. No doubt, the savvy Mr. Alexander chose these to show off a woman's gams. She wondered if she stayed in this position if he would notice.

"You just always go with it. You don't have a job, no worries, you don't know what you're doing tomorrow, not a problem." Ivy put her hand on her stomach. "I can't let go like you do. What's taking them so long?"

"Well, you have to go with it, what other choice do we have?" She continued to assess her legs.

Before Ivy got a chance to say something deep or meaningful, a knock at the front door interrupted them.

They both looked at the door and then back in the direction Wilson took.

The knock came again, but louder.

"What should we do?" Ivy bit her lip.

"Well, when people knock, the normal course of action is to open it." Though she didn't want to ruin how awesome her legs looked from the bar stool, she slid down and opened the door, only to be greeted by a huge man with not much hair holding a wrench. "Harvey! We've been waiting for you. Come on in."

The man smiled and trundled inside. "Is Wilson here?"

"Wait! You can't just let anyone in here. Hold on." Ivy rushed to the back. "Wilson!"

With a shrug, Giselle stood to the side to let Harvey enter. "So, you're here to do some installation?"

"Putting in the new glass washer and adjusting some things on the plumbing on the bar." Almost as if he wanted to prove his identity, he held up a toolbox and a plumber's wrench.

"Well, time is money, get to it." She pointed over to the bar.

Harvey grabbed his toolbox and hobbled over to the bar. "And you are?"

With it sort of dark, she grabbed a flashlight from his toolbox, propped herself back up on the stool and aimed it where Harvey was beginning his work. "Giselle, of course."

Wilson reappeared. "Well, Miss Giselle of course, I'd like to know what you think you're doing here?"

"My last name is Abromowitz." She crossed her legs.

"Thank you, but that didn't answer my question." He approached, giving her a good look at his form, a bit more muscular than his younger brother, and it was that bit she liked. "What are you doing here?"

She had now been asked this question multiple times and all in the name of trying to help. If everyone kept asking, it was apparent she needed to be somewhere else. She put the flashlight down and jumped off the stool. "Right now I'm leaving."

Kim Carmichael

Idolized

A HOLLYWOOD STARDUST NOVEL

Coming Soon from Irksome Rebel Press

An Excerpt

The limousine stopped in front of the Beverly Garland hotel and Ryder Scott held up his hand, a silent command telling the driver not to unlock the door quite yet. No one should ever enter a battle zone without a plan of attack, and he needed a moment to center himself and get the lay of the land.

While the set up was always the same, the players always changed. As usual, the red carpet trailed from the crowded curb on Sunset Boulevard all the way to the door of one of

Hollywood's trendiest hotels. In between point A and point B, a step and repeat emblazoned with the *Hollywood Starburst* movie logo provided the perfect background for the stars to stop, strike a pose, and answer a question or two before heading into the after-party celebrating the movie premiere of the sequel that had waited over twenty years to be told.

After several deep breaths, he lowered his hand giving the go signal. The second the telltale click of the doors being unlocked echoed through the vehicle, a nameless uniformed person opened the door into the war zone.

His strategy firmly planted in his mind, Ryder put one foot on that red carpet and paused, allowing the rest of him to remain in the shadows of car interior. All too soon, the focus of the photographers would pull away from the step and repeat to find out who was in the last limo, though they knew the answer. All his co-stars had already arrived.

At times like this, it was critical to stay hydrated and ensure his pH was optimized, so he downed the last of his alkaline water before achieving his desired result.

At last, two photographers turned toward the limo, and once a third followed suit, Ryder took his time exiting the car.

In one fluid motion he stood, flashed the one-sided smile that made him a star, and waved. Once the roar of the crowd gathered around the front of the hotel amplified, the smile became a bit more real, and he took his place in line behind his co-stars. All the better to remain in a defensive position as well as provide the much needed grand finale of arrivals. He lived by the motto, last in, first out, and above all else, leave everyone in a state of want.

Logan Alexander with his wife, Ivy, by his side and his kid, Curtis, in his arms went first. The once villain of the group, Logan turned his reputation around when he not only fell in love with the woman interviewing him, but resurrected and helped direct the sequel to their genre changing movie, *Hollywood Stardust*.

"Logan." One of the news reporters came forward. "What did you think of the final cut of *Hollywood Starburst*?"

"I think the sequel turned out exactly as we envisioned, and we stayed true to the story." He nodded, and his little toddler reached for the microphone, causing all of them to chuckle.

"When does the filming of *Hollywood Stardom* begin?" The woman let the little boy hold the microphone handle with her.

In a startling twist to the *Hollywood Stardust* story, there was a third and final movie planned, *Hollywood Stardom*. Even more surprising was that the four original actors would be reprising their roles. Of course, Ryder would be the penultimate star. He was the one with the body of work, the career to be envied, and the one who was even making his own movie.

"We will begin next month, and it's sure to be the perfect wrap-up for this set of characters." Logan took his wife's hand.

"Ivy, what was it like making your acting debut with your husband?" The reporter turned the mic to Mrs. Alexander.

The once camera shy girl not only did a cameo in this movie, but would be taking a full-fledged role in the next movie. Instead of the girl whose voice shook the first time she tried to interview him, now she faced the camera head on. "I couldn't have asked for a better director." She turned to her husband.

In a moment tailor-made for the Hollywood royalty they had become, the couple kissed and Logan led her into the hotel.

The couple in waiting, Drew Fulton, Ph.D. and Erin Holland-Fulton, took their position next. At long last, fans of the elusive happily ever after could rejoice. In a fairytale come to life, the geek and the leading lady in the original movie, reconnected after twenty years had tied the knot in a gala fit for any princess.

The happy little couple struck several media-friendly adorable poses, including several which included having Drew place his hands on Erin's barely visible baby bump.

Ryder gave a quick glance behind him, swearing he could still see the smoke trail on the bullet he dodged when he didn't end up with her. While Erin might have taught him many things on being an amazing lover, of utmost importance was her lesson on birth control. Don't enter a woman without it.

"Erin, you are positively glowing." The reporter began.

"It's a Hollywood Glow." Erin held on to Drew and put her hand over her stomach. "Among other things."

Well, no one could say Erin wasn't a sales person through and through. Within her first four words she plugged her and Drew's line of nutraceuticals. Not that she needed to, the stuff could barely be found on the high-end shelves, where it reigned as the crown prince of supplements. With a sneer, Ryder reached into his pocket and made sure he had his late night dose. Hell, the stuff worked.

"Exactly." The reporter nodded. "So, as the original Roxy, how do you feel the new cast did taking over for this installment of the story?"

Only someone who knew Erin would have noticed her grip tighten on her husband, and the slight quiver of her lower lip. Of all of them, Erin had the worst time allowing the role she defined be taken on by someone else.

Erin leaned forward. "They all did magnificent, but I can't say I'm not thrilled to have Roxy back."

Her answer was gracious and truthful, and Ryder gave her a thumbs-up even if she didn't see the gesture.

"Your fans are going to be thrilled." The reporter beamed at her and turned her attention to Drew. "Dr. Fulton, how does it feel to return to acting?"

"It feels right." Ever the serious one, Drew lifted his chin at the reporter and then took Erin inside.

Ready for his turn on the front line, Ryder no sooner stepped over to give these reporters a true photo opportunity than a stripe of black lace rushed in front of him, tripped and stumbled right into the center of the step and repeat.

When the woman stopped, clenched her fist and straightened up, two things happened. First, one luscious tendril of auburn hair tumbled free of its updo into her, eye giving the woman a sexy "just got out of bed and ready to get back in it" look.

Second, he recognized the woman. In fact, one could say she was one of his many benefactors, though not in his traditional sense, meaning he hadn't slept with her...yet.

Still, the woman media-blocked his entrance, and though he made sure to have no expression on his face, he waited to find out if he needed to fight.

"Cora Caine." The reporter tiptoed toward the intruder. "Welcome to the red carpet."

Yes, Cora Caine, the CEO of chargge.com.

Three years ago, when her web portal/search engine/multimedia site was purchased by the same company who owned the studio who produced *Hollywood Stardust*, she became a billionaire overnight. She also seemed to be the one pushing for the Stardust movies to continue.

Rather than answer, Cora glanced around and as if she finally realized she was in front of reporters and photographers, she struck her version of a pose.

More accurately, she put her hands on her hips and pursed her lips. "What was the question?"

Inside, Ryder winced. While the reporter hadn't asked a question, Cora's demeanor gave him some much needed intel. Apparently, Ms. Caine didn't intend to sabotage his moment in the limelight, but simply took the wrong way.

"Were you always a fan of the *Hollywood Stardust* movie? Is that why you became involved with the sequel?" Where the reporter was smooth with his costars, at having her flow disrupted, her voice shook.

"The original movie is one of the most beloved of all time. When my team ran our algorithms we decided that it would be a good investment." Cora crossed her arms over her chest, providing a barrier to the reporter and covering up one of her best assets.

Also, Ryder wasn't sure if she'd even answered the question. He was still back on the word algorithm. What the hell was an algorithm? Did anyone know?

"Oh, well, yes." The reporter's smile faded. "Your dress is gorgeous. Who are you wearing?"

Ah, the old standby question. It was also a gift on the reporter's part. Hopefully, Cora would take the hint and lower her arms, no one should be allowed to miss that body. All her curves were made for exploration. Instead of revealing the designer, Cora returned to that pursing her lips thing.

Sometimes the best battles were won purely on opportunity and coincidence. It was time for a surprise attack.

After a quick check of his tie, Ryder swooped in and came up right behind Ms. Caine. She gasped, but that didn't stop him. He put one hand on her waist, and with his other hand, he pulled the back of her dress, got a quick glimpse at the label and leaned into her ear. "Owen Blakeney, Blake Designs."

"Ryder Scott, what a surprise!" The reporter smiled again.

Cora twisted around to see him, her lock of hair hitting him in the face.

He corralled her hair and decided the best course of action was to take over. "The gorgeous Cora Caine is wearing an Owen Blakeney dress that fits her better than any glove I've ever seen, and as luck would have it, I have one of his tuxedos on tonight."

"Are you ready to reprise your role as William?" the reporter asked.

"I think the more accurate question would be, is William ready for me?" He chuckled and slid his hand up Cora's rib cage. Hey, he'd saved her ass, he might as well get a little touchy-feely.

"Are you pleased with the outcome of the second movie?" As the reporter asked yet another question, Cora tensed like she wanted to walk.

In an effort to keep the media monstrosity in place, he tightened his hold on her and continued to speak for her. "With all the unique circumstances, I think this was a perfect way to tell the story. Now, I believe it's time to walk the rest of the red carpet." He gave the reporter a wink and with his arm around her waist, guided Cora toward the hotel entrance.

"You can let go of me now, Mr. Scott." She put her hand over his.

"Why would I do that? It feels like it belongs here." They continued toward the doors, and he nodded at no one in particular.

"I can guarantee that no part of you belongs on any part of me." The doormen did their jobs, but before she entered she turned to him.

"I don't think anyone, let alone you, can guarantee that." To prove his point, he let his hand skim down to the swell of her backside. The angle of the curve let him know if he delved a little deeper he would get quite the magnificent handful.

Her green eyes darkened, and they stared at each other.

"What are you looking at?" She didn't walk away, but she did narrow her eyes.

Though he had met Cora a few times, he'd never had the opportunity to be this close up to her. In fact, she was quite attractive, actually beautiful, with feminine little features in complete contrast to her harder than steel attitude. Part of him wanted to take a bite, but the other part was afraid he would chip one of his teeth and his caps were damn expensive. "Why don't you use one of your algorithms and figure it out?" He purposely lowered his eyes to her copious cleavage. "Instead of snapping at me, maybe you should thank me for saving your ass out there."

"My ass did not need saving." She raised her chin.

"I think that's where you and I need to agree to disagree." With a quick glance back to ensure at least a few of the cameras were on them, he gave into his want from earlier and finally let his palm graze over the aforementioned body part. Oh, he was spot on, her ass was perfection.

Her eyes ablaze, she dramatically grabbed his hand and plucked it off her. "My algorithm tells me this is done." She spun on her heel and stomped into the hotel.

Once more, Ryder looked back at the media. Even more people were focused on him and gave them a slight bow. Those gathered let out a collective *awww*. "I better get inside." He widened his eyes to garner any last bit of sympathy and paused to allow the photographers to get their shot before following his impromptu date. Tomorrow's stories would have him plastered everywhere. Job well done, Ryder. Job well done.

About the Author

Kim Carmichael

Kim Carmichael began writing nine years ago when her love of happy endings inspired her to create her own.

A Southern California native, Kim's contemporary romance combines Hollywood magic with pop culture to create quirky characters set against some of most unique and colorful settings in the world.

With a weakness for designer purses, bad boys and techno geeks, Kim married her own computer whiz after he proved he could keep her all her gadgets running and finally admitted handbags were an investment.

Kim is a PAN member of the Romance Writers of America, as well as some small specialty chapters. A multi-published author, Kim's books can be found all over the world.

When not writing, she can usually be found slathered in sunscreen trolling Los Angeles and helping top doctors build their practices.

To find out more about Kim Carmichael visit:

Website: www.kimcarmichaelnovels.com

Hollywood Stardust Website: www.chargge.com

Facebook: http://www.facebook.com/kimcarmichaelnovels

Twitter: @kimcarmichael4

http://www.amazon.com/Kim-Carmichael/e/B0098RNFUI

www.ingramcontent.com/pod-product-compliance
Lightning Source LLC
Chambersburg PA
CBHW071629260626
47170CB00001B/19